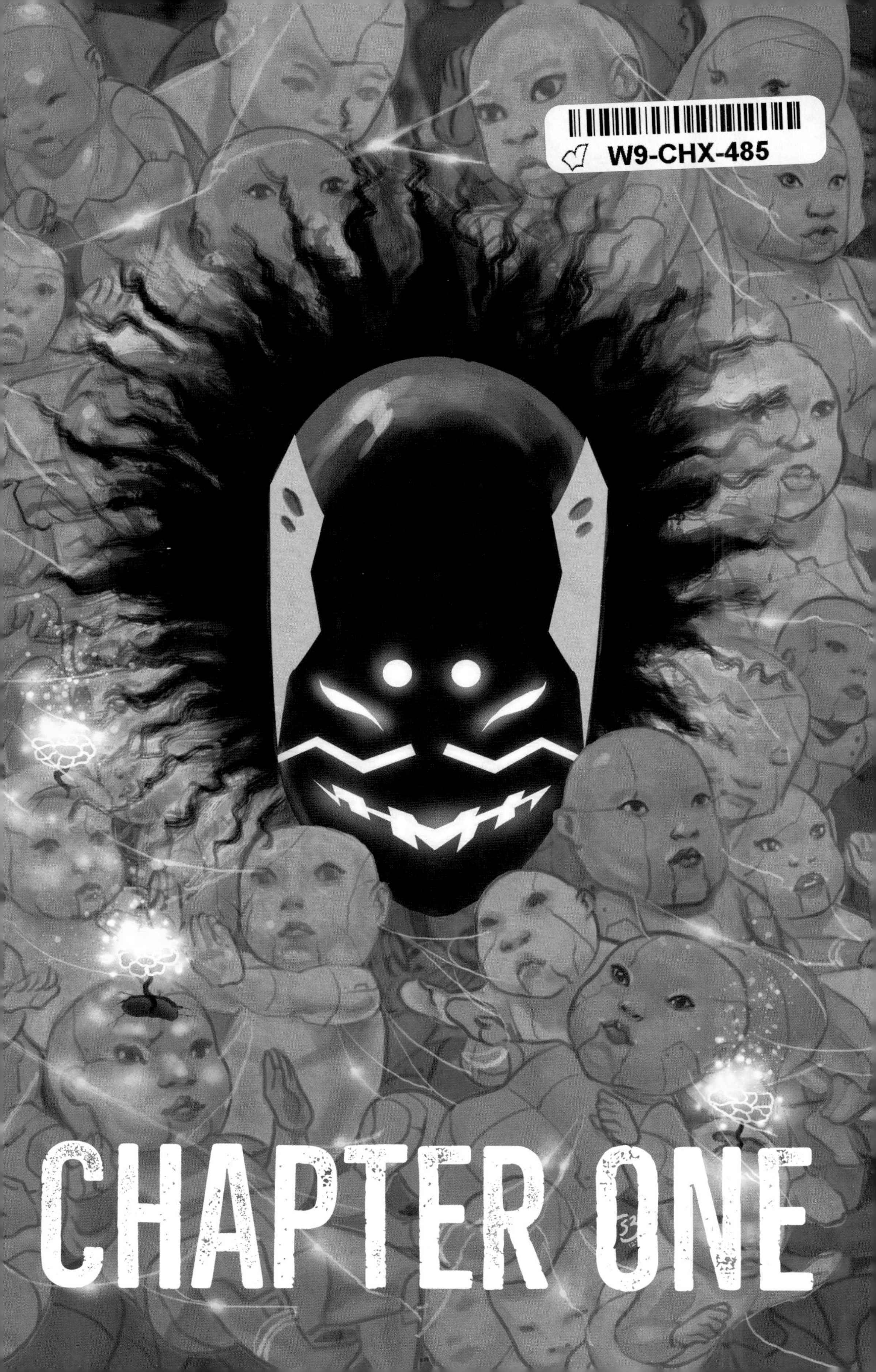
CHAPTER ONE

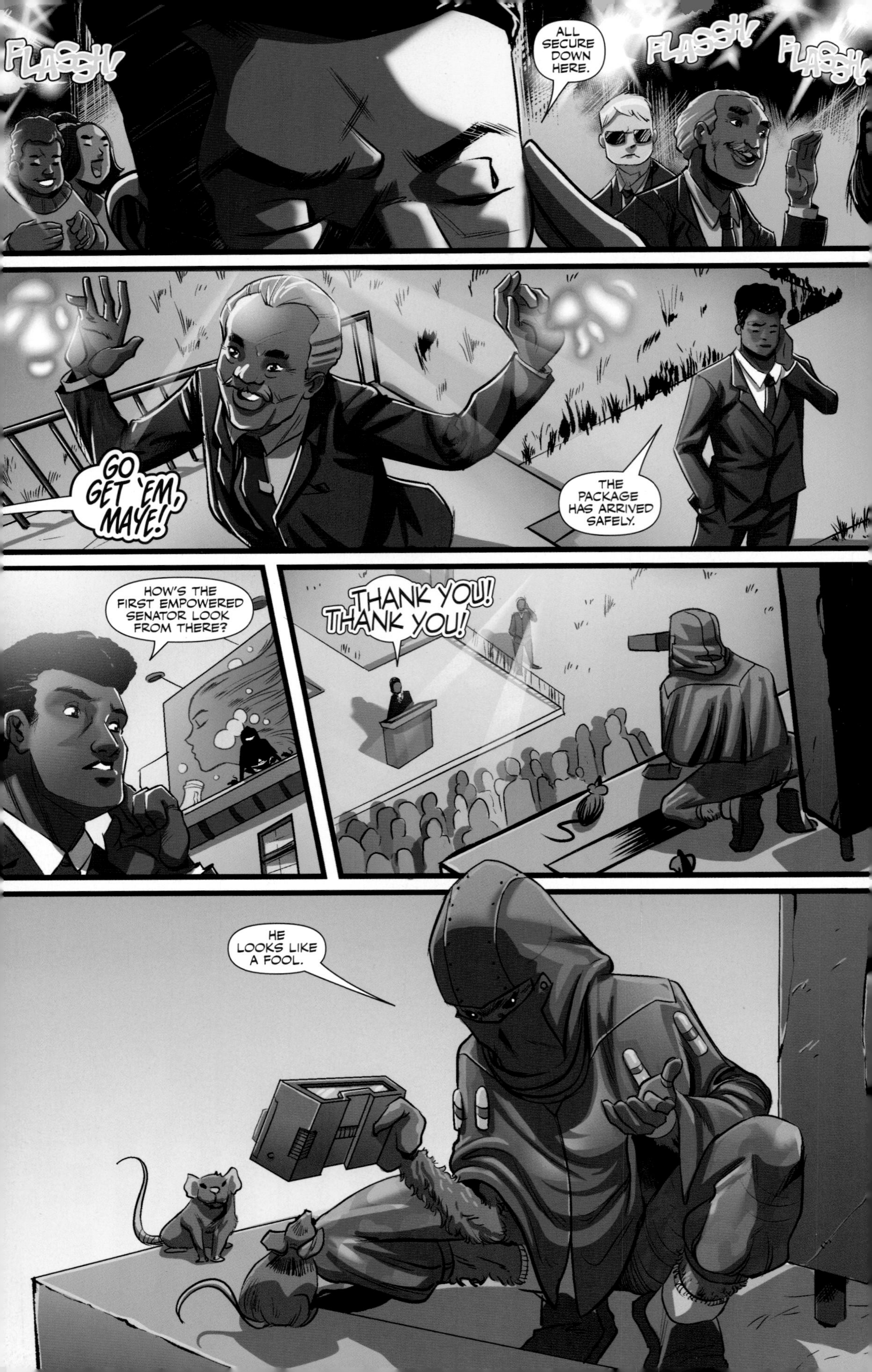
FLASSH!
ALL SECURE DOWN HERE.
FLASSH!
FLASSH!
GO GET 'EM, MAYE!
THE PACKAGE HAS ARRIVED SAFELY.
HOW'S THE FIRST EMPOWERED SENATOR LOOK FROM THERE?
THANK YOU! THANK YOU!
HE LOOKS LIKE A FOOL.

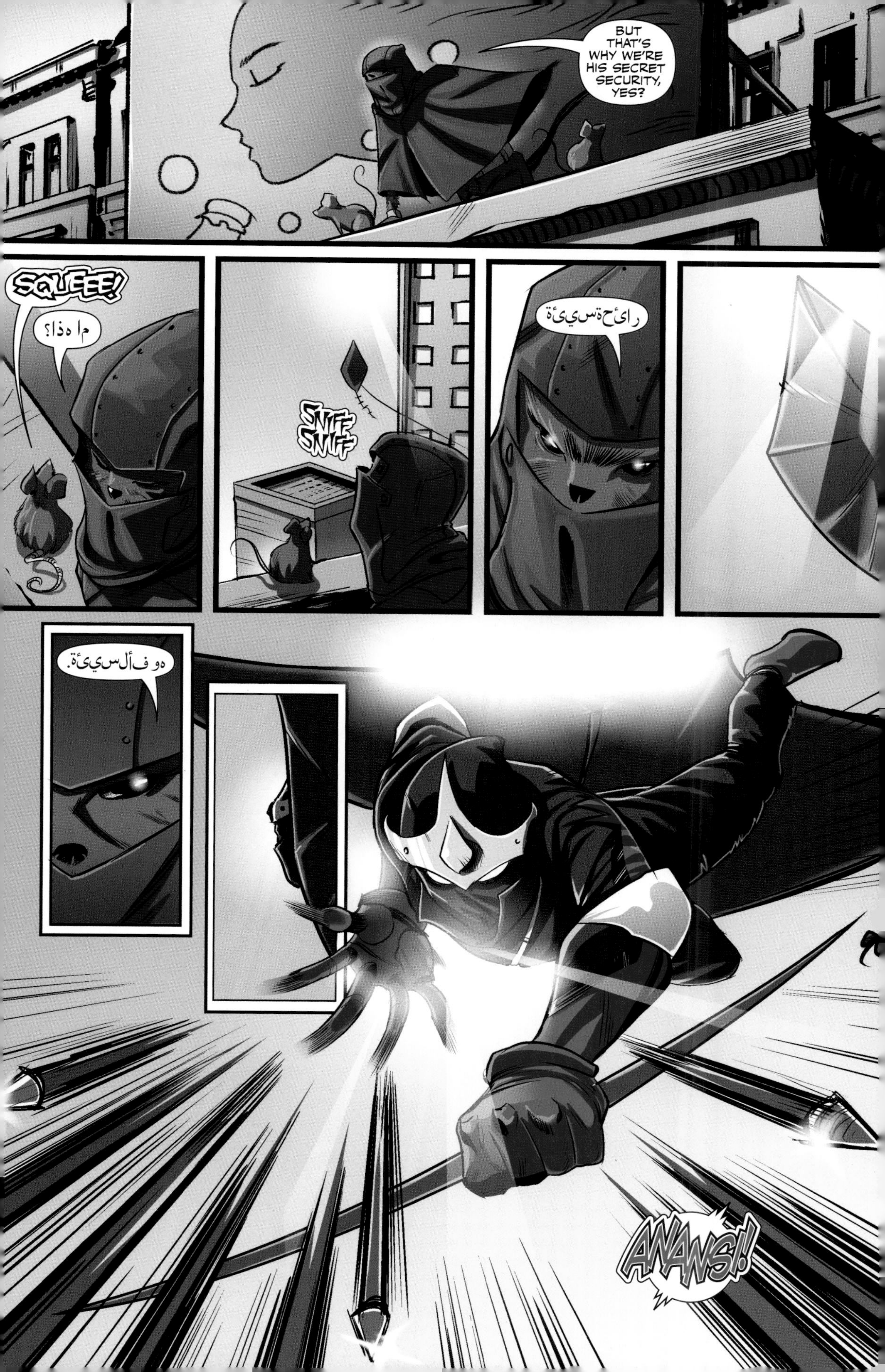
BUT THAT'S WHY WE'RE HIS SECRET SECURITY, YES?
SQUEEE!
ما هذا؟
SNIFF SNIFF
رائحة سيئة
هو فأل سيئة.
ANANSI!

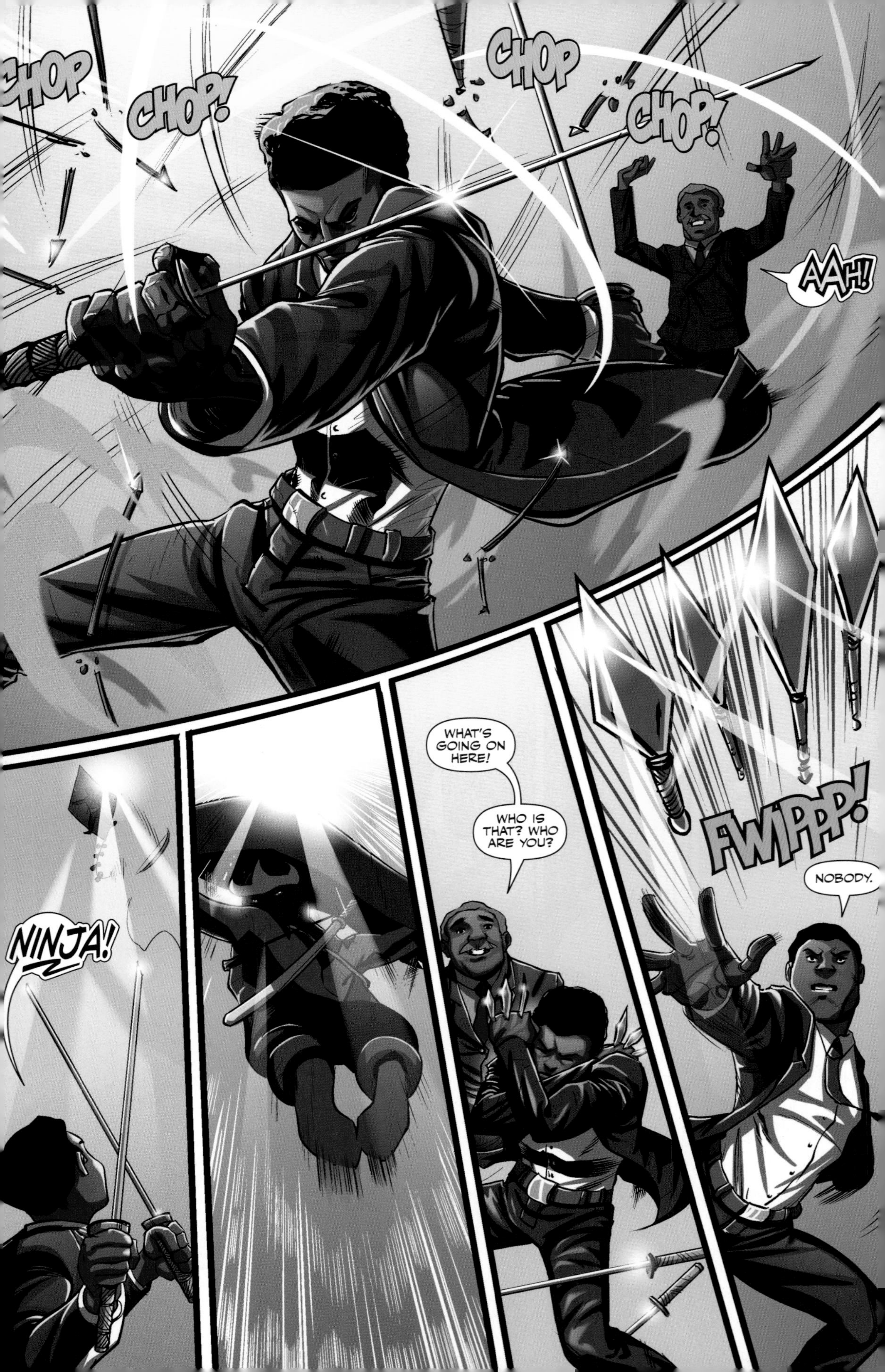
CHOP
CHOP!
CHOP
CHOP!
AAH!
FWIPPP!
NOBODY.
WHAT'S GOING ON HERE!
WHO IS THAT? WHO ARE YOU?
NINJA!

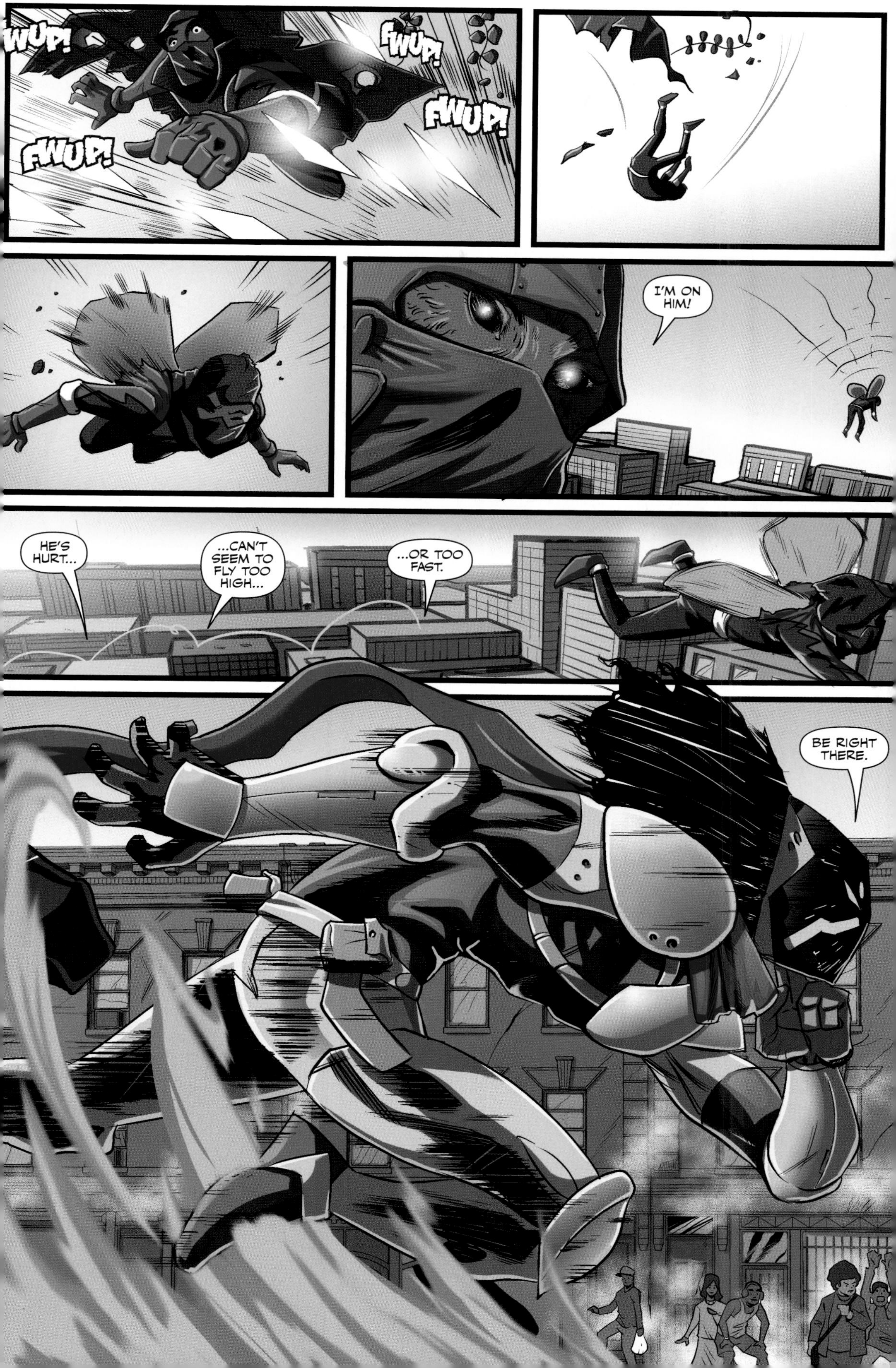

WUP!
FWUP!
FWUP!
FWUP!
I'M ON HIM!
HE'S HURT...
...CAN'T SEEM TO FLY TOO HIGH...
...OR TOO FAST.
BE RIGHT THERE.

THWIZZ!

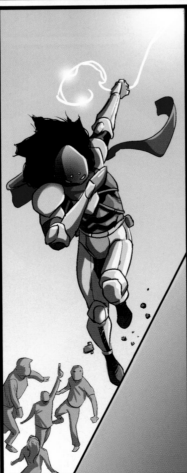

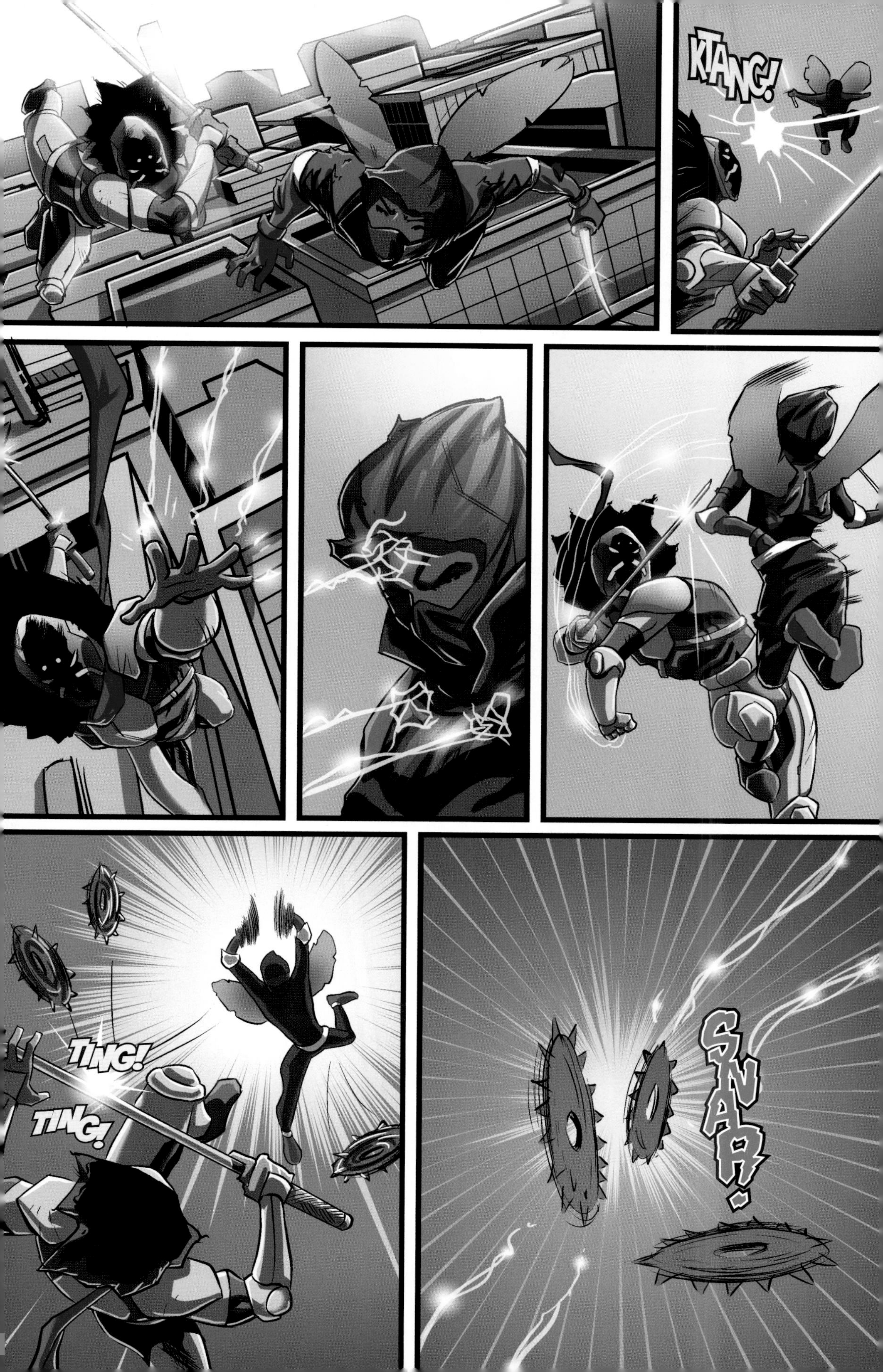
KTANG!
TING!
TING!
SNAP!

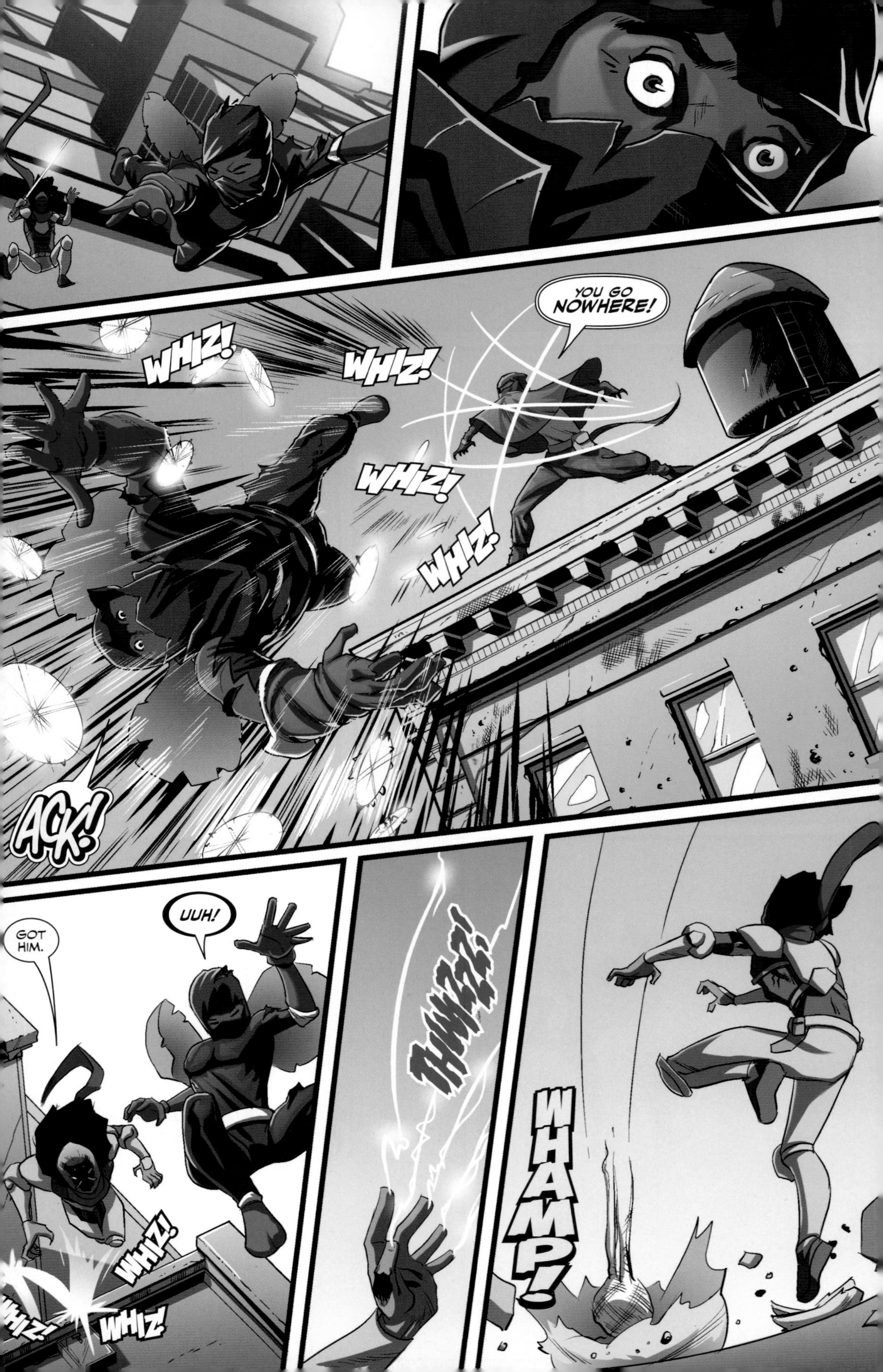
YOU GO NOWHERE!
WHIZ!
WHIZ!
WHIZ!
WHIZ!
ACK!
GOT HIM.
UUH!
WHIZ!
WHIZ!
WHIZ!
THWZZZZ!
WHAMP!

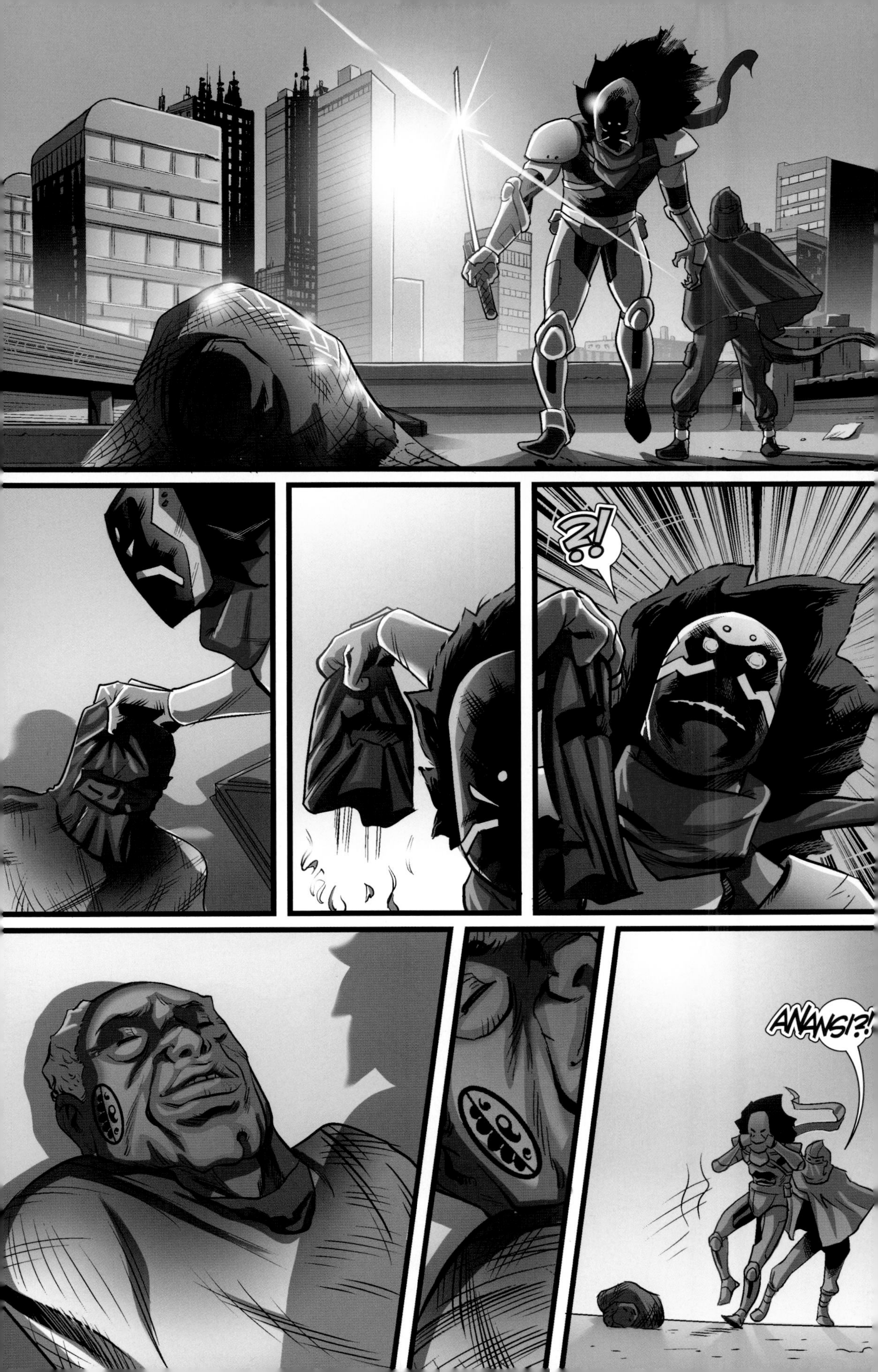
?!
ANANSI!?!

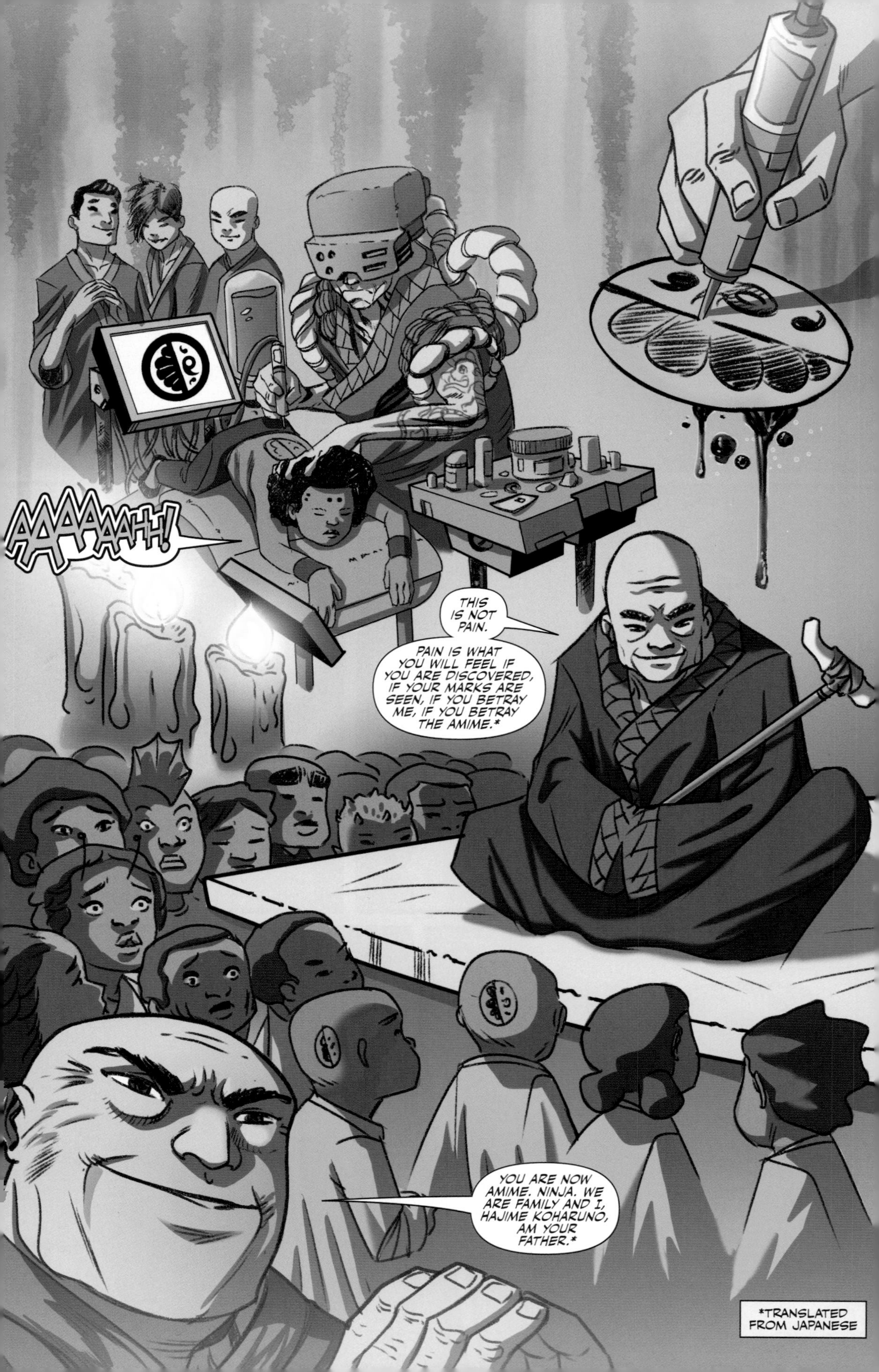
AAAAAAHH!
THIS IS NOT PAIN.
PAIN IS WHAT YOU WILL FEEL IF YOU ARE DISCOVERED, IF YOUR MARKS ARE SEEN, IF YOU BETRAY ME, IF YOU BETRAY THE AMIME.*
YOU ARE NOW AMIME. NINJA. WE ARE FAMILY AND I, HAJIME KOHARUNO, AM YOUR FATHER.*
*TRANSLATED FROM JAPANESE

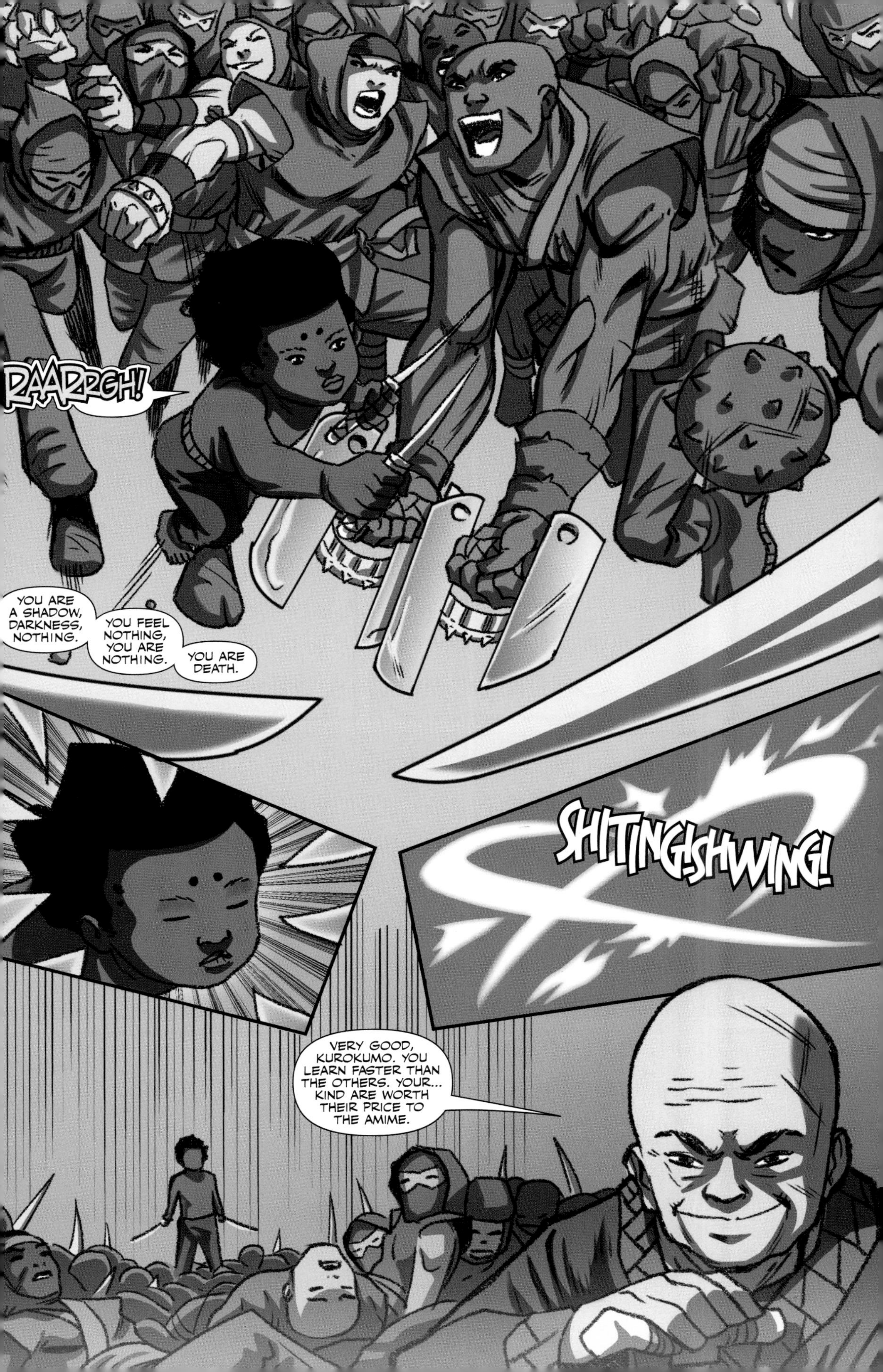
RAARRGH!
YOU ARE A SHADOW, DARKNESS, NOTHING.
YOU FEEL NOTHING, YOU ARE NOTHING.
YOU ARE DEATH.
SHITING!SHWING!
VERY GOOD, KUROKUMO. YOU LEARN FASTER THAN THE OTHERS. YOUR... KIND ARE WORTH THEIR PRICE TO THE AMIME.

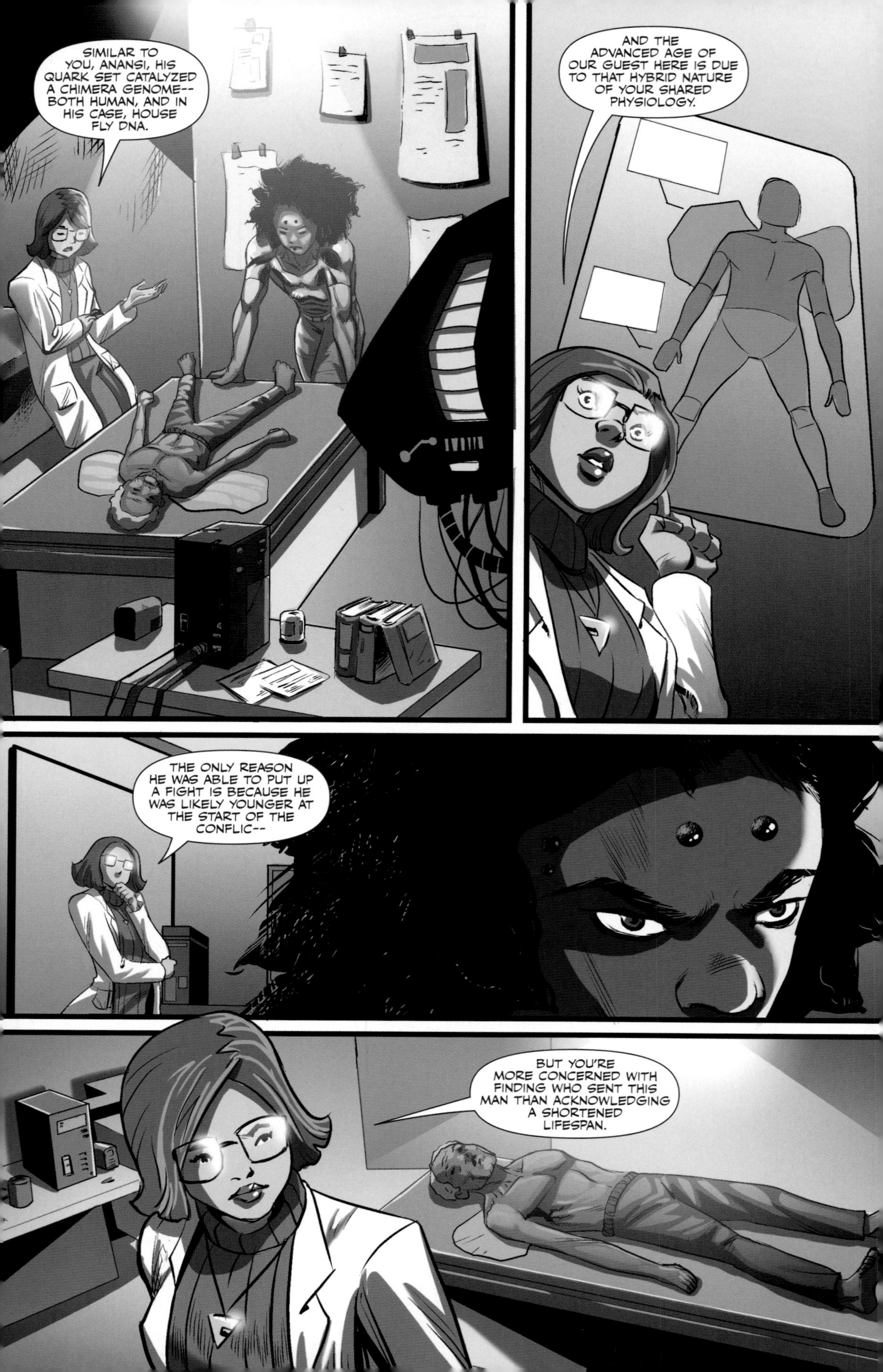
SIMILAR TO YOU, ANANSI, HIS QUARK SET CATALYZED A CHIMERA GENOME-- BOTH HUMAN, AND IN HIS CASE, HOUSE FLY DNA.
AND THE ADVANCED AGE OF OUR GUEST HERE IS DUE TO THAT HYBRID NATURE OF YOUR SHARED PHYSIOLOGY.
THE ONLY REASON HE WAS ABLE TO PUT UP A FIGHT IS BECAUSE HE WAS LIKELY YOUNGER AT THE START OF THE CONFLIC--
BUT YOU'RE MORE CONCERNED WITH FINDING WHO SENT THIS MAN THAN ACKNOWLEDGING A SHORTENED LIFESPAN.

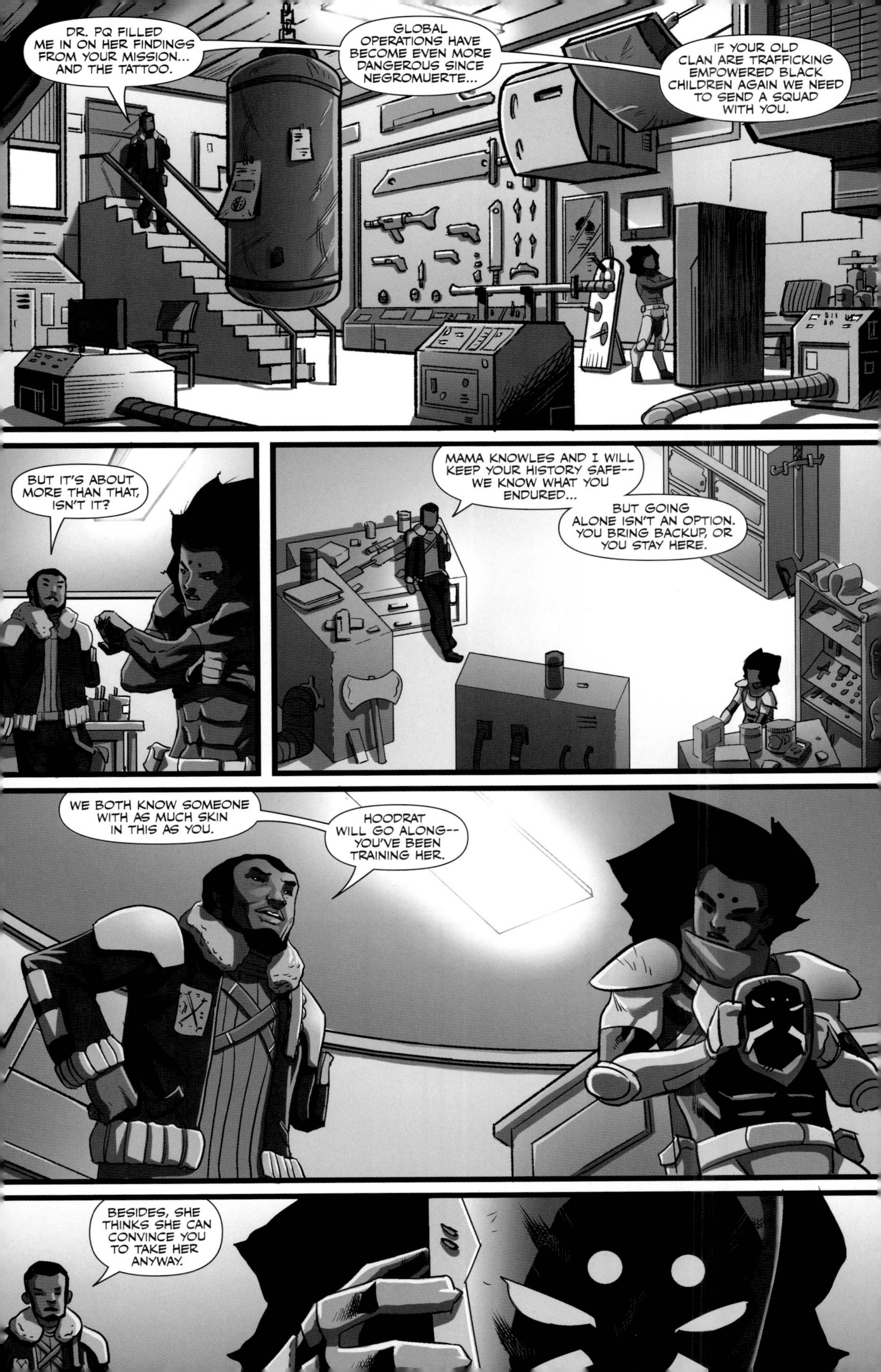
DR. PQ FILLED ME IN ON HER FINDINGS FROM YOUR MISSION... AND THE TATTOO.
GLOBAL OPERATIONS HAVE BECOME EVEN MORE DANGEROUS SINCE NEGROMUERTE...
IF YOUR OLD CLAN ARE TRAFFICKING EMPOWERED BLACK CHILDREN AGAIN WE NEED TO SEND A SQUAD WITH YOU.
BUT IT'S ABOUT MORE THAN THAT, ISN'T IT?
MAMA KNOWLES AND I WILL KEEP YOUR HISTORY SAFE-- WE KNOW WHAT YOU ENDURED...
BUT GOING ALONE ISN'T AN OPTION. YOU BRING BACKUP, OR YOU STAY HERE.
WE BOTH KNOW SOMEONE WITH AS MUCH SKIN IN THIS AS YOU.
HOODRAT WILL GO ALONG-- YOU'VE BEEN TRAINING HER.
BESIDES, SHE THINKS SHE CAN CONVINCE YOU TO TAKE HER ANYWAY.

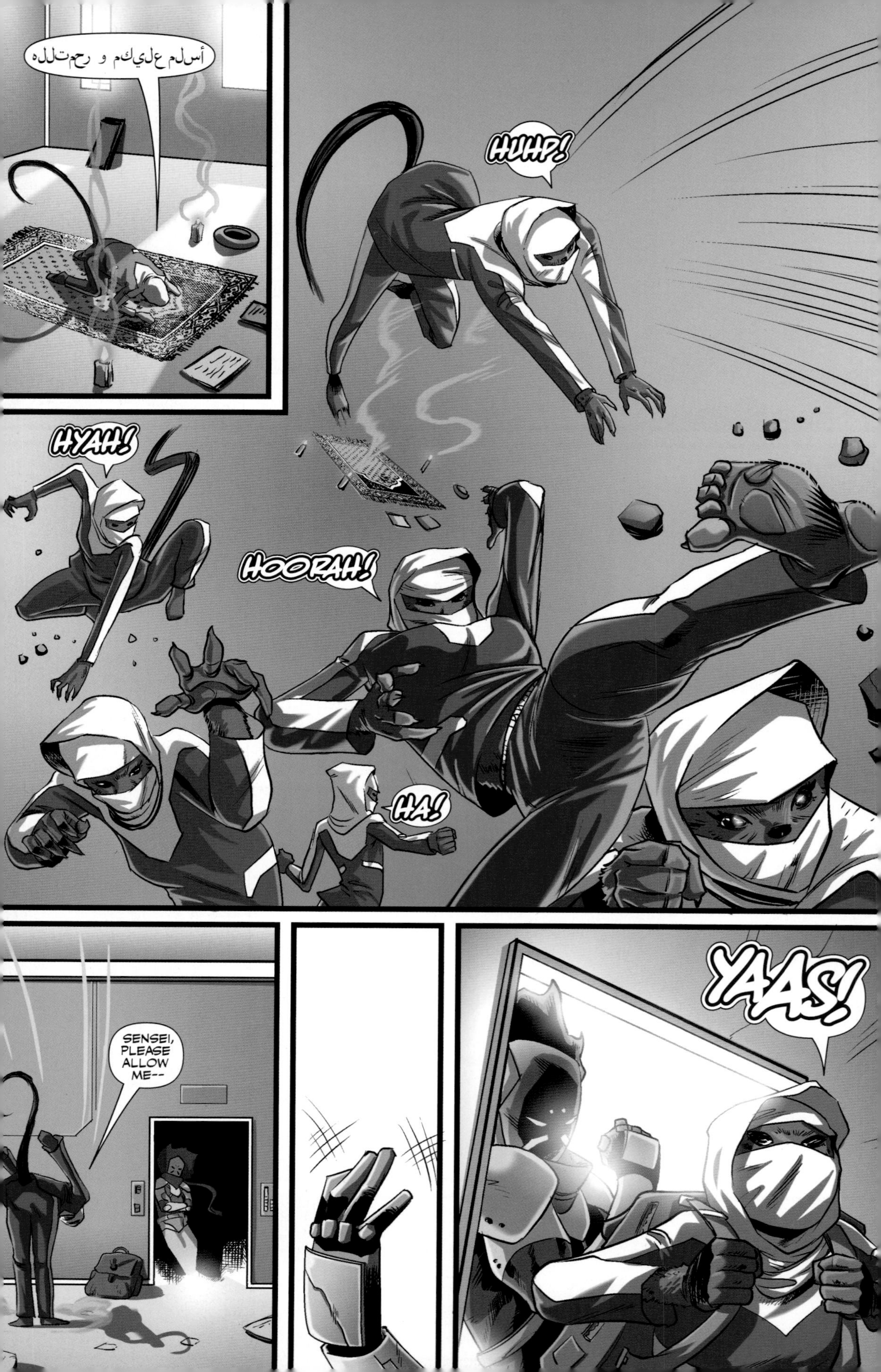
أسلم عليكم و رحمت الله
HUHP!
HYAH!
HOORAH!
HA!
SENSEI, PLEASE ALLOW ME--
YAAS!

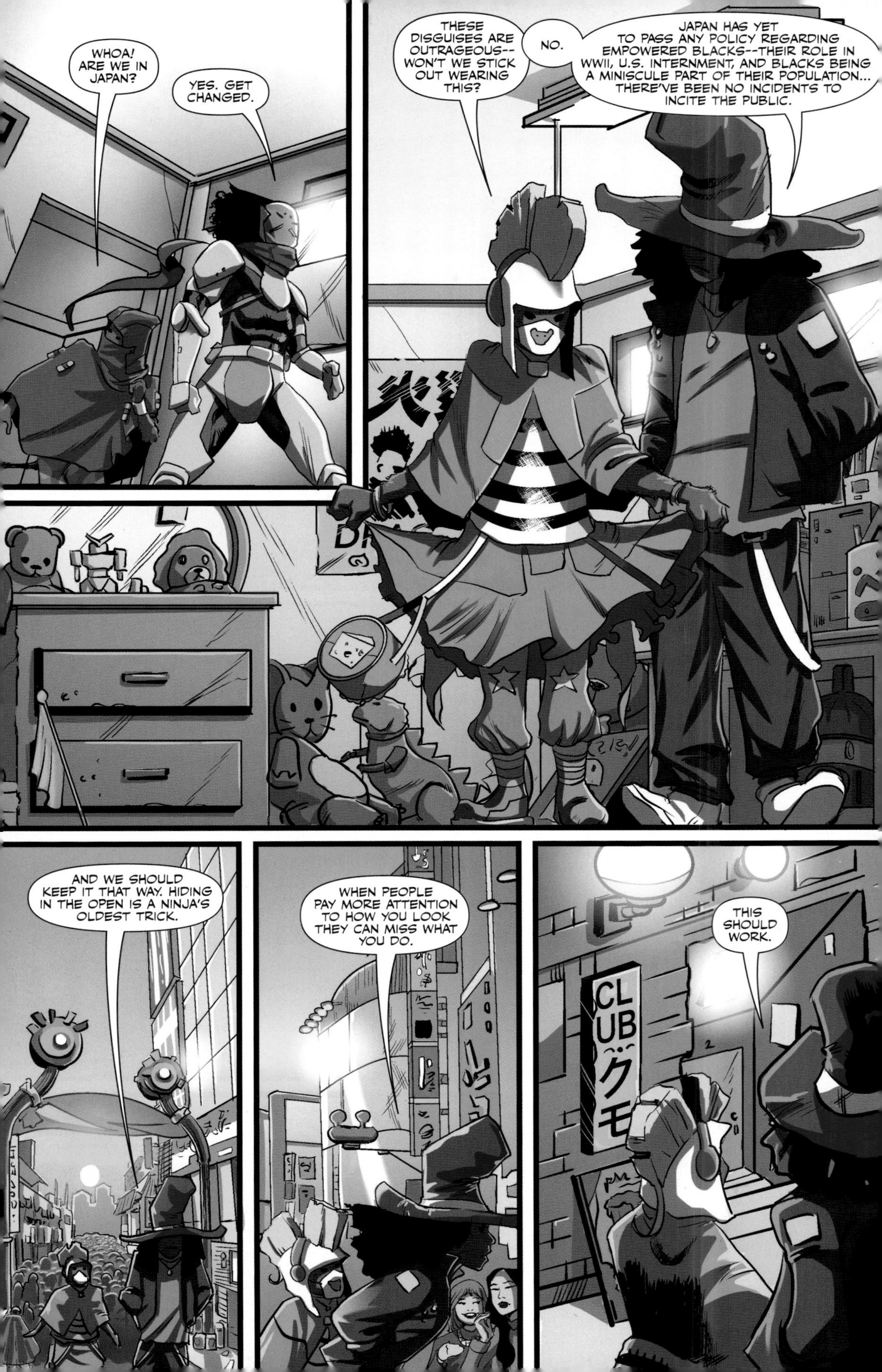
WHOA! ARE WE IN JAPAN?
YES. GET CHANGED.
THESE DISGUISES ARE OUTRAGEOUS-- WON'T WE STICK OUT WEARING THIS?
NO.
JAPAN HAS YET TO PASS ANY POLICY REGARDING EMPOWERED BLACKS--THEIR ROLE IN WWII, U.S. INTERNMENT, AND BLACKS BEING A MINISCULE PART OF THEIR POPULATION... THERE'VE BEEN NO INCIDENTS TO INCITE THE PUBLIC.
AND WE SHOULD KEEP IT THAT WAY. HIDING IN THE OPEN IS A NINJA'S OLDEST TRICK.
WHEN PEOPLE PAY MORE ATTENTION TO HOW YOU LOOK THEY CAN MISS WHAT YOU DO.
CLUB クモ
THIS SHOULD WORK.

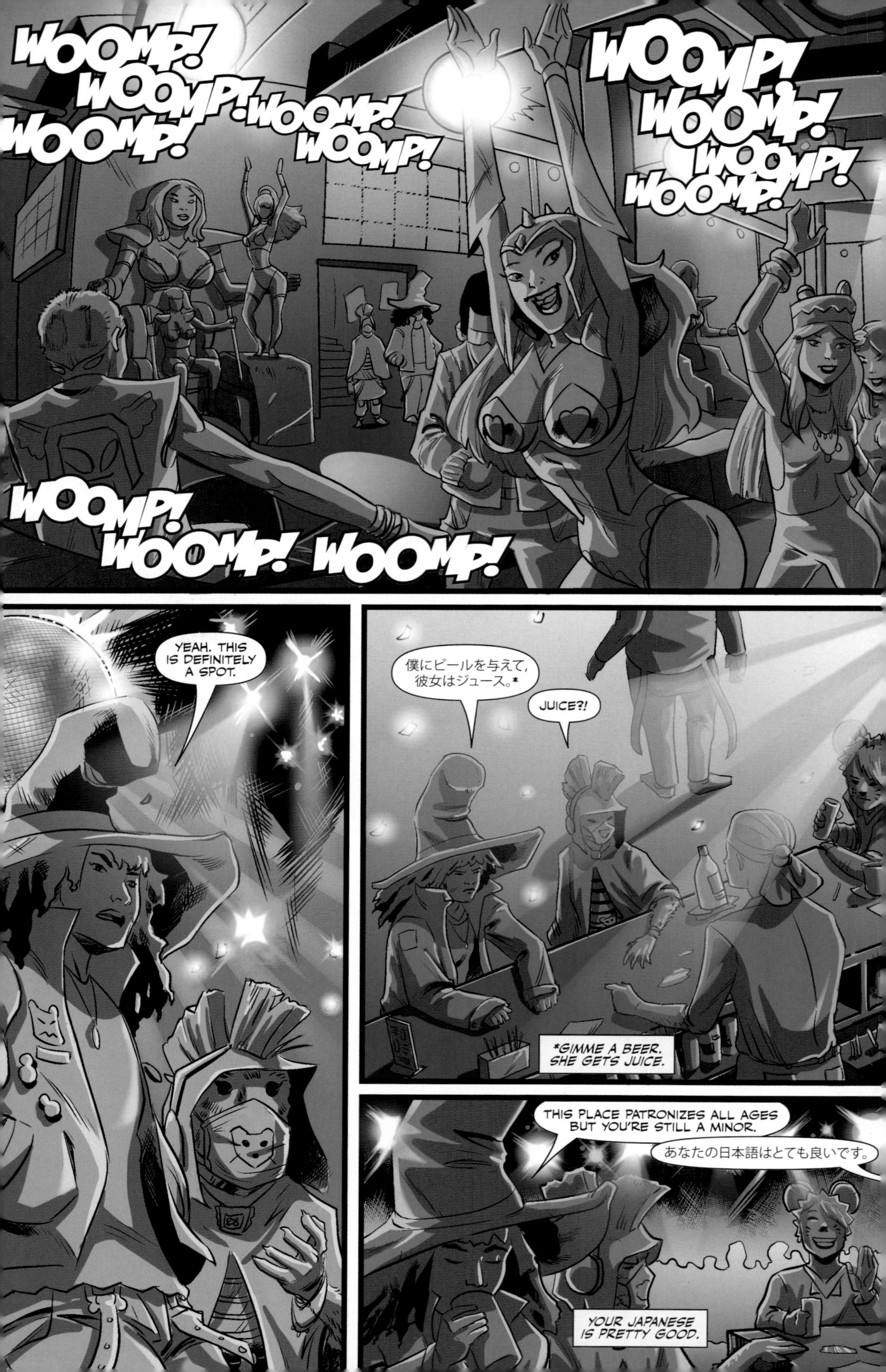
WOOMP! WOOMP! WOOMP! WOOMP! WOOMP!
WOOMP! WOOMP! WOOMP! WOOMP!
WOOMP! WOOMP! WOOMP!
YEAH. THIS IS DEFINITELY A SPOT.
僕にビールを与えて，彼女はジュース。*
JUICE?!
*GIMME A BEER. SHE GETS JUICE.
THIS PLACE PATRONIZES ALL AGES BUT YOU'RE STILL A MINOR.
あなたの日本語はとても良いです。
YOUR JAPANESE IS PRETTY GOOD.

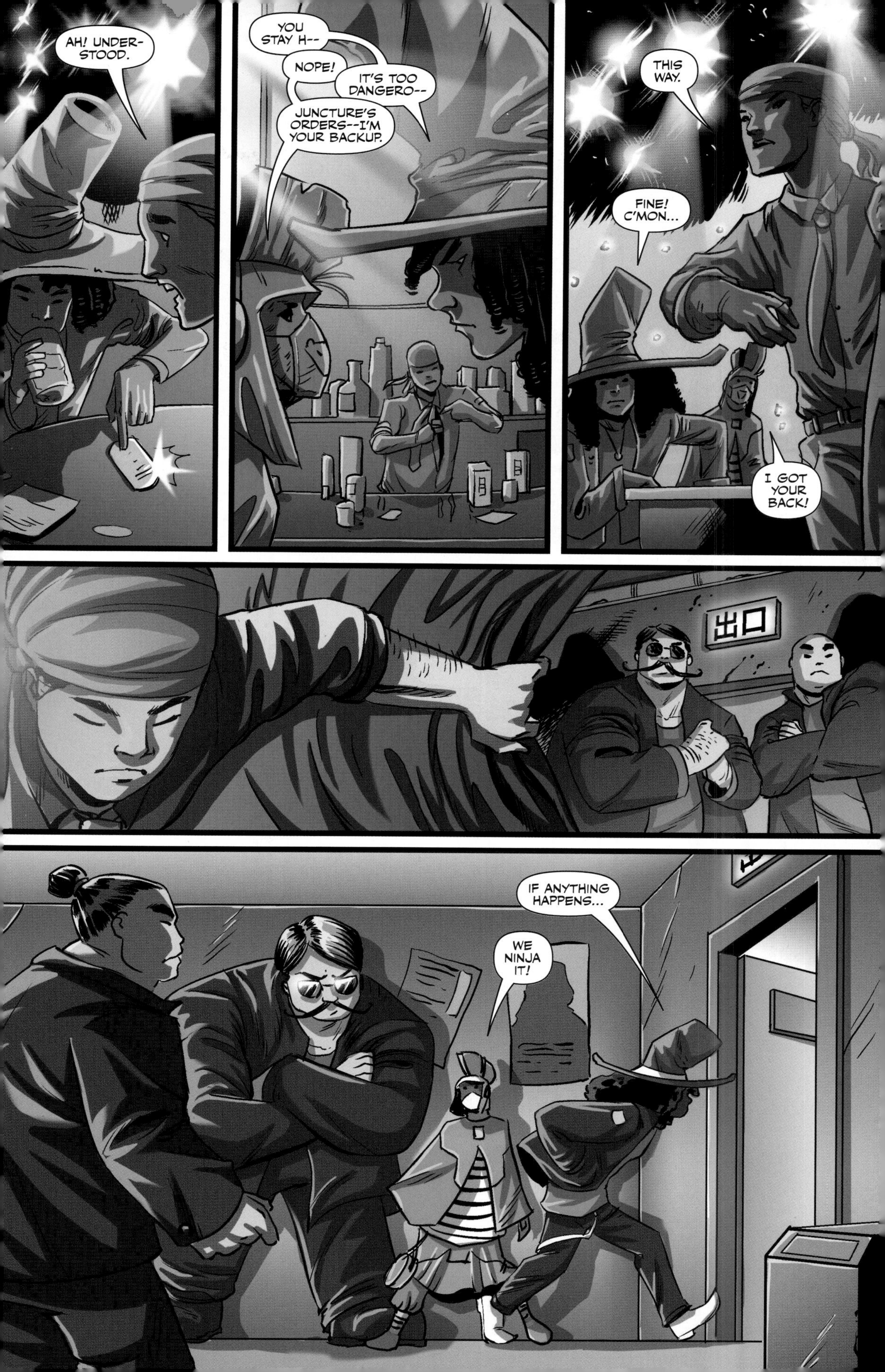
AH! UNDER-STOOD.
YOU STAY H--
NOPE!
IT'S TOO DANGERO--
JUNCTURE'S ORDERS--I'M YOUR BACKUP.
THIS WAY.
FINE! C'MON...
I GOT YOUR BACK!
出口
IF ANYTHING HAPPENS...
WE NINJA IT!

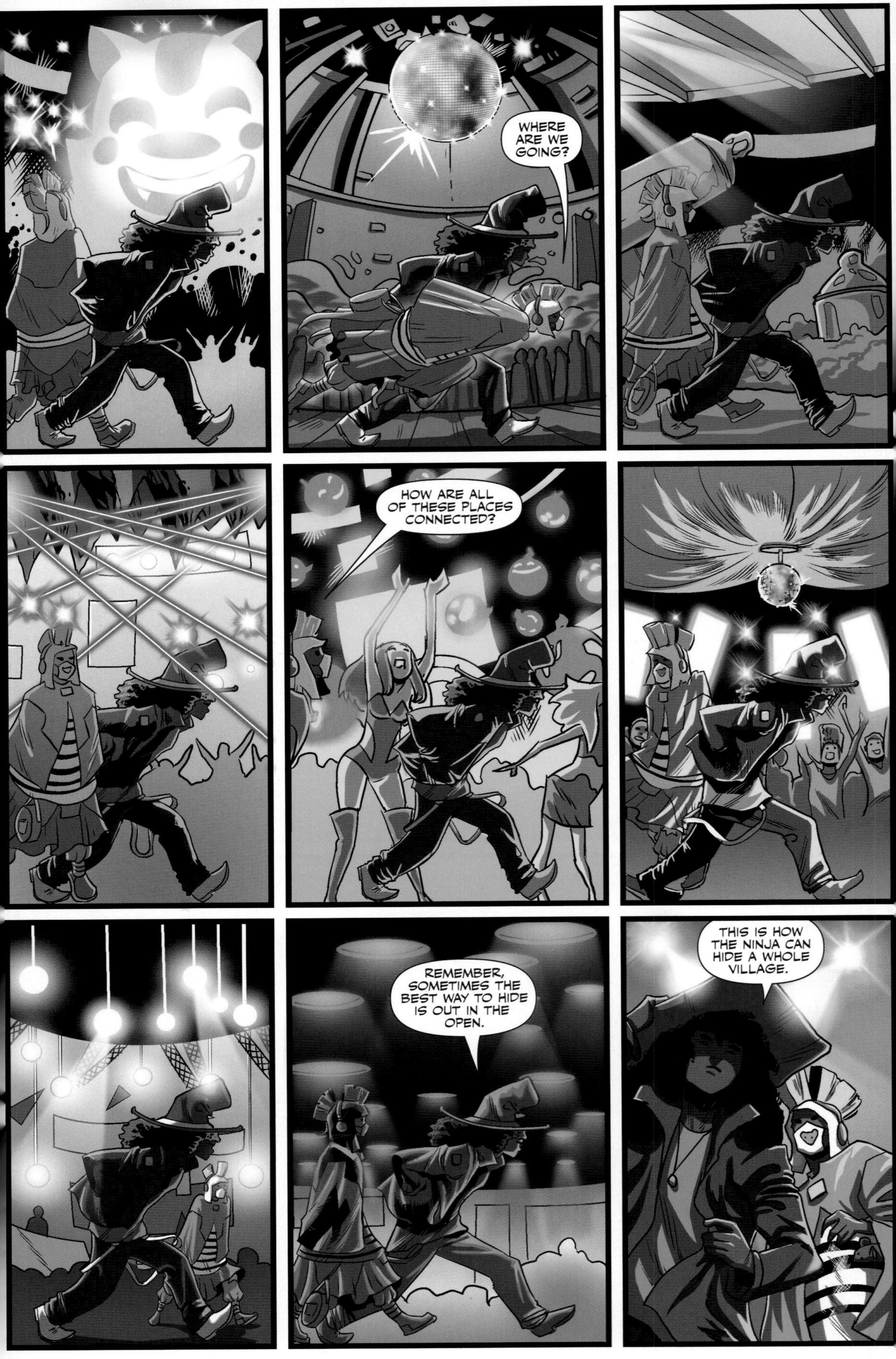
WHERE ARE WE GOING?
HOW ARE ALL OF THESE PLACES CONNECTED?
REMEMBER, SOMETIMES THE BEST WAY TO HIDE IS OUT IN THE OPEN.
THIS IS HOW THE NINJA CAN HIDE A WHOLE VILLAGE.

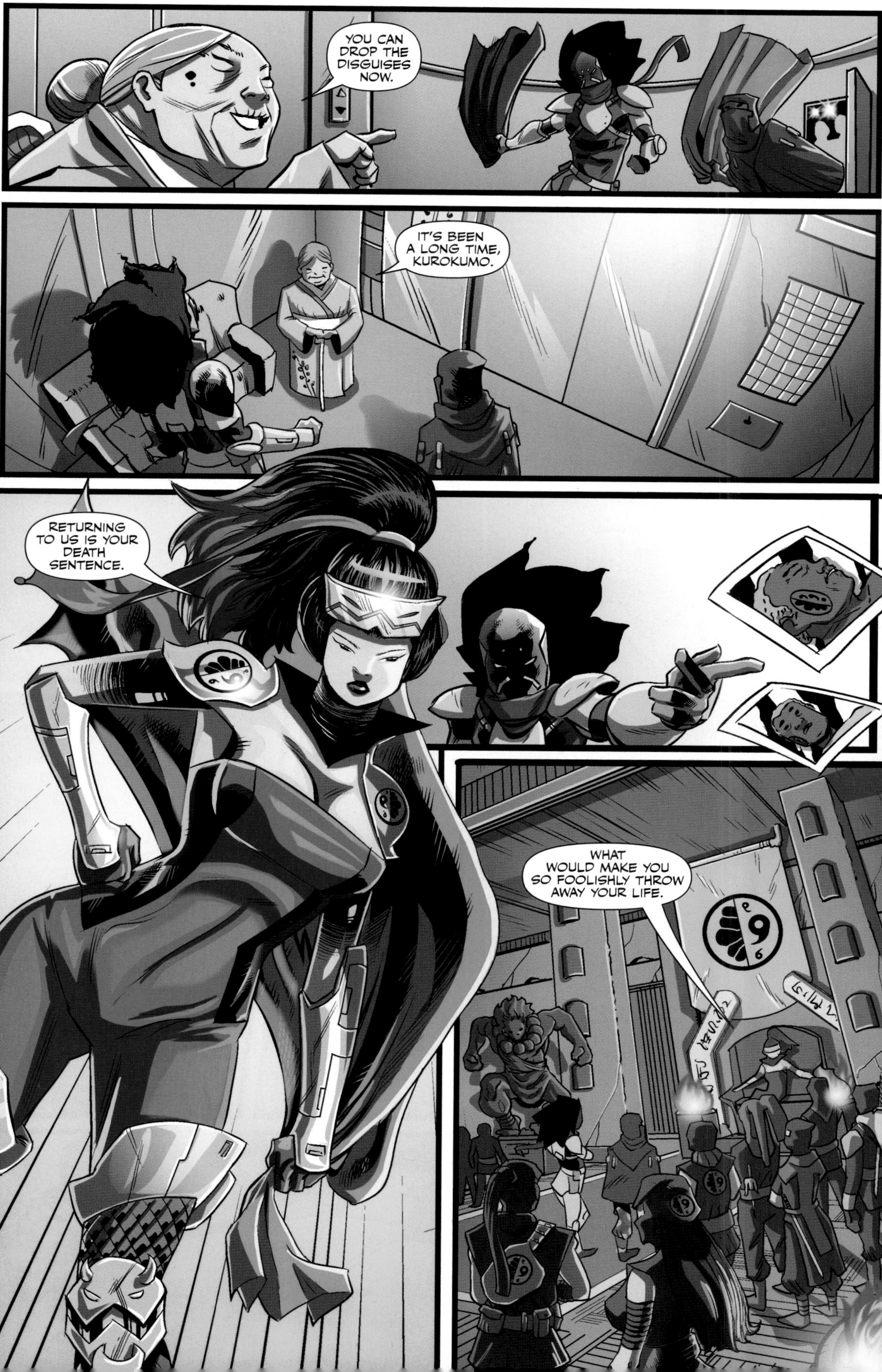

YOU CAN DROP THE DISGUISES NOW.
IT'S BEEN A LONG TIME, KUROKUMO.
RETURNING TO US IS YOUR DEATH SENTENCE.
WHAT WOULD MAKE YOU SO FOOLISHLY THROW AWAY YOUR LIFE.

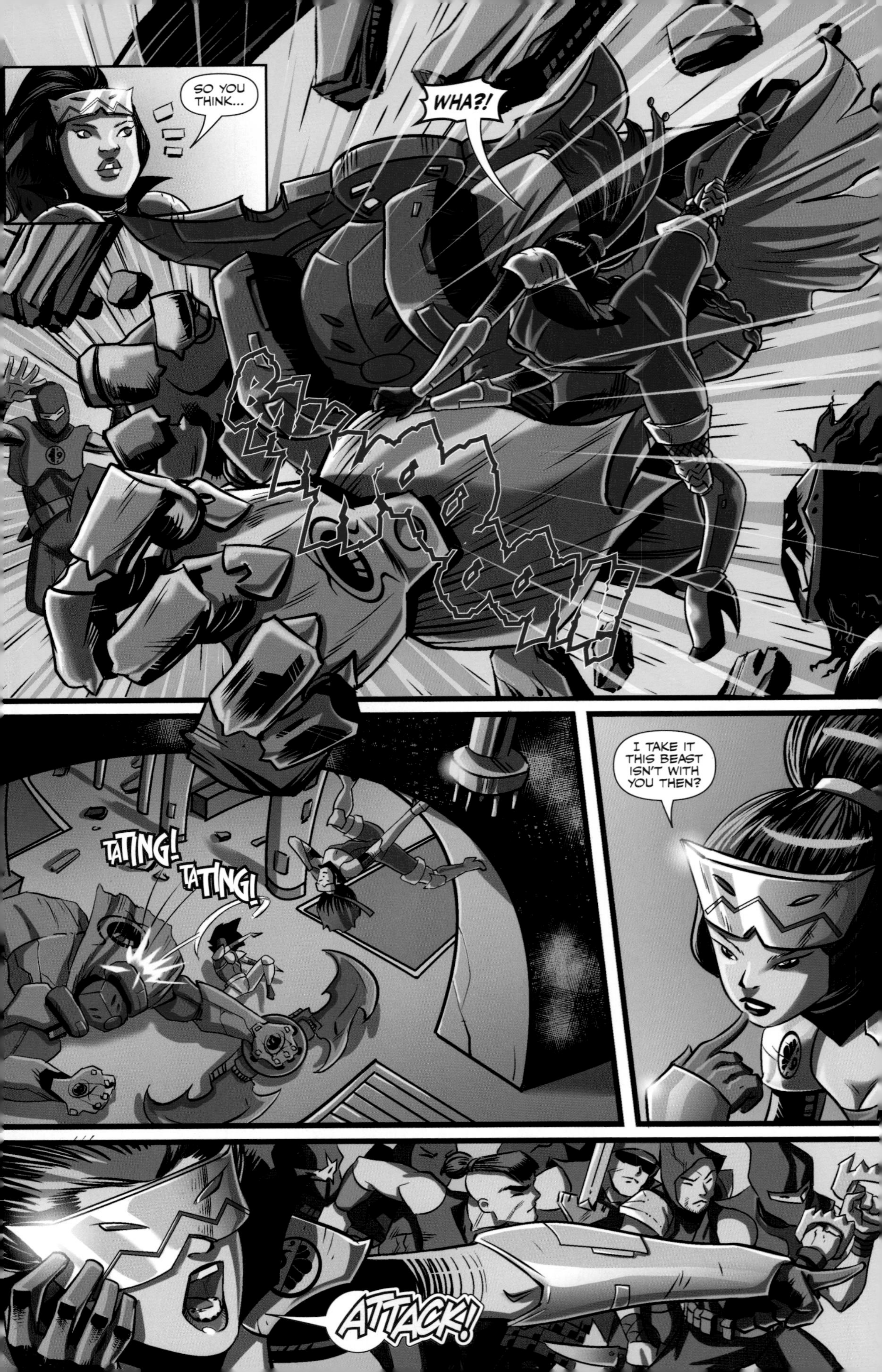
SO YOU THINK...
WHA?!
TATING!
TATING!
I TAKE IT THIS BEAST ISN'T WITH YOU THEN?
ATTACK!

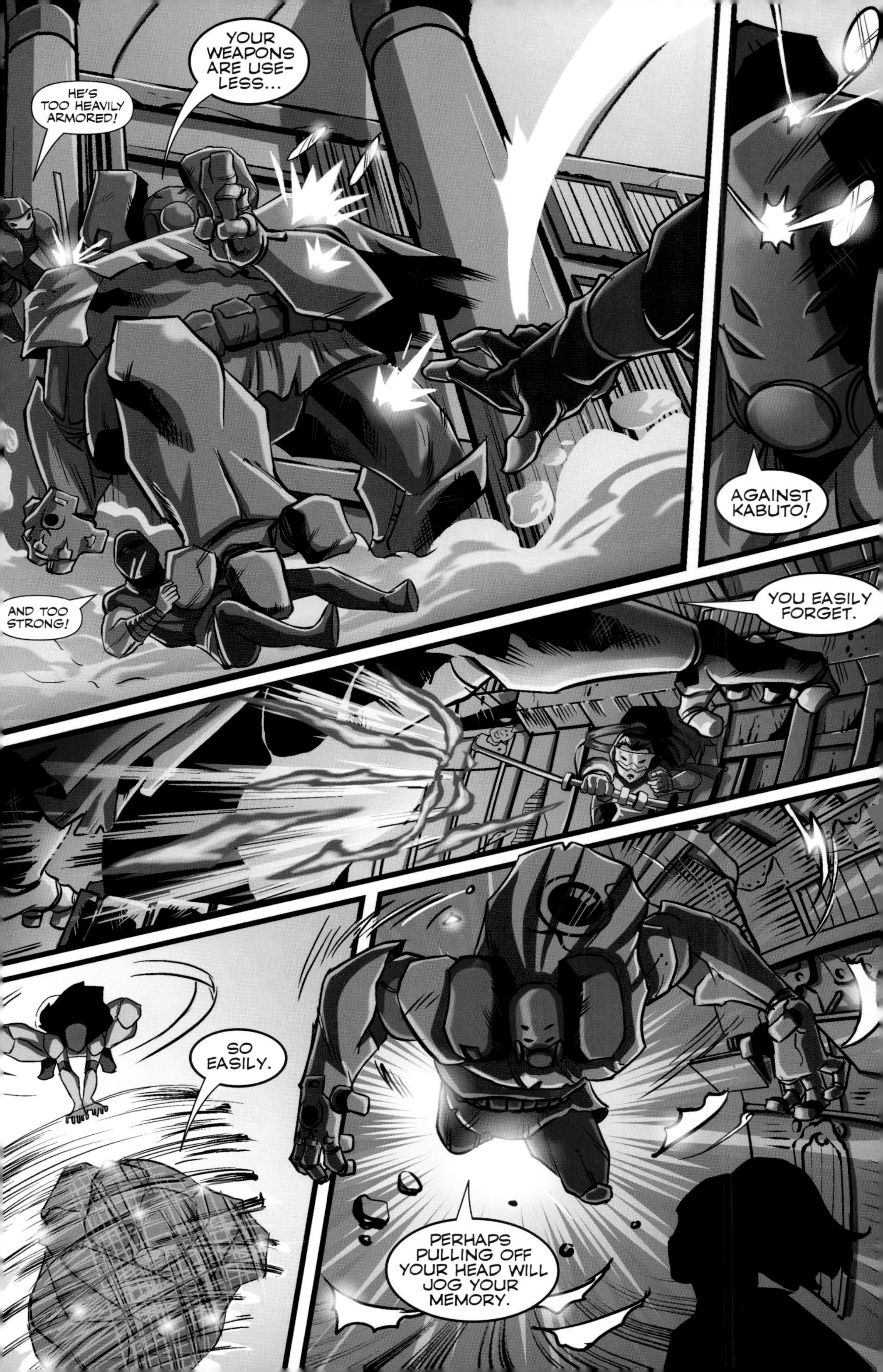
HE'S TOO HEAVILY ARMORED!
YOUR WEAPONS ARE USE-LESS...
AGAINST KABUTO!
AND TOO STRONG!
YOU EASILY FORGET.
SO EASILY.
PERHAPS PULLING OFF YOUR HEAD WILL JOG YOUR MEMORY.

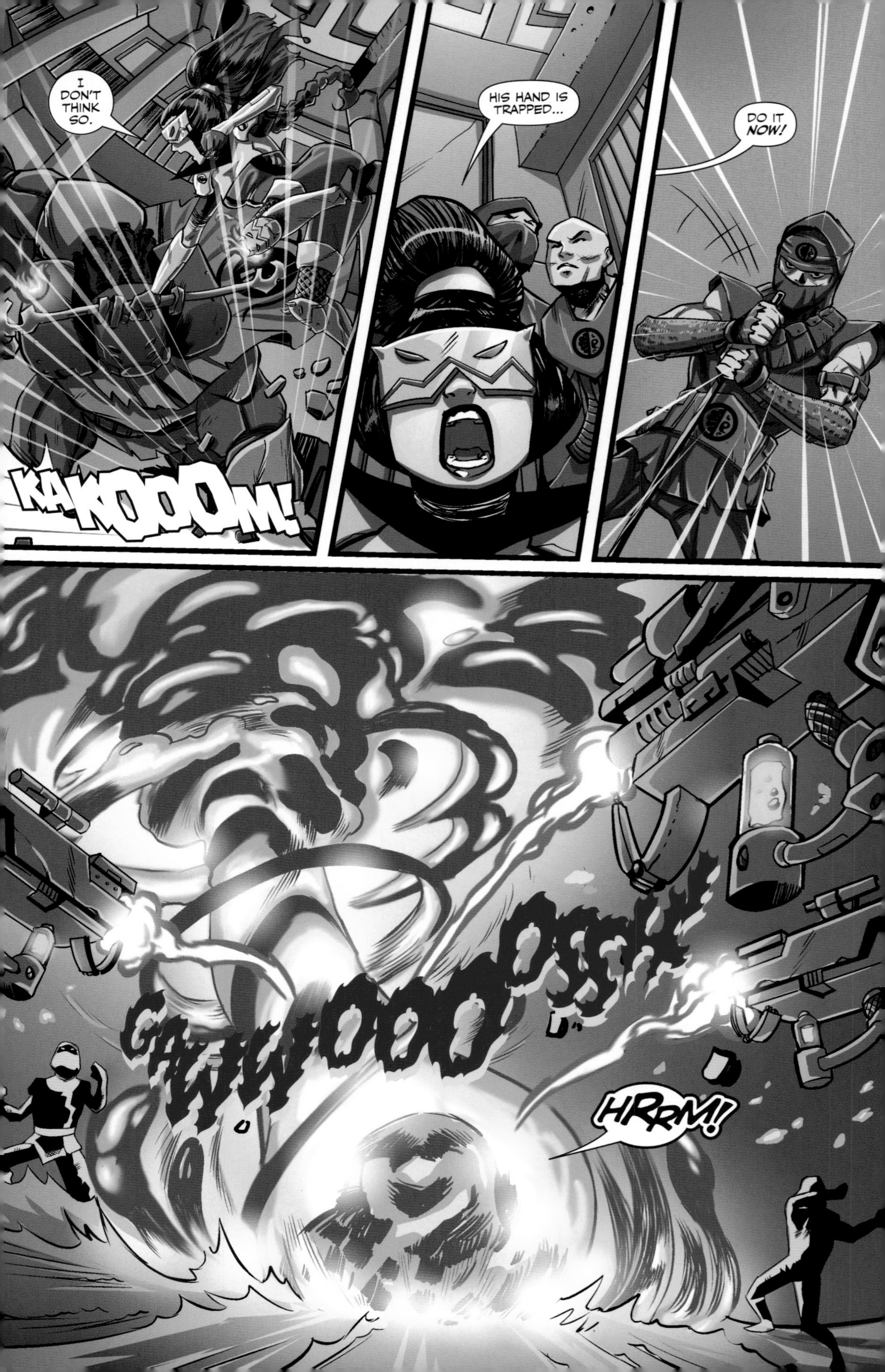
I DON'T THINK SO.
KAKOOOM!
HIS HAND IS TRAPPED...
DO IT NOW!
HRRM!

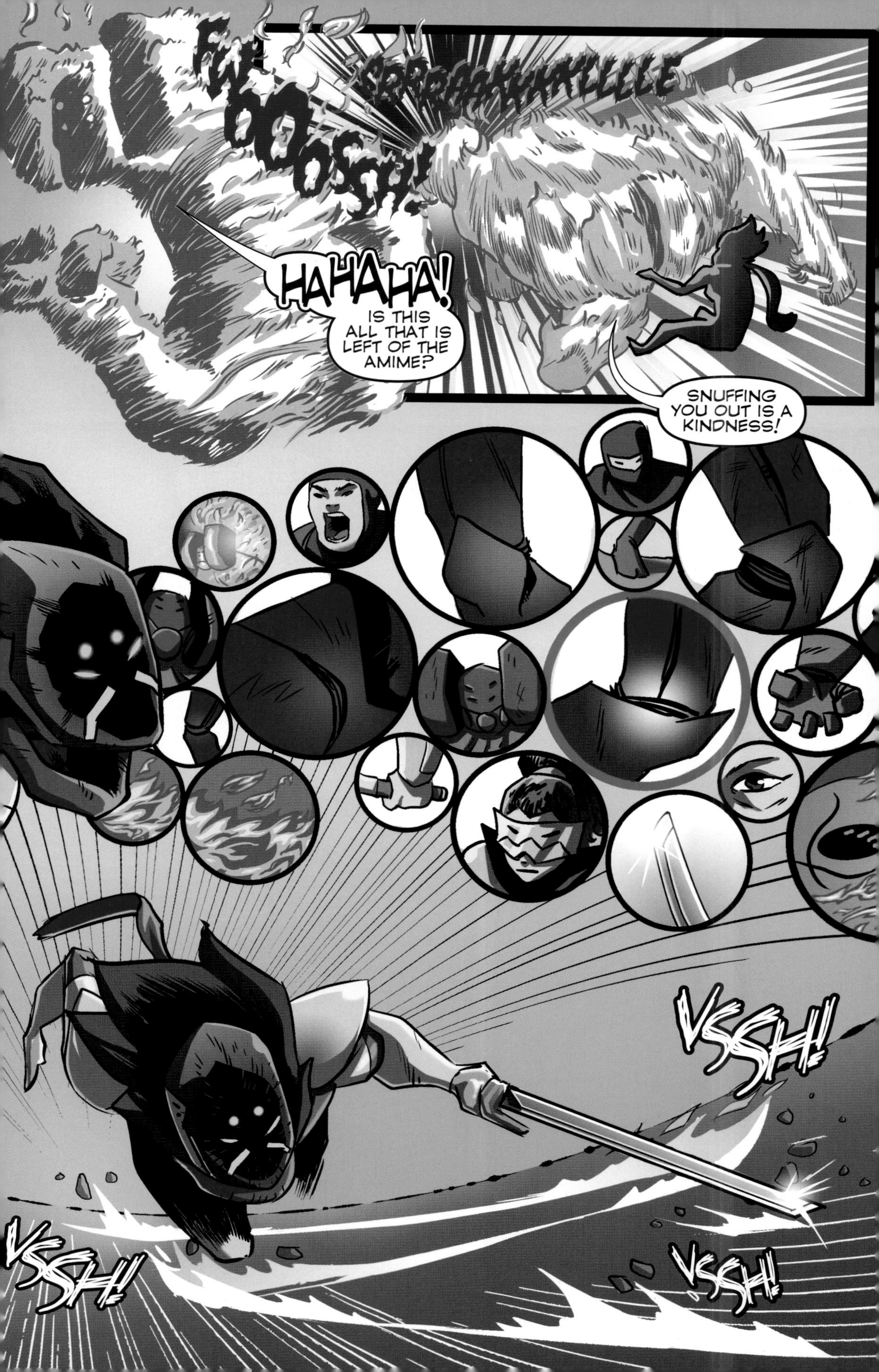
FWOOOSSH!
HAHAHA! IS THIS ALL THAT IS LEFT OF THE AMIME?
SNUFFING YOU OUT IS A KINDNESS!
VSSH!
VSSH!
VSSH!

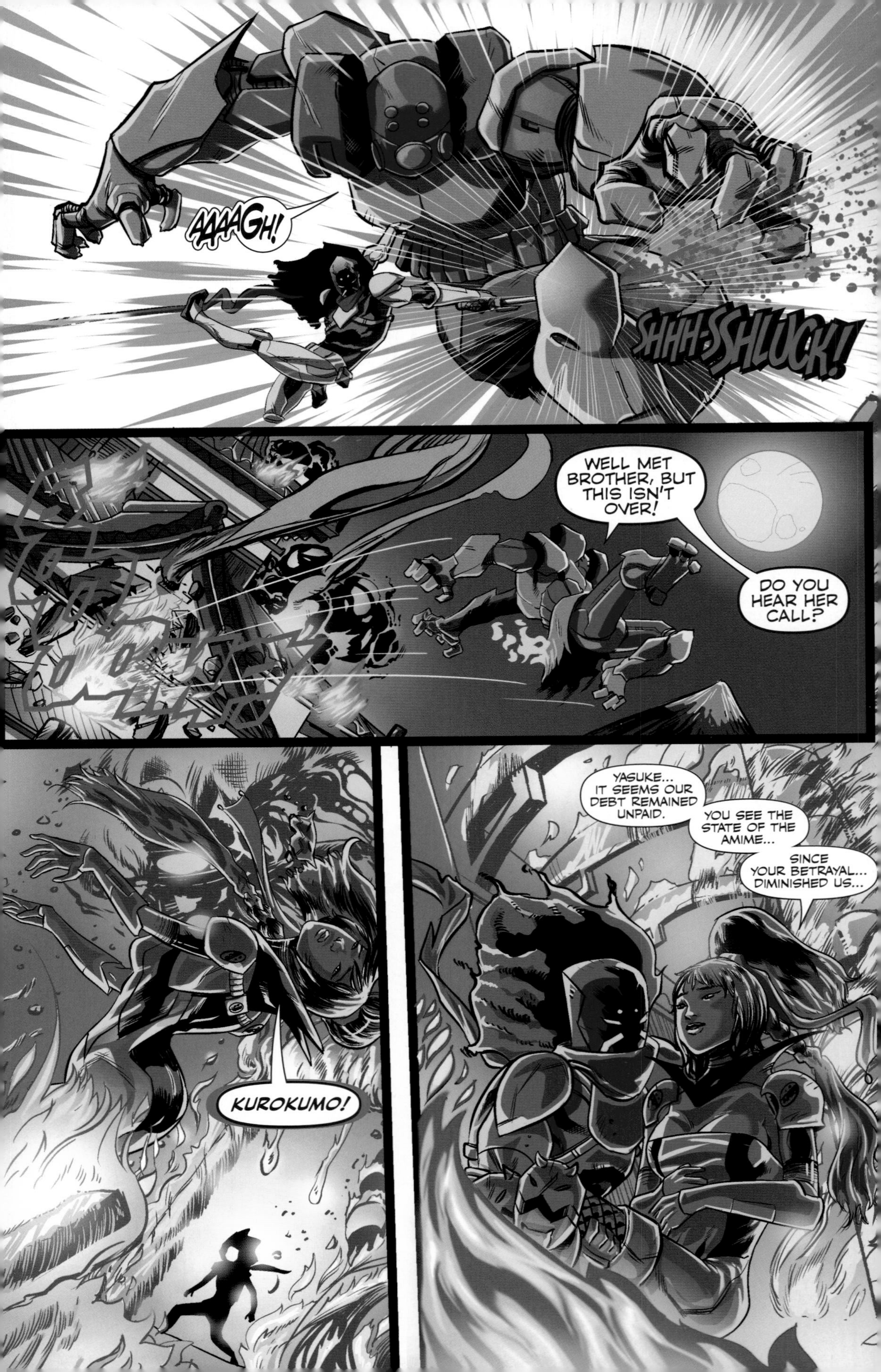
AAAAGH!
SHHH-SSHLUCK!
WELL MET BROTHER, BUT THIS ISN'T OVER!
DO YOU HEAR HER CALL?
KUROKUMO!
YASUKE... IT SEEMS OUR DEBT REMAINED UNPAID.
YOU SEE THE STATE OF THE AMIME...
SINCE YOUR BETRAYAL... DIMINISHED US...

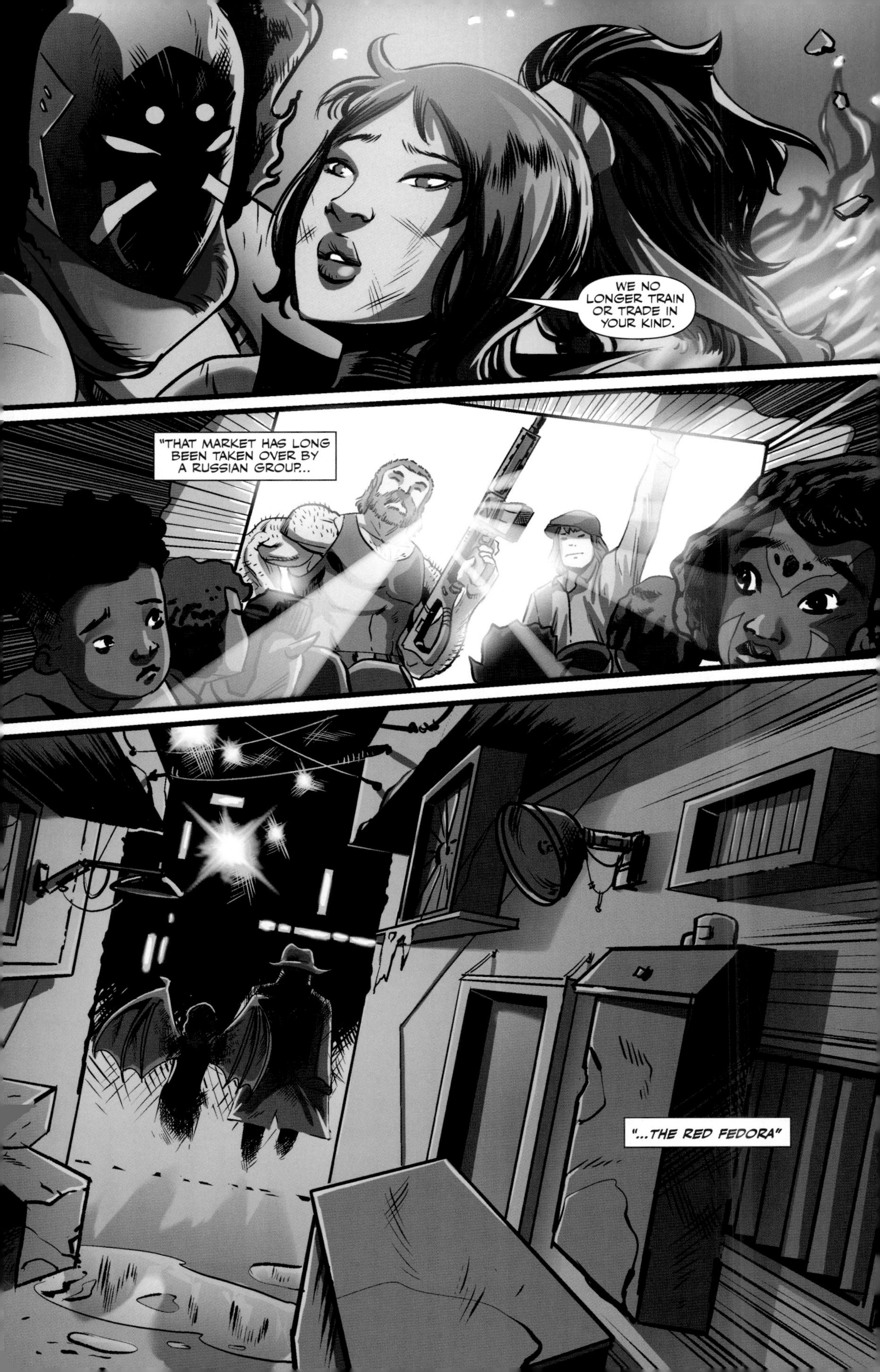
WE NO LONGER TRAIN OR TRADE IN YOUR KIND.
"THAT MARKET HAS LONG BEEN TAKEN OVER BY A RUSSIAN GROUP...
"...THE RED FEDORA"

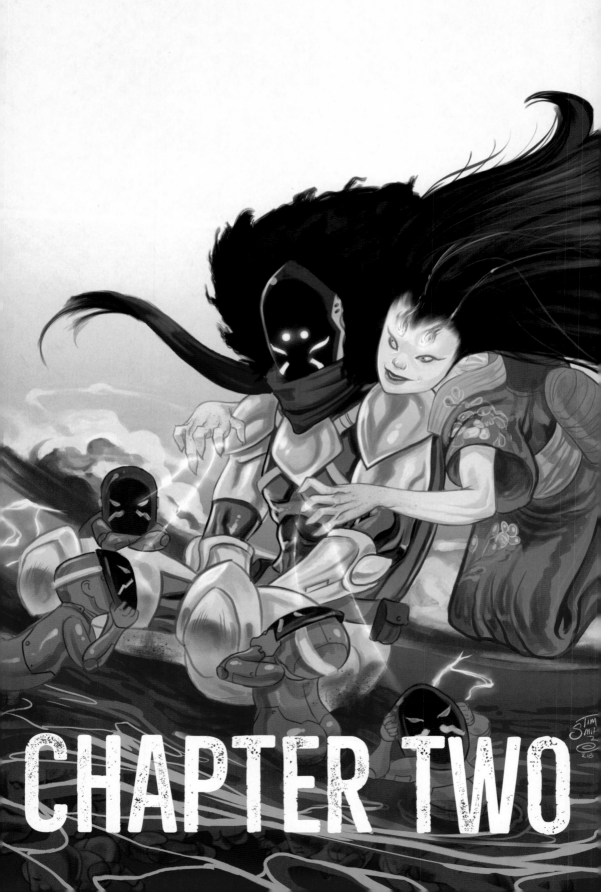

CHAPTER TWO

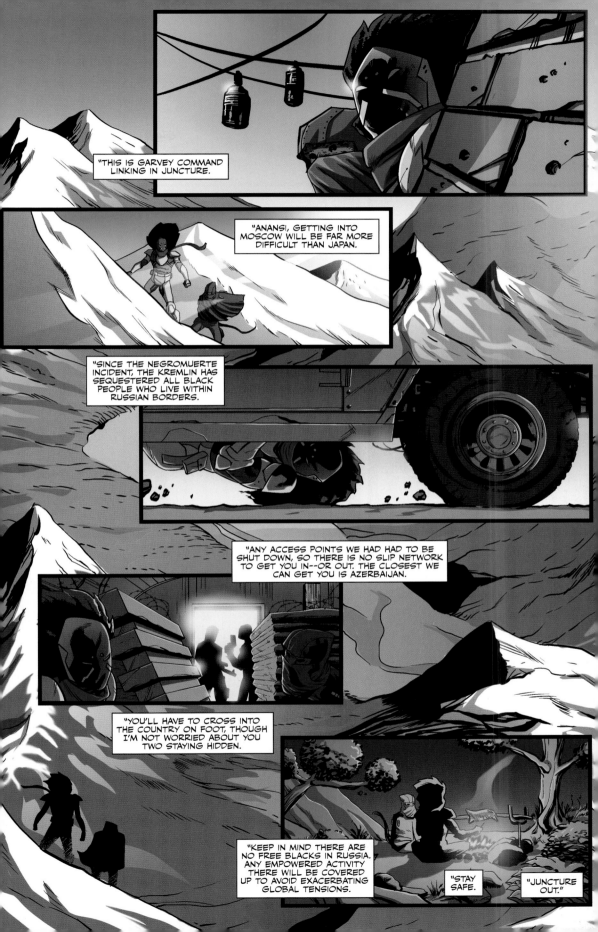

"THIS IS GARVEY COMMAND LINKING IN JUNCTURE.

"ANANSI, GETTING INTO MOSCOW WILL BE FAR MORE DIFFICULT THAN JAPAN.

"SINCE THE NEGROMUERTE INCIDENT, THE KREMLIN HAS SEQUESTERED ALL BLACK PEOPLE WHO LIVE WITHIN RUSSIAN BORDERS.

"ANY ACCESS POINTS WE HAD HAD TO BE SHUT DOWN, SO THERE IS NO SLIP NETWORK TO GET YOU IN--OR OUT. THE CLOSEST WE CAN GET YOU IS AZERBAIJAN.

"YOU'LL HAVE TO CROSS INTO THE COUNTRY ON FOOT, THOUGH I'M NOT WORRIED ABOUT YOU TWO STAYING HIDDEN.

"KEEP IN MIND THERE ARE NO FREE BLACKS IN RUSSIA. ANY EMPOWERED ACTIVITY THERE WILL BE COVERED UP TO AVOID EXACERBATING GLOBAL TENSIONS.

"STAY SAFE.

"JUNCTURE OUT."

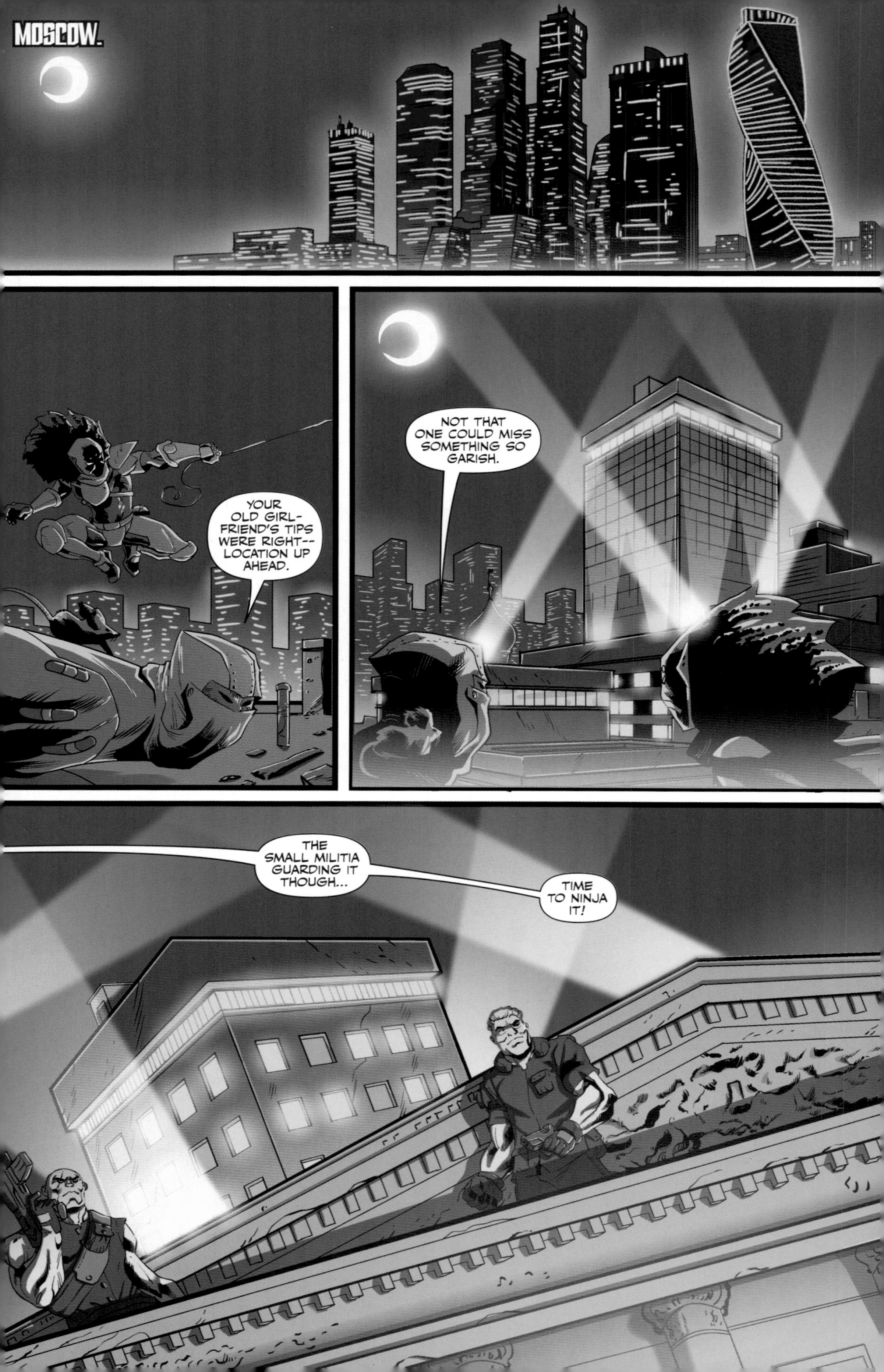
MOSCOW.
YOUR OLD GIRL-FRIEND'S TIPS WERE RIGHT-- LOCATION UP AHEAD.
NOT THAT ONE COULD MISS SOMETHING SO GARISH.
THE SMALL MILITIA GUARDING IT THOUGH...
TIME TO NINJA IT!

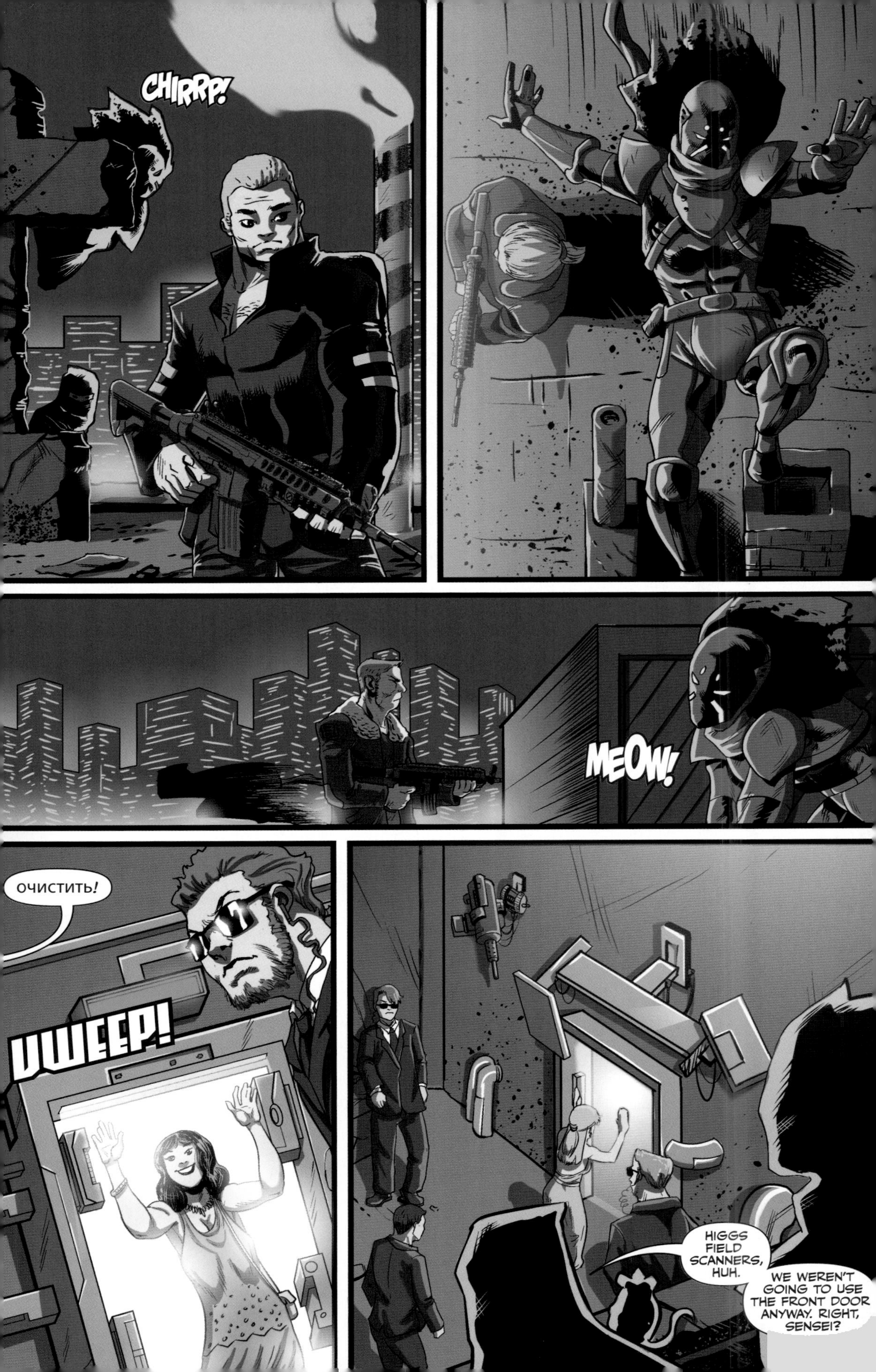
CHIRRP!
MEOW!
очистить!
VWEEP!
HIGGS FIELD SCANNERS, HUH.
WE WEREN'T GOING TO USE THE FRONT DOOR ANYWAY. RIGHT, SENSEI?

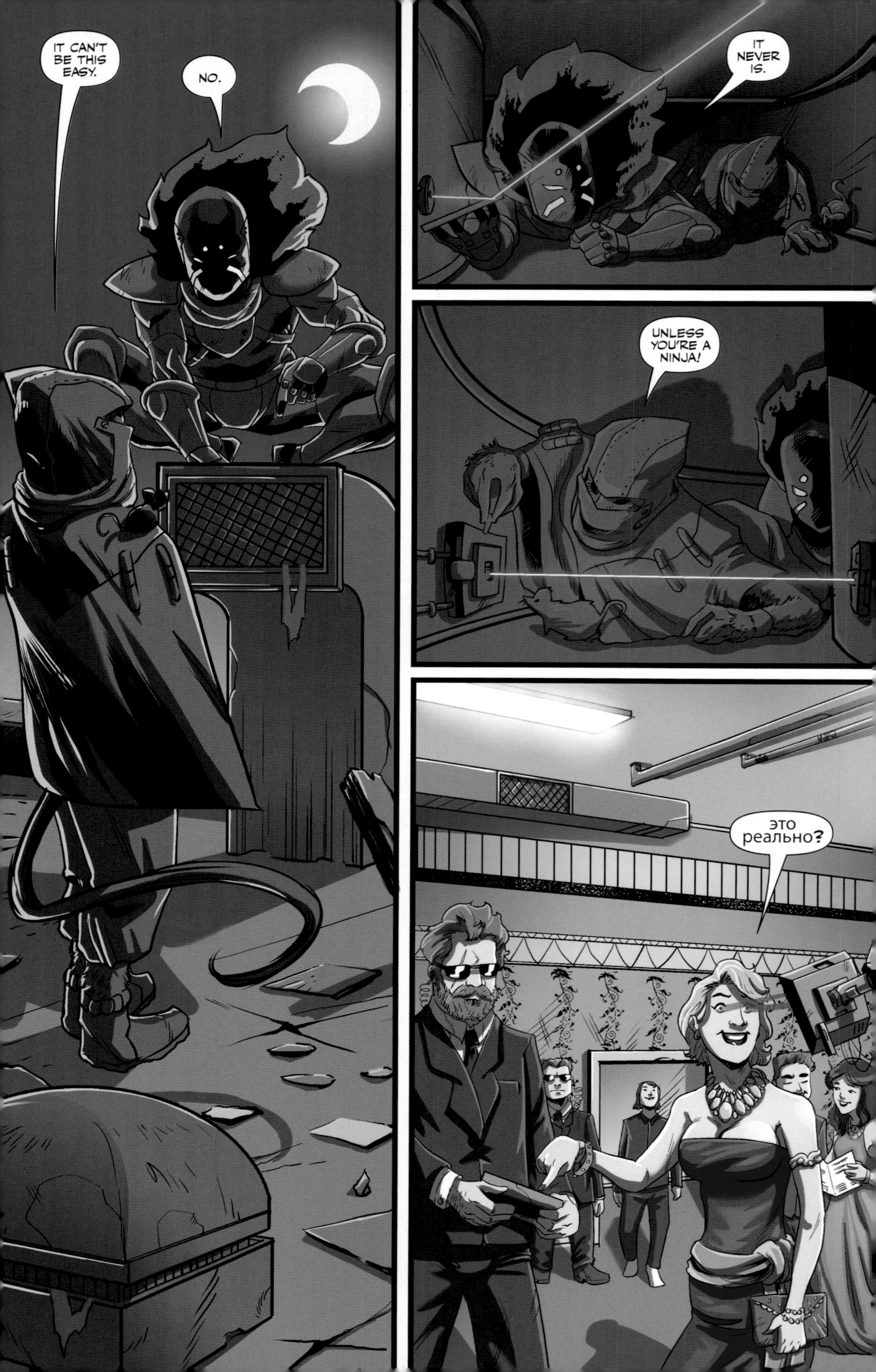
IT CAN'T BE THIS EASY.
NO.
IT NEVER IS.
UNLESS YOU'RE A NINJA!
это реально?

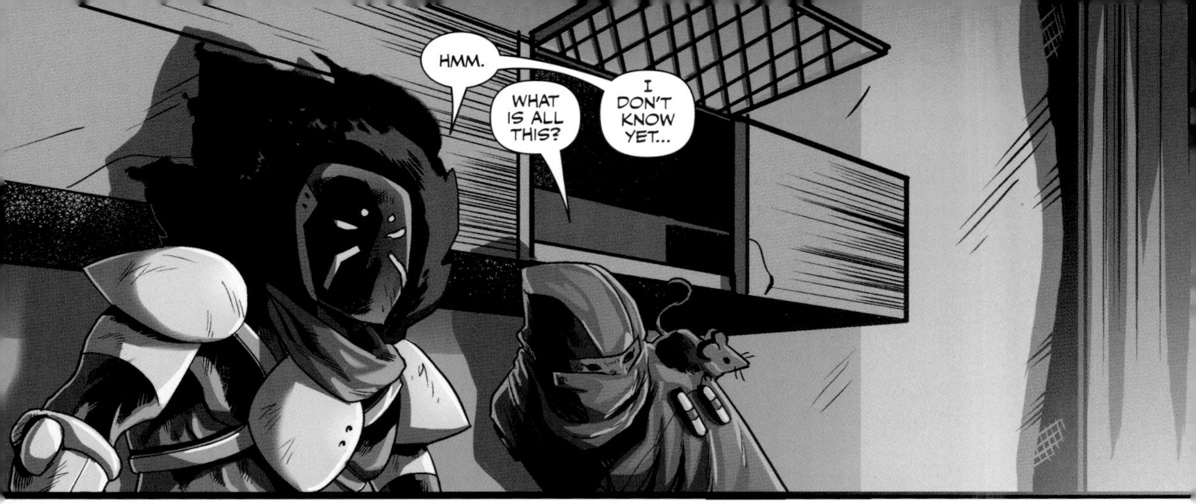
HMM.
WHAT IS ALL THIS?
I DON'T KNOW YET...

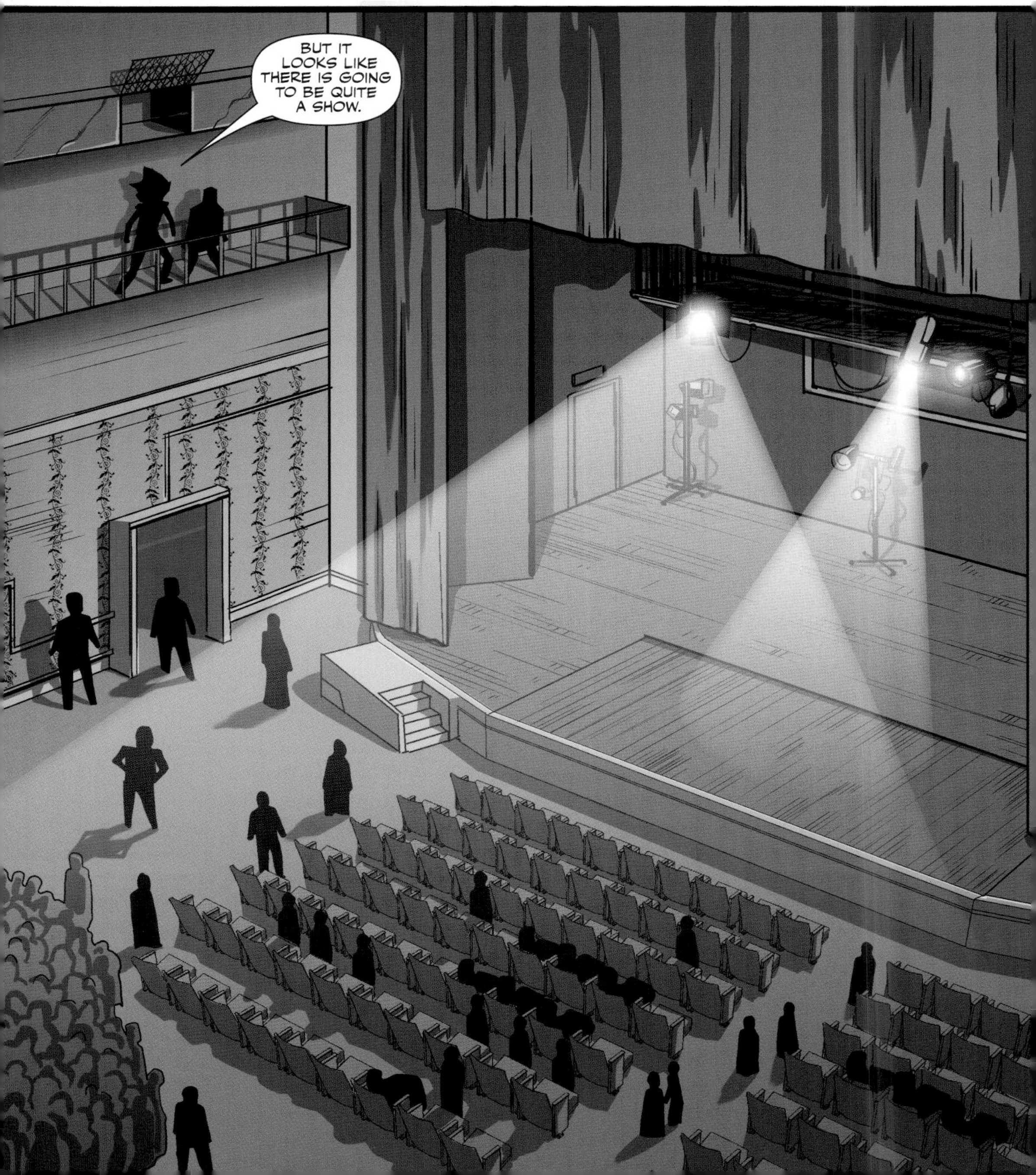
BUT IT LOOKS LIKE THERE IS GOING TO BE QUITE A SHOW.

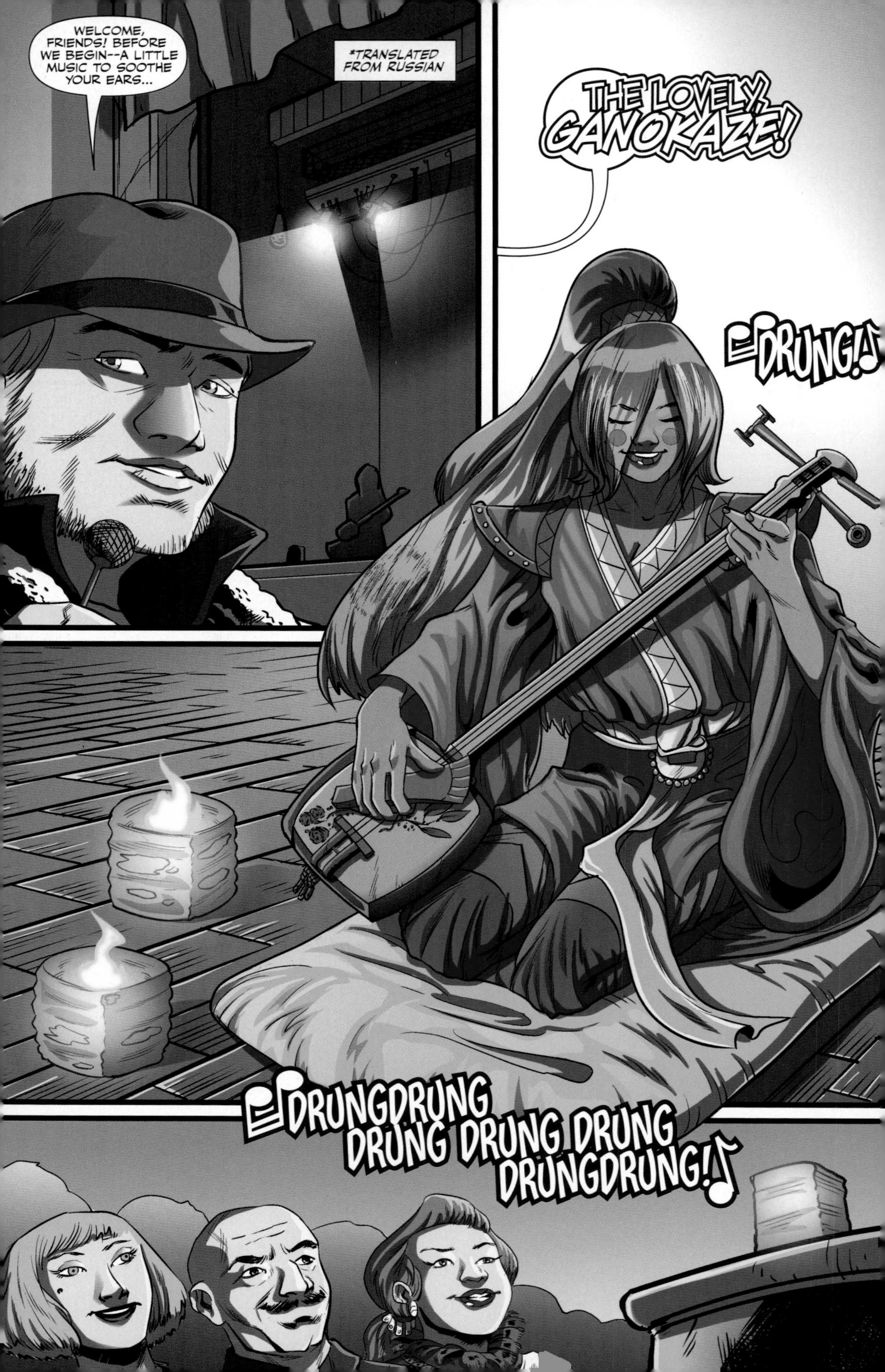

WELCOME, FRIENDS! BEFORE WE BEGIN--A LITTLE MUSIC TO SOOTHE YOUR EARS...
*TRANSLATED FROM RUSSIAN
THE LOVELY, GANOKAZE!
DRUNG!
DRUNGDRUNG DRUNG DRUNG DRUNG DRUNGDRUNG!

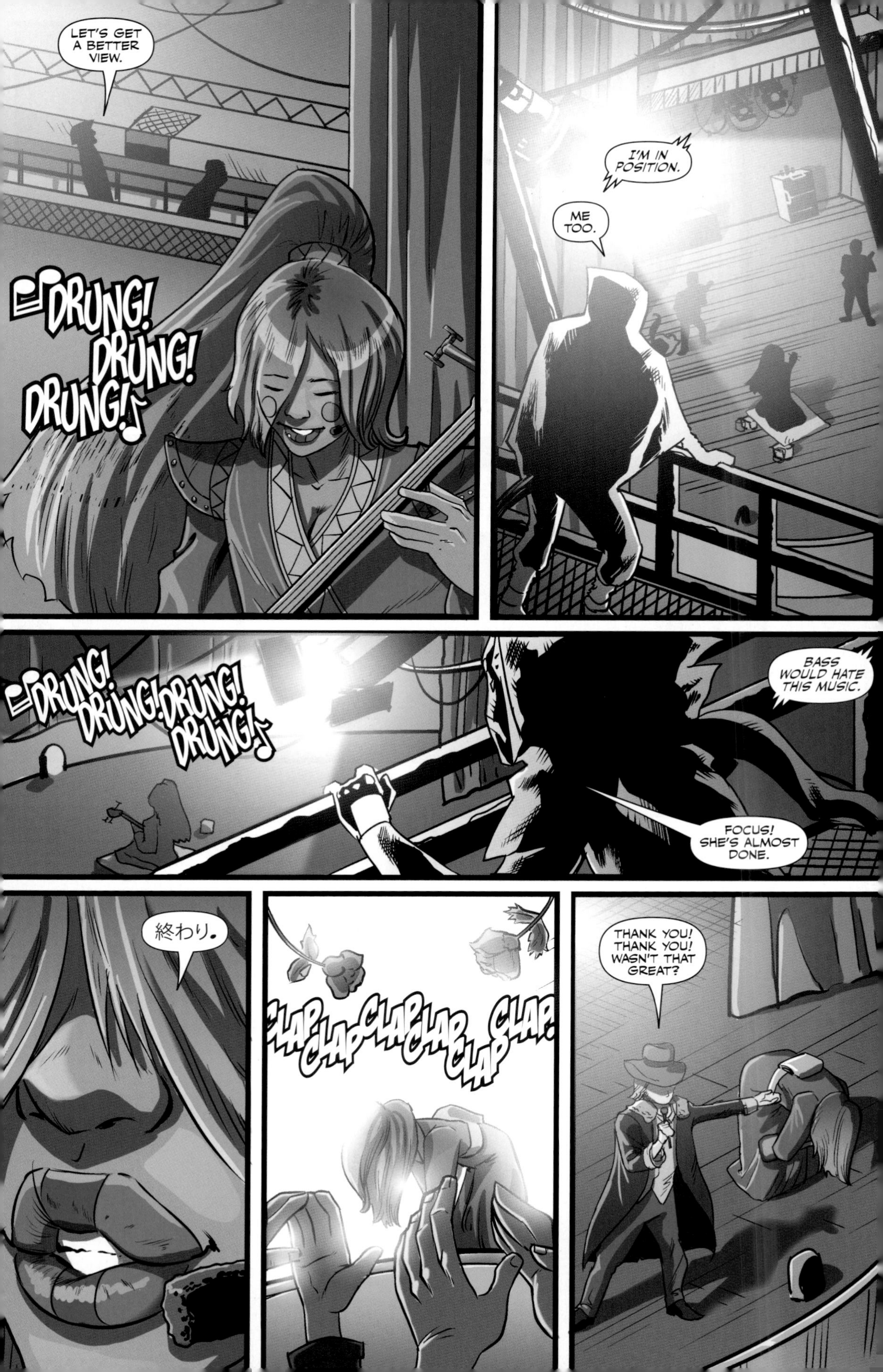
LET'S GET A BETTER VIEW.
DRUNG! DRUNG! DRUNG!
I'M IN POSITION.
ME TOO.
DRUNG! DRUNG! DRUNG! DRUNG!
BASS WOULD HATE THIS MUSIC.
FOCUS! SHE'S ALMOST DONE.
終わり。
CLAP CLAP CLAP CLAP CLAP CLAP CLAP
THANK YOU! THANK YOU! WASN'T THAT GREAT?

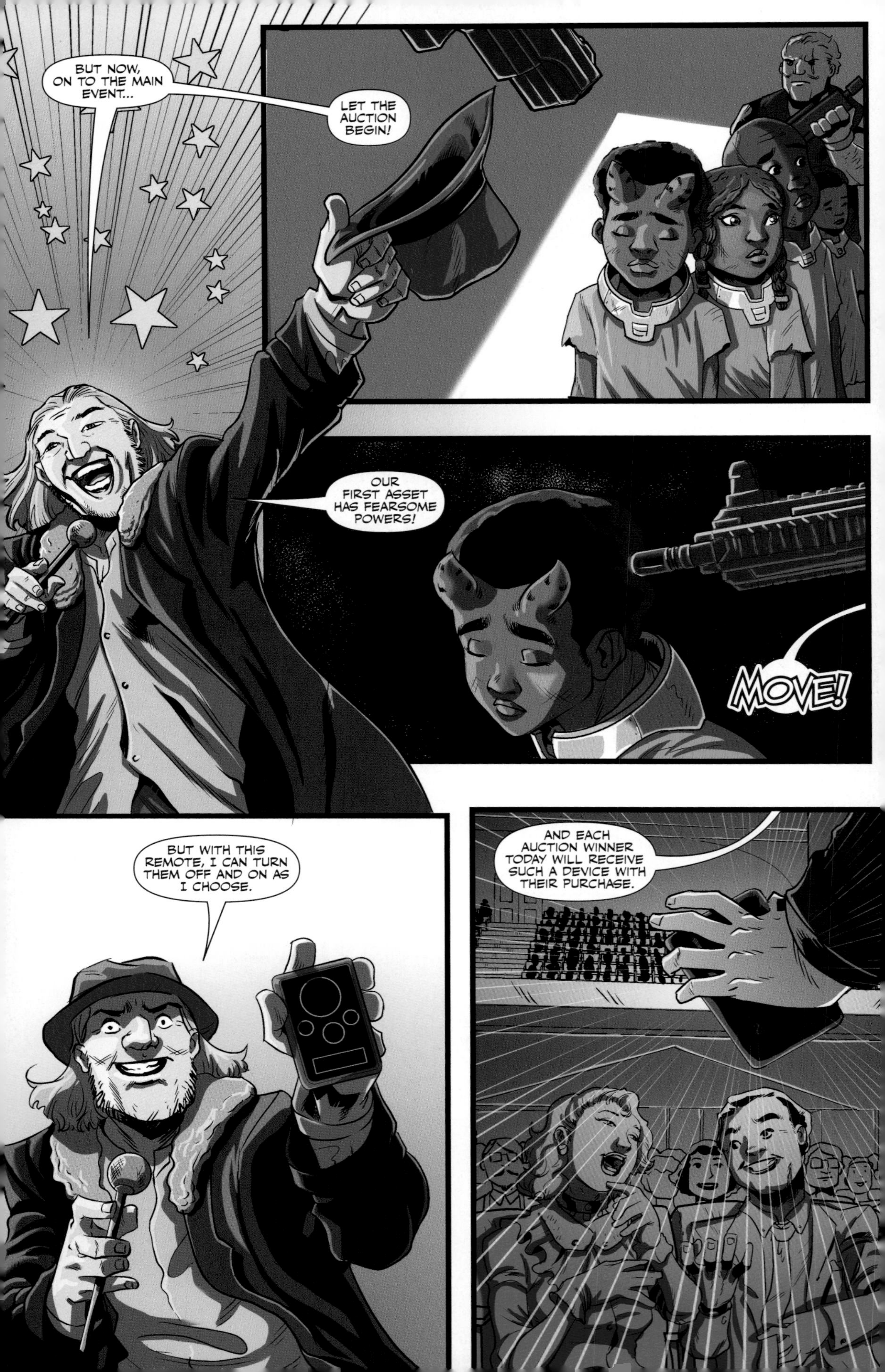
BUT NOW, ON TO THE MAIN EVENT...
LET THE AUCTION BEGIN!
OUR FIRST ASSET HAS FEARSOME POWERS!
MOVE!
BUT WITH THIS REMOTE, I CAN TURN THEM OFF AND ON AS I CHOOSE.
AND EACH AUCTION WINNER TODAY WILL RECEIVE SUCH A DEVICE WITH THEIR PURCHASE.

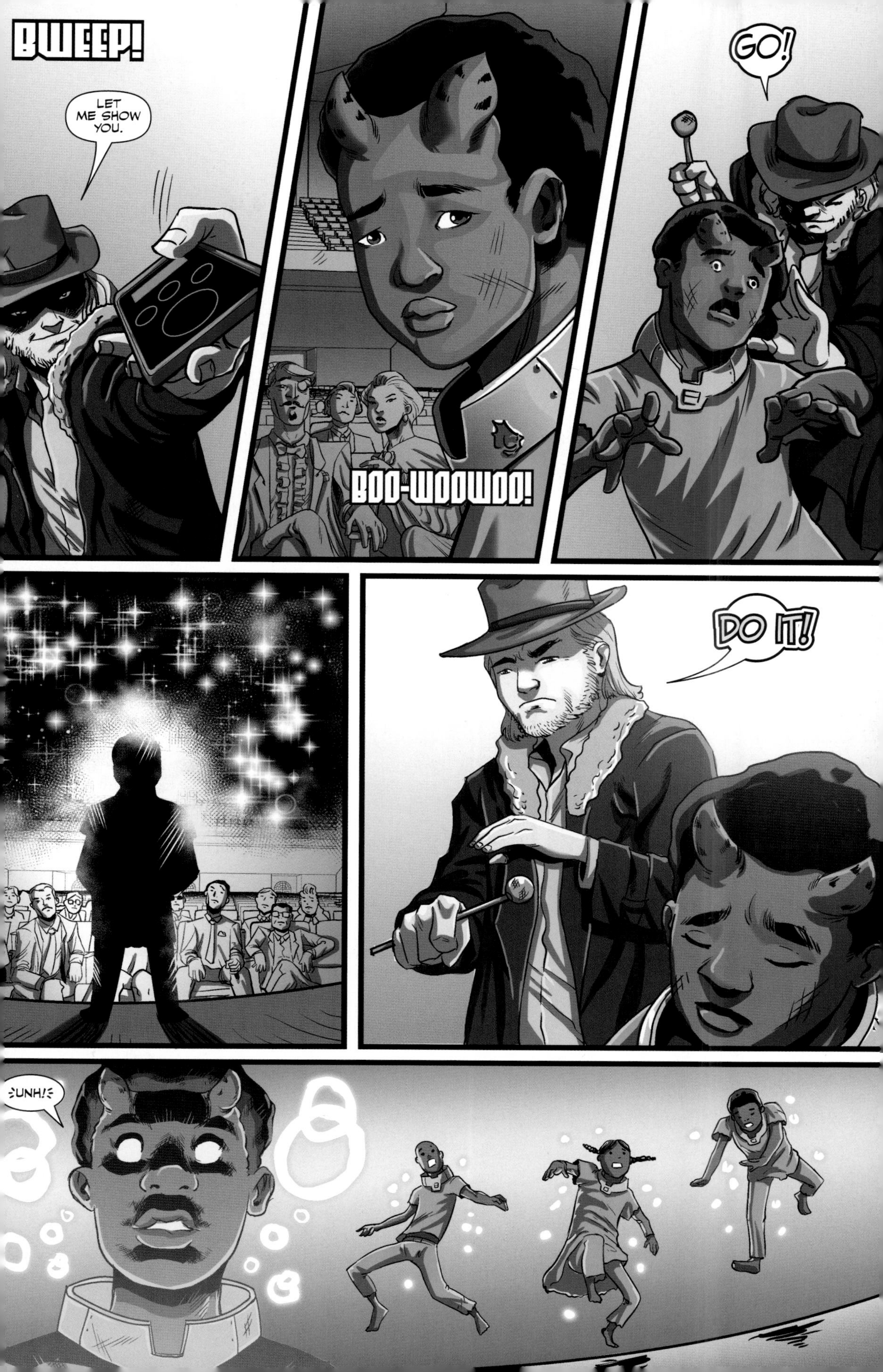
BWEEP!
LET ME SHOW YOU.
BOO-WOOWOO!
GO!
DO IT!
UNH!

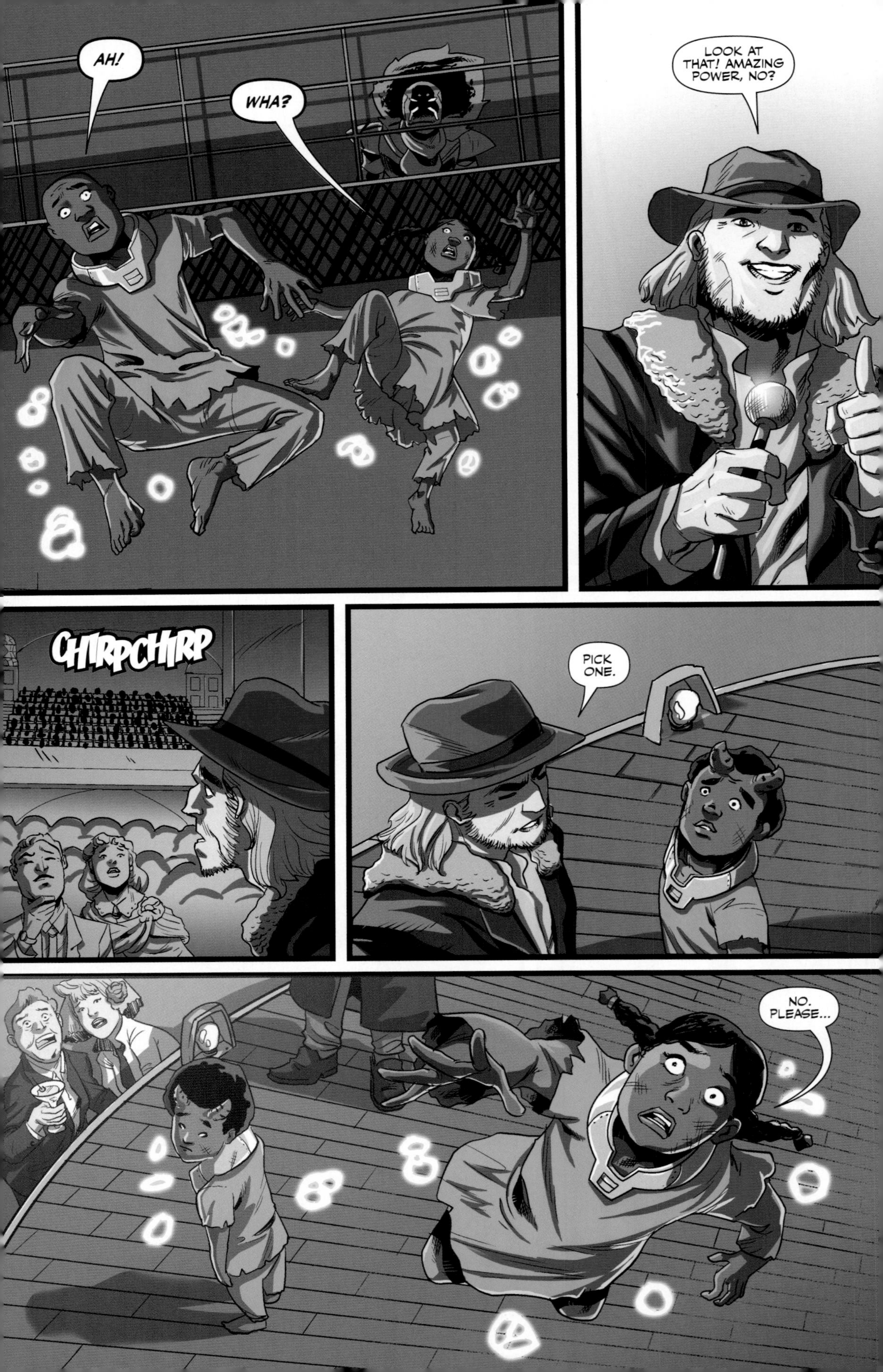
AH!
WHA?
LOOK AT THAT! AMAZING POWER, NO?
CHIRPCHIRP
PICK ONE.
NO. PLEASE...

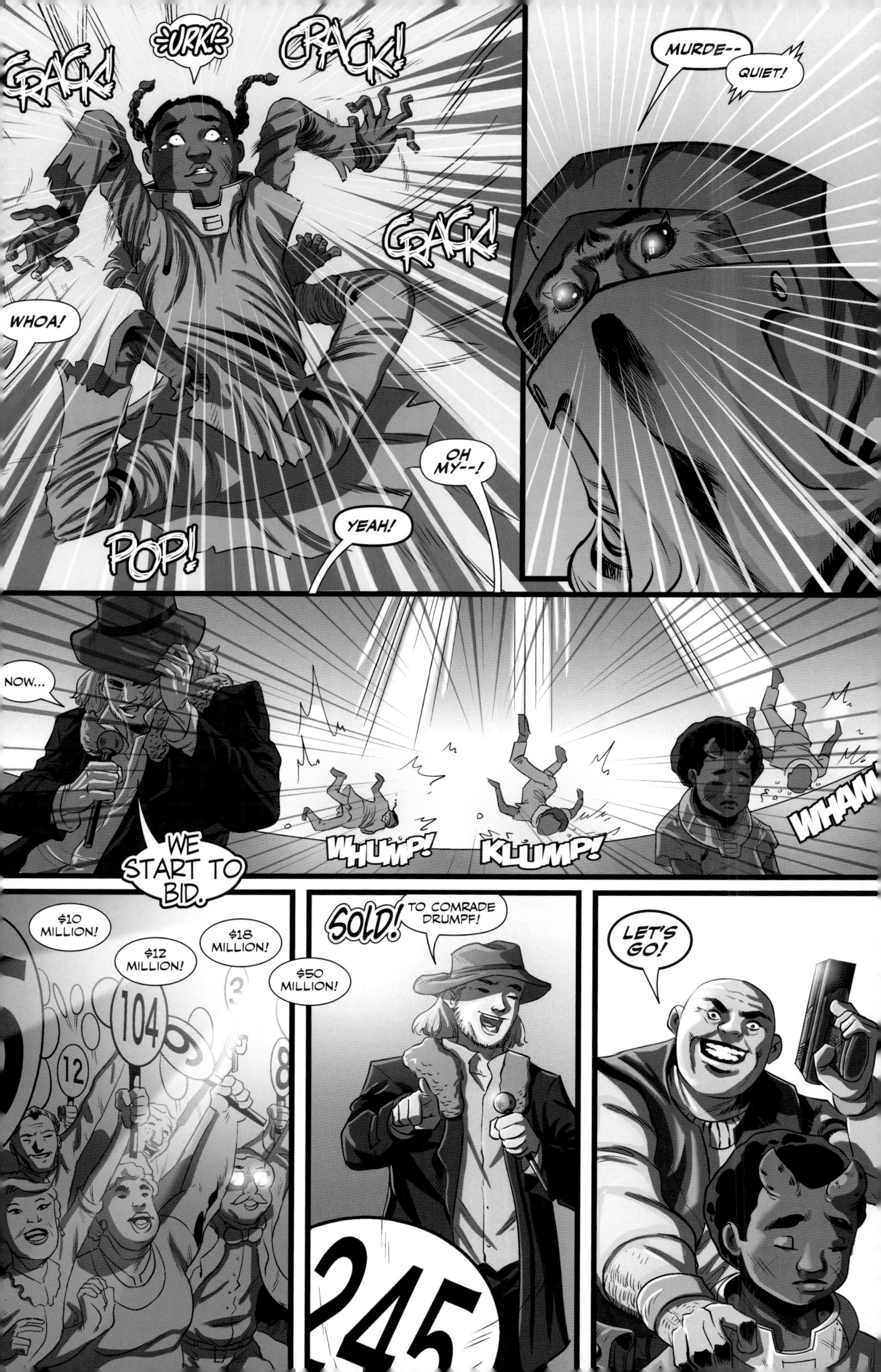
CRACK!
URK!
CRACK!
CRACK!
WHOA!
OH MY--!
YEAH!
POP!
MURDE--
QUIET!
NOW...
WE START TO BID.
WHUMP!
KLUMP!
WHAM
$10 MILLION!
$12 MILLION!
$18 MILLION!
$50 MILLION!
104
12
SOLD!
TO COMRADE DRUMPF!
245
LET'S GO!

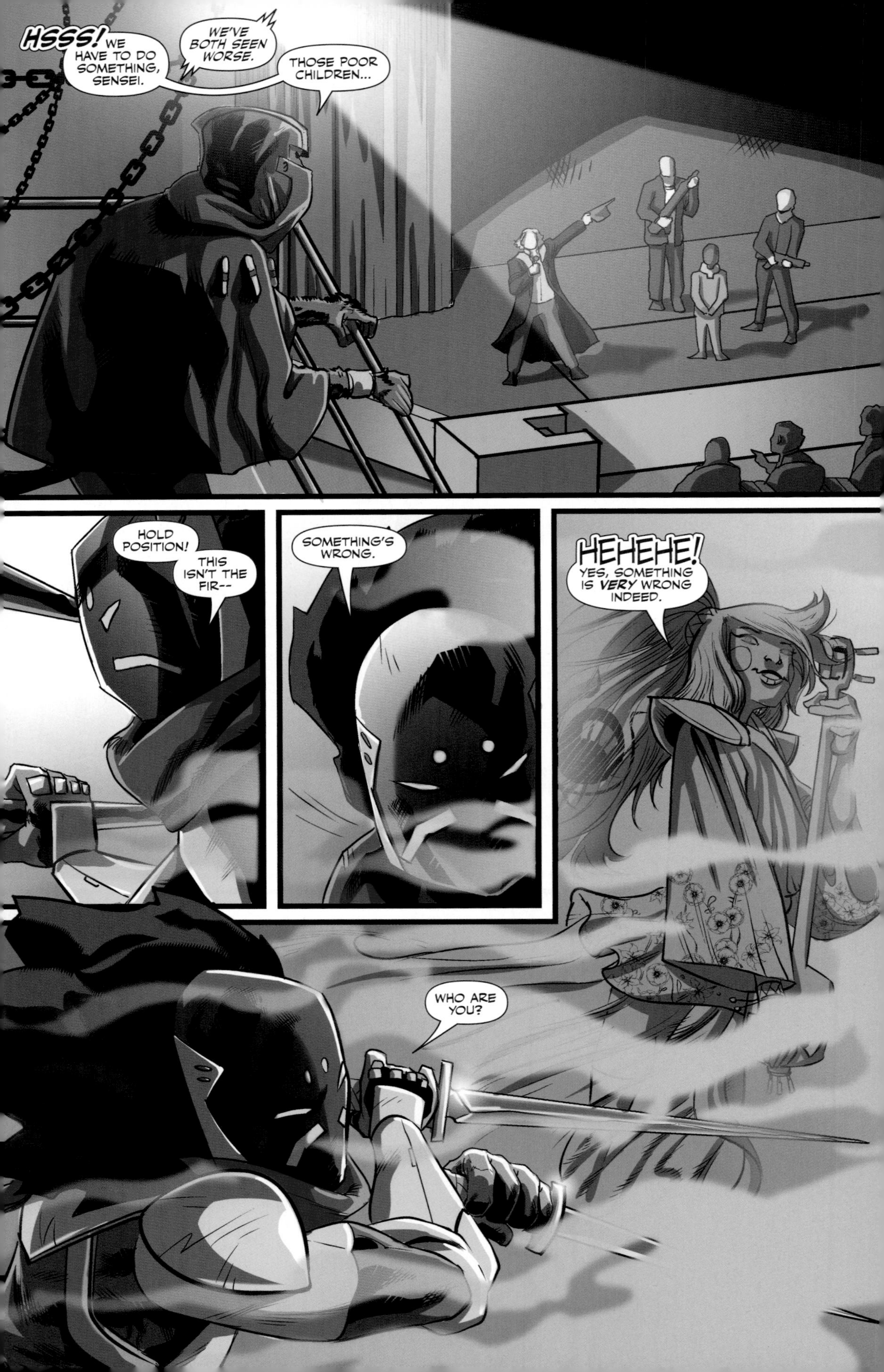
HSSS! WE HAVE TO DO SOMETHING, SENSEI.
WE'VE BOTH SEEN WORSE.
THOSE POOR CHILDREN...
HOLD POSITION!
THIS ISN'T THE FIR--
SOMETHING'S WRONG.
HEHEHE!
YES, SOMETHING IS *VERY* WRONG INDEED.
WHO ARE YOU?

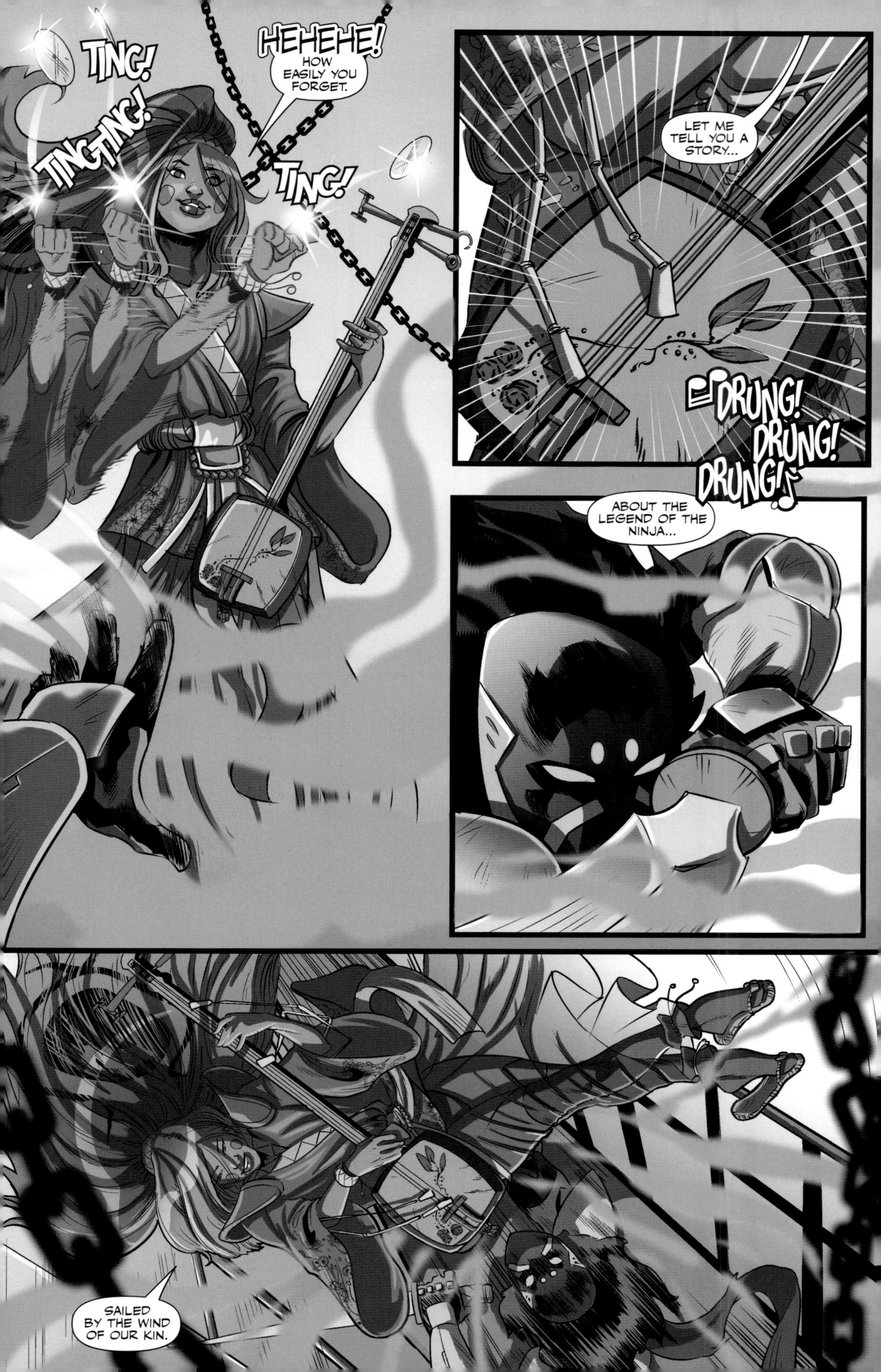
TING!
TINGTING!
HEHEHE! HOW EASILY YOU FORGET.
TING!
LET ME TELL YOU A STORY...
DRUNG! DRUNG! DRUNG!
ABOUT THE LEGEND OF THE NINJA...
SAILED BY THE WIND OF OUR KIN.

IT'S A TRAGIC TALE...

TAP

FILLED WITH BETRAYAL...

AND THE DEATH OF A HERO.

SENSEI, COME IN.

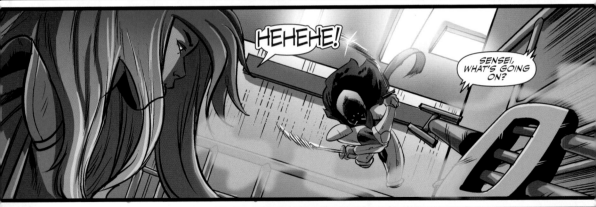

HEHEHE!

SENSEI, WHAT'S GOING ON?

WHY ISN'T HE ANSWERING?

SOMETHING'S HAPPENING ON THE STAGE.

AND NOW FOR OUR NEXT ITEM!

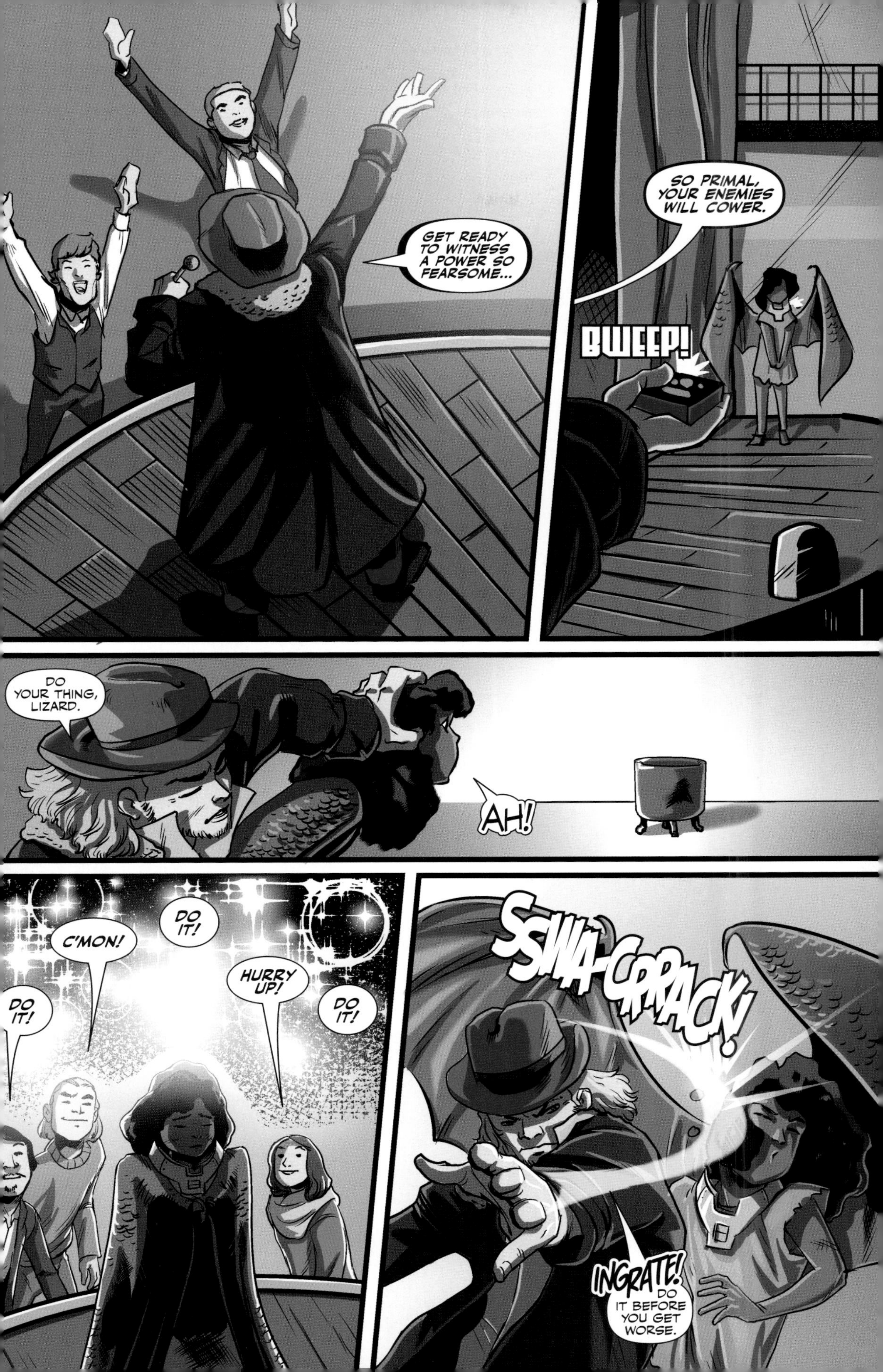
GET READY TO WITNESS A POWER SO FEARSOME...
SO PRIMAL, YOUR ENEMIES WILL COWER.
BWEEP!
DO YOUR THING, LIZARD.
AH!
C'MON!
DO IT!
DO IT!
HURRY UP!
DO IT!
SSWA-CRRACK!
INGRATE!
DO IT BEFORE YOU GET WORSE.

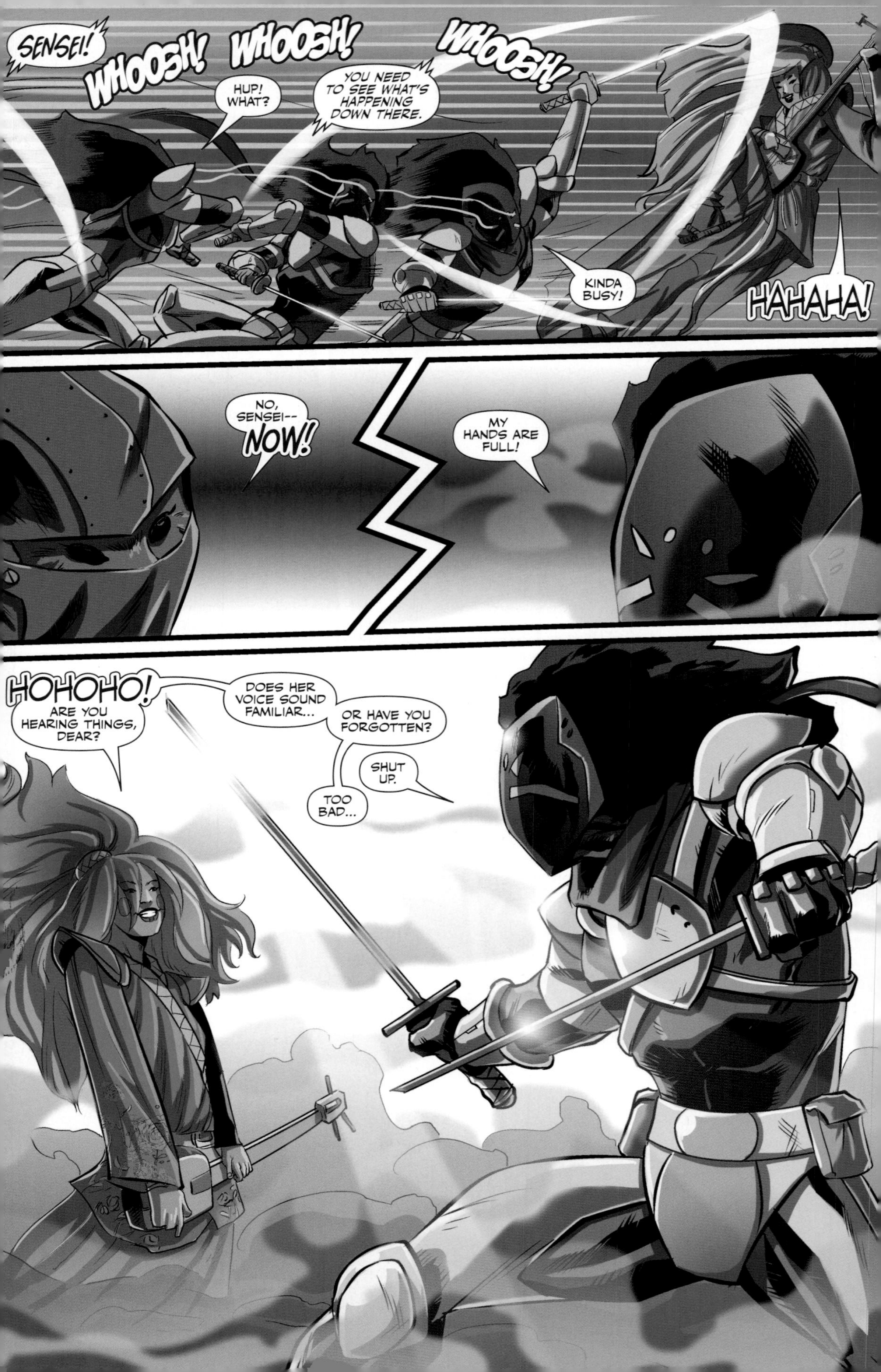
SENSEI!
WHOOSH!
HUP! WHAT?
WHOOSH!
YOU NEED TO SEE WHAT'S HAPPENING DOWN THERE.
WHOOSH!
KINDA BUSY!
HAHAHA!
NO, SENSEI-- NOW!
MY HANDS ARE FULL!
HOHOHO!
ARE YOU HEARING THINGS, DEAR?
DOES HER VOICE SOUND FAMILIAR...
OR HAVE YOU FORGOTTEN?
SHUT UP.
TOO BAD...

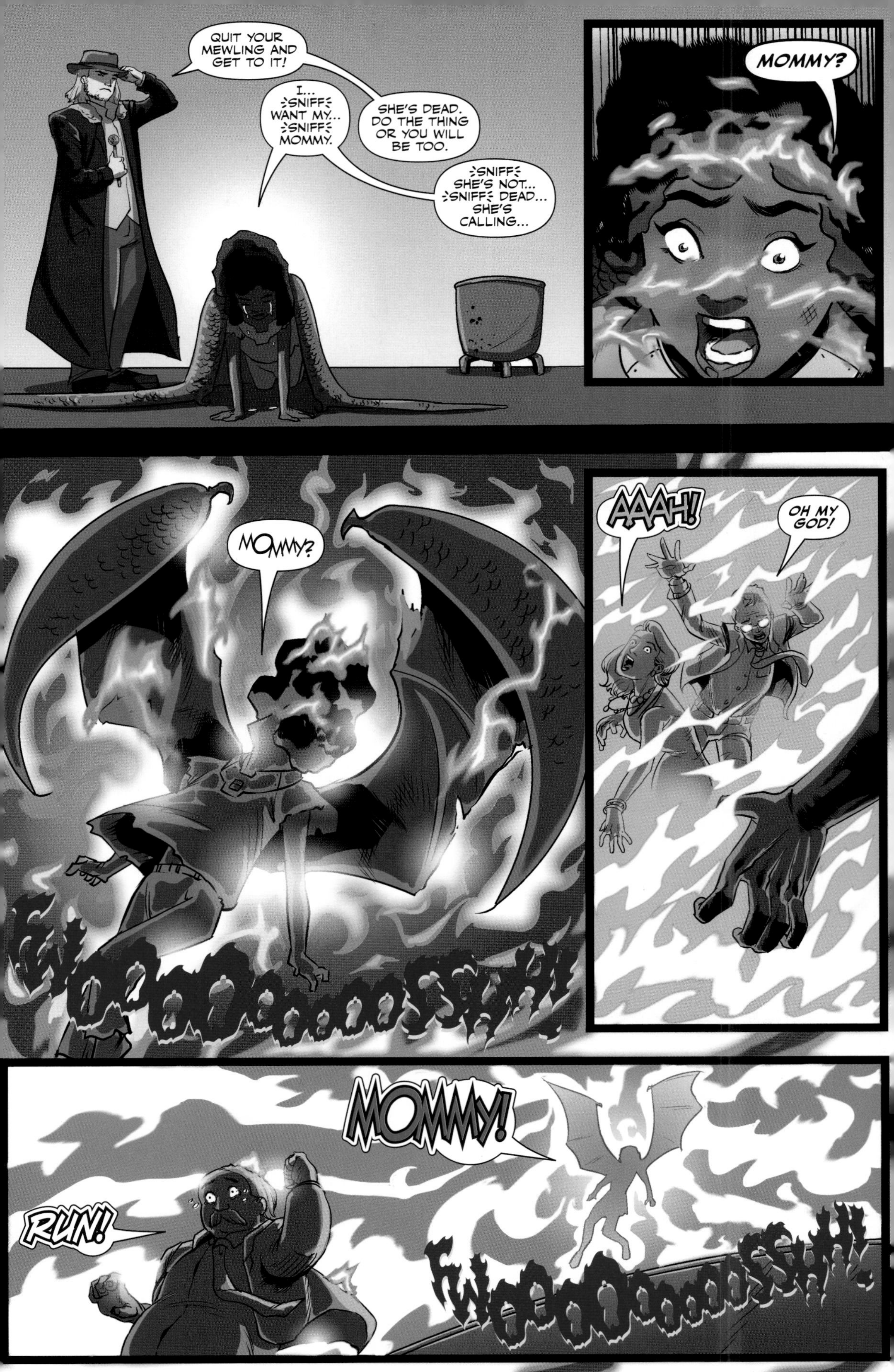
QUIT YOUR MEWLING AND GET TO IT!
I... ⁝SNIFF⁝ WANT MY... ⁝SNIFF⁝ MOMMY.
SHE'S DEAD. DO THE THING OR YOU WILL BE TOO.
⁝SNIFF⁝ SHE'S NOT... ⁝SNIFF⁝ DEAD... SHE'S CALLING...
MOMMY?
MOMMY?
FWOOOOoooooSSHH!
AAAH!
OH MY GOD!
MOMMY!
RUN!
FWOOOOoooooSSHH!

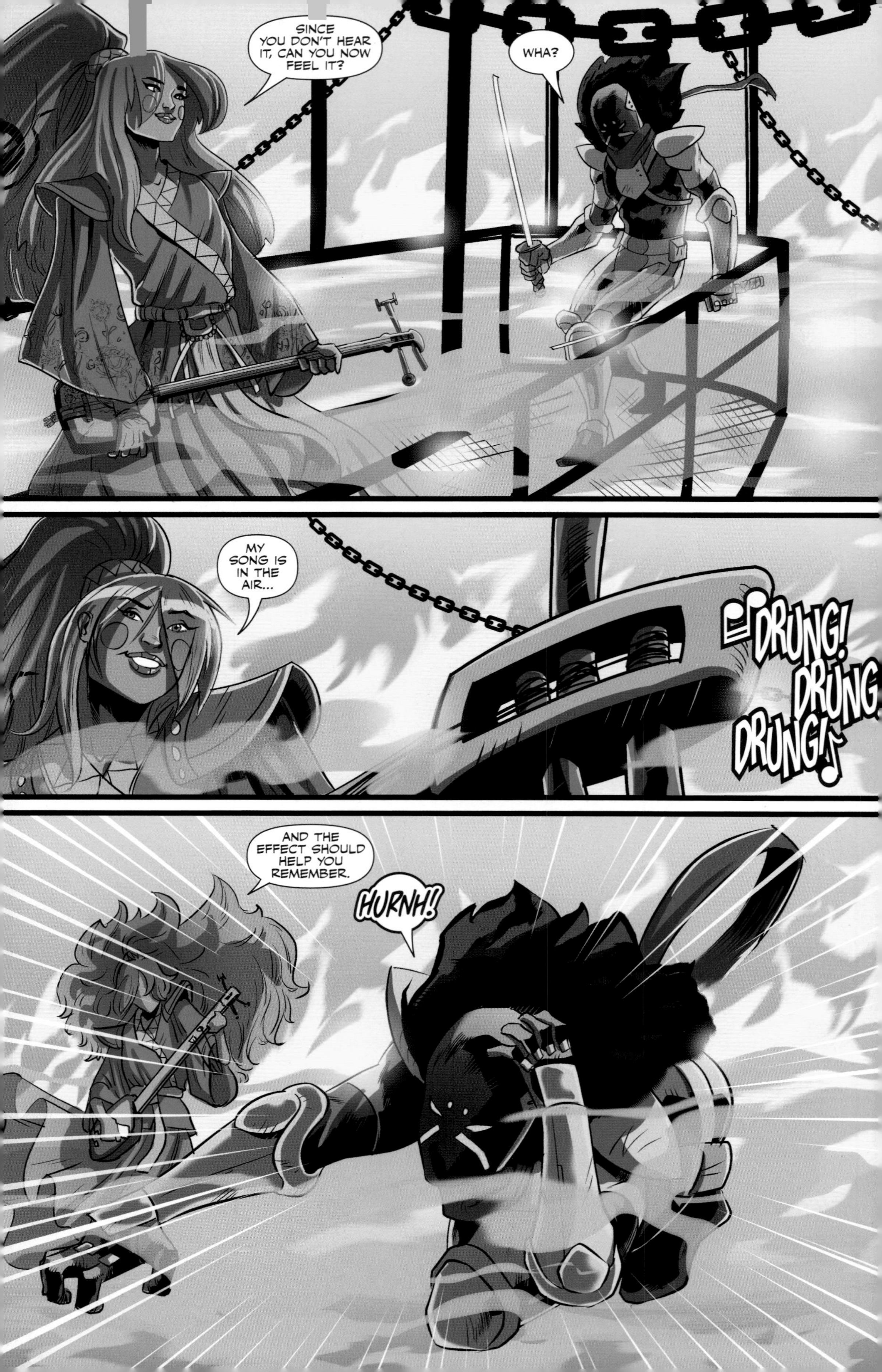
SINCE YOU DON'T HEAR IT, CAN YOU NOW FEEL IT?
WHA?
MY SONG IS IN THE AIR...
DRUNG! DRUNG DRUNG!
AND THE EFFECT SHOULD HELP YOU REMEMBER.
HURNH!

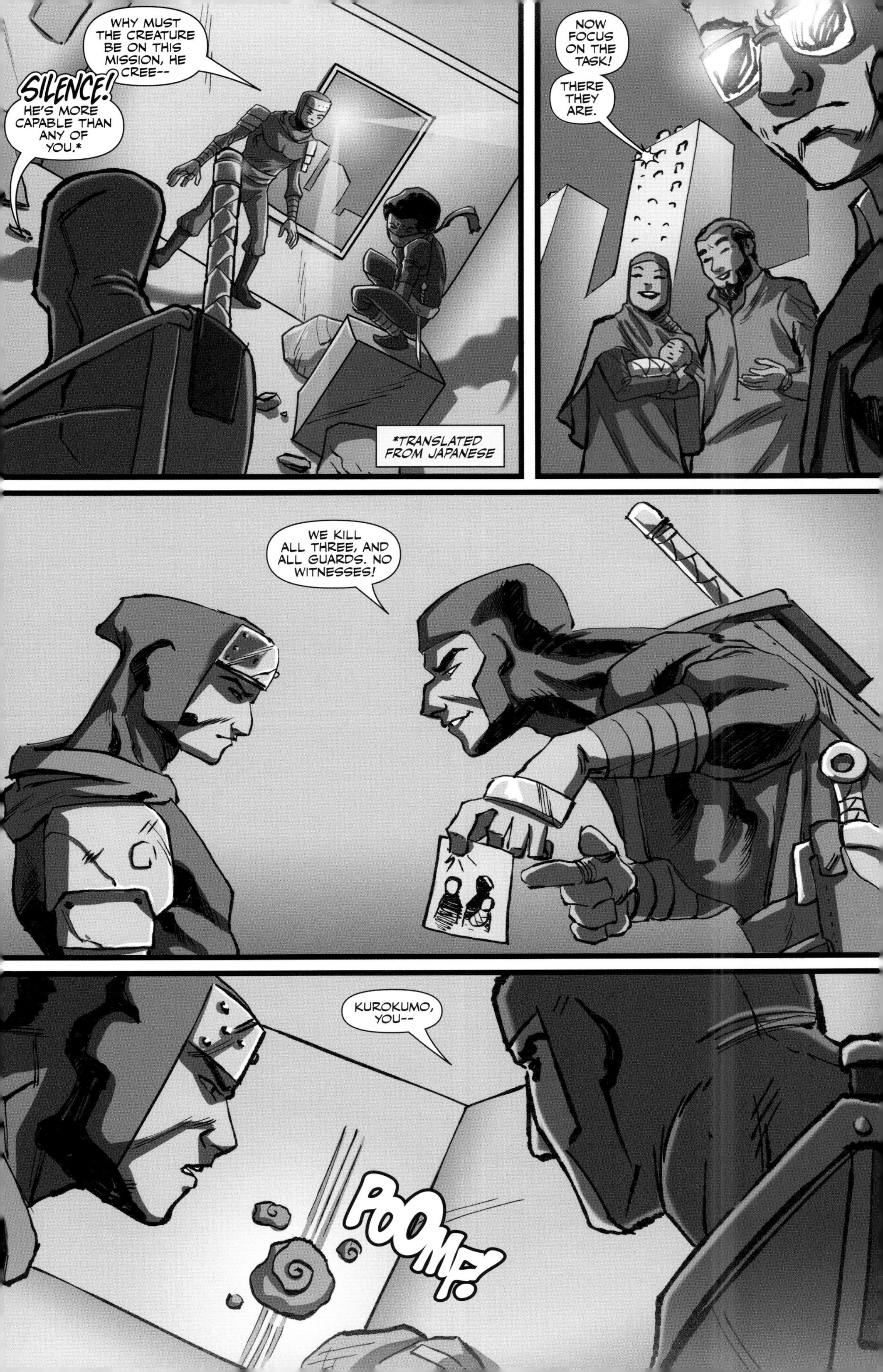
WHY MUST THE CREATURE BE ON THIS MISSION, HE CREE--
SILENCE! HE'S MORE CAPABLE THAN ANY OF YOU.*
*TRANSLATED FROM JAPANESE
NOW FOCUS ON THE TASK!
THERE THEY ARE.
WE KILL ALL THREE, AND ALL GUARDS. NO WITNESSES!
KUROKUMO, YOU--
POOMF!

FOOL! YOU ARE NO NINJA!

WHUKRACK!

AWK!

BUT YOU WILL BE...

SHLUCK!

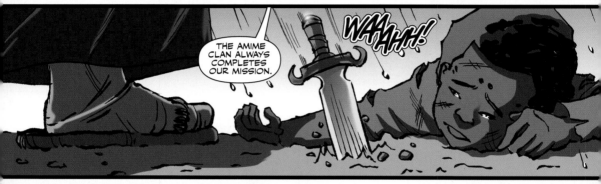

THE AMIME CLAN ALWAYS COMPLETES OUR MISSION.

WAAAHH!

YOU ARE A WEAPON...

DO WHAT YOU WERE MADE FOR!

WAAAHH!

KRAKA-BOOM

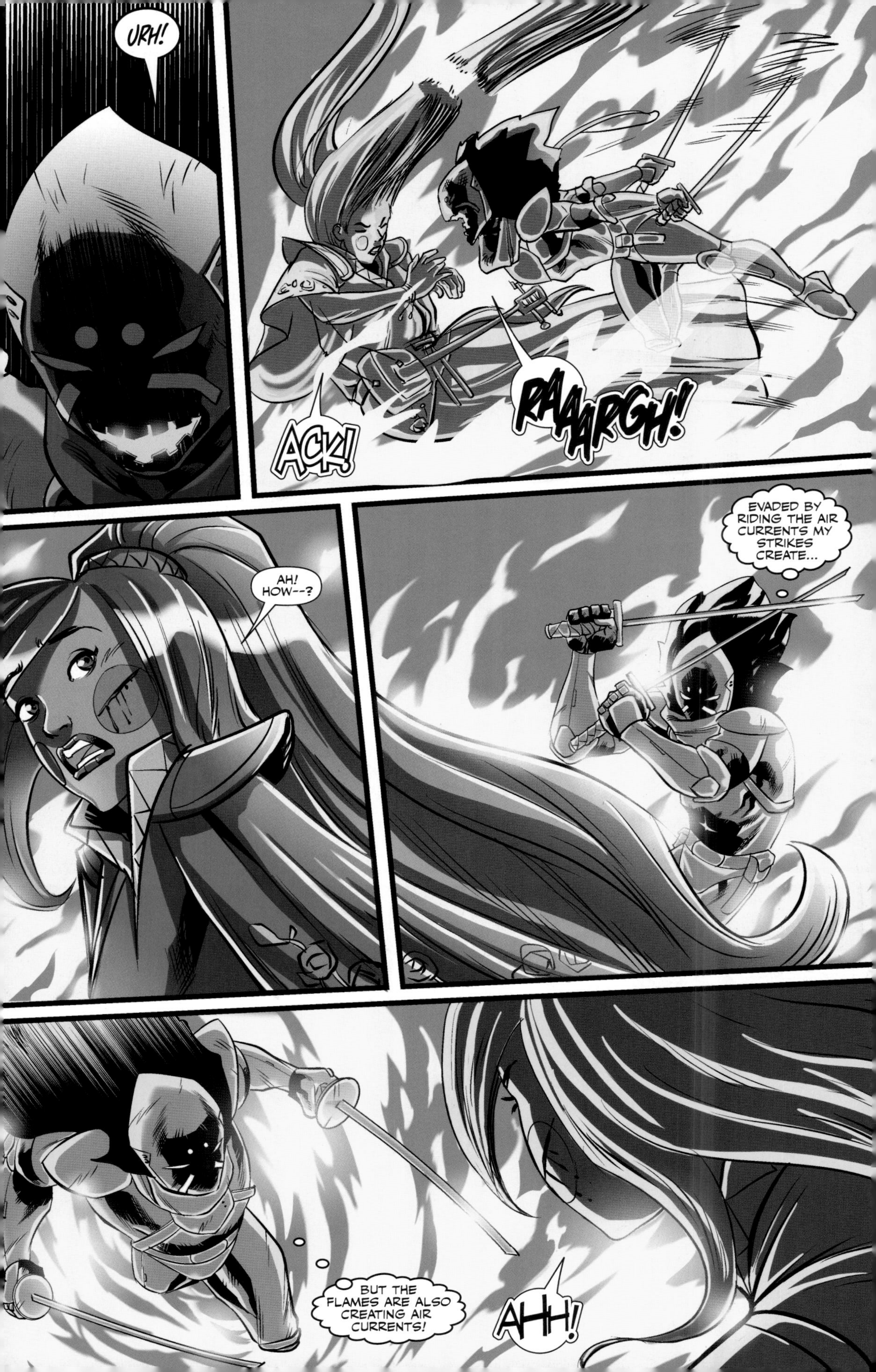
URH!
ACK!
RAAAARGH!
AH! HOW--?
EVADED BY RIDING THE AIR CURRENTS MY STRIKES CREATE...
BUT THE FLAMES ARE ALSO CREATING AIR CURRENTS!
AHH!

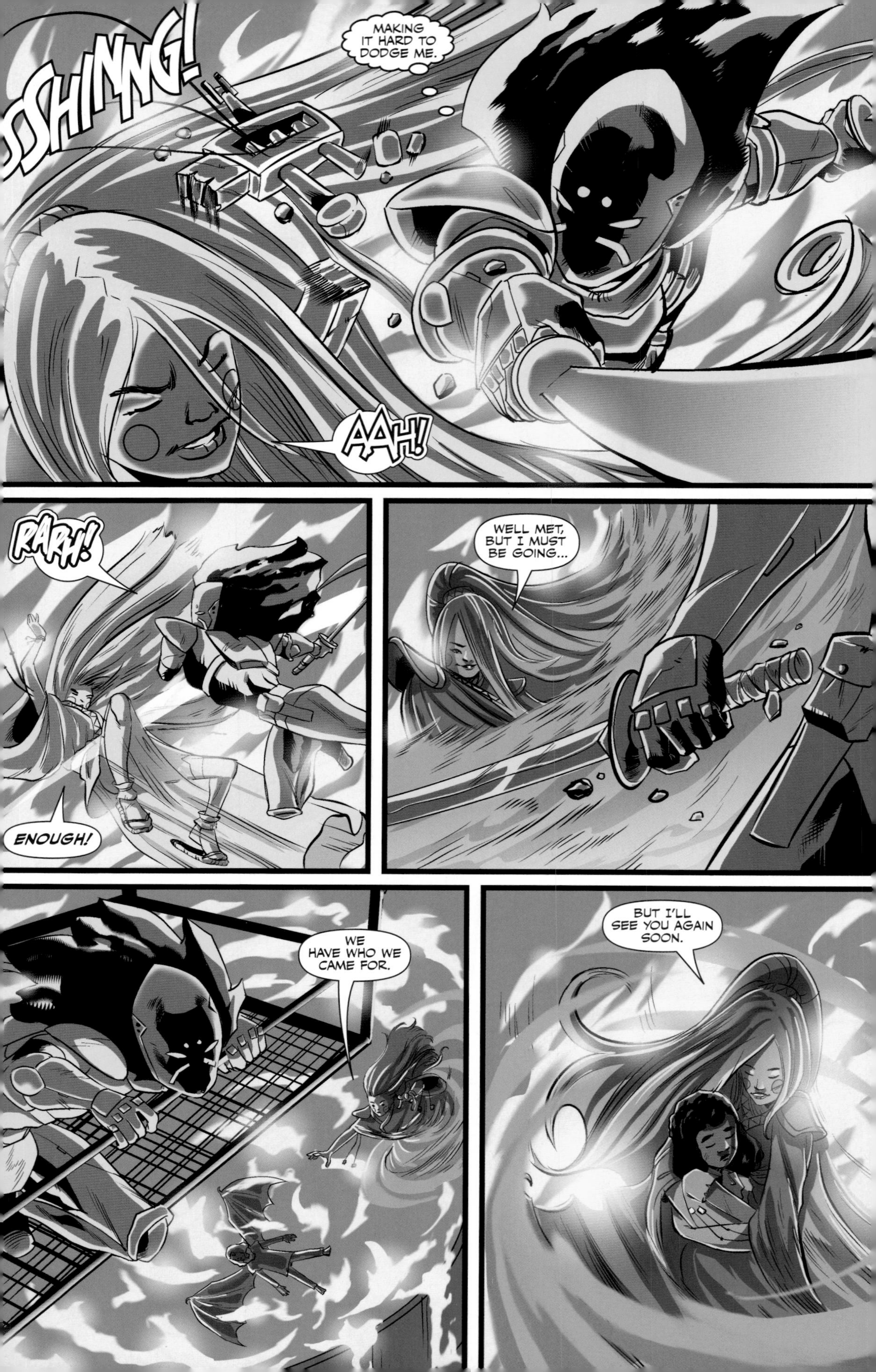
SSHINNG!
MAKING IT HARD TO DODGE ME.
AAH!
RARH!
ENOUGH!
WELL MET, BUT I MUST BE GOING...
WE HAVE WHO WE CAME FOR.
BUT I'LL SEE YOU AGAIN SOON.

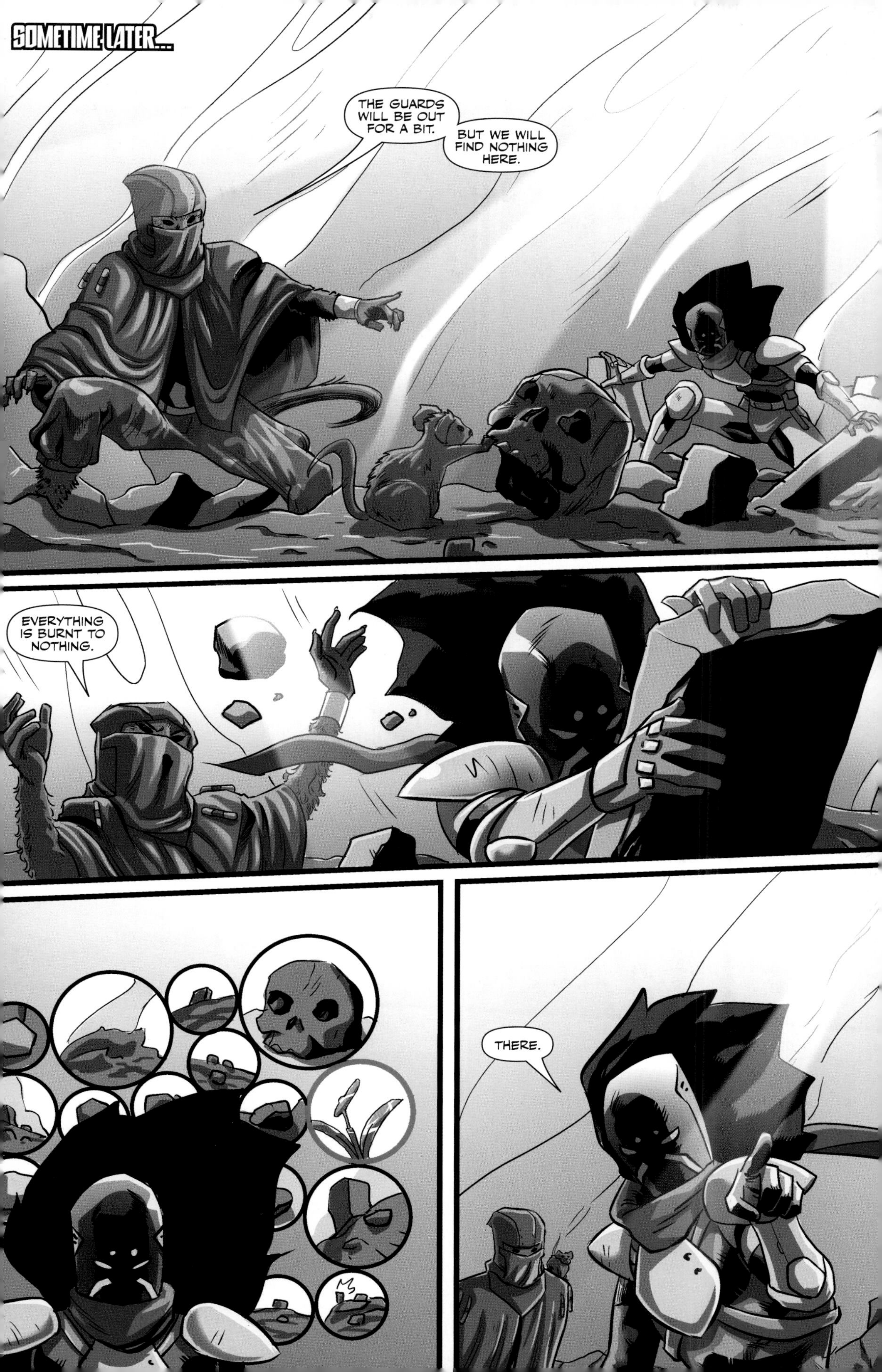
SOMETIME LATER...
THE GUARDS WILL BE OUT FOR A BIT.
BUT WE WILL FIND NOTHING HERE.
EVERYTHING IS BURNT TO NOTHING.
THERE.

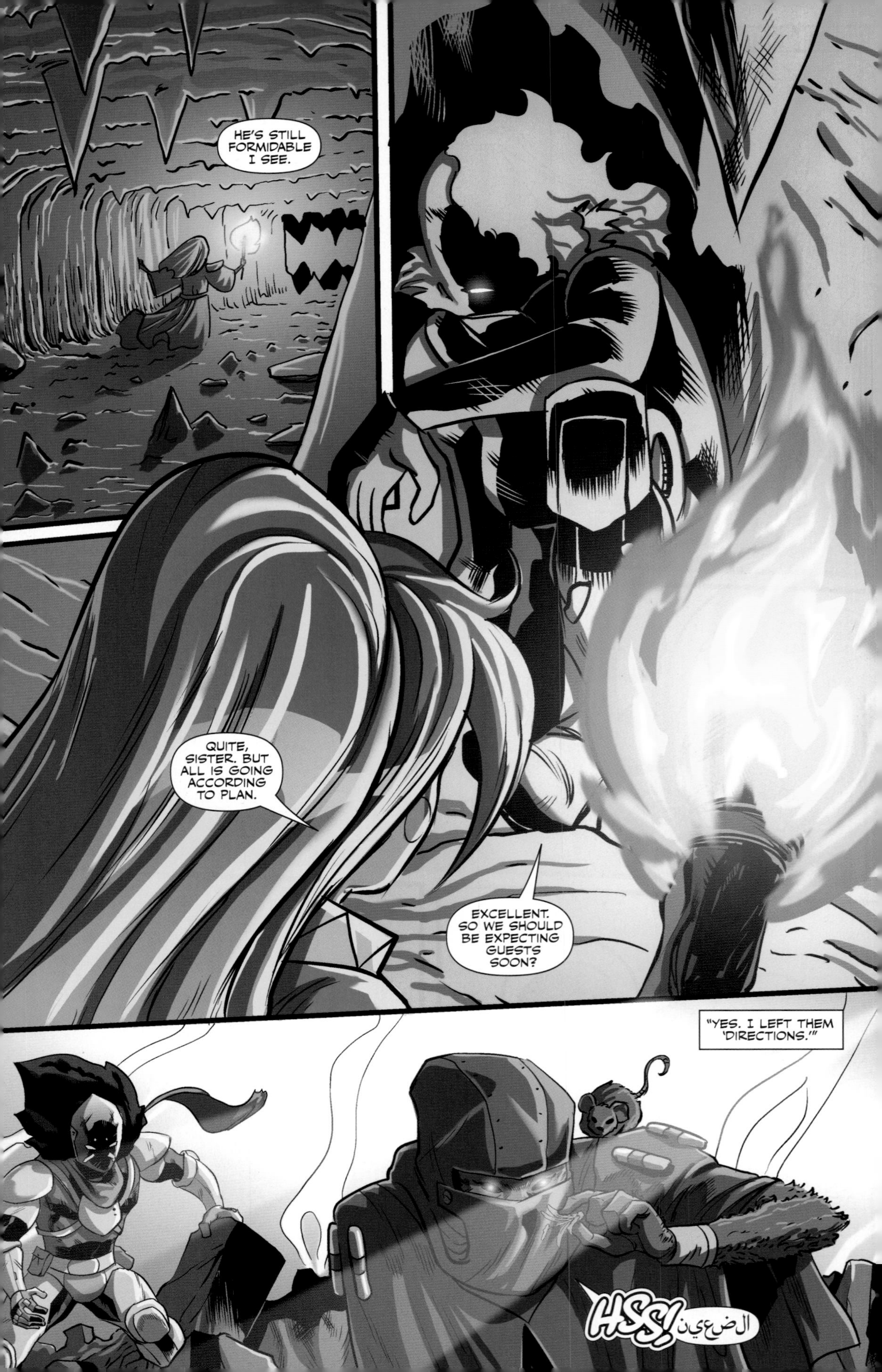
HE'S STILL FORMIDABLE I SEE.
QUITE, SISTER. BUT ALL IS GOING ACCORDING TO PLAN.
EXCELLENT. SO WE SHOULD BE EXPECTING GUESTS SOON?
"YES. I LEFT THEM 'DIRECTIONS.'"
HSS!

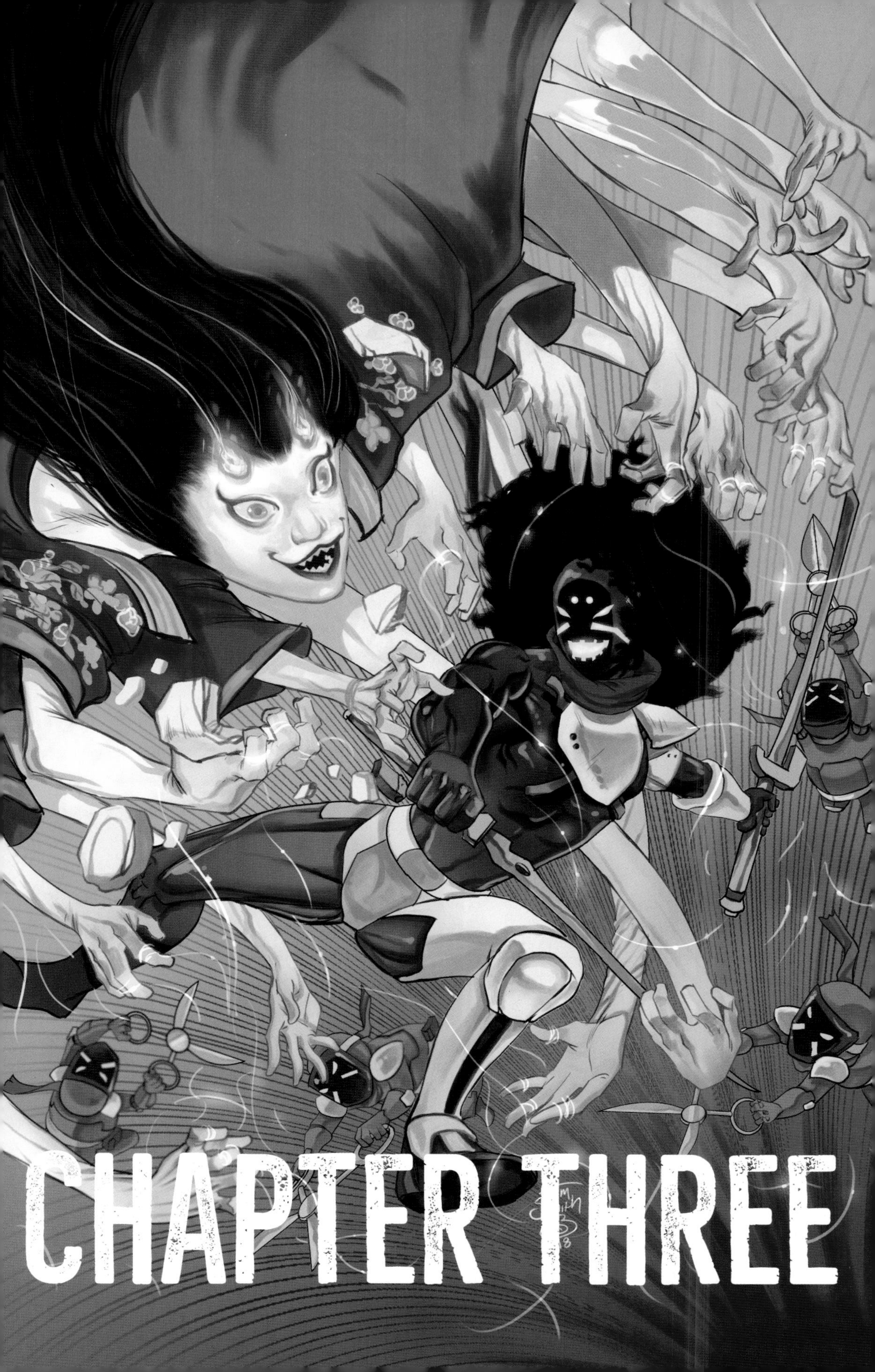

CHAPTER THREE

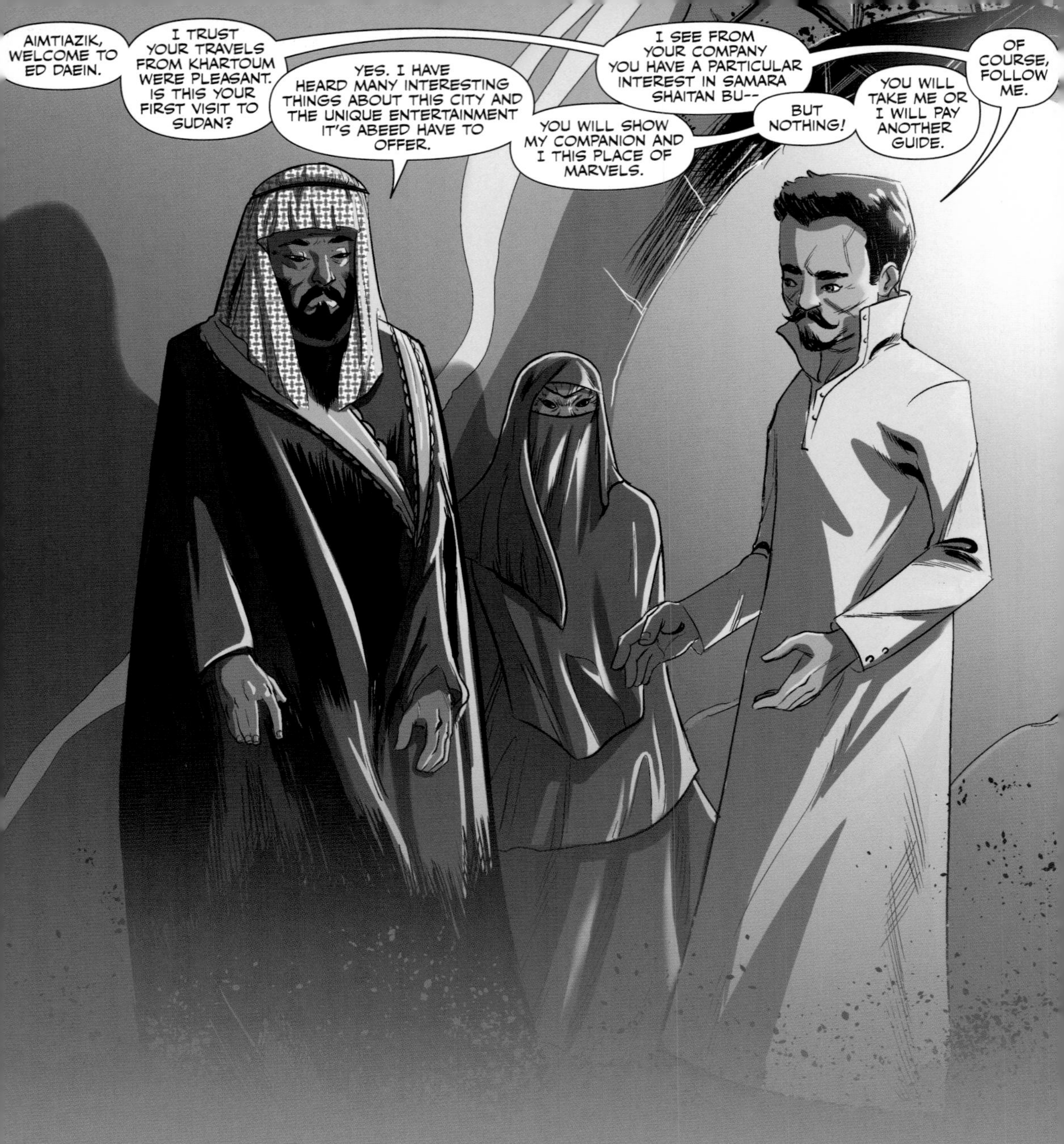
AIMTIAZIK, WELCOME TO ED DAEIN.
I TRUST YOUR TRAVELS FROM KHARTOUM WERE PLEASANT. IS THIS YOUR FIRST VISIT TO SUDAN?
YES. I HAVE HEARD MANY INTERESTING THINGS ABOUT THIS CITY AND THE UNIQUE ENTERTAINMENT IT'S ABEED HAVE TO OFFER.
I SEE FROM YOUR COMPANY YOU HAVE A PARTICULAR INTEREST IN SAMARA SHAITAN BU--
YOU WILL SHOW MY COMPANION AND I THIS PLACE OF MARVELS.
BUT NOTHING!
YOU WILL TAKE ME OR I WILL PAY ANOTHER GUIDE.
OF COURSE, FOLLOW ME.

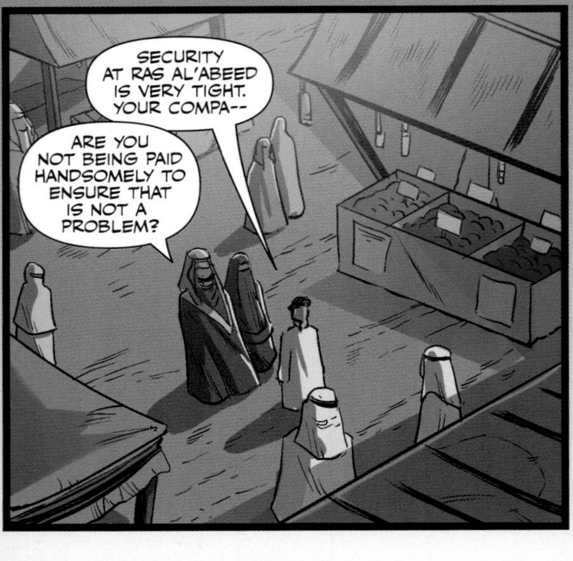
SECURITY AT RAS AL'ABEED IS VERY TIGHT. YOUR COMPA--
ARE YOU NOT BEING PAID HANDSOMELY TO ENSURE THAT IS NOT A PROBLEM?

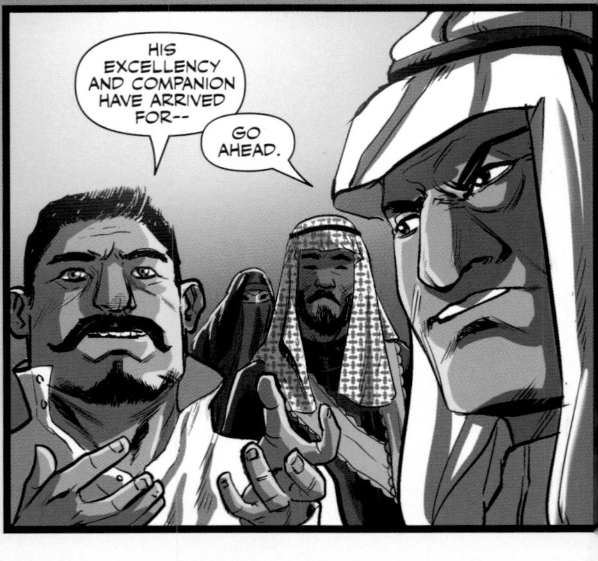
HIS EXCELLENCY AND COMPANION HAVE ARRIVED FOR--
GO AHEAD.

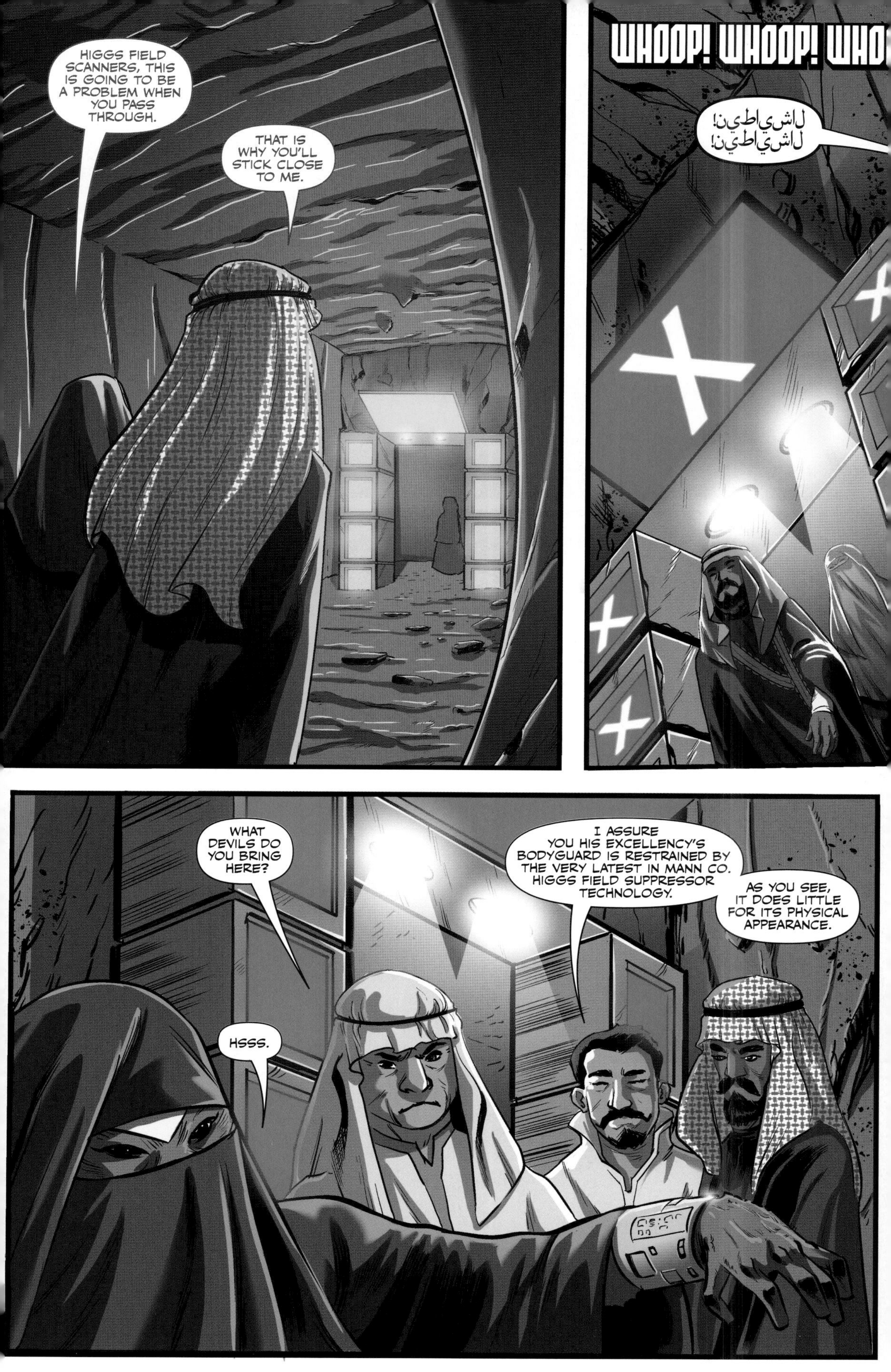
HIGGS FIELD SCANNERS, THIS IS GOING TO BE A PROBLEM WHEN YOU PASS THROUGH.
THAT IS WHY YOU'LL STICK CLOSE TO ME.
WHOOP! WHOOP! WHO
لاشياطين!
لاشياطين!
WHAT DEVILS DO YOU BRING HERE?
HSSS.
I ASSURE YOU HIS EXCELLENCY'S BODYGUARD IS RESTRAINED BY THE VERY LATEST IN MANN CO. HIGGS FIELD SUPPRESSOR TECHNOLOGY.
AS YOU SEE, IT DOES LITTLE FOR ITS PHYSICAL APPEARANCE.

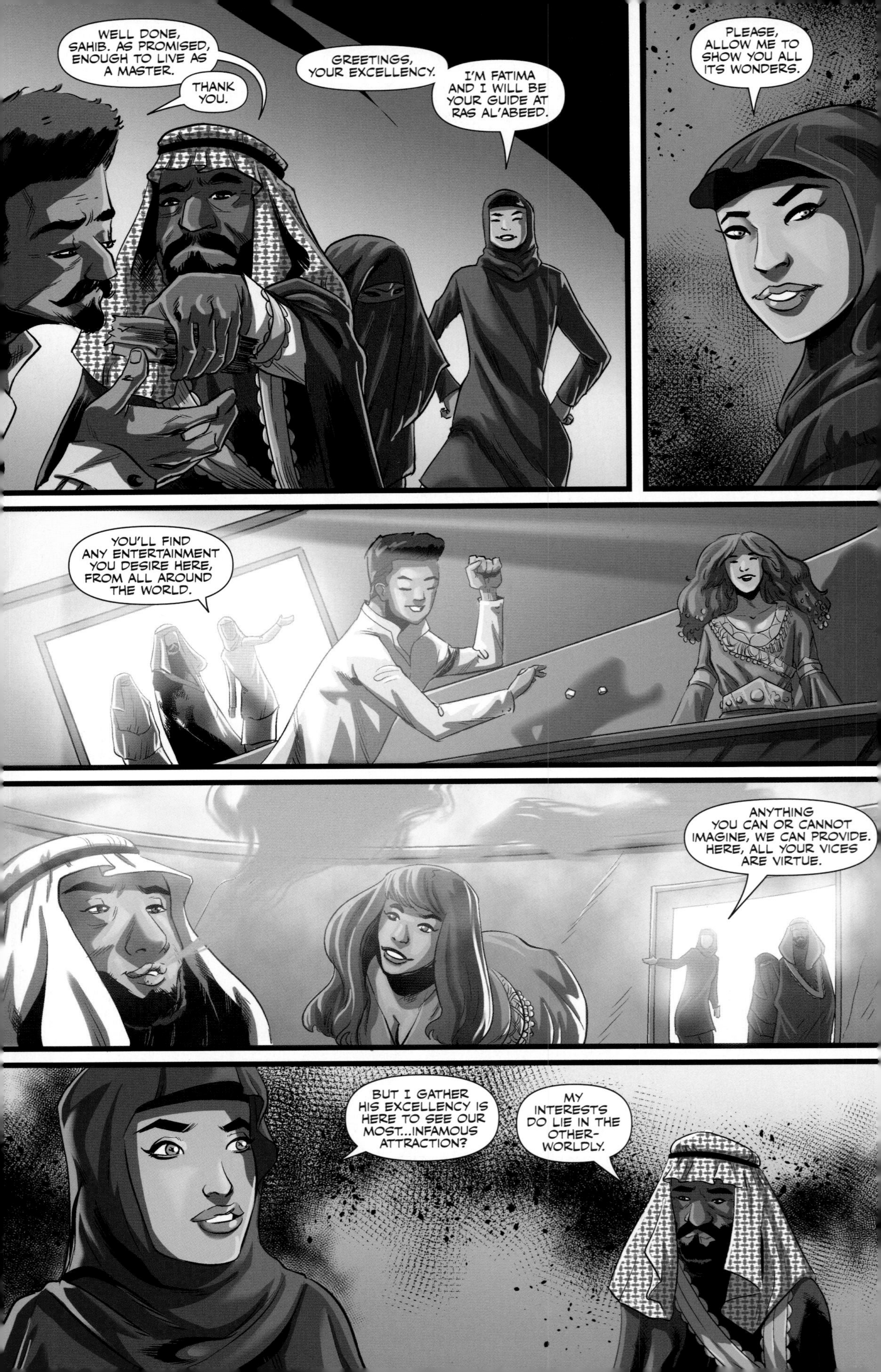
WELL DONE, SAHIB. AS PROMISED, ENOUGH TO LIVE AS A MASTER.
THANK YOU.
GREETINGS, YOUR EXCELLENCY.
I'M FATIMA AND I WILL BE YOUR GUIDE AT RAS AL'ABEED.
PLEASE, ALLOW ME TO SHOW YOU ALL ITS WONDERS.
YOU'LL FIND ANY ENTERTAINMENT YOU DESIRE HERE, FROM ALL AROUND THE WORLD.
ANYTHING YOU CAN OR CANNOT IMAGINE, WE CAN PROVIDE. HERE, ALL YOUR VICES ARE VIRTUE.
BUT I GATHER HIS EXCELLENCY IS HERE TO SEE OUR MOST...INFAMOUS ATTRACTION?
MY INTERESTS DO LIE IN THE OTHER-WORLDLY.

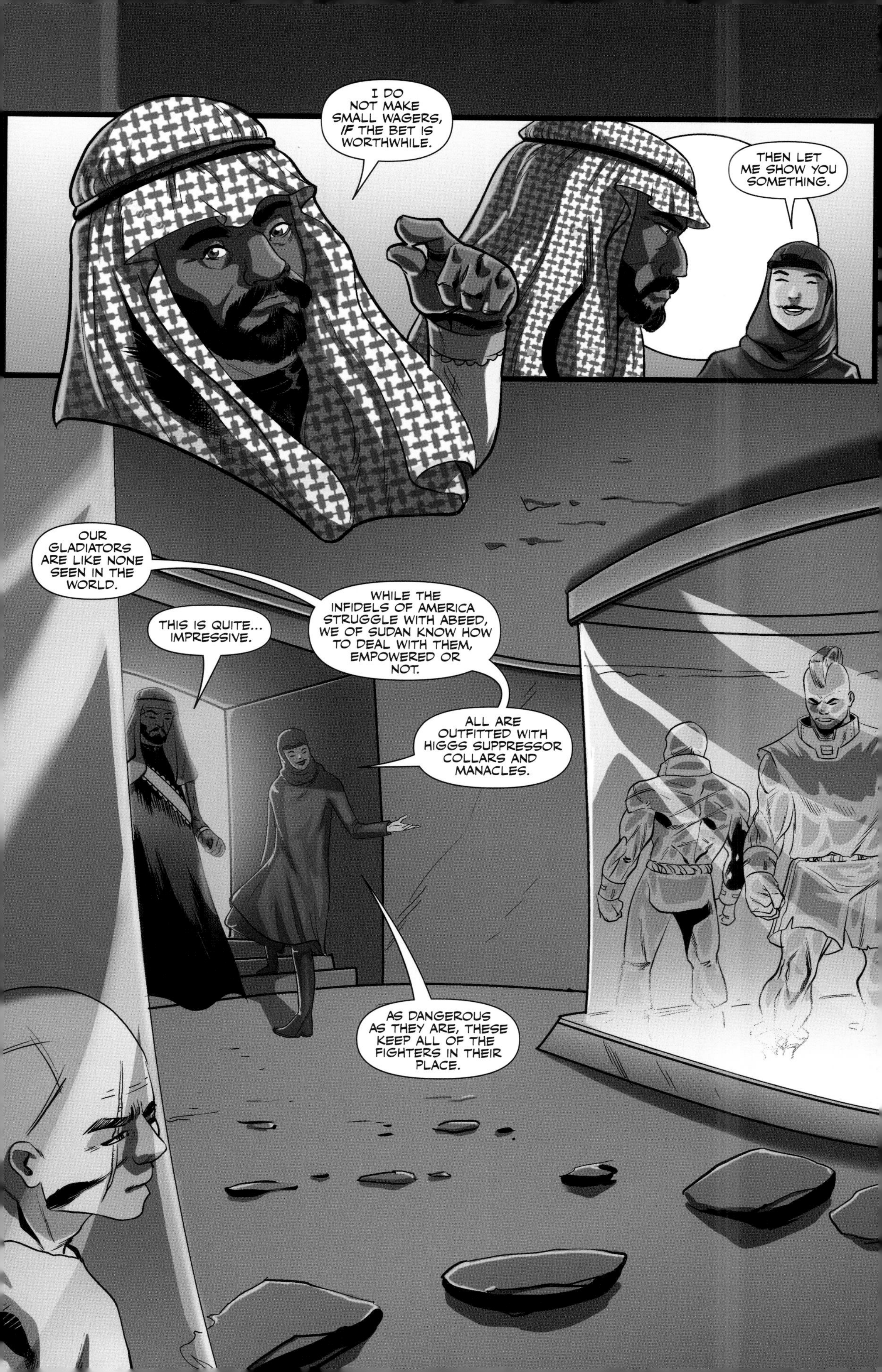
I DO NOT MAKE SMALL WAGERS, *IF* THE BET IS WORTHWHILE.
THEN LET ME SHOW YOU SOMETHING.
OUR GLADIATORS ARE LIKE NONE SEEN IN THE WORLD.
THIS IS QUITE... IMPRESSIVE.
WHILE THE INFIDELS OF AMERICA STRUGGLE WITH ABEED, WE OF SUDAN KNOW HOW TO DEAL WITH THEM, EMPOWERED OR NOT.
ALL ARE OUTFITTED WITH HIGGS SUPPRESSOR COLLARS AND MANACLES.
AS DANGEROUS AS THEY ARE, THESE KEEP ALL OF THE FIGHTERS IN THEIR PLACE.

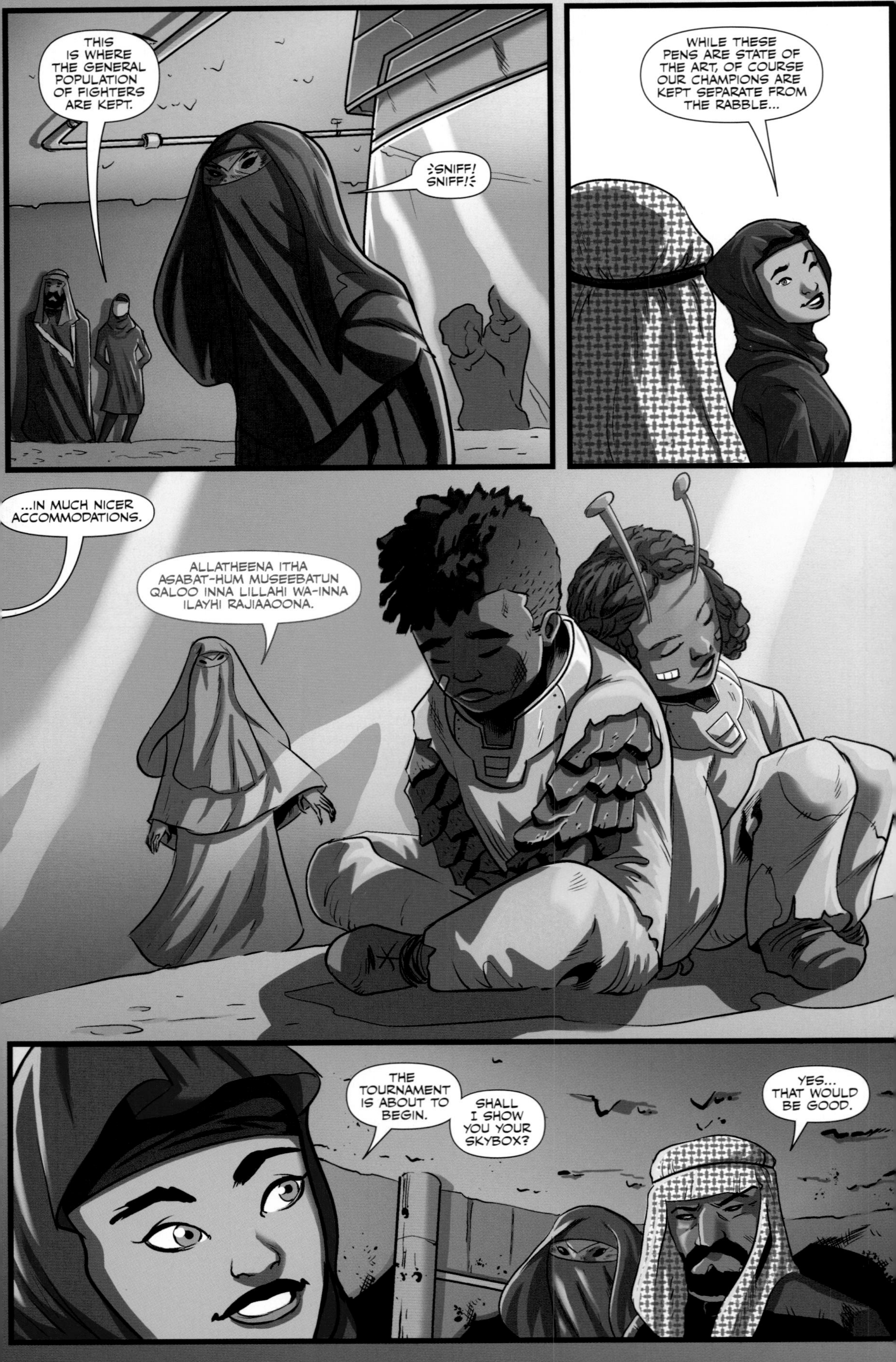
THIS IS WHERE THE GENERAL POPULATION OF FIGHTERS ARE KEPT.
SNIFF! SNIFF!
WHILE THESE PENS ARE STATE OF THE ART, OF COURSE OUR CHAMPIONS ARE KEPT SEPARATE FROM THE RABBLE...
...IN MUCH NICER ACCOMMODATIONS.
ALLATHEENA ITHA ASABAT-HUM MUSEEBATUN QALOO INNA LILLAHI WA-INNA ILAYHI RAJIAAOONA.
THE TOURNAMENT IS ABOUT TO BEGIN.
SHALL I SHOW YOU YOUR SKYBOX?
YES... THAT WOULD BE GOOD.

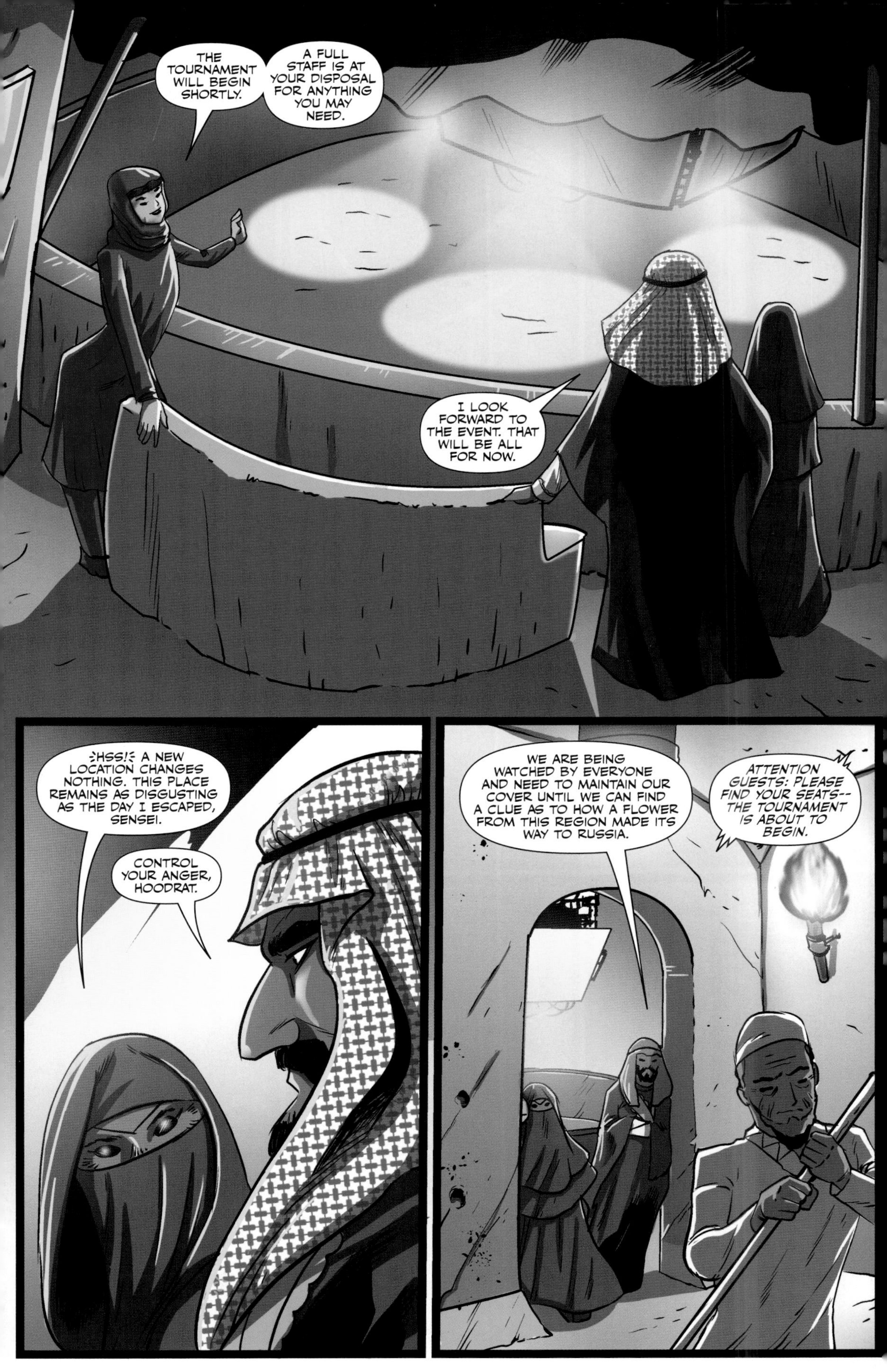
THE TOURNAMENT WILL BEGIN SHORTLY.
A FULL STAFF IS AT YOUR DISPOSAL FOR ANYTHING YOU MAY NEED.
I LOOK FORWARD TO THE EVENT. THAT WILL BE ALL FOR NOW.
HSS! A NEW LOCATION CHANGES NOTHING. THIS PLACE REMAINS AS DISGUSTING AS THE DAY I ESCAPED, SENSEI.
CONTROL YOUR ANGER, HOODRAT.
WE ARE BEING WATCHED BY EVERYONE AND NEED TO MAINTAIN OUR COVER UNTIL WE CAN FIND A CLUE AS TO HOW A FLOWER FROM THIS REGION MADE ITS WAY TO RUSSIA.
ATTENTION GUESTS: PLEASE FIND YOUR SEATS-- THE TOURNAMENT IS ABOUT TO BEGIN.

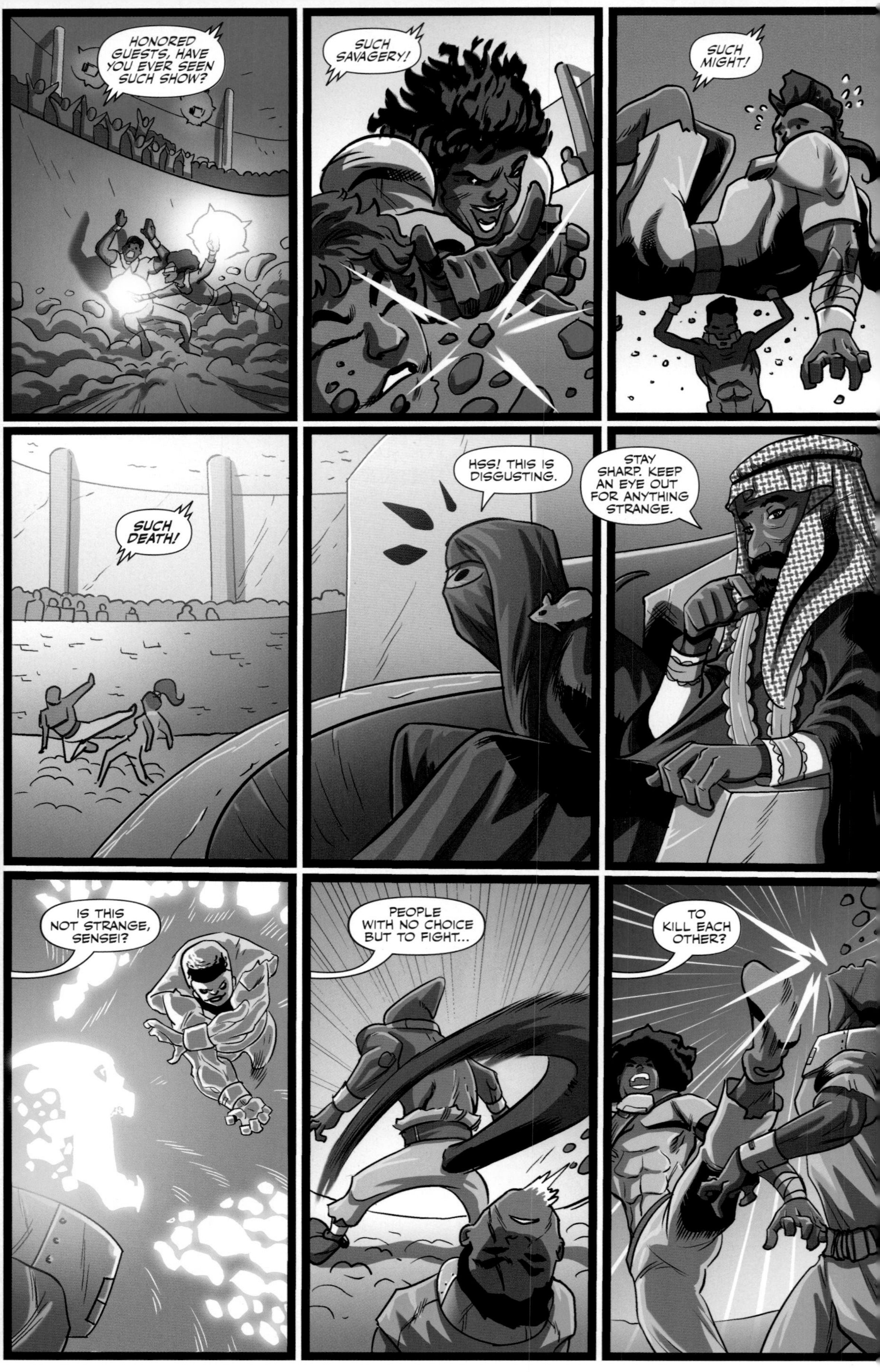
HONORED GUESTS, HAVE YOU EVER SEEN SUCH SHOW?
SUCH SAVAGERY!
SUCH MIGHT!
SUCH DEATH!
HSS! THIS IS DISGUSTING.
STAY SHARP. KEEP AN EYE OUT FOR ANYTHING STRANGE.
IS THIS NOT STRANGE, SENSEI?
PEOPLE WITH NO CHOICE BUT TO FIGHT...
TO KILL EACH OTHER?

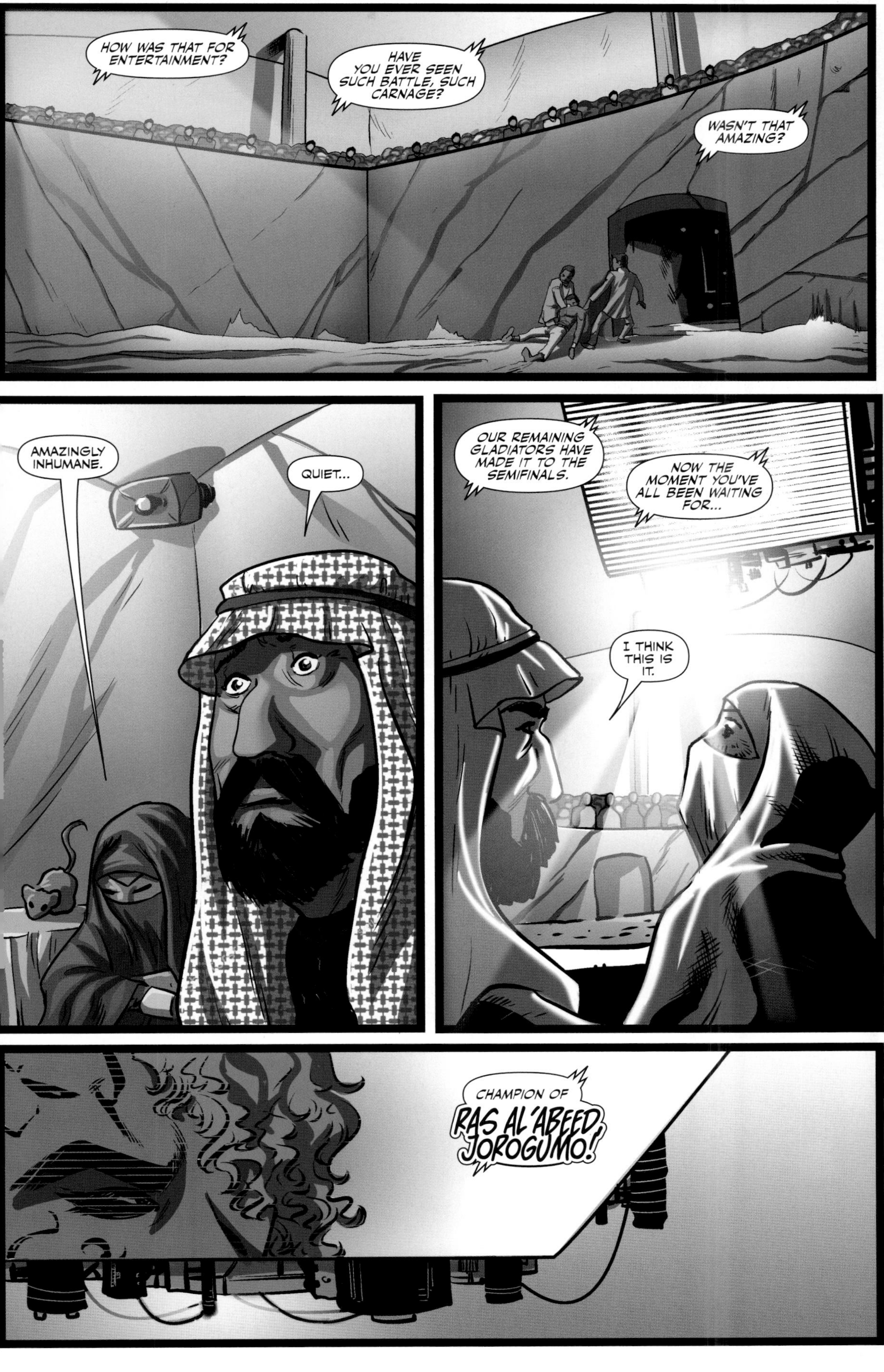
HOW WAS THAT FOR ENTERTAINMENT?
HAVE YOU EVER SEEN SUCH BATTLE, SUCH CARNAGE?
WASN'T THAT AMAZING?
AMAZINGLY INHUMANE.
QUIET...
OUR REMAINING GLADIATORS HAVE MADE IT TO THE SEMIFINALS.
NOW THE MOMENT YOU'VE ALL BEEN WAITING FOR...
I THINK THIS IS IT.
CHAMPION OF RAS AL'ABEED, JOROGUMO!

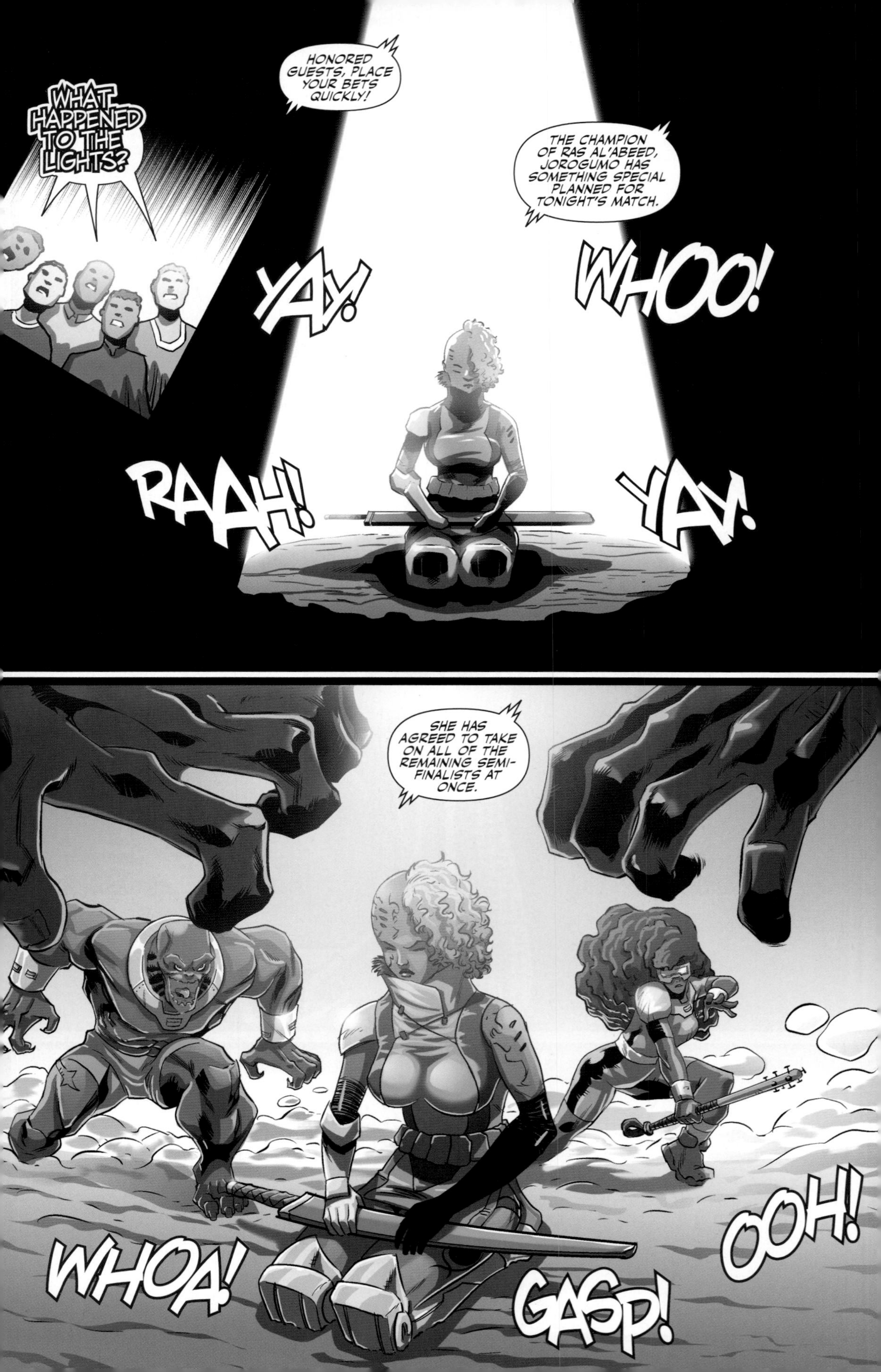
WHAT HAPPENED TO THE LIGHTS?
HONORED GUESTS, PLACE YOUR BETS QUICKLY!
THE CHAMPION OF RAS AL'ABEED, JOROGUMO HAS SOMETHING SPECIAL PLANNED FOR TONIGHT'S MATCH.
YAY!
WHOO!
RAAH!
YAY!
SHE HAS AGREED TO TAKE ON ALL OF THE REMAINING SEMI-FINALISTS AT ONCE.
WHOA!
GASP!
OOH!

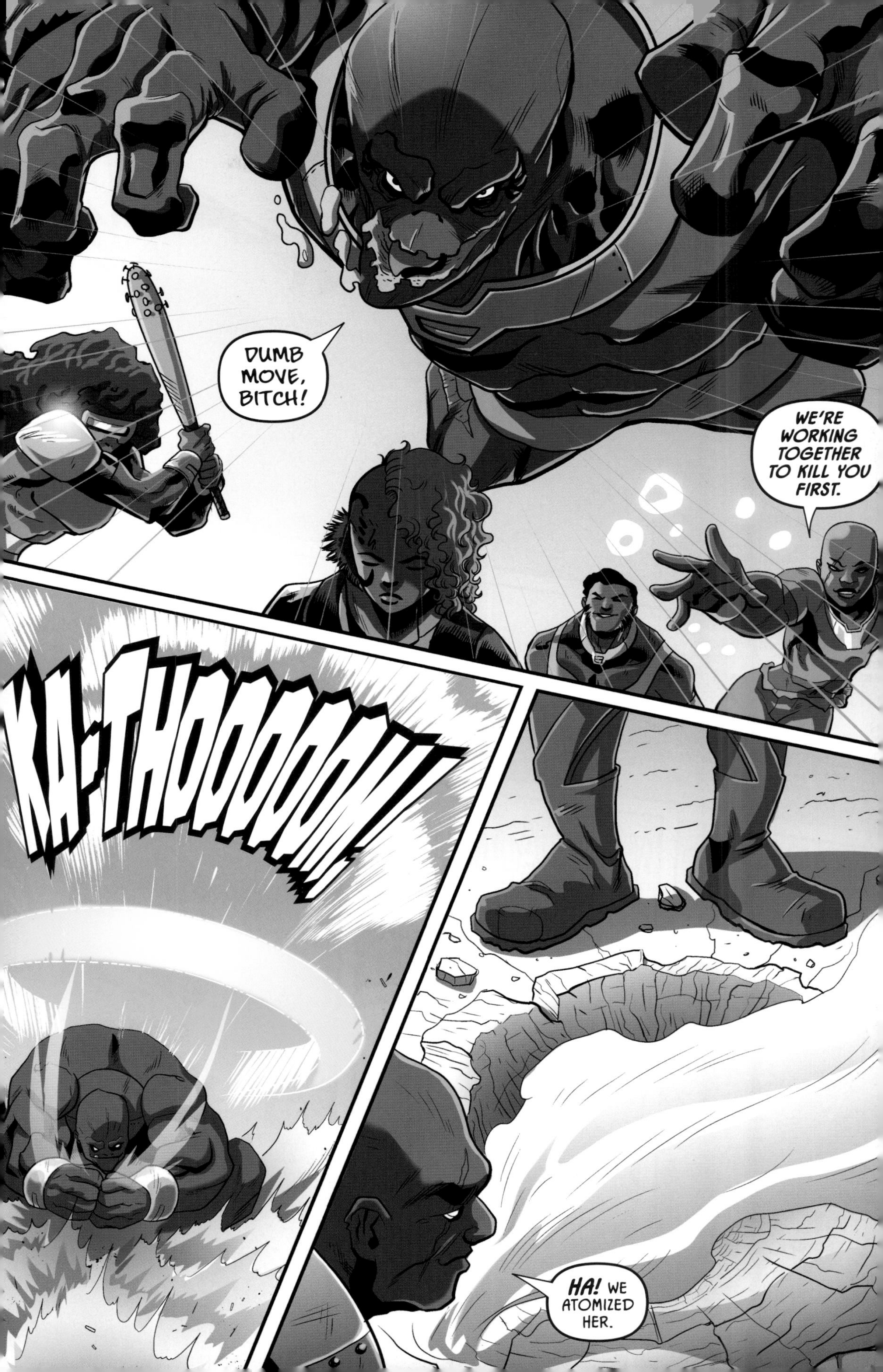
DUMB MOVE, BITCH!
WE'RE WORKING TOGETHER TO KILL YOU FIRST.
KA-THOOOOOM!
HA! WE ATOMIZED HER.

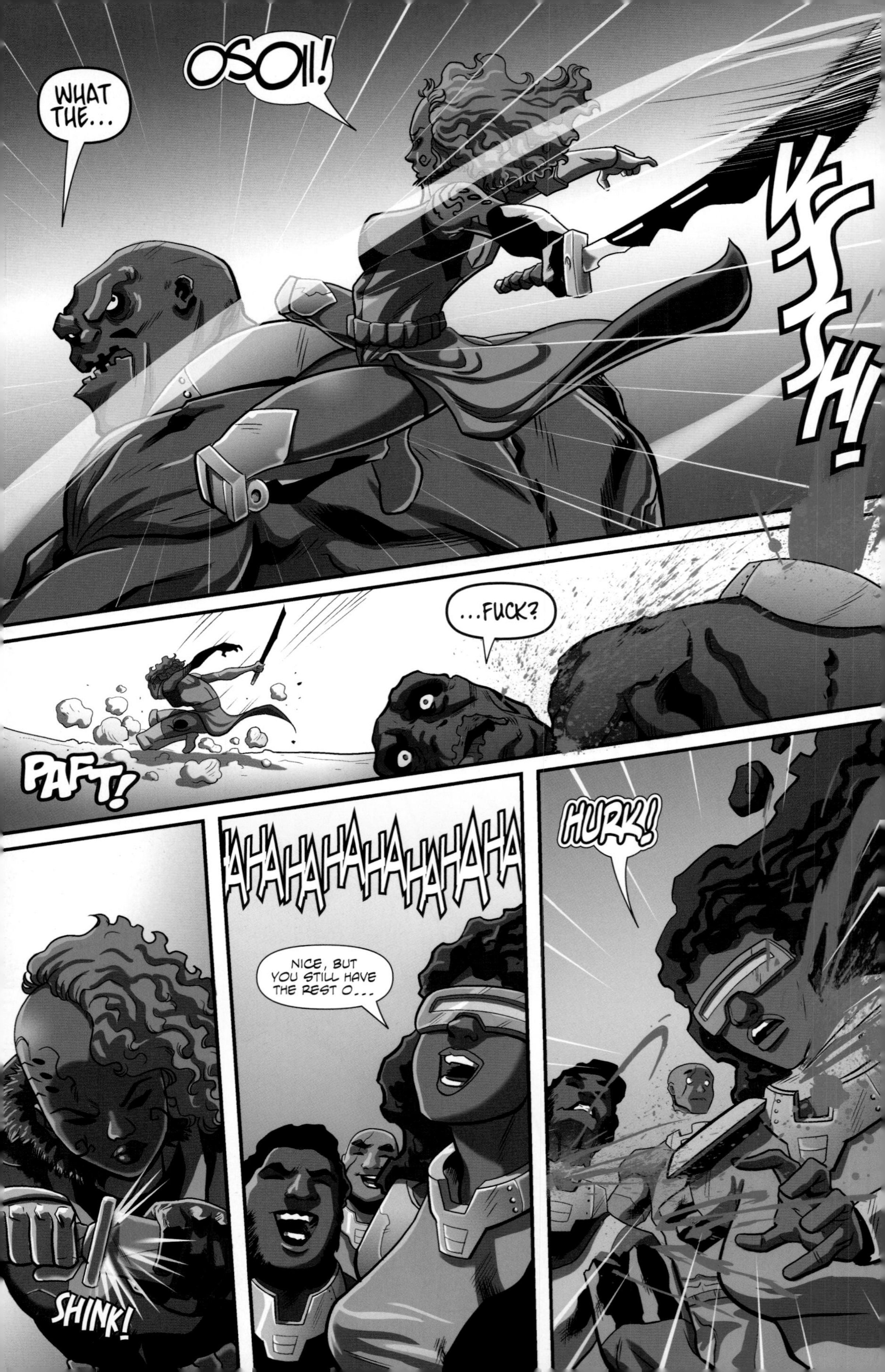
WHAT THE...
OSOII!
KE-T-SH!
...FUCK?
PAFT!
SHINK!
AHAHAHAHAHAHAHAHA
NICE, BUT YOU STILL HAVE THE REST O...
HURK!

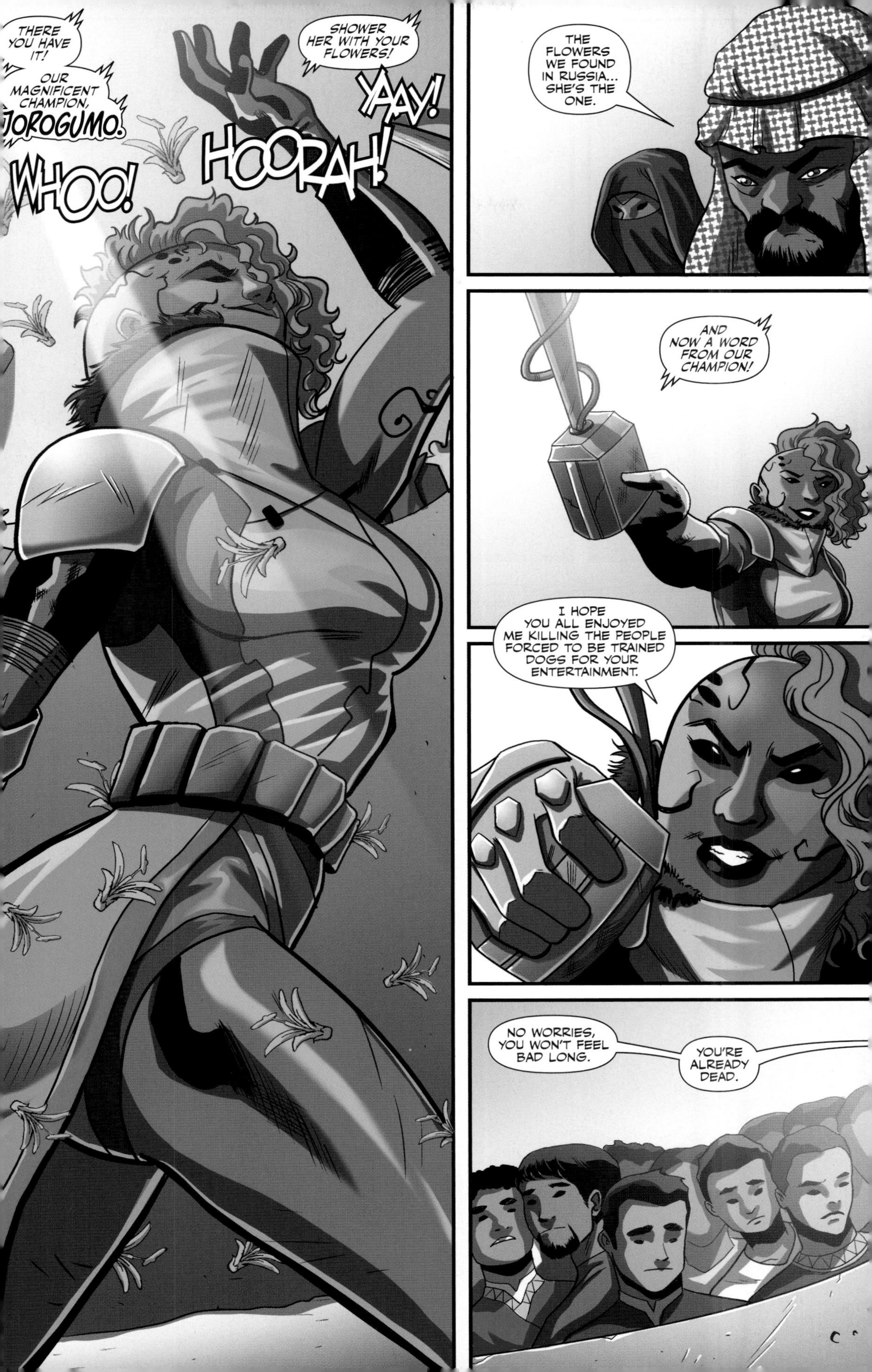
THERE YOU HAVE IT!
OUR MAGNIFICENT CHAMPION, JOROGUMO.
SHOWER HER WITH YOUR FLOWERS!
YAAY!
HOORAH!
WHOO!
THE FLOWERS WE FOUND IN RUSSIA... SHE'S THE ONE.
AND NOW A WORD FROM OUR CHAMPION!
I HOPE YOU ALL ENJOYED ME KILLING THE PEOPLE FORCED TO BE TRAINED DOGS FOR YOUR ENTERTAINMENT.
NO WORRIES, YOU WON'T FEEL BAD LONG.
YOU'RE ALREADY DEAD.

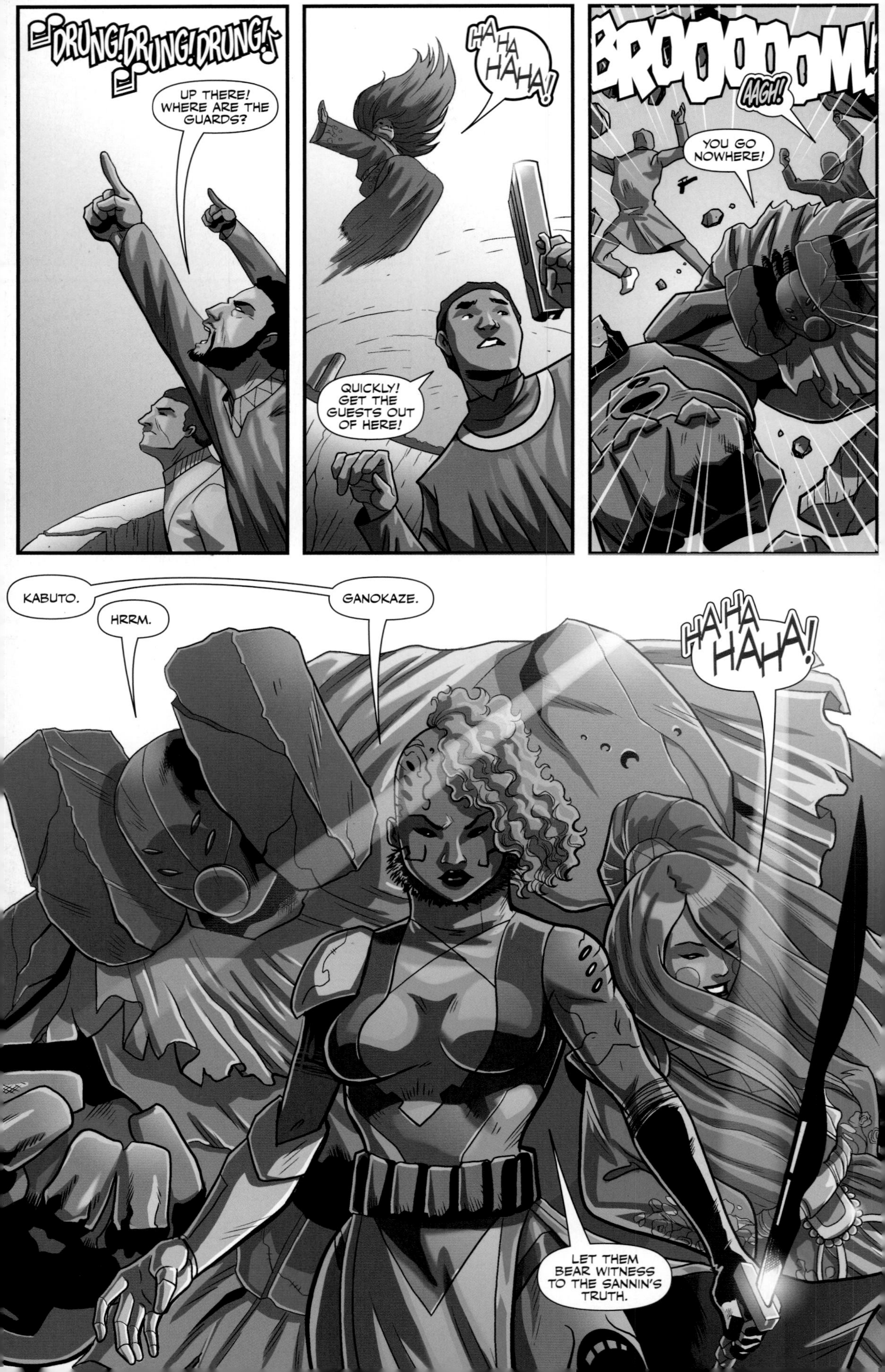
DRUNG! DRUNG! DRUNG!
UP THERE! WHERE ARE THE GUARDS?
HA HA HAHA!
QUICKLY! GET THE GUESTS OUT OF HERE!
BROOOOOM!
AAGH!
YOU GO NOWHERE!
KABUTO.
HRRM.
GANOKAZE.
HAHA HAHA!
LET THEM BEAR WITNESS TO THE SANNIN'S TRUTH.

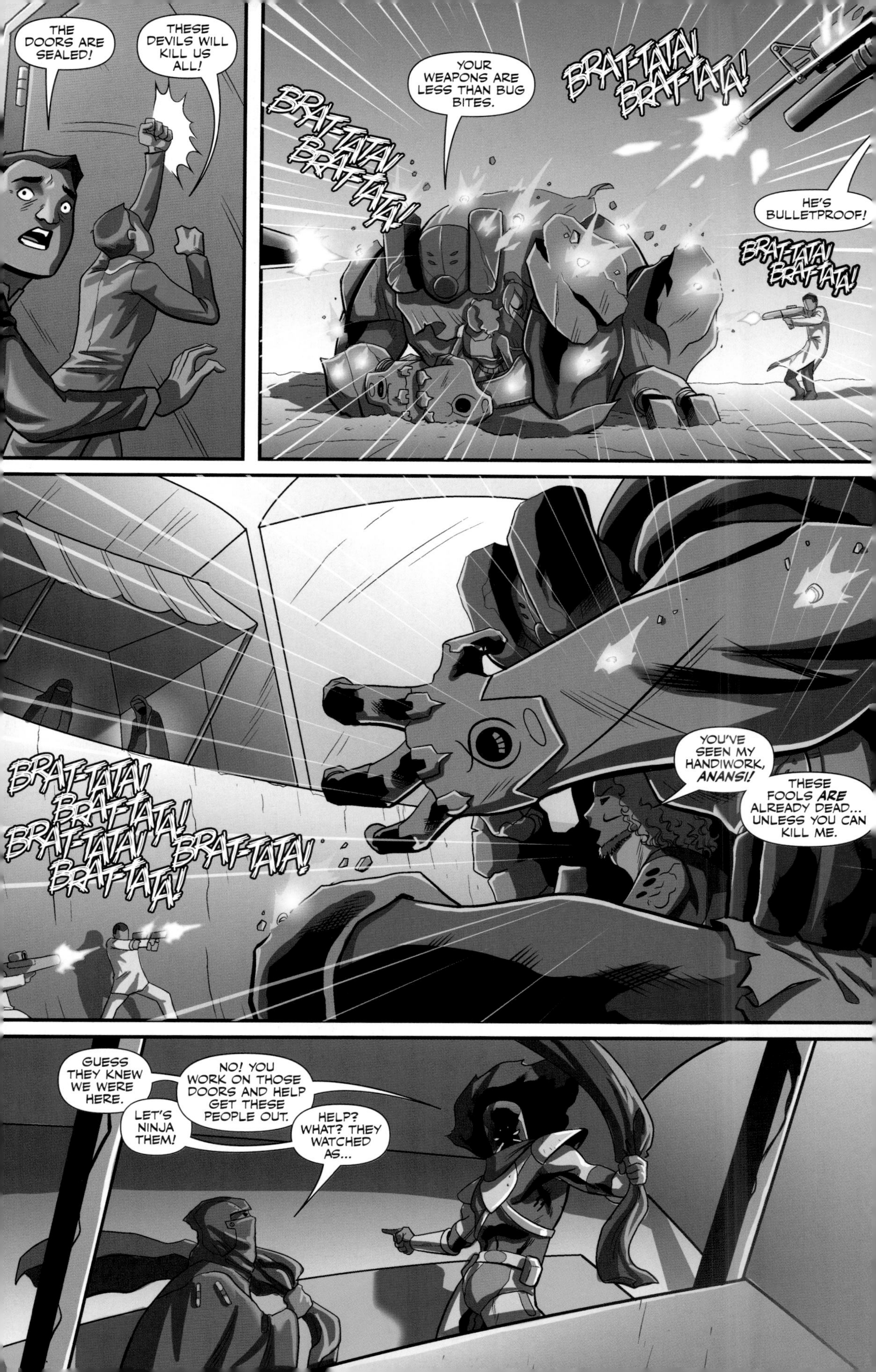
THE DOORS ARE SEALED!
THESE DEVILS WILL KILL US ALL!
YOUR WEAPONS ARE LESS THAN BUG BITES.
BRAT-TATA! BRAT-TATA!
BRAT-TATA! BRAT-TATA!
HE'S BULLETPROOF!
BRAT-TATA! BRAT-TATA!
BRAT-TATA! BRAT-TATA! BRAT-TATA! BRAT-TATA! BRAT-TATA!
YOU'VE SEEN MY HANDIWORK, ANANSI!
THESE FOOLS ARE ALREADY DEAD... UNLESS YOU CAN KILL ME.
GUESS THEY KNEW WE WERE HERE.
LET'S NINJA THEM!
NO! YOU WORK ON THOSE DOORS AND HELP GET THESE PEOPLE OUT.
HELP? WHAT? THEY WATCHED AS...

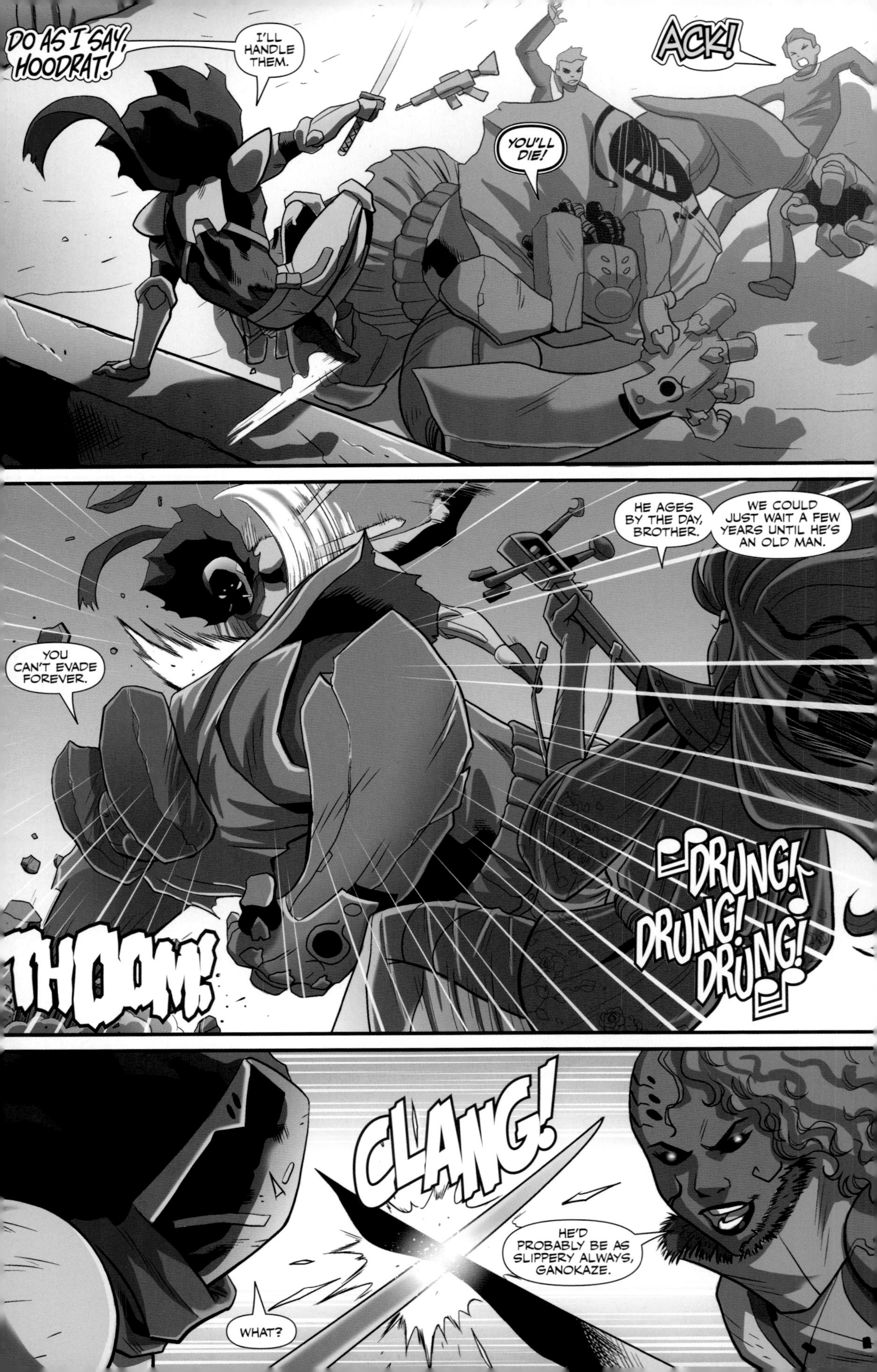
DO AS I SAY, HOODRAT!
I'LL HANDLE THEM.
ACK!
YOU'LL DIE!
HE AGES BY THE DAY, BROTHER.
WE COULD JUST WAIT A FEW YEARS UNTIL HE'S AN OLD MAN.
YOU CAN'T EVADE FOREVER.
DRUNG! DRUNG! DRUNG!
THOOM!
CLANG!
HE'D PROBABLY BE AS SLIPPERY ALWAYS, GANOKAZE.
WHAT?

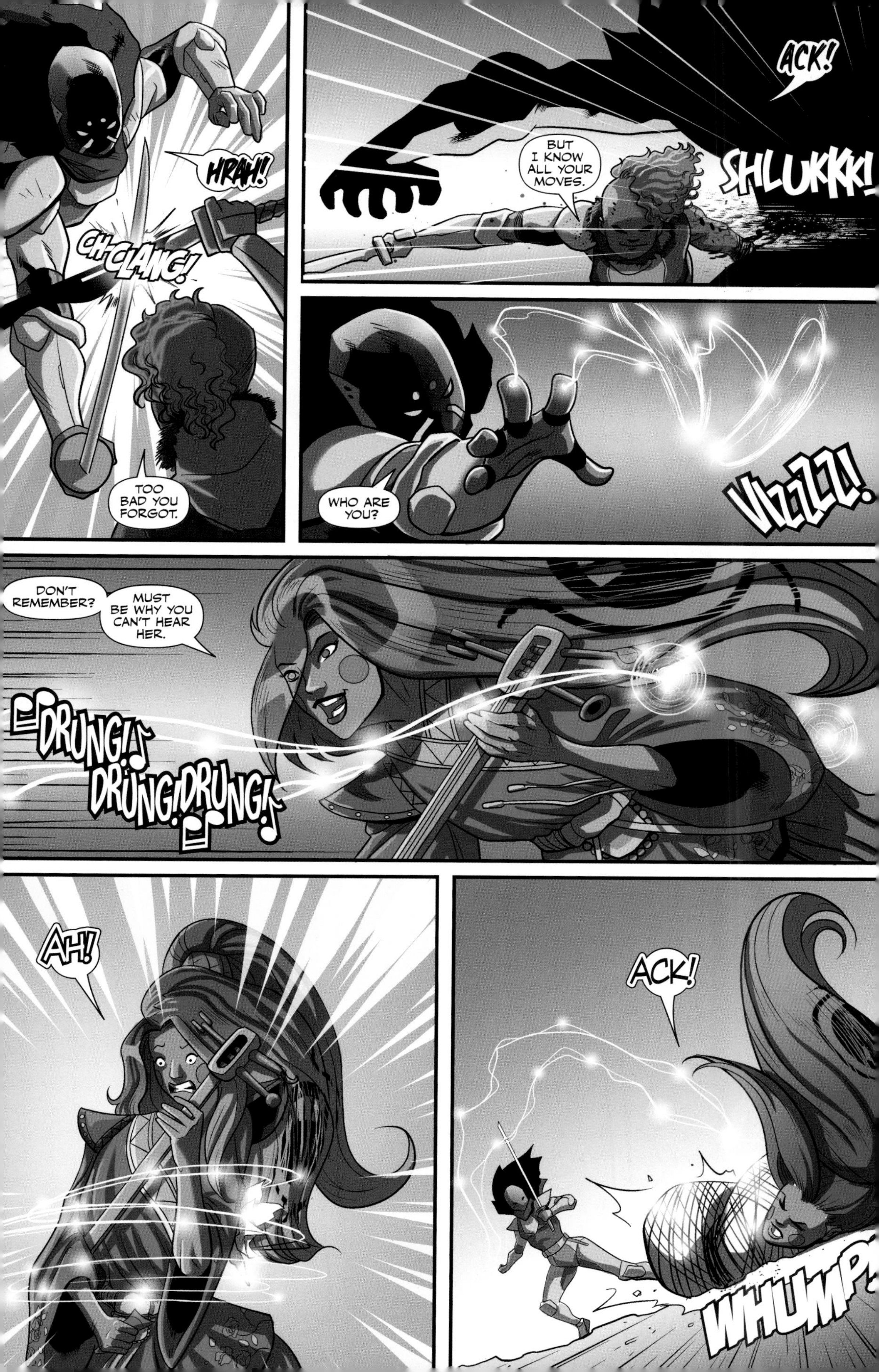
HRAH!
CH-CLANG!
TOO BAD YOU FORGOT.
ACK!
BUT I KNOW ALL YOUR MOVES.
SHLUKKK!
WHO ARE YOU?
VIZZZZ!
DON'T REMEMBER?
MUST BE WHY YOU CAN'T HEAR HER.
DRUNG!
DRUNG! DRUNG!
AH!
ACK!
WHUMP!

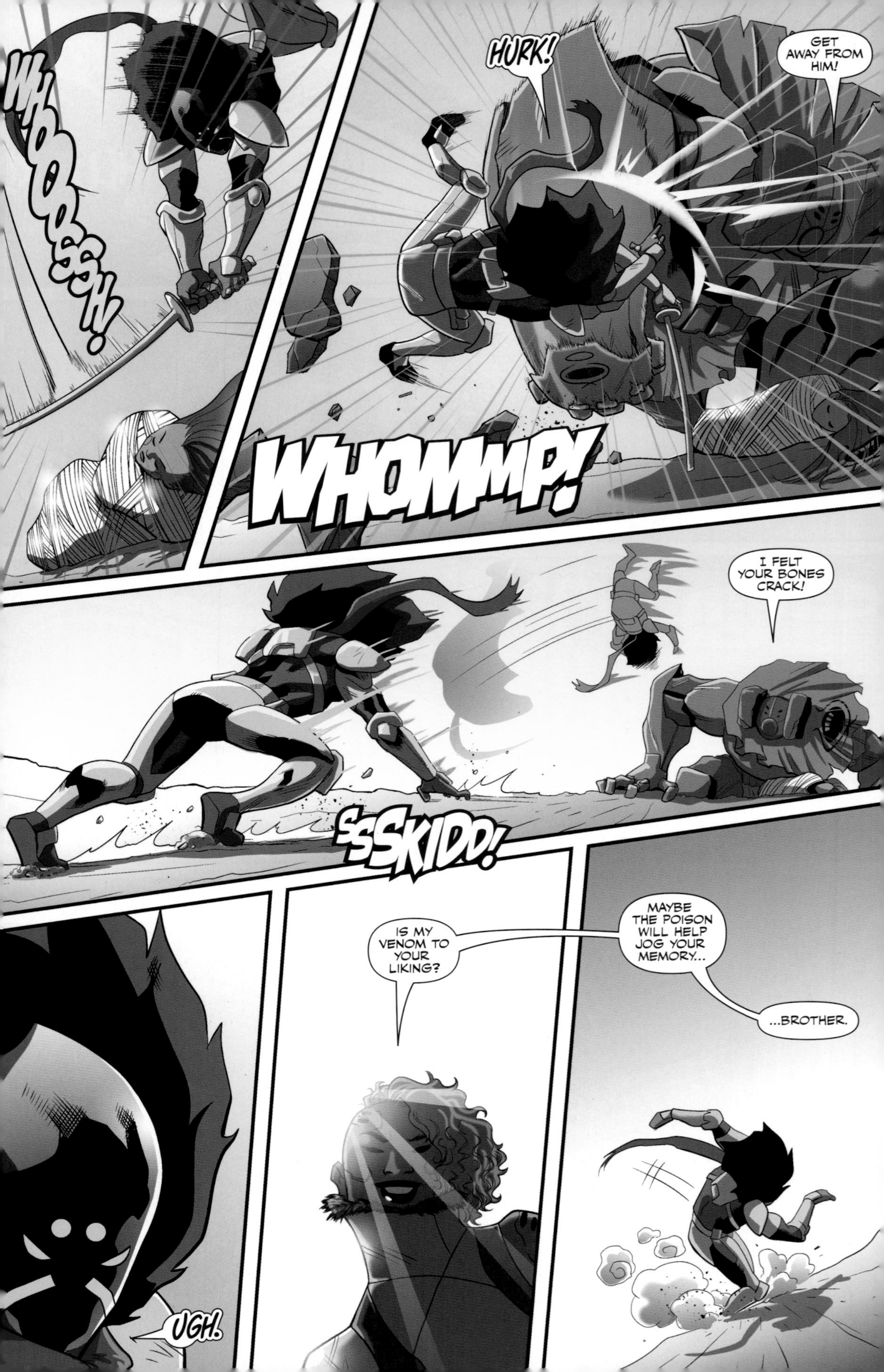
WHOOOOSSH!
HURK!
GET AWAY FROM HIM!
WHOMMP!
I FELT YOUR BONES CRACK!
SSSKIDD!
UGH.
IS MY VENOM TO YOUR LIKING?
MAYBE THE POISON WILL HELP JOG YOUR MEMORY...
...BROTHER.

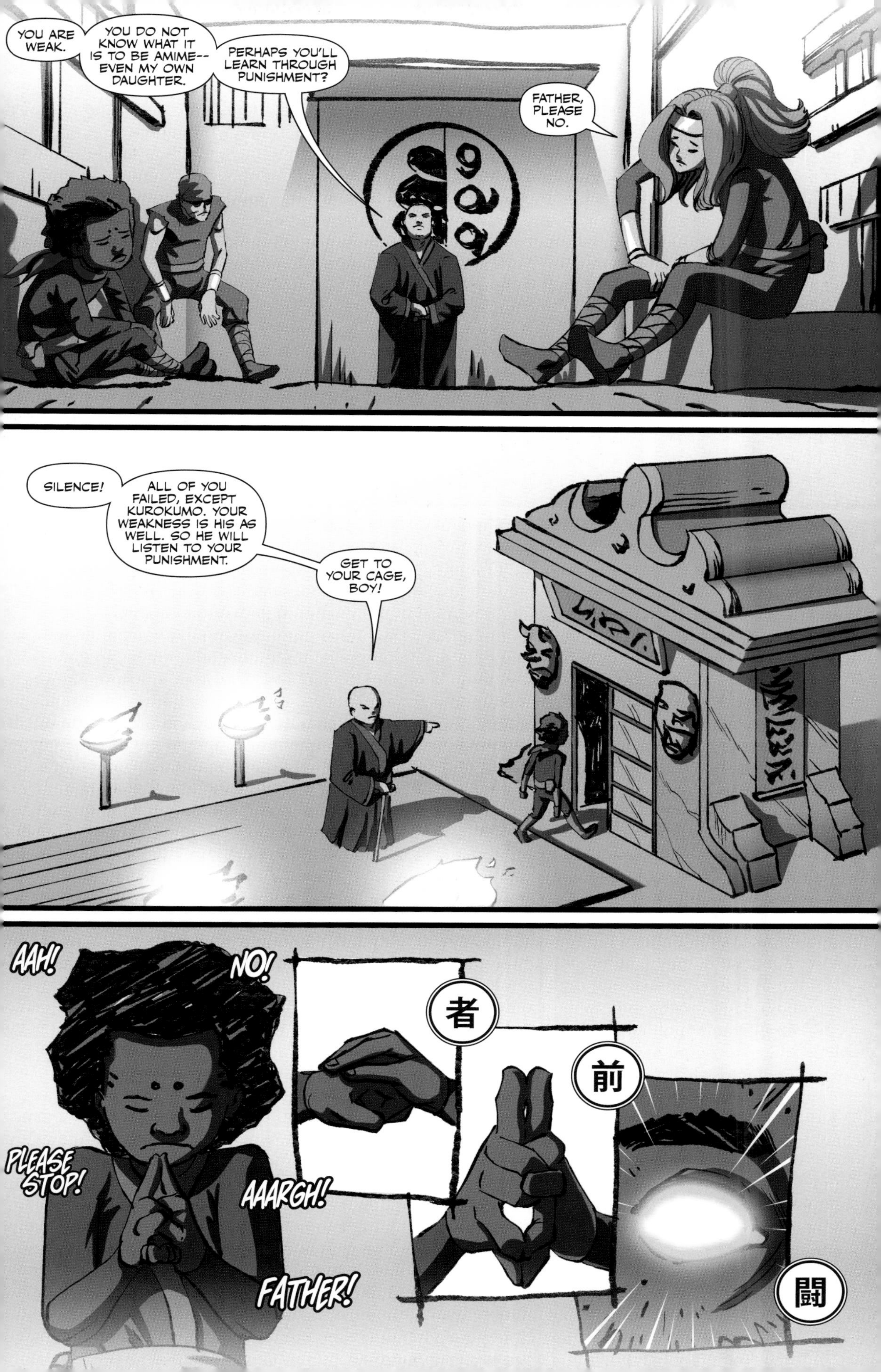
YOU ARE WEAK.
YOU DO NOT KNOW WHAT IT IS TO BE AMIME-- EVEN MY OWN DAUGHTER.
PERHAPS YOU'LL LEARN THROUGH PUNISHMENT?
FATHER, PLEASE NO.
SILENCE!
ALL OF YOU FAILED, EXCEPT KUROKUMO. YOUR WEAKNESS IS HIS AS WELL. SO HE WILL LISTEN TO YOUR PUNISHMENT.
GET TO YOUR CAGE, BOY!
AAH!
NO!
PLEASE STOP!
AAARGH!
FATHER!
者
前
闘

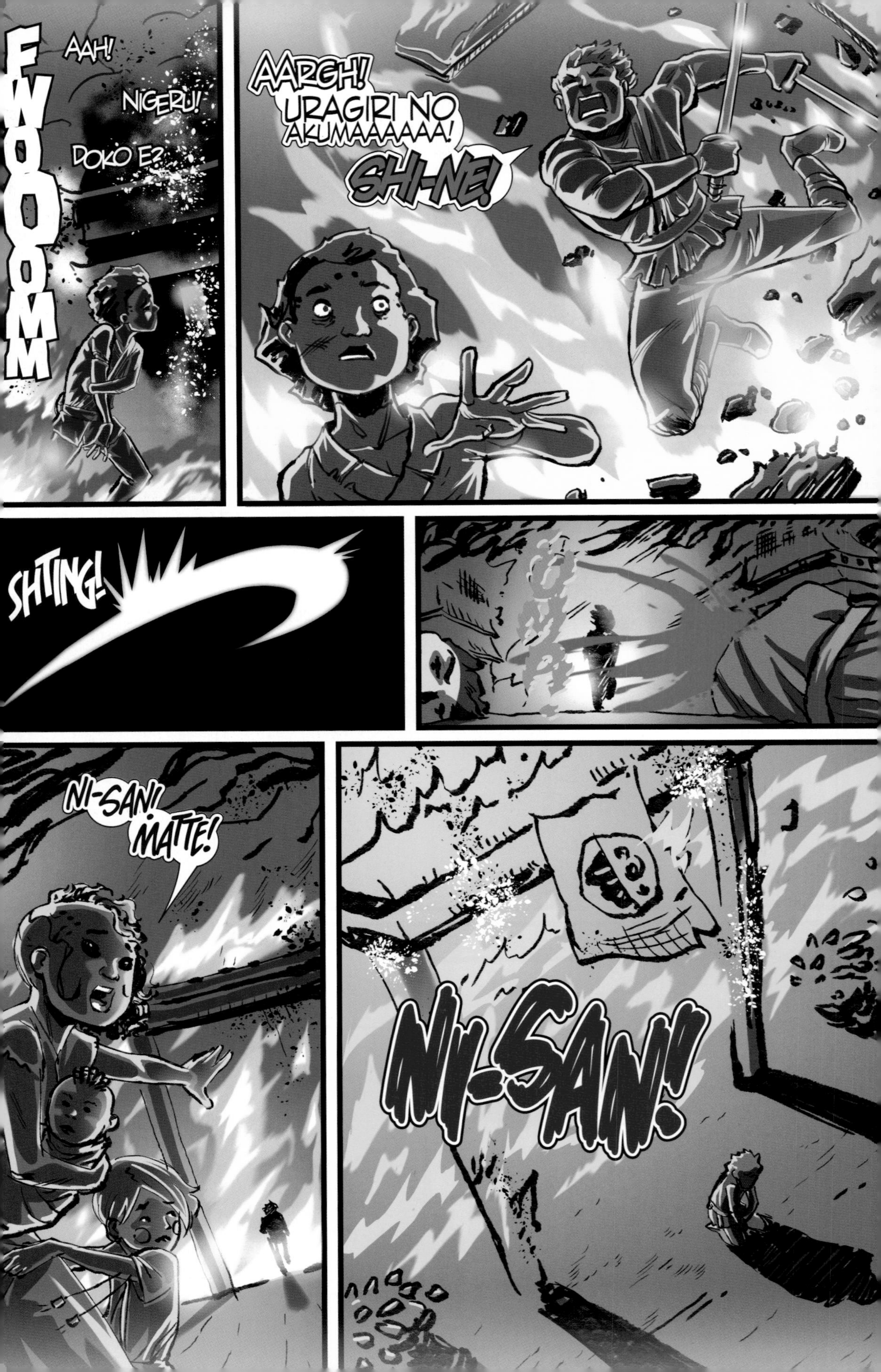
FWOOOMM
AAH!
NIGERU!
DOKO E?
AARGH! URAGIRI NO AKUMAAAAAAA!
SHI-NE!
SHTING!
NI-SAN! MATTE!
NI-SAN!

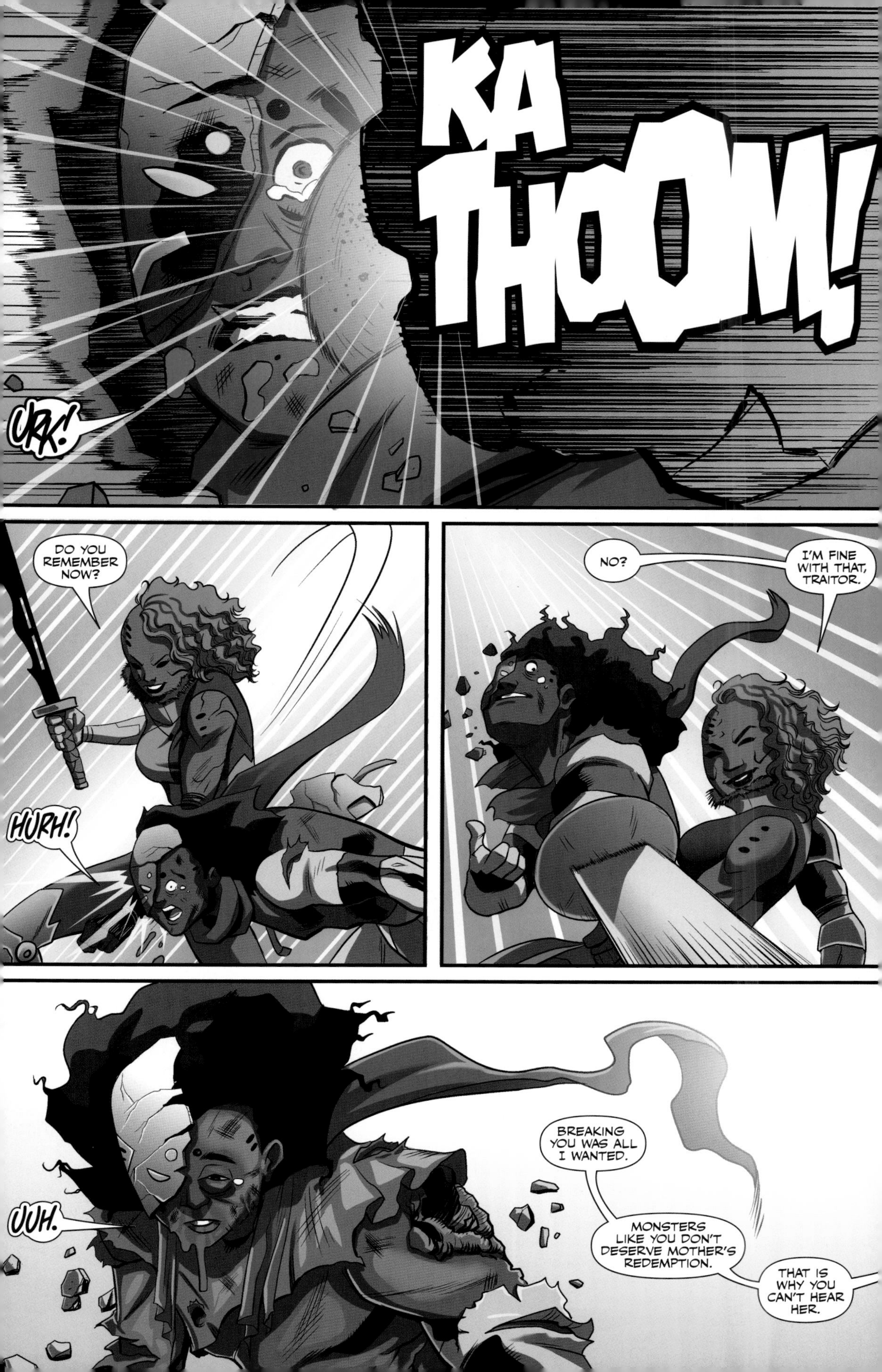
KA THOOM!
URK!
DO YOU REMEMBER NOW?
HURH!
NO?
I'M FINE WITH THAT, TRAITOR.
BREAKING YOU WAS ALL I WANTED.
MONSTERS LIKE YOU DON'T DESERVE MOTHER'S REDEMPTION.
THAT IS WHY YOU CAN'T HEAR HER.
UUH.

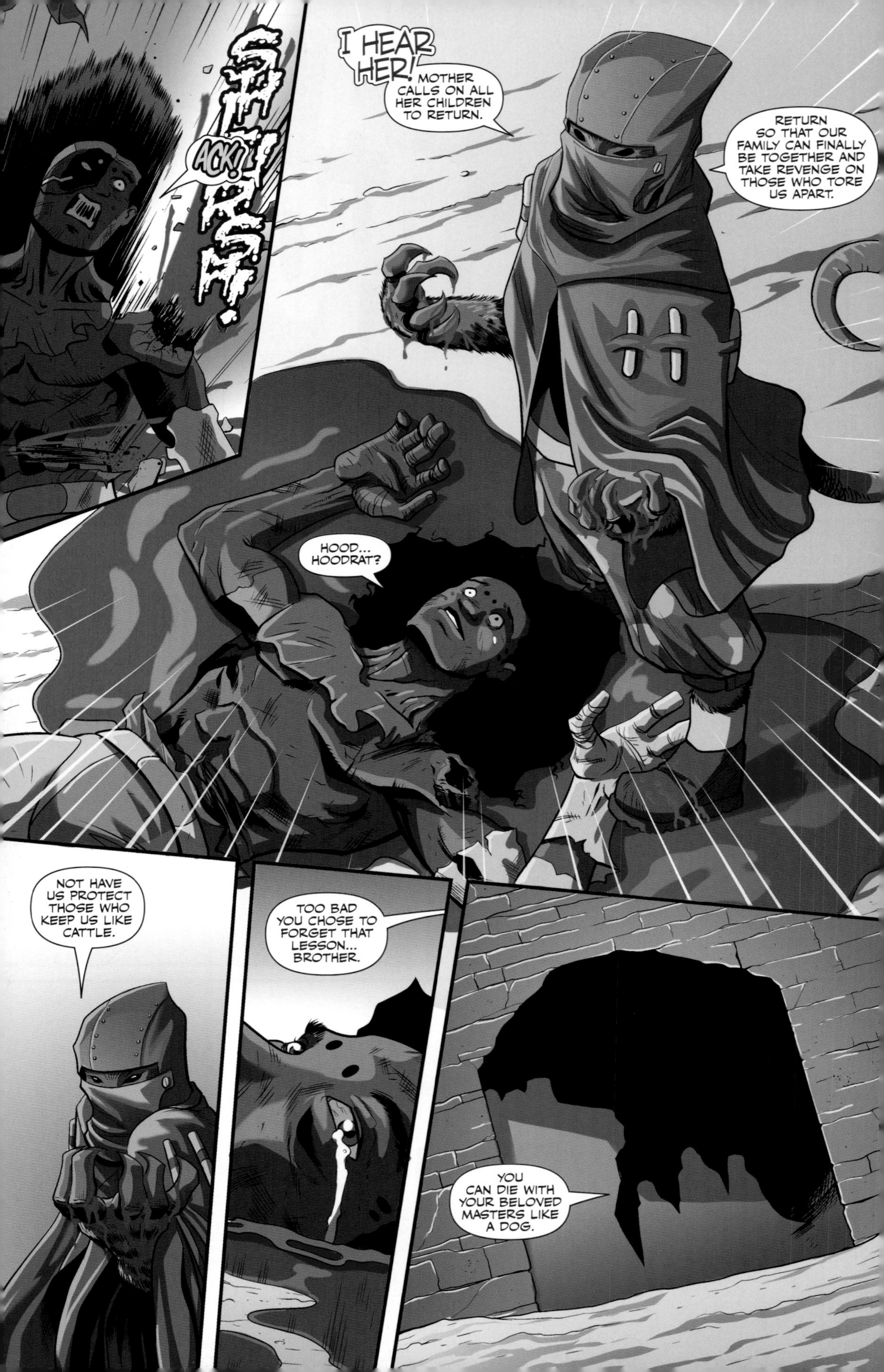
ACK!
I HEAR HER! MOTHER CALLS ON ALL HER CHILDREN TO RETURN.
RETURN SO THAT OUR FAMILY CAN FINALLY BE TOGETHER AND TAKE REVENGE ON THOSE WHO TORE US APART.
HOOD... HOODRAT?
NOT HAVE US PROTECT THOSE WHO KEEP US LIKE CATTLE.
TOO BAD YOU CHOSE TO FORGET THAT LESSON... BROTHER.
YOU CAN DIE WITH YOUR BELOVED MASTERS LIKE A DOG.

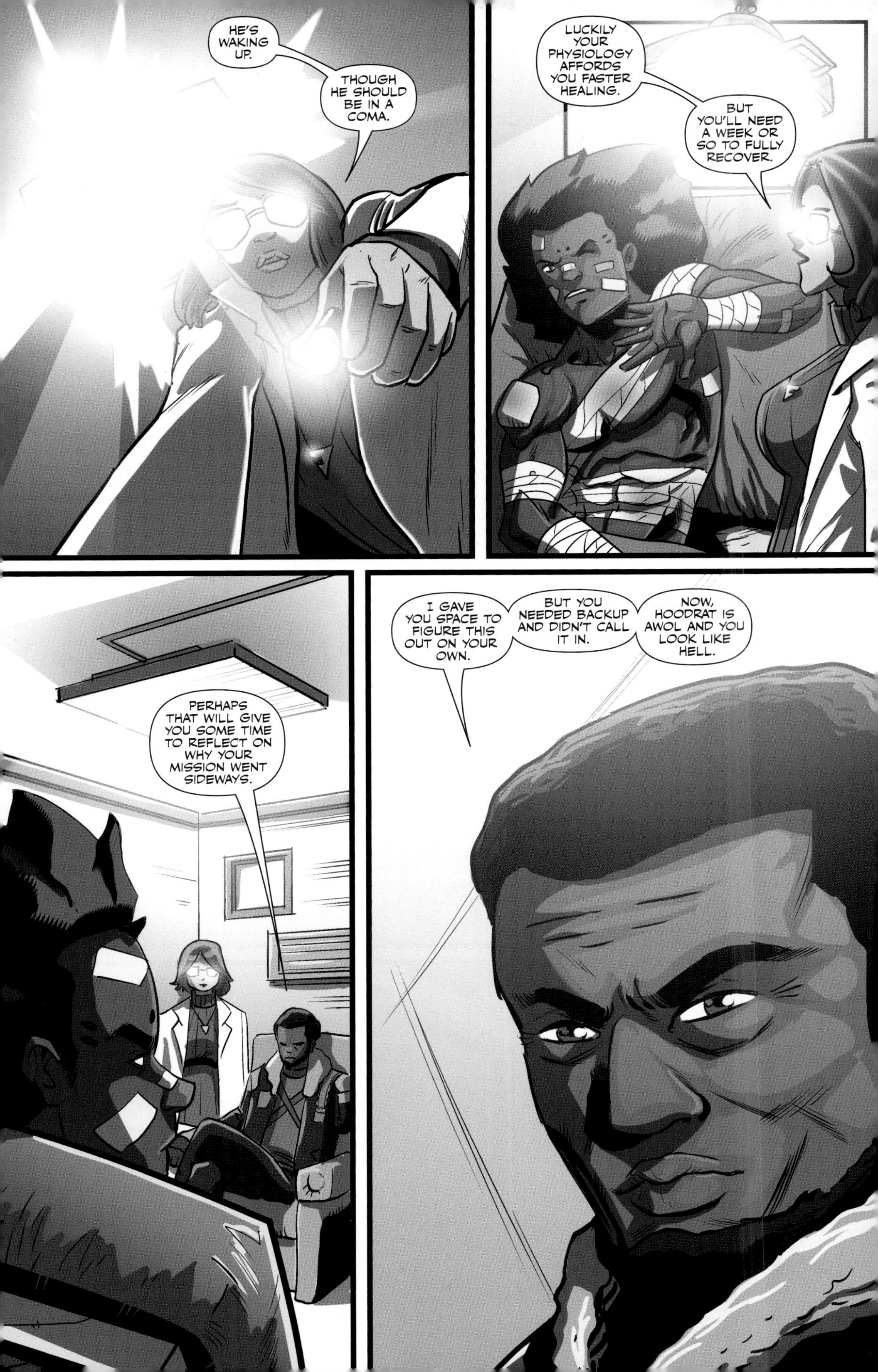
HE'S WAKING UP.
THOUGH HE SHOULD BE IN A COMA.
LUCKILY YOUR PHYSIOLOGY AFFORDS YOU FASTER HEALING.
BUT YOU'LL NEED A WEEK OR SO TO FULLY RECOVER.
PERHAPS THAT WILL GIVE YOU SOME TIME TO REFLECT ON WHY YOUR MISSION WENT SIDEWAYS.
I GAVE YOU SPACE TO FIGURE THIS OUT ON YOUR OWN.
BUT YOU NEEDED BACKUP AND DIDN'T CALL IT IN.
NOW, HOODRAT IS AWOL AND YOU LOOK LIKE HELL.

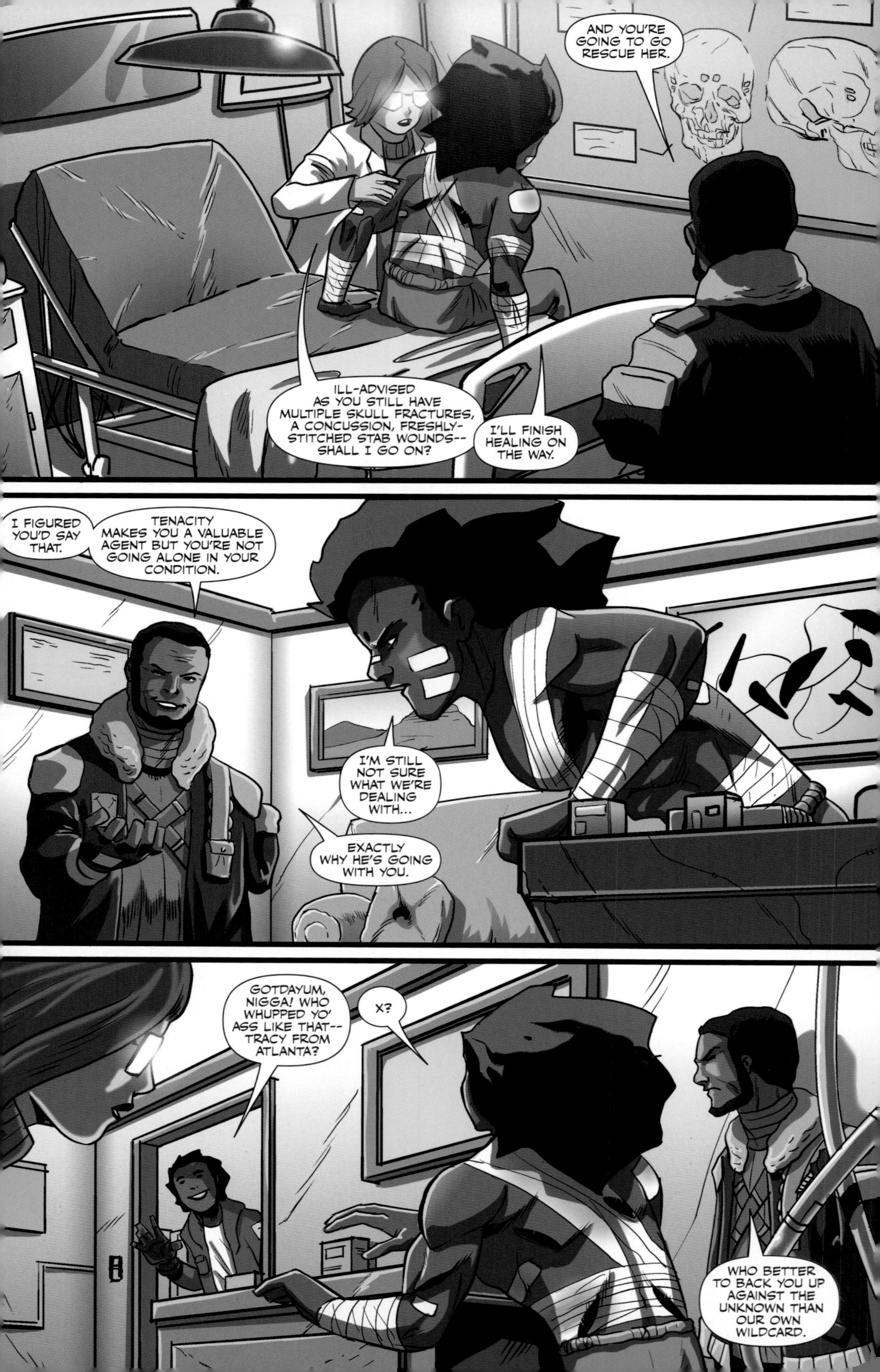
AND YOU'RE GOING TO GO RESCUE HER.
ILL-ADVISED AS YOU STILL HAVE MULTIPLE SKULL FRACTURES, A CONCUSSION, FRESHLY-STITCHED STAB WOUNDS-- SHALL I GO ON?
I'LL FINISH HEALING ON THE WAY.
I FIGURED YOU'D SAY THAT.
TENACITY MAKES YOU A VALUABLE AGENT BUT YOU'RE NOT GOING ALONE IN YOUR CONDITION.
I'M STILL NOT SURE WHAT WE'RE DEALING WITH...
EXACTLY WHY HE'S GOING WITH YOU.
GOTDAYUM, NIGGA! WHO WHUPPED YO' ASS LIKE THAT-- TRACY FROM ATLANTA?
X?
WHO BETTER TO BACK YOU UP AGAINST THE UNKNOWN THAN OUR OWN WILDCARD.

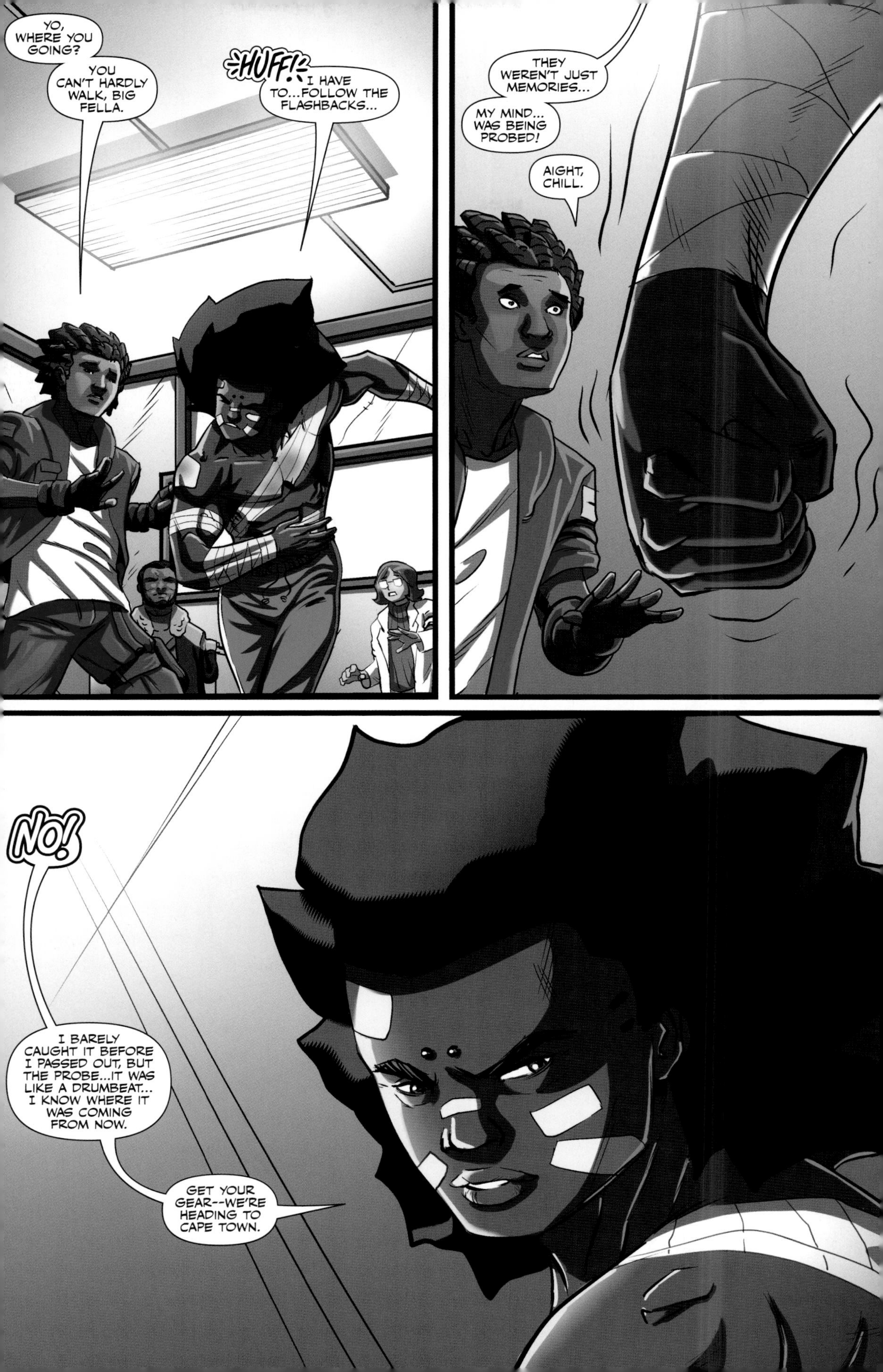
YO, WHERE YOU GOING?
YOU CAN'T HARDLY WALK, BIG FELLA.
HUFF!
I HAVE TO...FOLLOW THE FLASHBACKS...
THEY WEREN'T JUST MEMORIES...
MY MIND... WAS BEING PROBED!
AIGHT, CHILL.
NO!
I BARELY CAUGHT IT BEFORE I PASSED OUT, BUT THE PROBE...IT WAS LIKE A DRUMBEAT... I KNOW WHERE IT WAS COMING FROM NOW.
GET YOUR GEAR--WE'RE HEADING TO CAPE TOWN.

CHAPTER FOUR

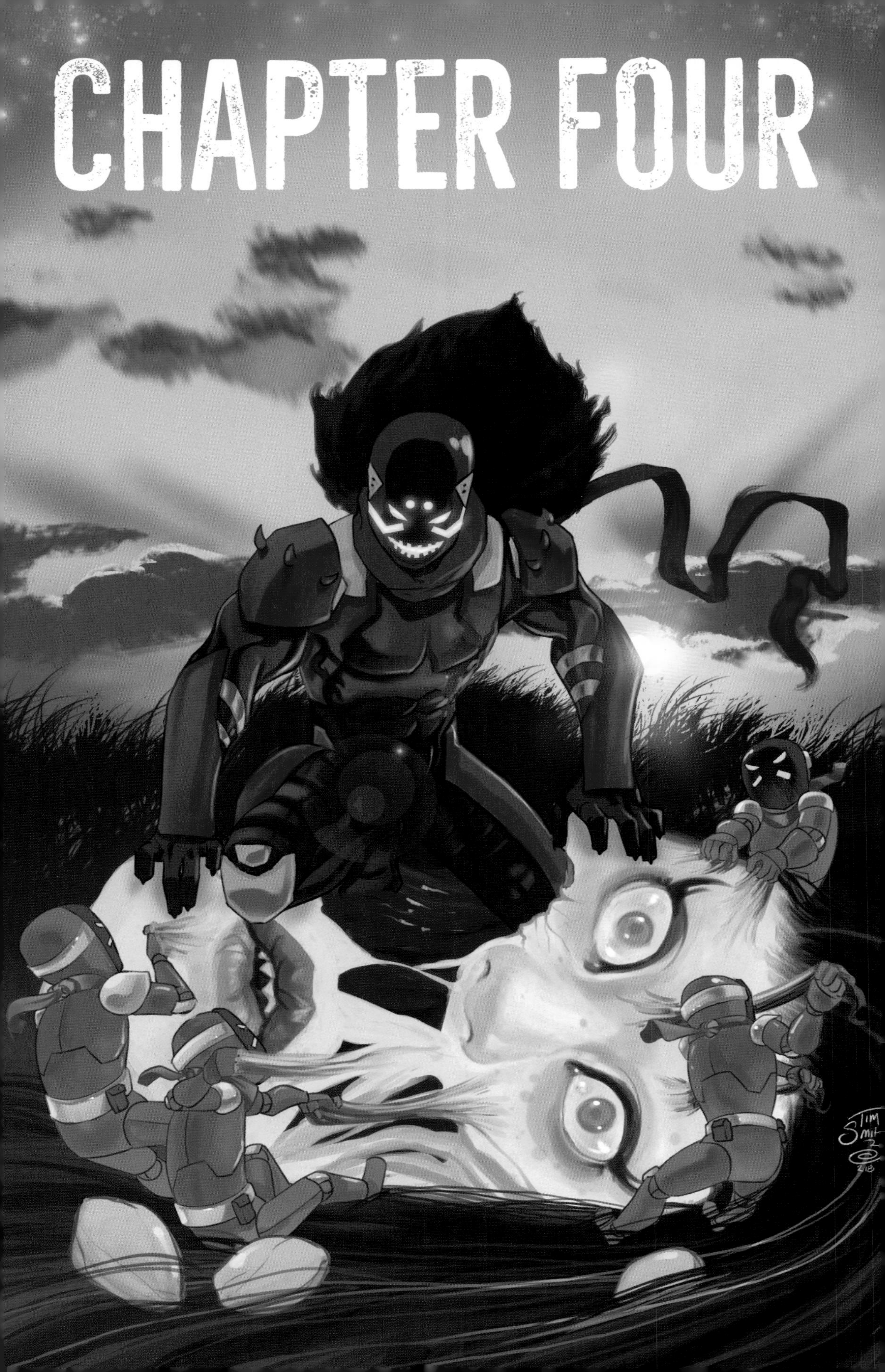

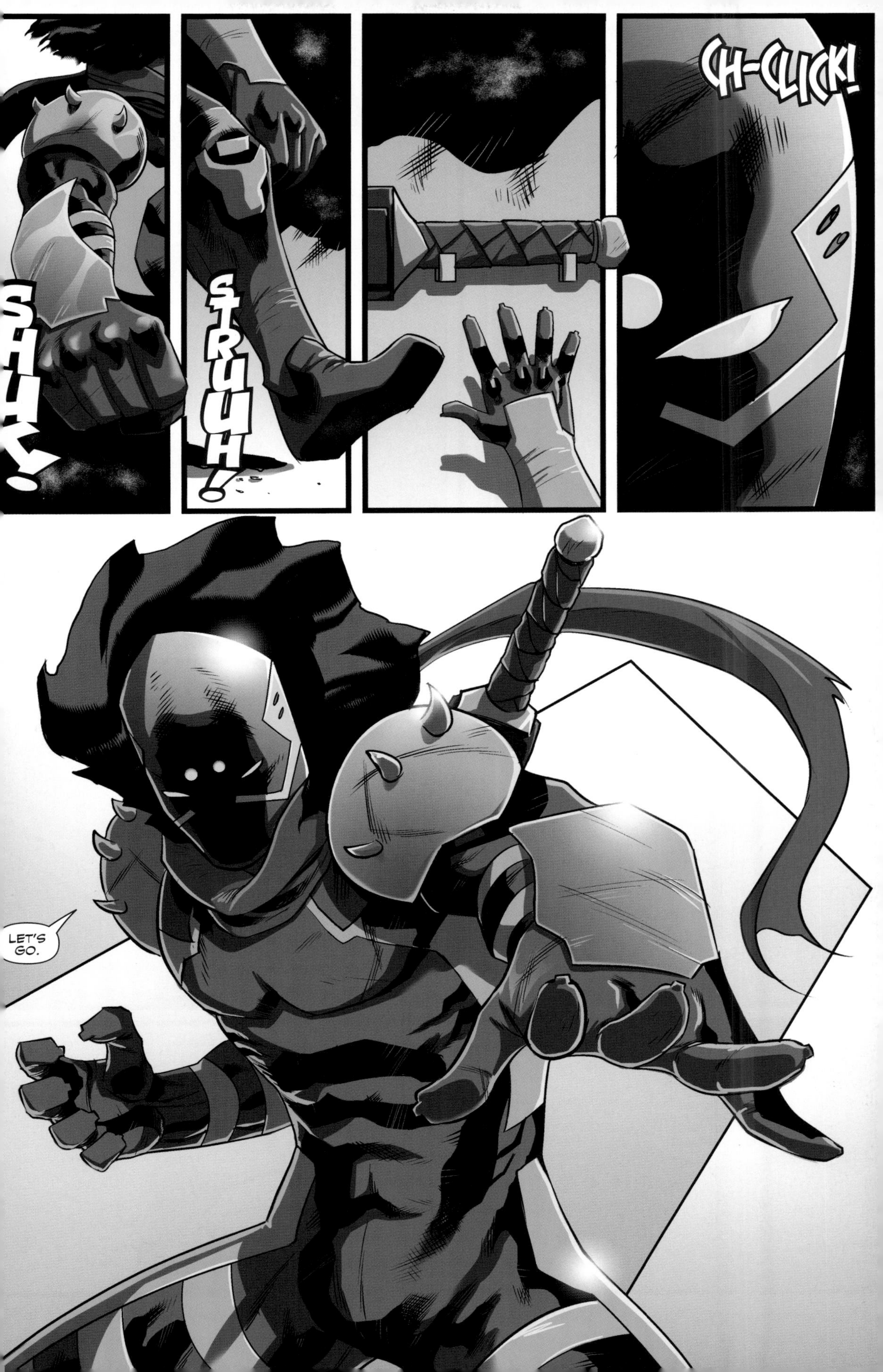
SHUK!
STRUUH!
CH-CLICK!
LET'S GO.

DAMN! YOU TOOK LONG ENOUGH, BRUH! NEW SUIT IS DOPE.

SO WE GOING TO AFRICA, HUH? THE MOTHERLAND! HOW'D YOU KNOW WHERE WE GOTTA GO?

A FEELING...

WHOEVER'S BEEN DIGGING IN MY MIND...I SOMEHOW FELT WHERE THEY ARE BROADCASTING FROM.

HOW DO YOU PLAN ON GETTING US THERE?

OH, I GOT'CHOO! DON'T WORRY.

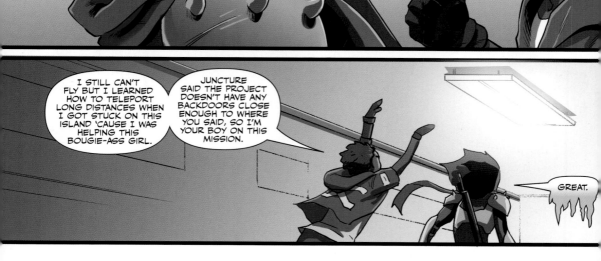

I STILL CAN'T FLY BUT I LEARNED HOW TO TELEPORT LONG DISTANCES WHEN I GOT STUCK ON THIS ISLAND 'CAUSE I WAS HELPING THIS BOUGIE-ASS GIRL.

JUNCTURE SAID THE PROJECT DOESN'T HAVE ANY BACKDOORS CLOSE ENOUGH TO WHERE YOU SAID, SO I'M YOUR BOY ON THIS MISSION.

GREAT.

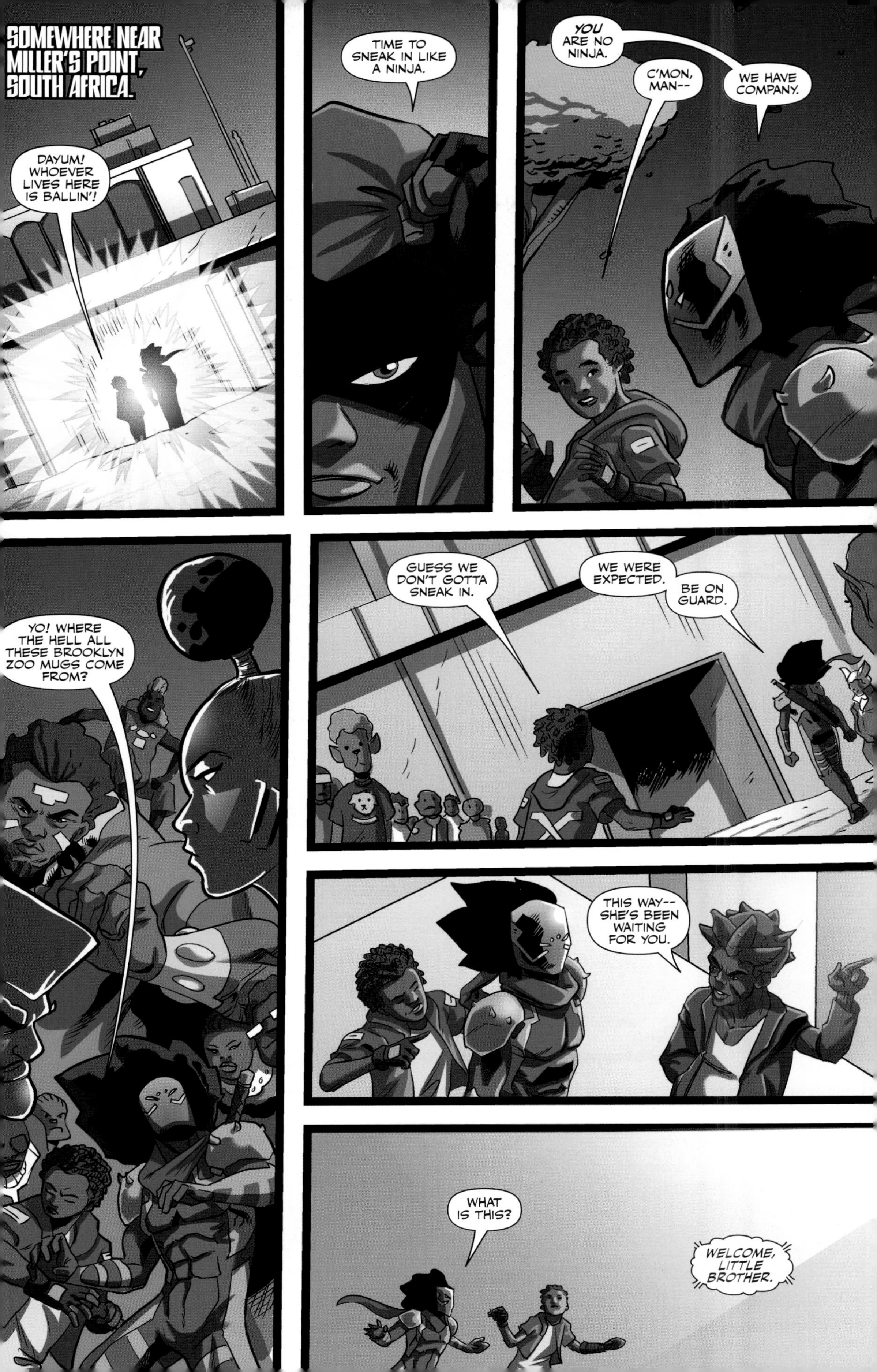
SOMEWHERE NEAR MILLER'S POINT, SOUTH AFRICA.
DAYUM! WHOEVER LIVES HERE IS BALLIN'!
TIME TO SNEAK IN LIKE A NINJA.
YOU ARE NO NINJA.
C'MON, MAN--
WE HAVE COMPANY.
YO! WHERE THE HELL ALL THESE BROOKLYN ZOO MUGS COME FROM?
GUESS WE DON'T GOTTA SNEAK IN.
WE WERE EXPECTED.
BE ON GUARD.
THIS WAY-- SHE'S BEEN WAITING FOR YOU.
WHAT IS THIS?
WELCOME, LITTLE BROTHER.

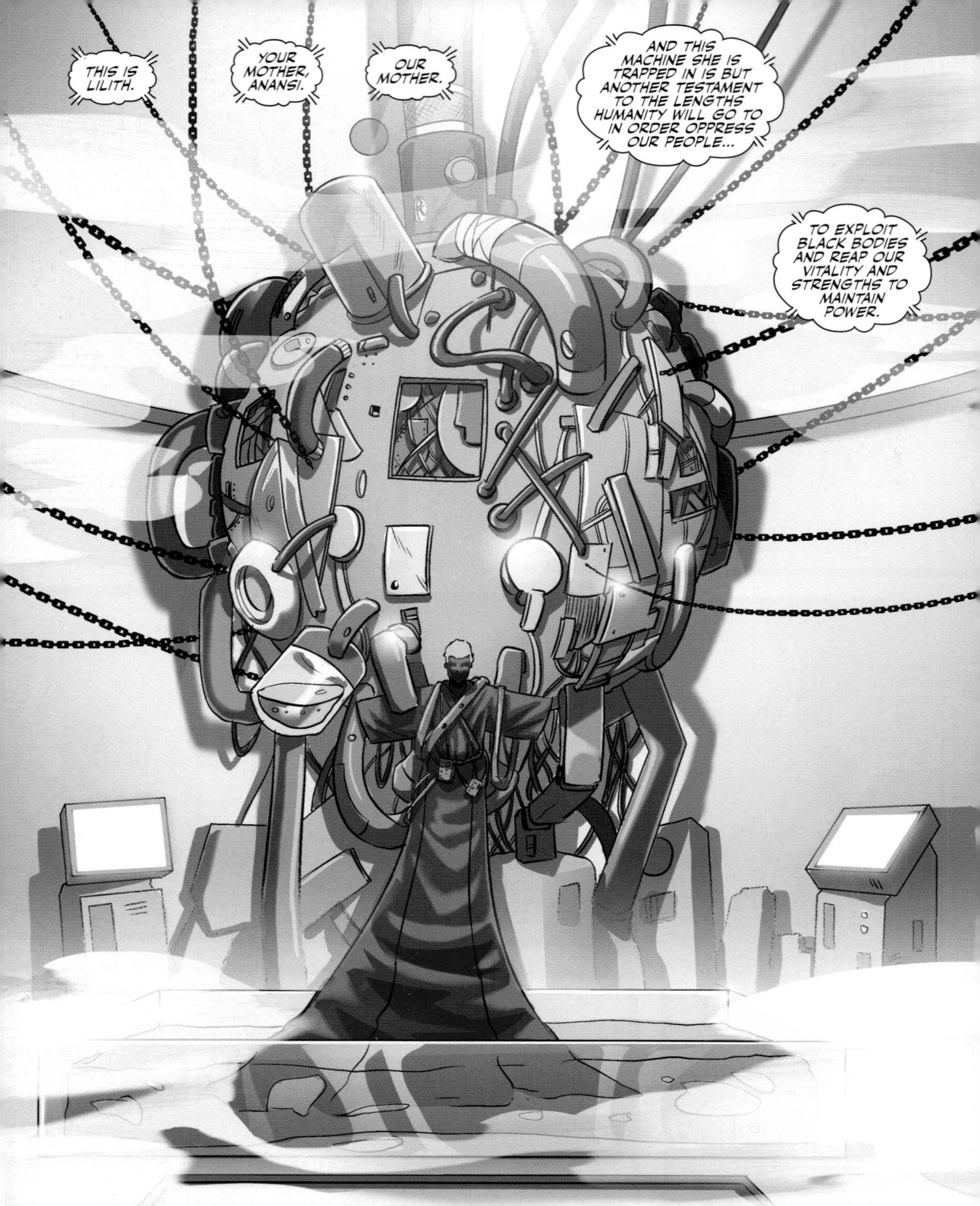
THIS IS LILITH.
YOUR MOTHER, ANANSI.
OUR MOTHER.
AND THIS MACHINE SHE IS TRAPPED IN IS BUT ANOTHER TESTAMENT TO THE LENGTHS HUMANITY WILL GO TO IN ORDER OPPRESS OUR PEOPLE...
TO EXPLOIT BLACK BODIES AND REAP OUR VITALITY AND STRENGTHS TO MAINTAIN POWER.

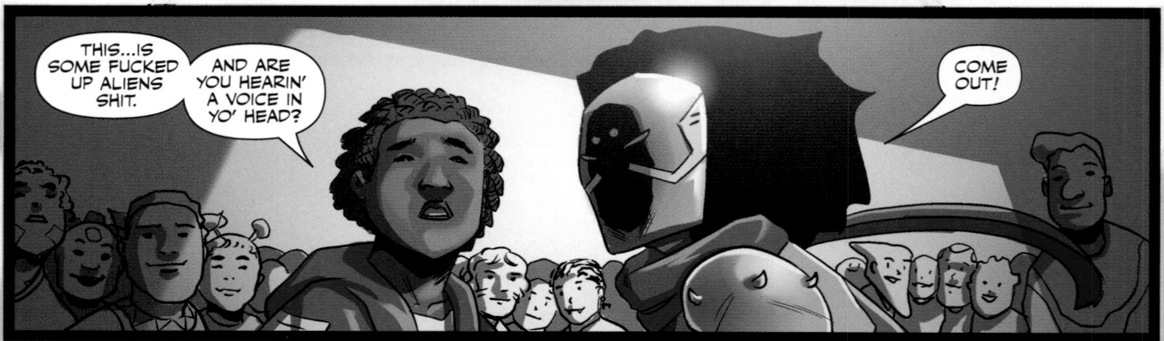
THIS...IS SOME FUCKED UP ALIENS SHIT.
AND ARE YOU HEARIN' A VOICE IN YO' HEAD?
COME OUT!

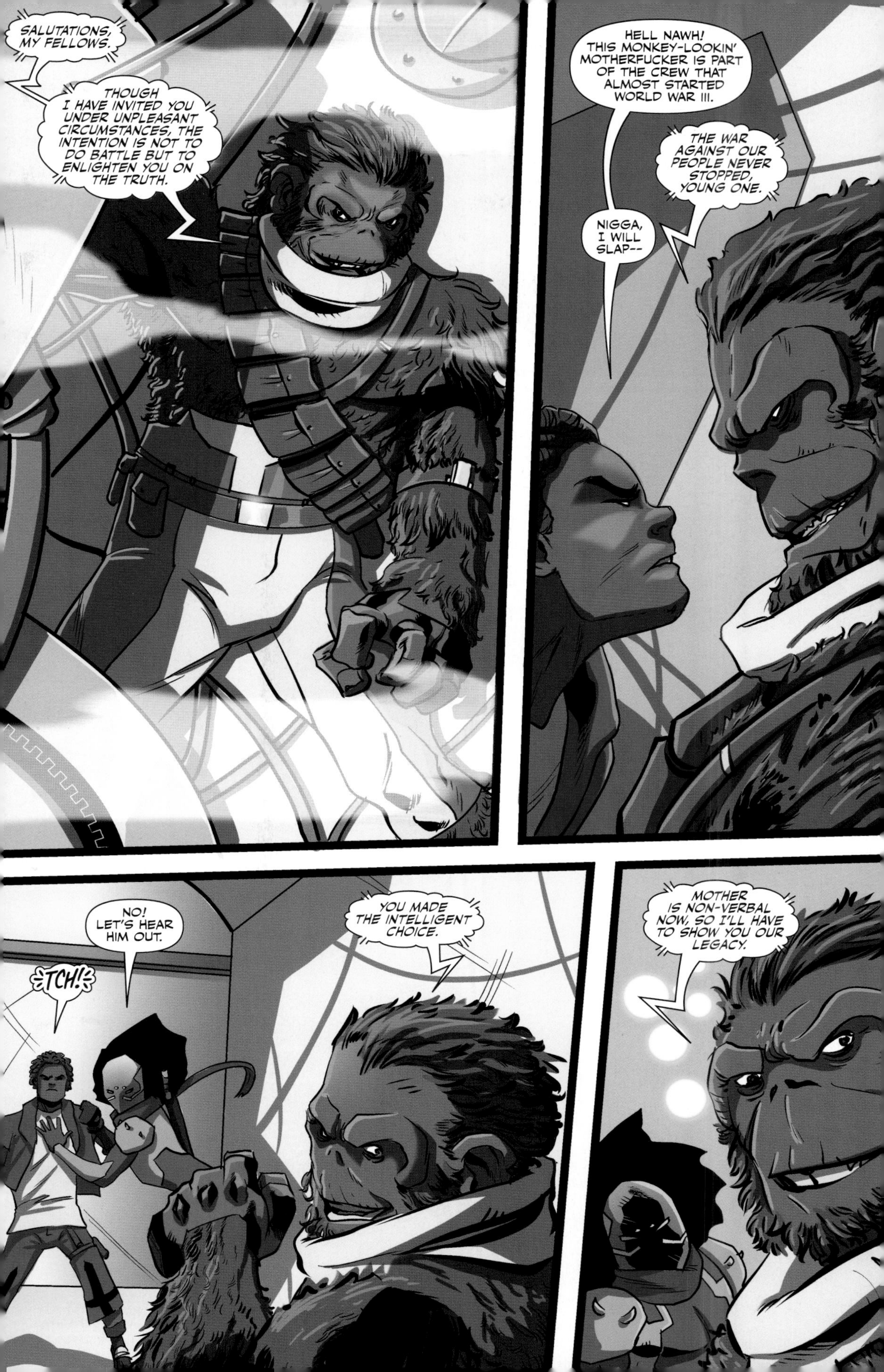

SALUTATIONS, MY FELLOWS.
THOUGH I HAVE INVITED YOU UNDER UNPLEASANT CIRCUMSTANCES, THE INTENTION IS NOT TO DO BATTLE BUT TO ENLIGHTEN YOU ON THE TRUTH.
HELL NAWH! THIS MONKEY-LOOKIN' MOTHERFUCKER IS PART OF THE CREW THAT ALMOST STARTED WORLD WAR III.
THE WAR AGAINST OUR PEOPLE NEVER STOPPED, YOUNG ONE.
NIGGA, I WILL SLAP--
NO! LET'S HEAR HIM OUT.
TCH!
YOU MADE THE INTELLIGENT CHOICE.
MOTHER IS NON-VERBAL NOW, SO I'LL HAVE TO SHOW YOU OUR LEGACY.

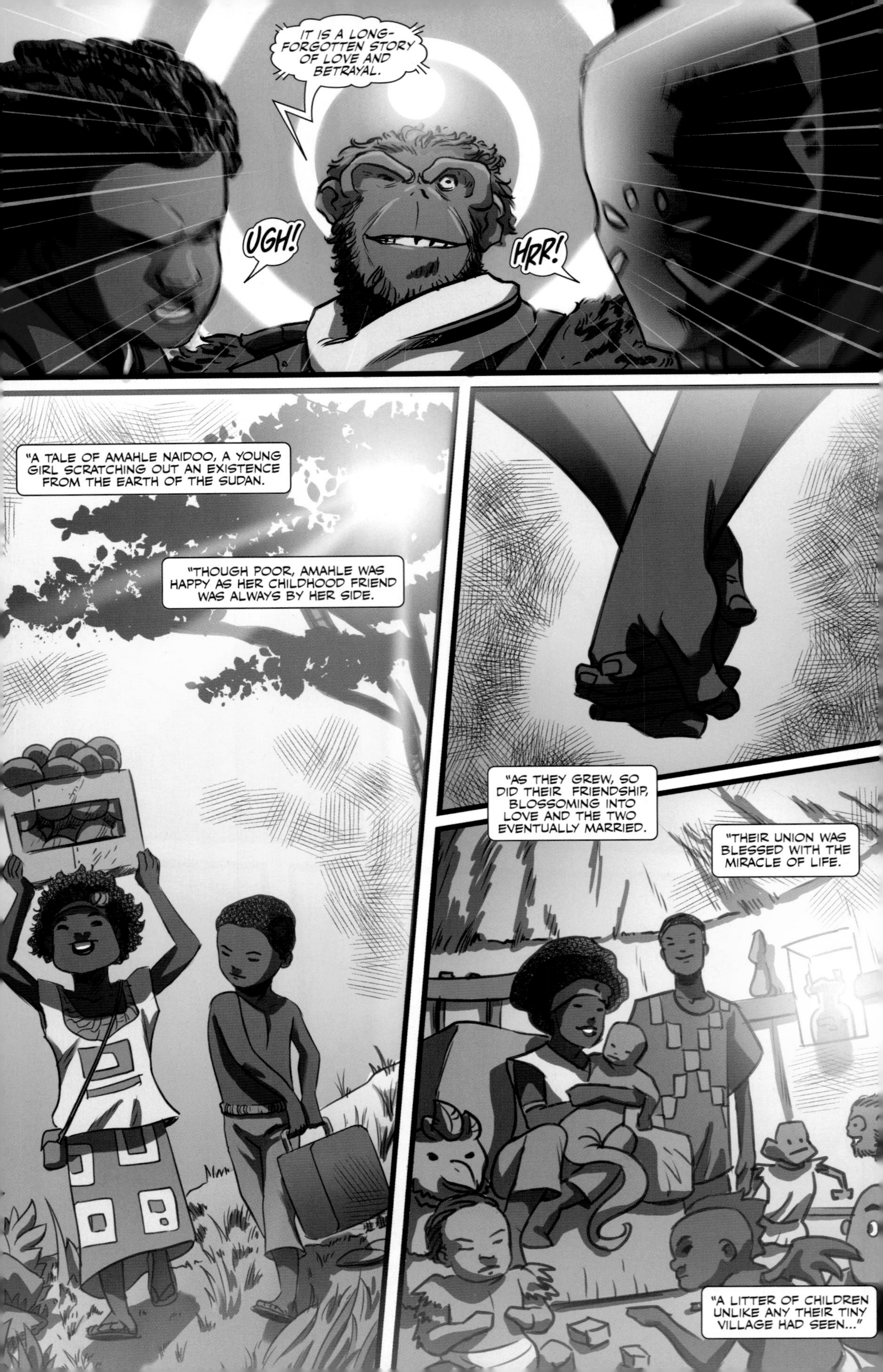
IT IS A LONG-FORGOTTEN STORY OF LOVE AND BETRAYAL.
UGH!
HRR!
"A TALE OF AMAHLE NAIDOO, A YOUNG GIRL SCRATCHING OUT AN EXISTENCE FROM THE EARTH OF THE SUDAN.
"THOUGH POOR, AMAHLE WAS HAPPY AS HER CHILDHOOD FRIEND WAS ALWAYS BY HER SIDE.
"AS THEY GREW, SO DID THEIR FRIENDSHIP, BLOSSOMING INTO LOVE AND THE TWO EVENTUALLY MARRIED.
"THEIR UNION WAS BLESSED WITH THE MIRACLE OF LIFE.
"A LITTER OF CHILDREN UNLIKE ANY THEIR TINY VILLAGE HAD SEEN..."

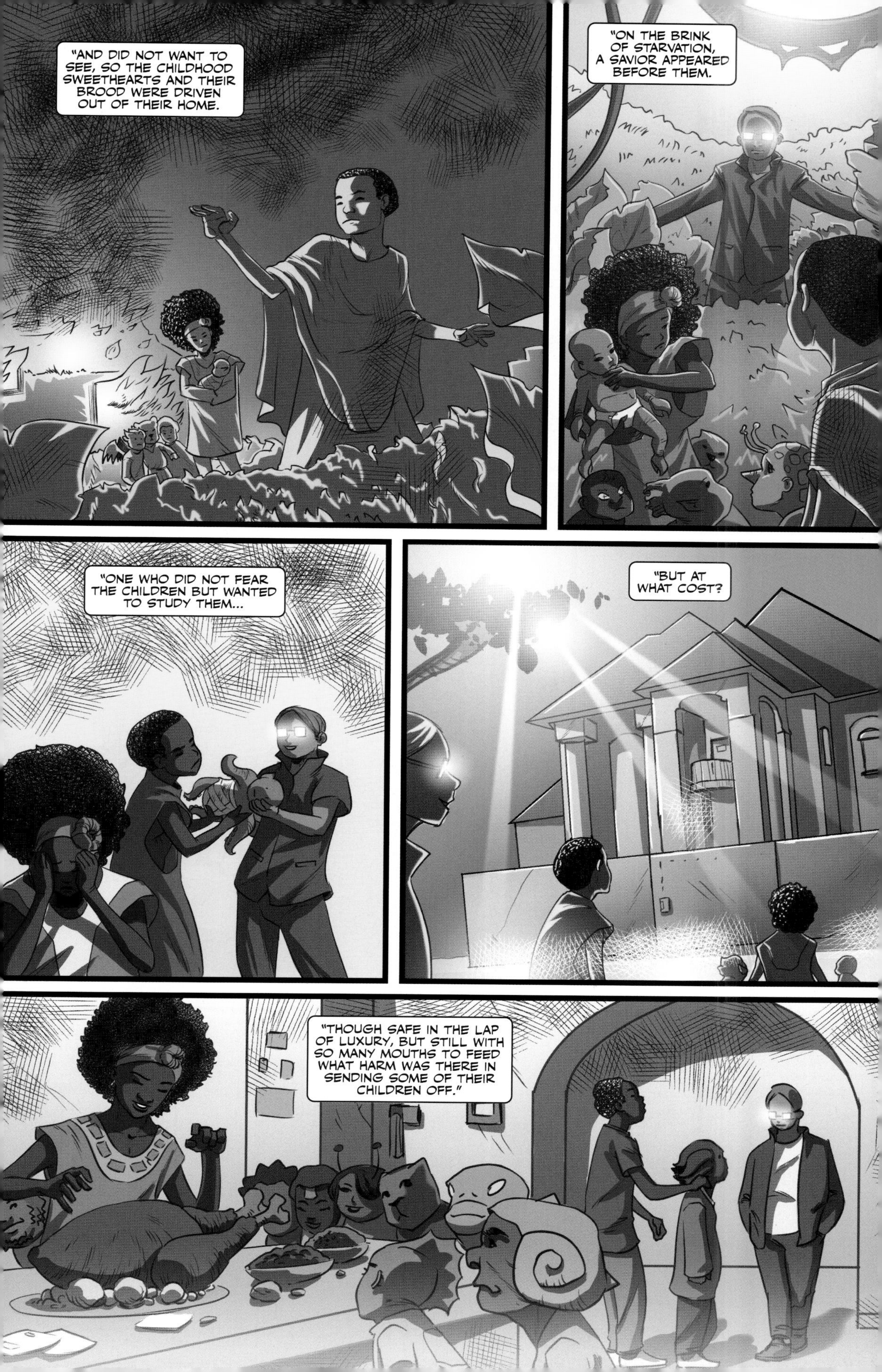
"AND DID NOT WANT TO SEE, SO THE CHILDHOOD SWEETHEARTS AND THEIR BROOD WERE DRIVEN OUT OF THEIR HOME.
"ON THE BRINK OF STARVATION, A SAVIOR APPEARED BEFORE THEM.
"ONE WHO DID NOT FEAR THE CHILDREN BUT WANTED TO STUDY THEM...
"BUT AT WHAT COST?
"THOUGH SAFE IN THE LAP OF LUXURY, BUT STILL WITH SO MANY MOUTHS TO FEED WHAT HARM WAS THERE IN SENDING SOME OF THEIR CHILDREN OFF."

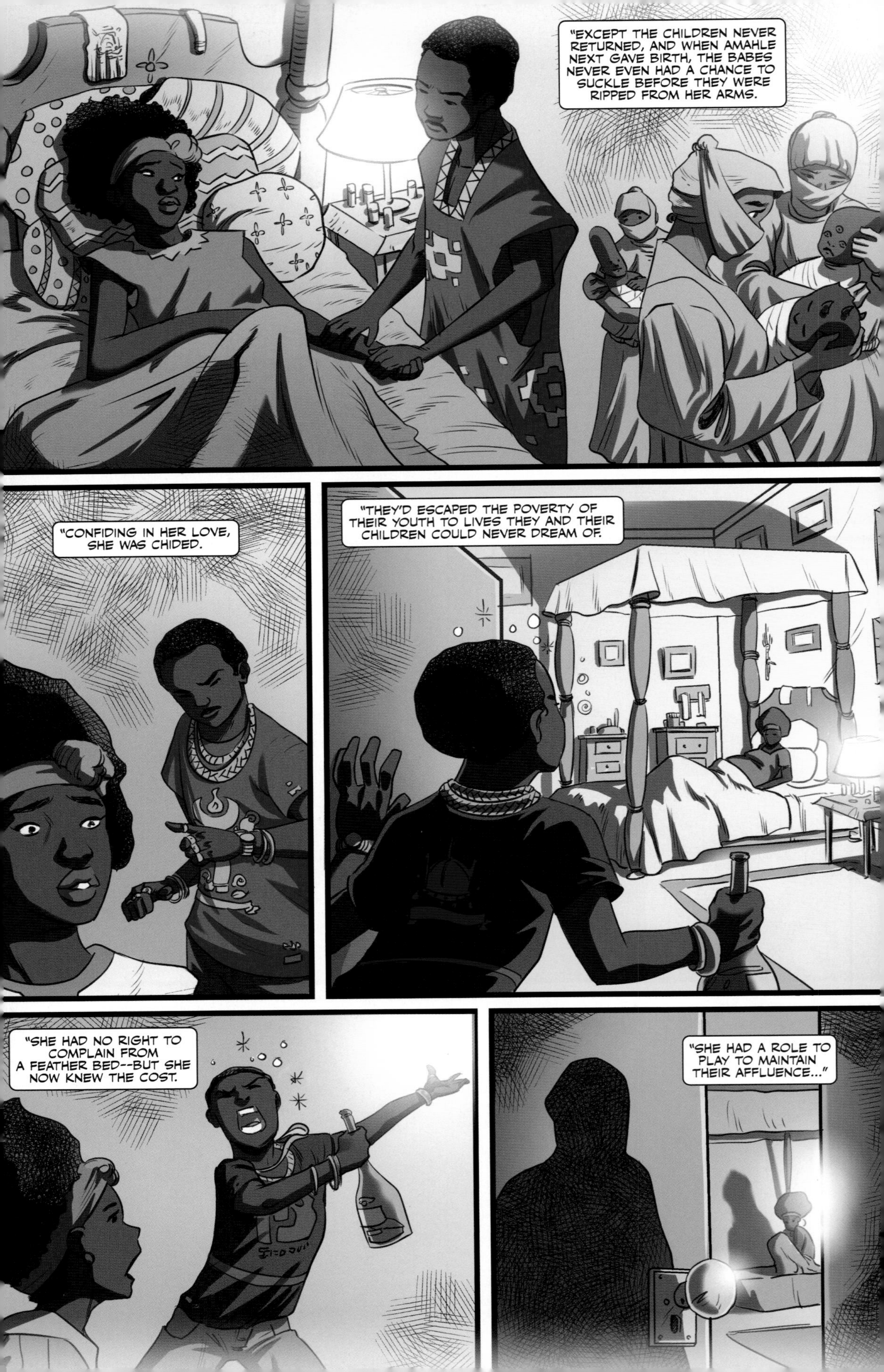
"EXCEPT THE CHILDREN NEVER RETURNED, AND WHEN AMAHLE NEXT GAVE BIRTH, THE BABES NEVER EVEN HAD A CHANCE TO SUCKLE BEFORE THEY WERE RIPPED FROM HER ARMS.
"CONFIDING IN HER LOVE, SHE WAS CHIDED.
"THEY'D ESCAPED THE POVERTY OF THEIR YOUTH TO LIVES THEY AND THEIR CHILDREN COULD NEVER DREAM OF.
"SHE HAD NO RIGHT TO COMPLAIN FROM A FEATHER BED--BUT SHE NOW KNEW THE COST.
"SHE HAD A ROLE TO PLAY TO MAINTAIN THEIR AFFLUENCE..."

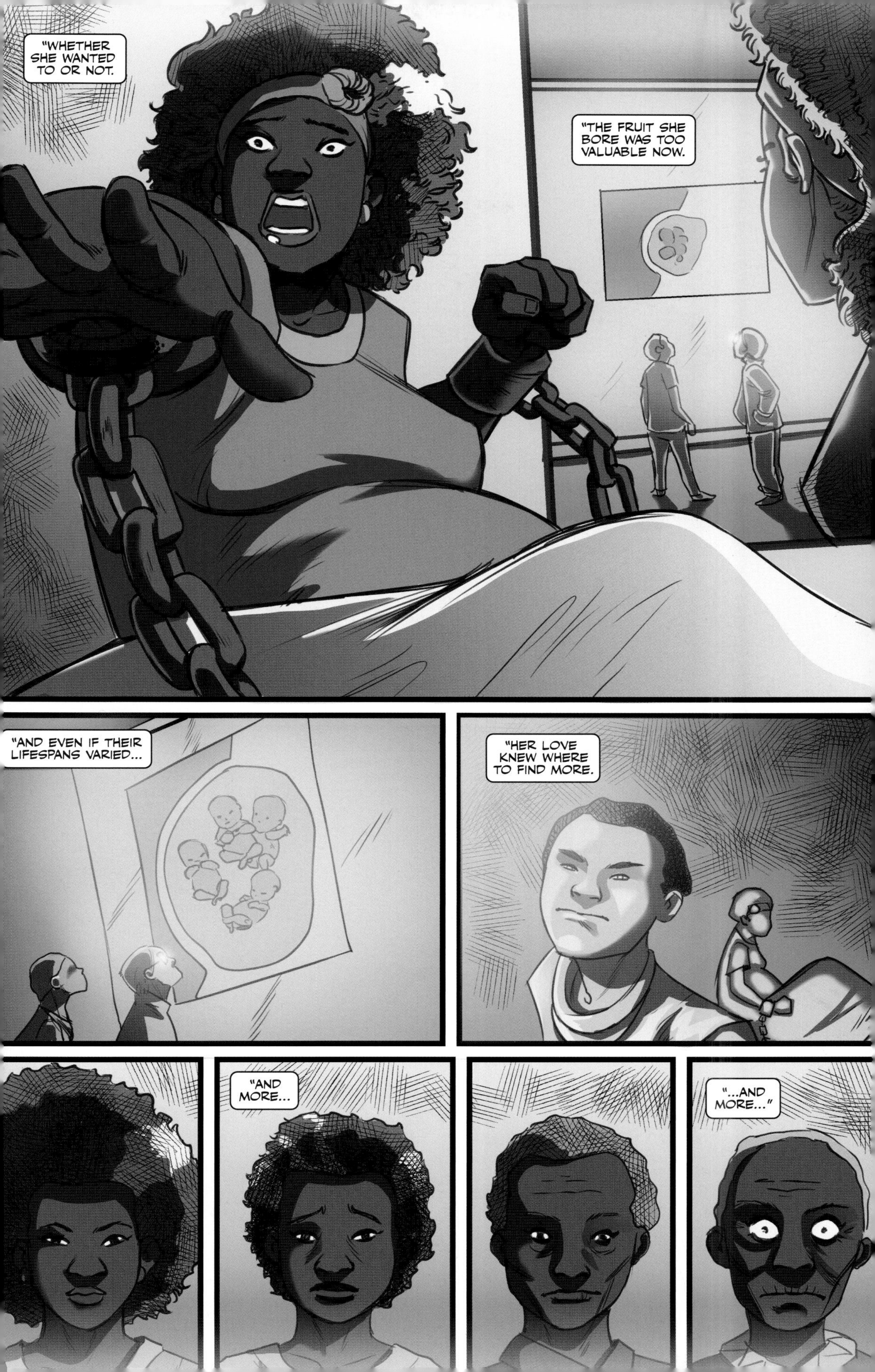
"WHETHER SHE WANTED TO OR NOT.
"THE FRUIT SHE BORE WAS TOO VALUABLE NOW.
"AND EVEN IF THEIR LIFESPANS VARIED...
"HER LOVE KNEW WHERE TO FIND MORE.
"AND MORE...
"...AND MORE..."

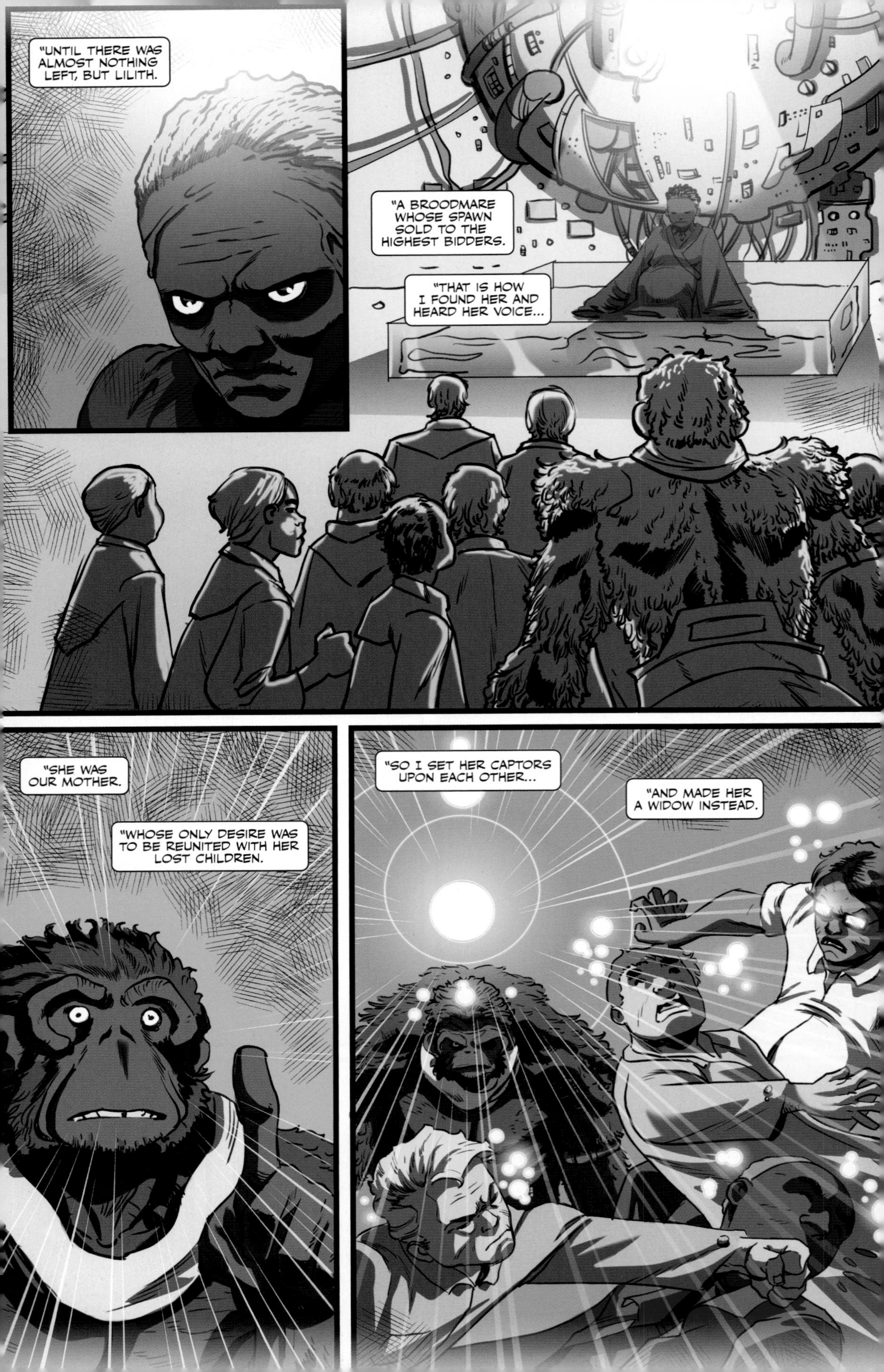
"UNTIL THERE WAS ALMOST NOTHING LEFT, BUT LILITH.
"A BROODMARE WHOSE SPAWN SOLD TO THE HIGHEST BIDDERS.
"THAT IS HOW I FOUND HER AND HEARD HER VOICE...
"SHE WAS OUR MOTHER.
"WHOSE ONLY DESIRE WAS TO BE REUNITED WITH HER LOST CHILDREN.
"SO I SET HER CAPTORS UPON EACH OTHER...
"AND MADE HER A WIDOW INSTEAD.

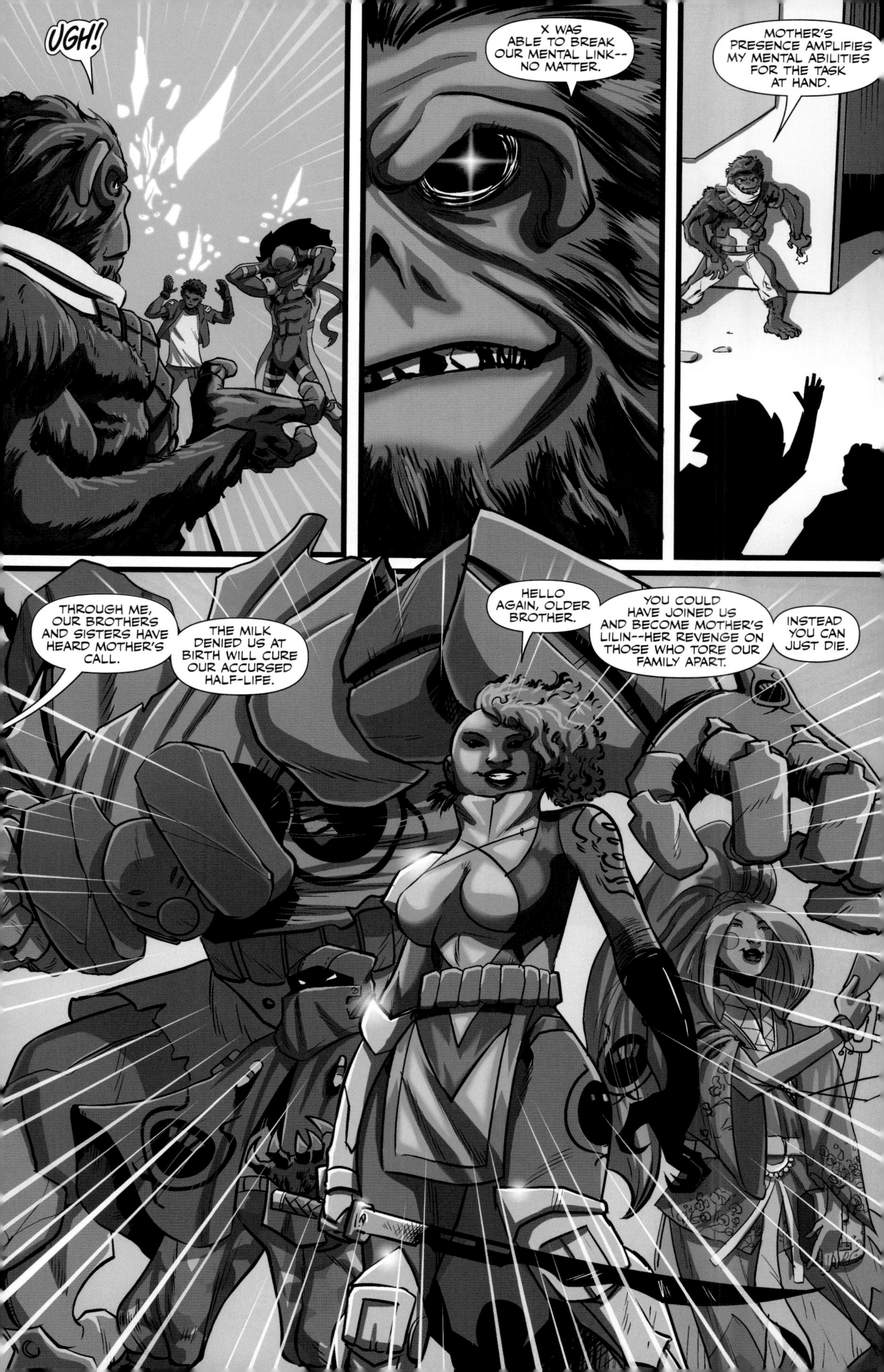
UGH!
X WAS ABLE TO BREAK OUR MENTAL LINK-- NO MATTER.
MOTHER'S PRESENCE AMPLIFIES MY MENTAL ABILITIES FOR THE TASK AT HAND.
THROUGH ME, OUR BROTHERS AND SISTERS HAVE HEARD MOTHER'S CALL.
THE MILK DENIED US AT BIRTH WILL CURE OUR ACCURSED HALF-LIFE.
HELLO AGAIN, OLDER BROTHER.
YOU COULD HAVE JOINED US AND BECOME MOTHER'S LILIN--HER REVENGE ON THOSE WHO TORE OUR FAMILY APART.
INSTEAD YOU CAN JUST DIE.

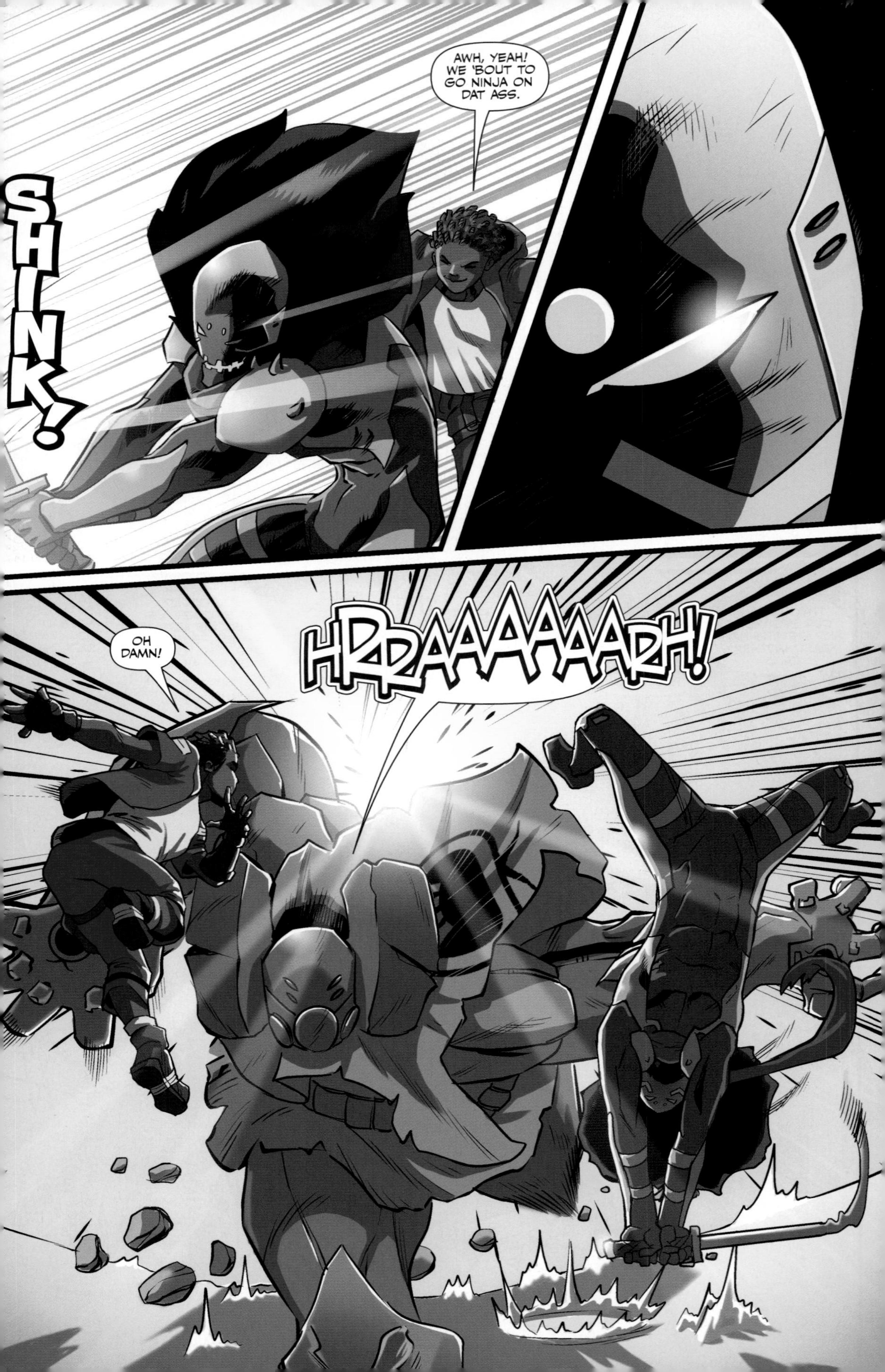
AWH, YEAH! WE 'BOUT TO GO NINJA ON DAT ASS.
SHINK!
OH DAMN!
HRRAAAAAAARH!

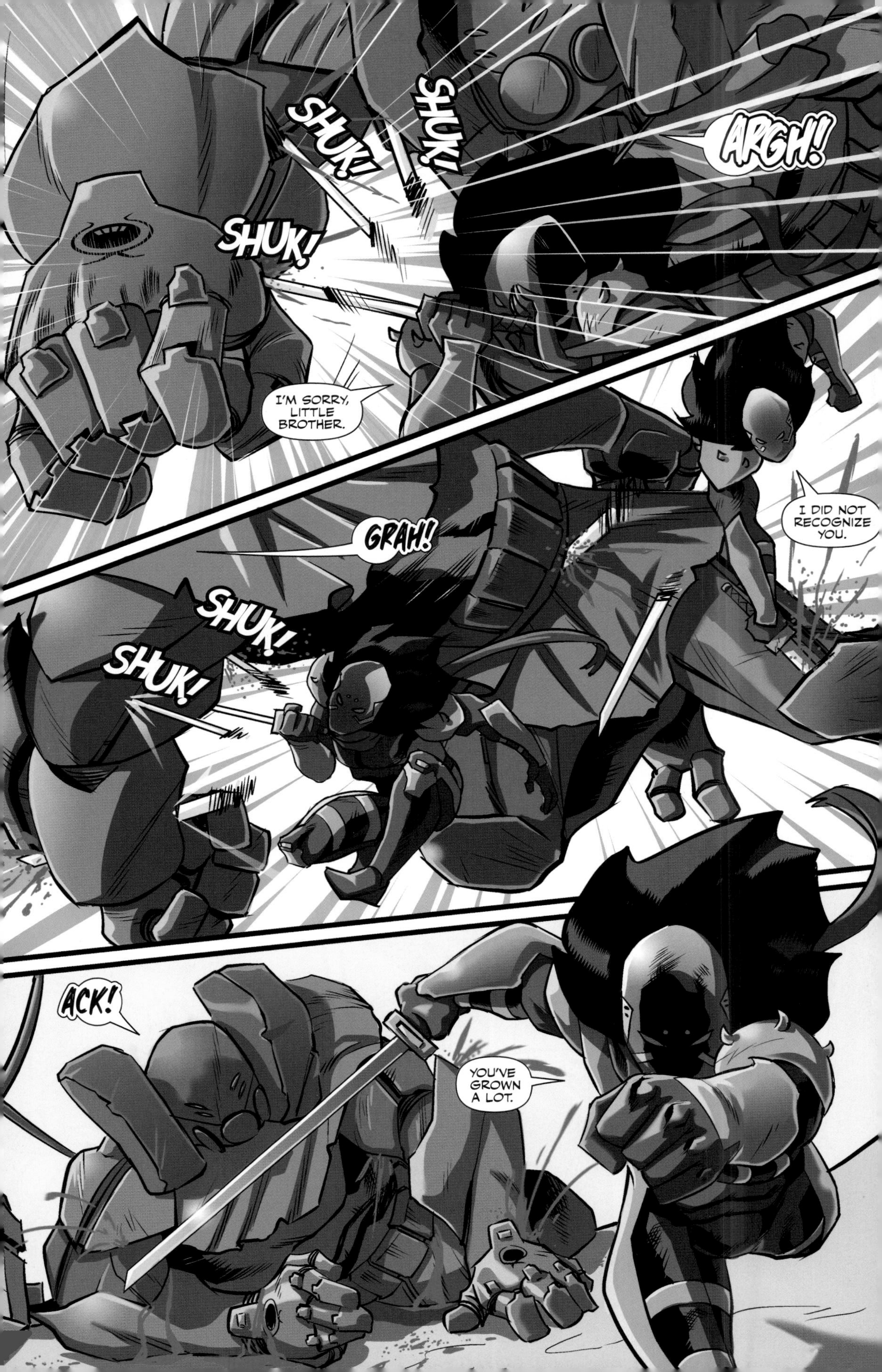
SHUK!
SHUK!
ARGH!
SHUK!
I'M SORRY, LITTLE BROTHER.
I DID NOT RECOGNIZE YOU.
GRAH!
SHUK!
SHUK!
ACK!
YOU'VE GROWN A LOT.

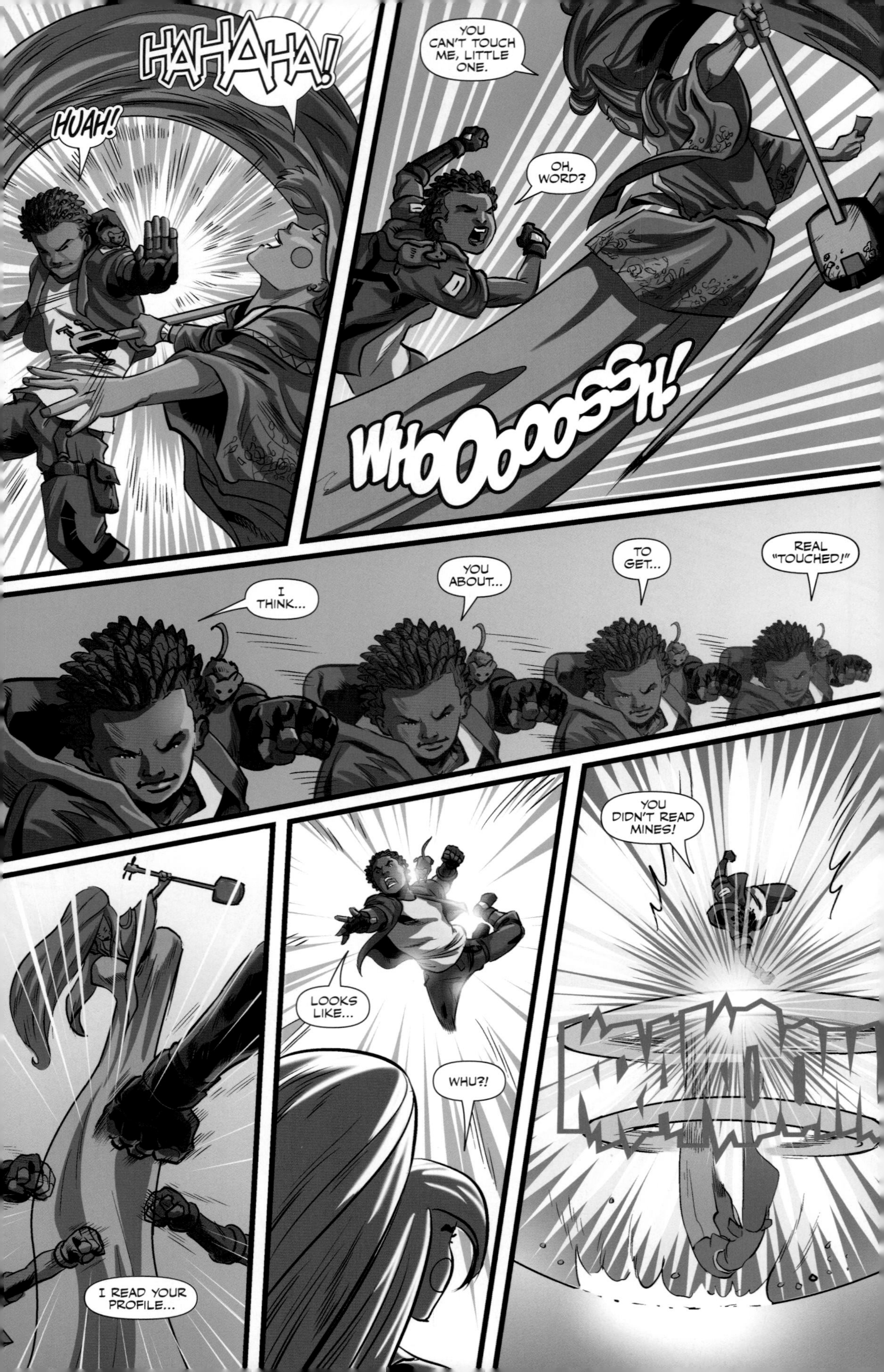
HUAH!
HAHAHA!
YOU CAN'T TOUCH ME, LITTLE ONE.
OH, WORD?
WHOOOOOOSSH!
I THINK...
YOU ABOUT...
TO GET...
REAL "TOUCHED!"
I READ YOUR PROFILE...
LOOKS LIKE...
WHU?!
YOU DIDN'T READ MINES!

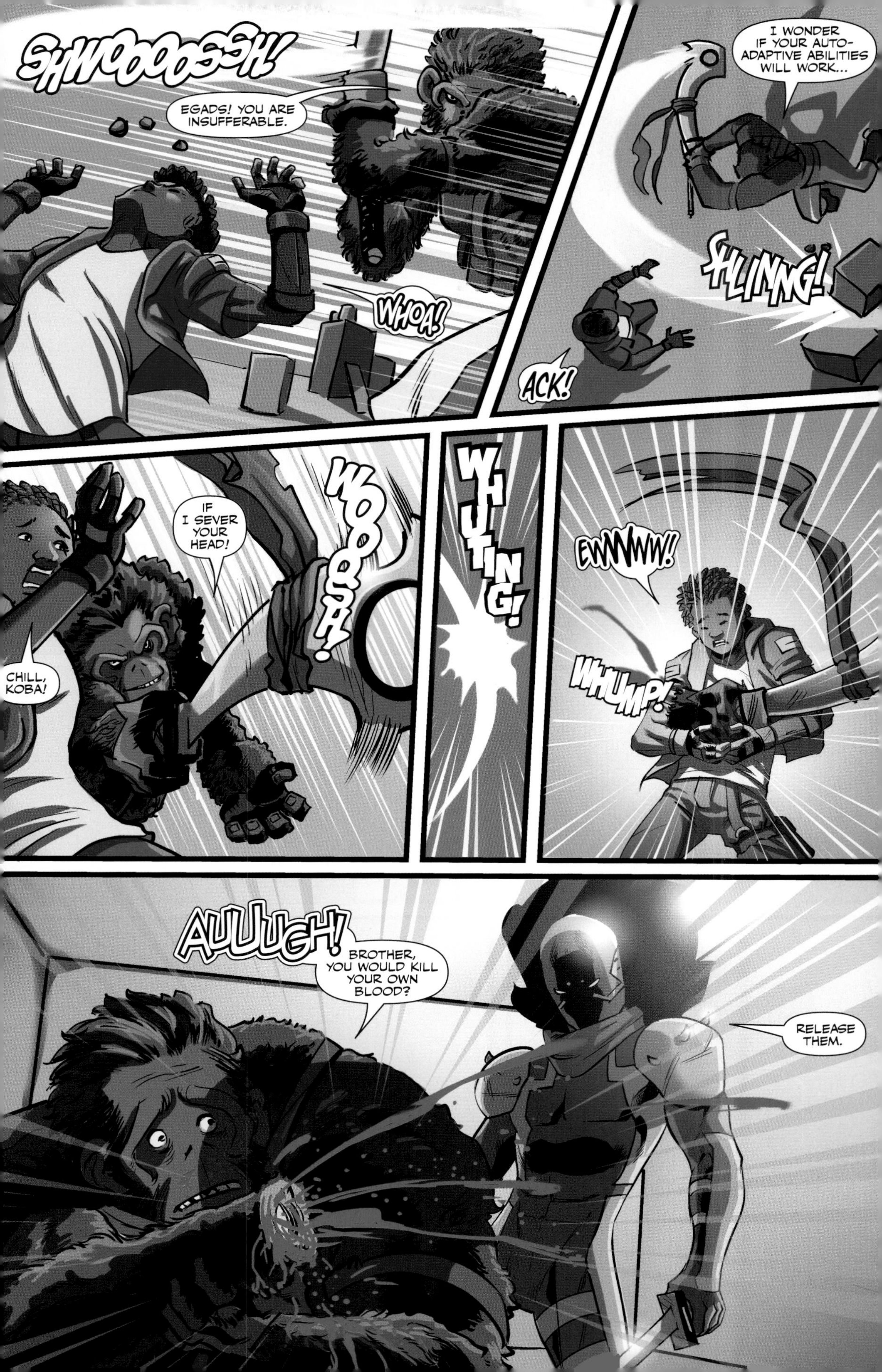
SHWOOOOSSH!
EGADS! YOU ARE INSUFFERABLE.
WHOA!
I WONDER IF YOUR AUTO-ADAPTIVE ABILITIES WILL WORK...
SHLINNG!
ACK!
IF I SEVER YOUR HEAD!
WOOOSH!
CHILL, KOBA!
WHUTING!
EWWWW!
WHUMP!
AUUUGH!
BROTHER, YOU WOULD KILL YOUR OWN BLOOD?
RELEASE THEM.

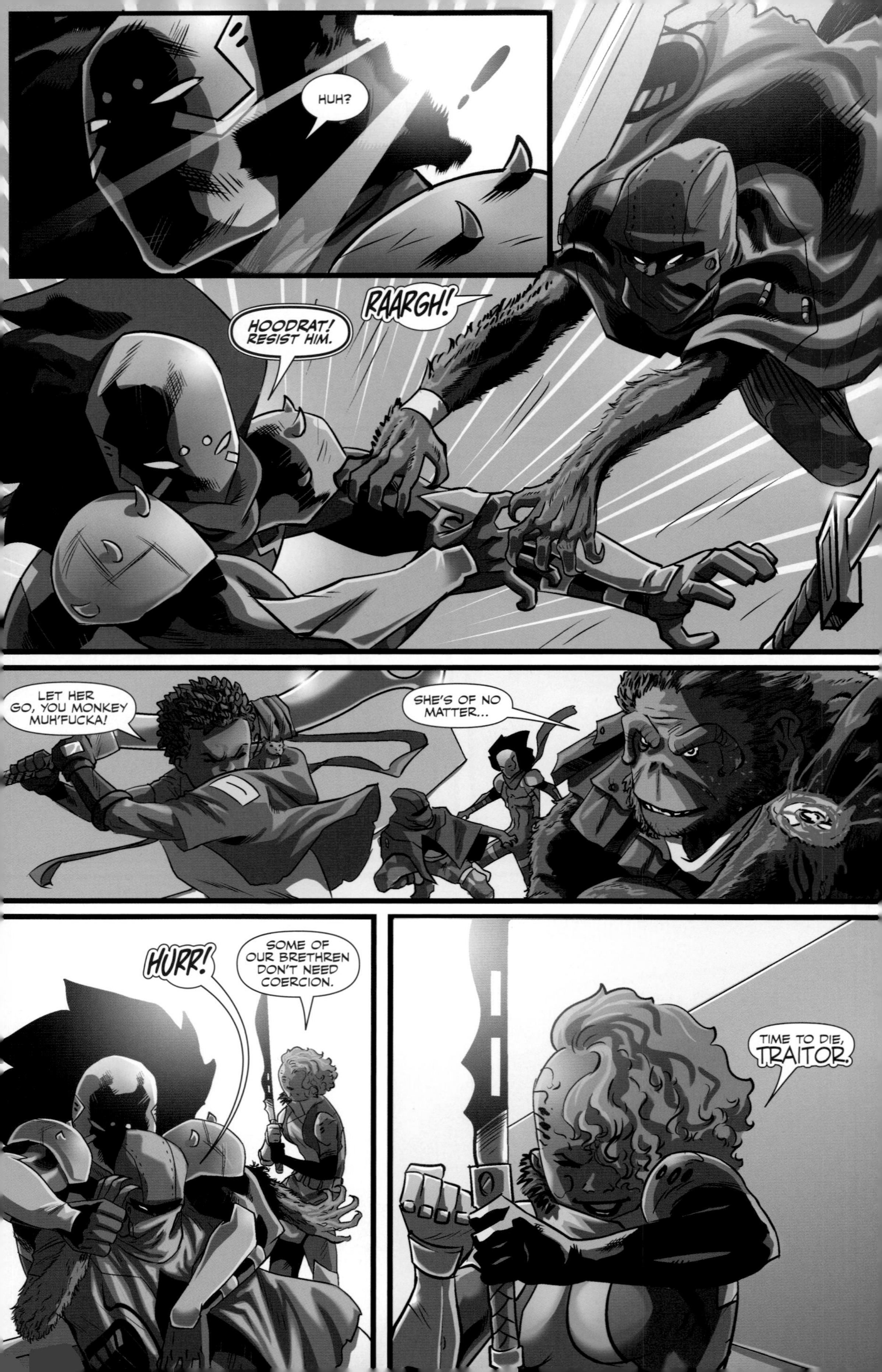

HUH?
RAARGH!
HOODRAT! RESIST HIM.
LET HER GO, YOU MONKEY MUH'FUCKA!
SHE'S OF NO MATTER...
HURR!
SOME OF OUR BRETHREN DON'T NEED COERCION.
TIME TO DIE, TRAITOR.

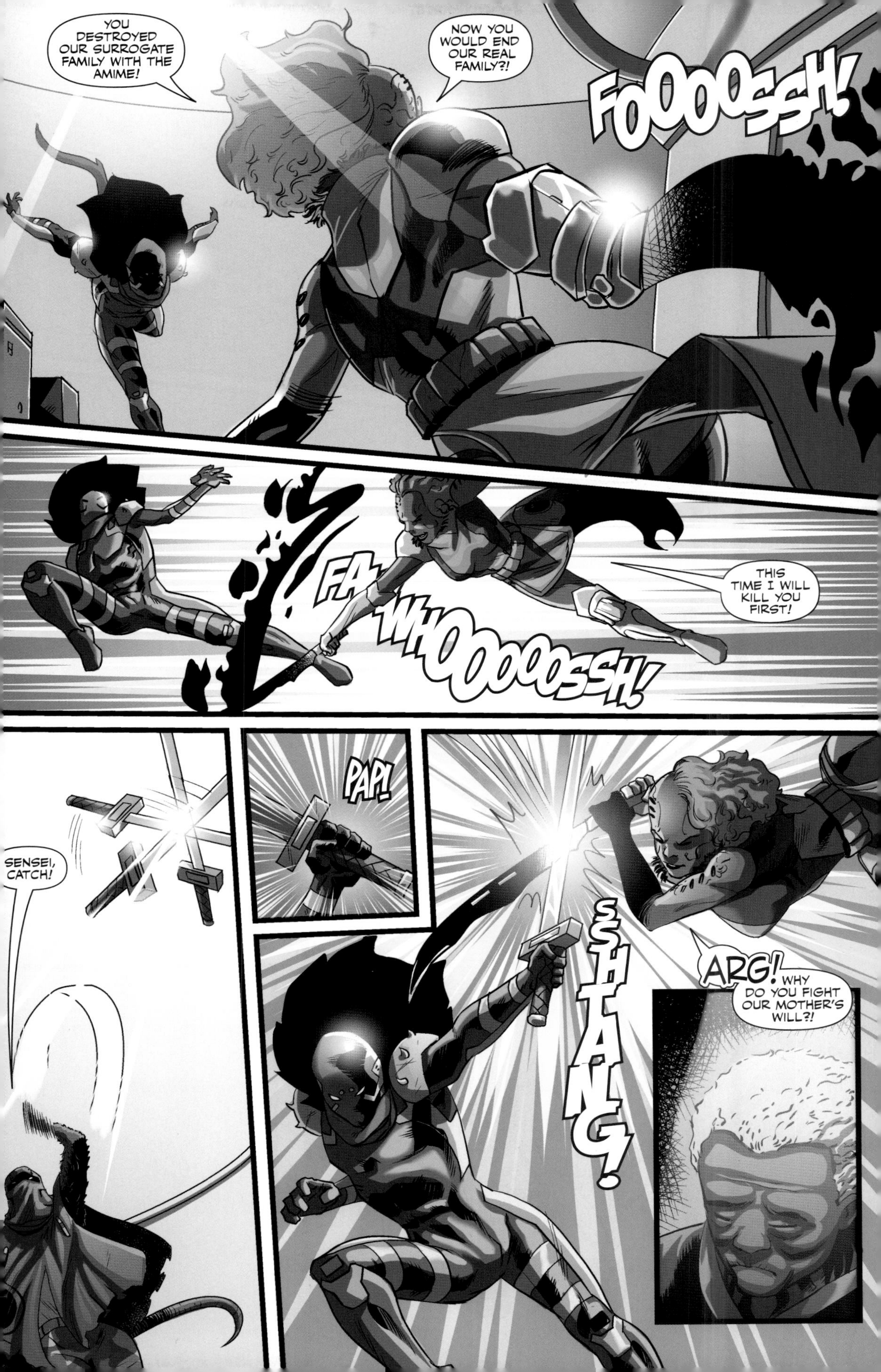
YOU DESTROYED OUR SURROGATE FAMILY WITH THE AMIME!
NOW YOU WOULD END OUR REAL FAMILY?!
FOOOOSSH!
FA-WHOOOOOOSSH!
THIS TIME I WILL KILL YOU FIRST!
SENSEI, CATCH!
PAP!
SSHTANG!
ARG! WHY DO YOU FIGHT OUR MOTHER'S WILL?!

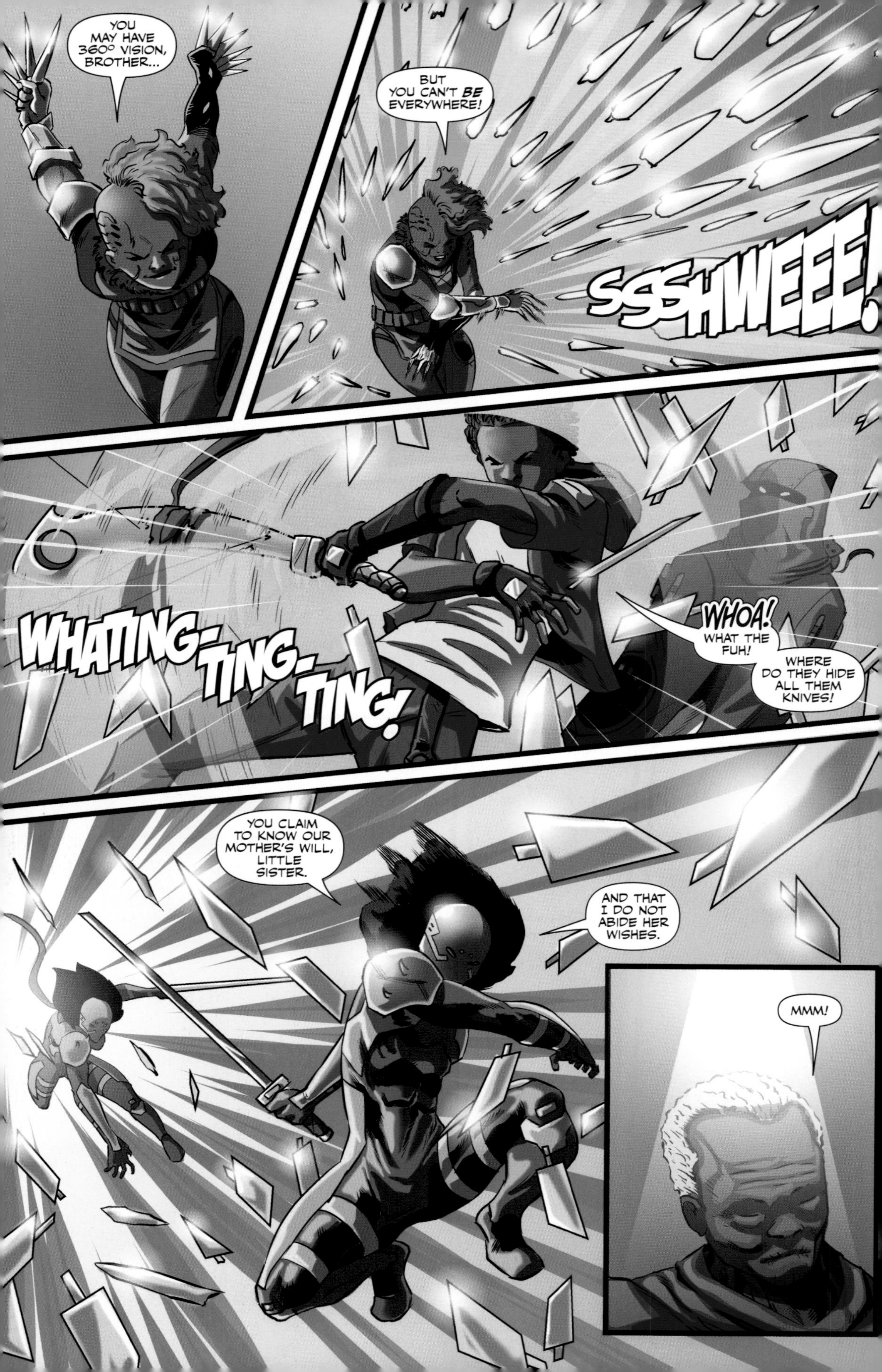

YOU MAY HAVE 360° VISION, BROTHER...
BUT YOU CAN'T *BE* EVERYWHERE!
SSSHWEEE!
WHATING-TING-TING!
WHOA! WHAT THE FUH!
WHERE DO THEY HIDE ALL THEM KNIVES!
YOU CLAIM TO KNOW OUR MOTHER'S WILL, LITTLE SISTER.
AND THAT I DO NOT ABIDE HER WISHES.
MMM!

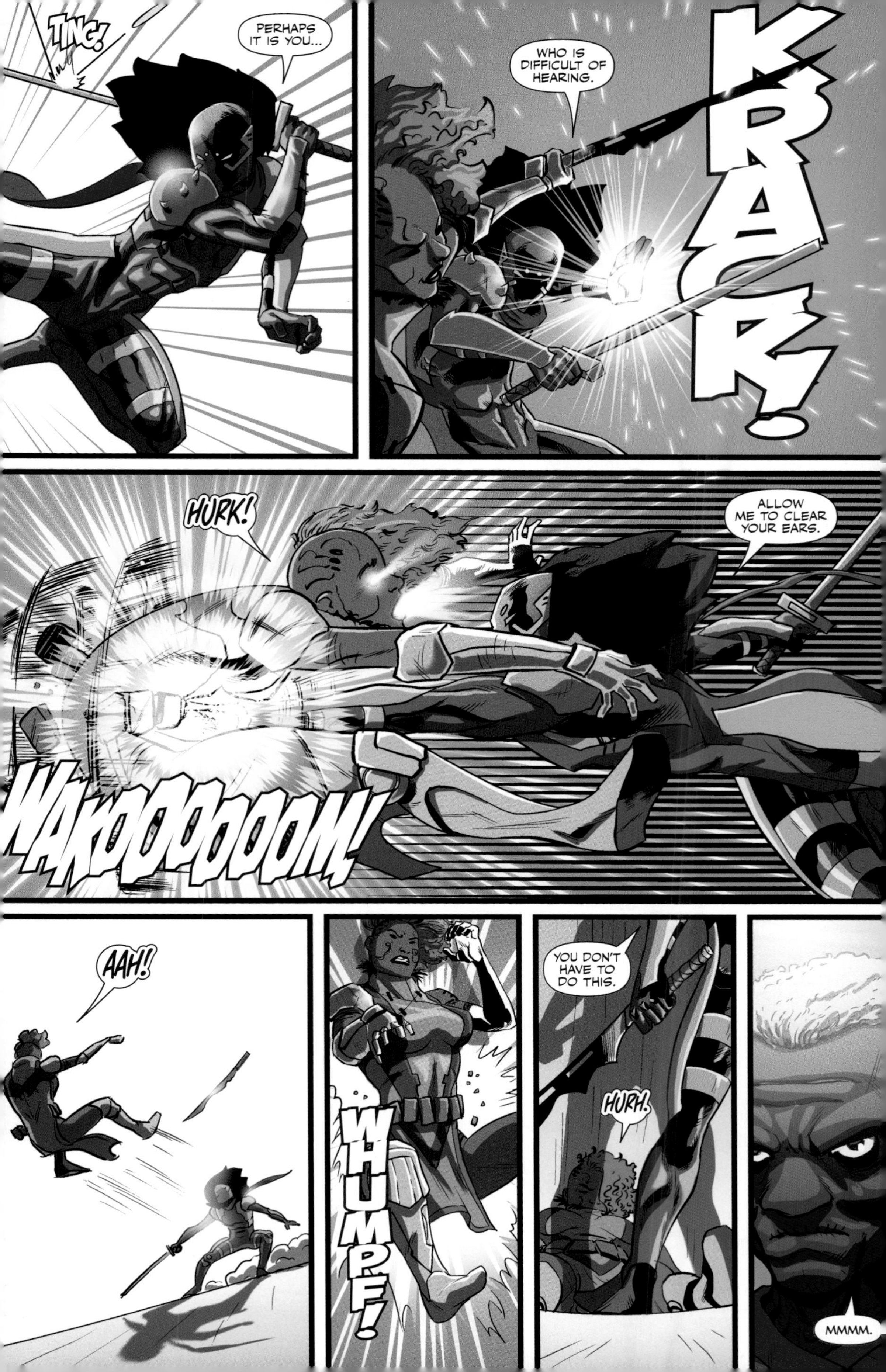
TING!
PERHAPS IT IS YOU...
WHO IS DIFFICULT OF HEARING.
KRAR!
HURK!
ALLOW ME TO CLEAR YOUR EARS.
WAKOOOOOOOM!
AAH!
WHUMPF!
YOU DON'T HAVE TO DO THIS.
HURH.
MMMM.

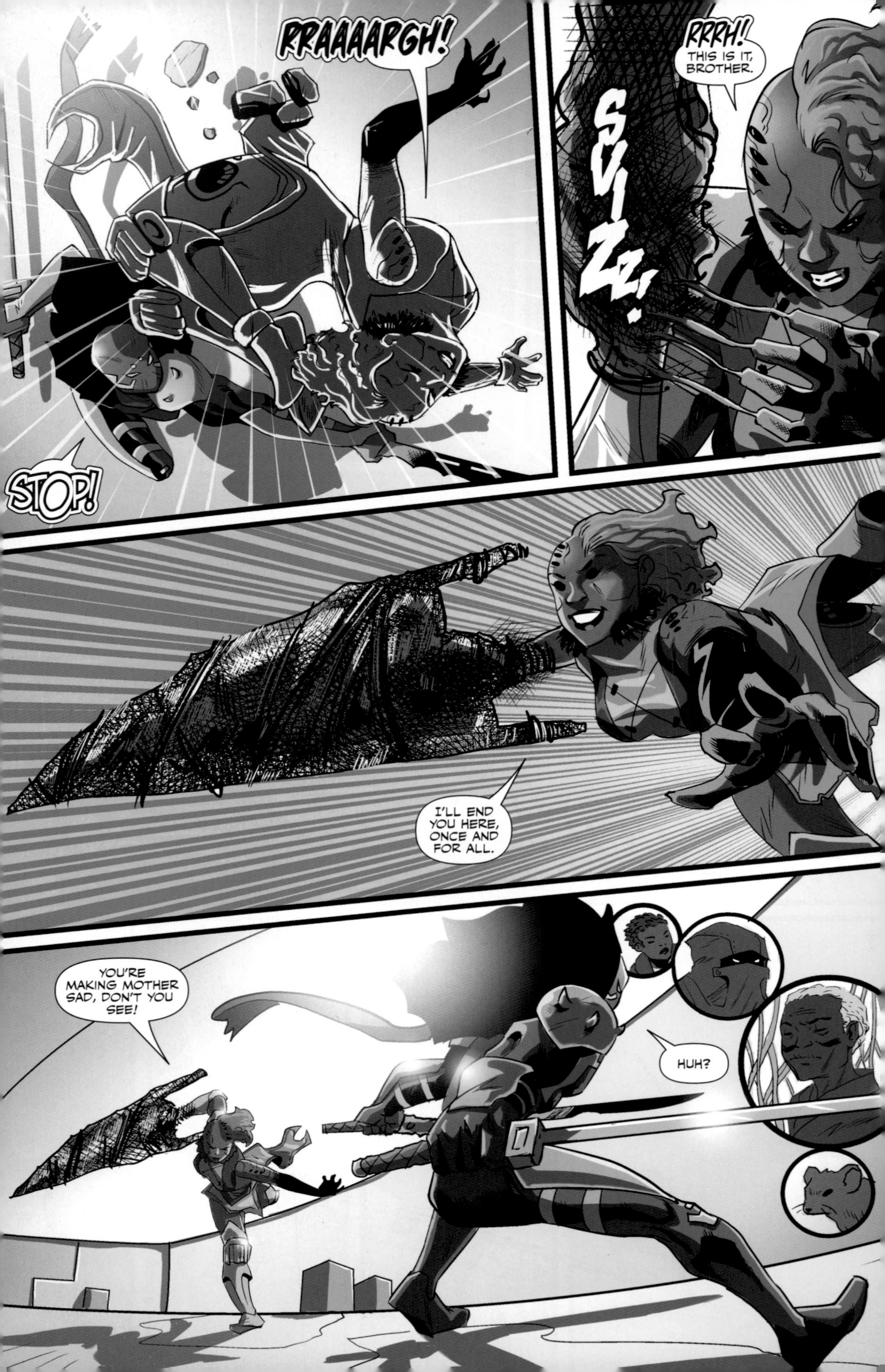
RRAAAARGH!
STOP!
RRRH!
THIS IS IT, BROTHER.
SVIZZ!
I'LL END YOU HERE, ONCE AND FOR ALL.
YOU'RE MAKING MOTHER SAD, DON'T YOU SEE!
HUH?

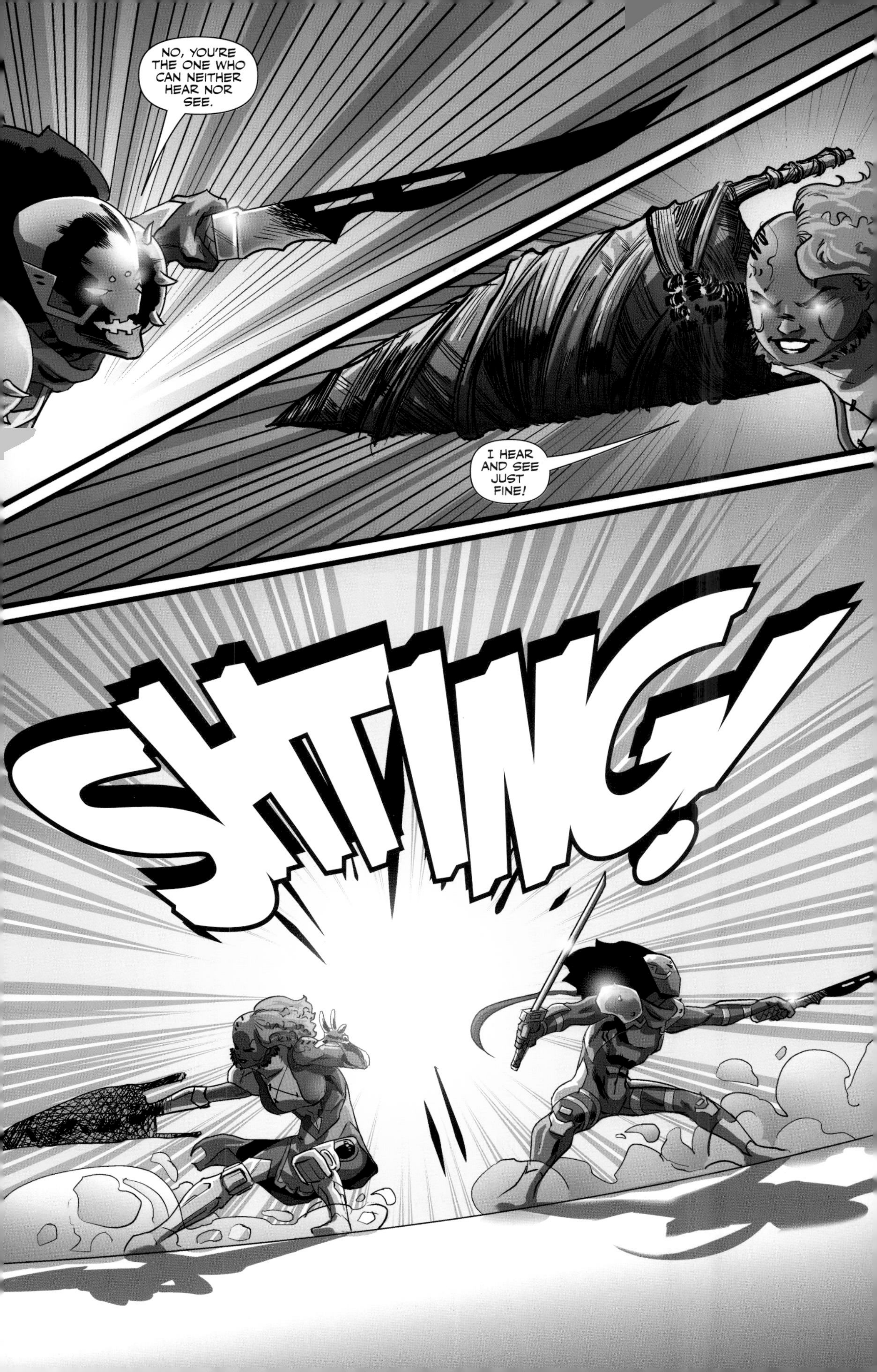
NO, YOU'RE THE ONE WHO CAN NEITHER HEAR NOR SEE.
I HEAR AND SEE JUST FINE!
SHTING!

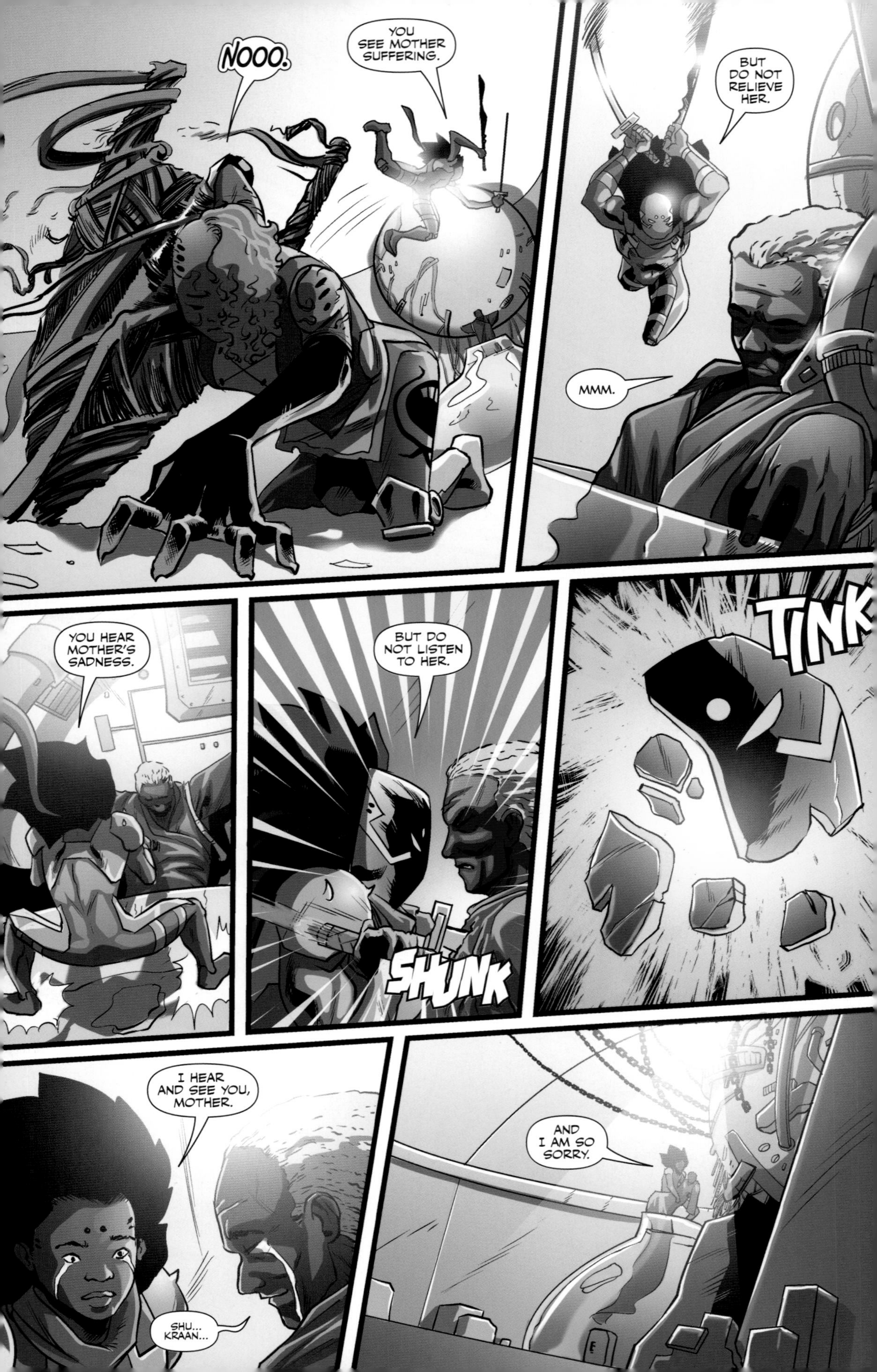
NOOO.
YOU SEE MOTHER SUFFERING.
BUT DO NOT RELIEVE HER.
MMM.
YOU HEAR MOTHER'S SADNESS.
BUT DO NOT LISTEN TO HER.
SHUNK
TINK
I HEAR AND SEE YOU, MOTHER.
SHU... KRAAN...
AND I AM SO SORRY.

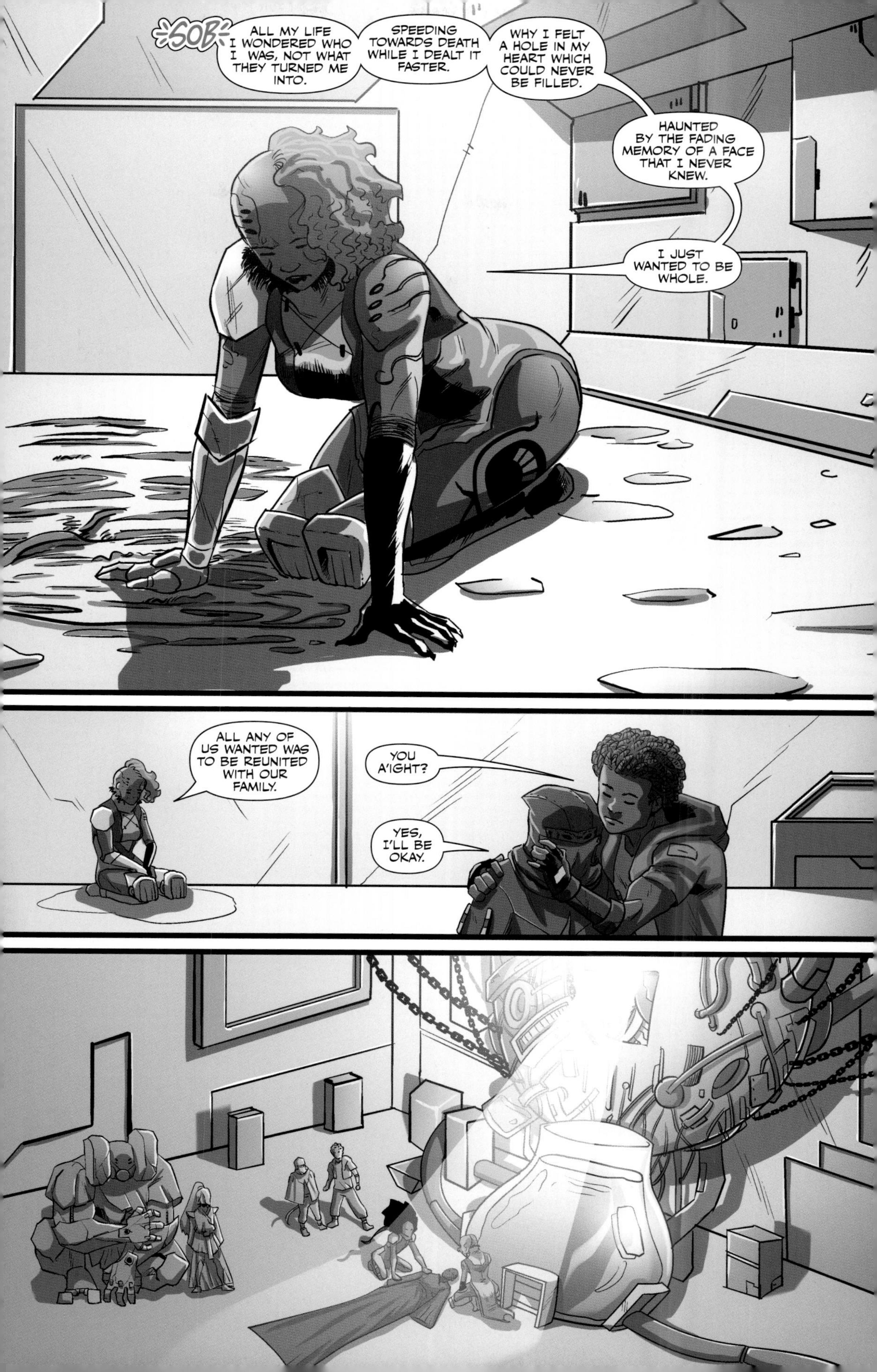
SOB
ALL MY LIFE I WONDERED WHO I WAS, NOT WHAT THEY TURNED ME INTO.
SPEEDING TOWARDS DEATH WHILE I DEALT IT FASTER.
WHY I FELT A HOLE IN MY HEART WHICH COULD NEVER BE FILLED.
HAUNTED BY THE FADING MEMORY OF A FACE THAT I NEVER KNEW.
I JUST WANTED TO BE WHOLE.
ALL ANY OF US WANTED WAS TO BE REUNITED WITH OUR FAMILY.
YOU A'IGHT?
YES, I'LL BE OKAY.

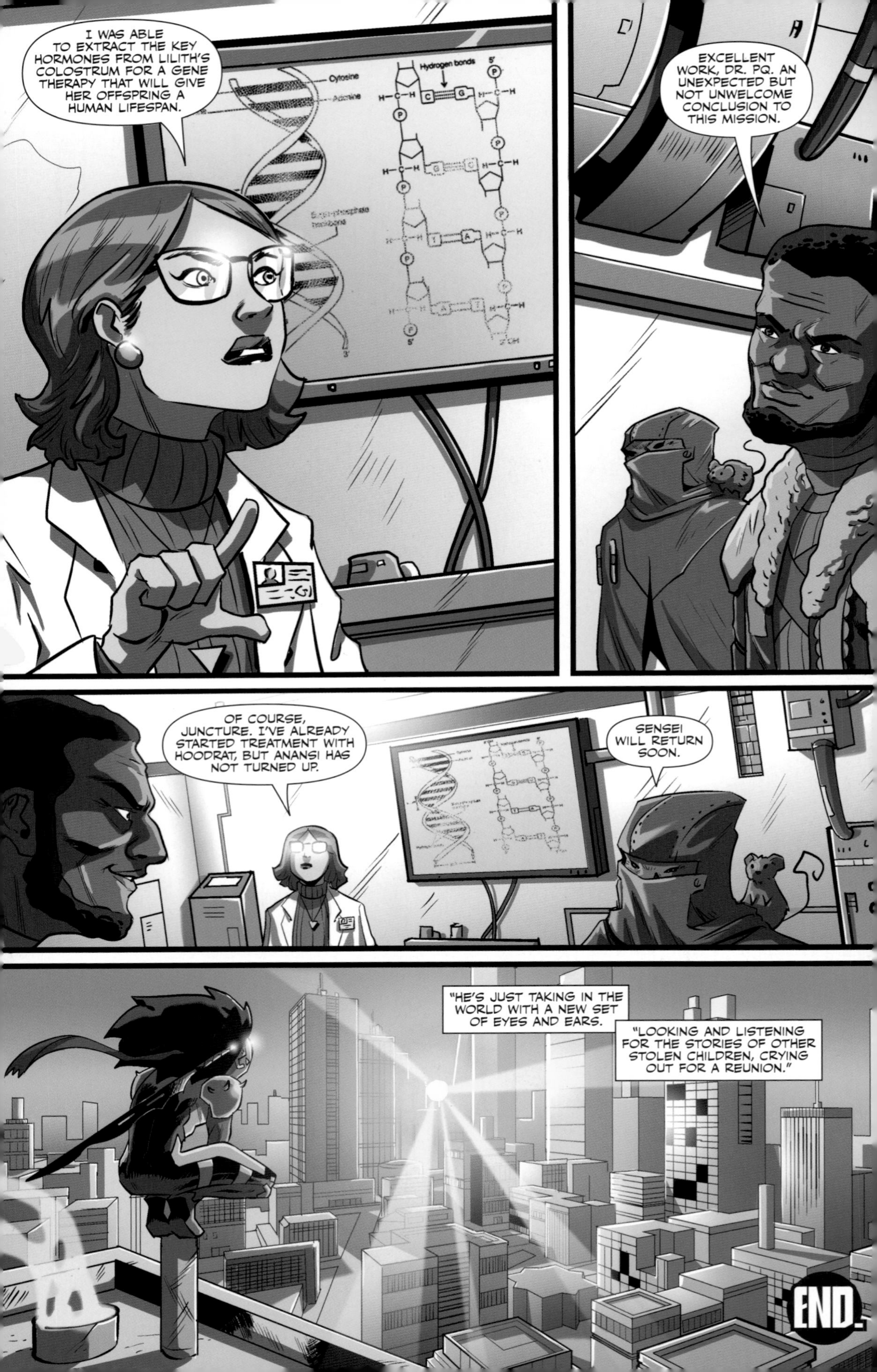
I WAS ABLE TO EXTRACT THE KEY HORMONES FROM LILITH'S COLOSTRUM FOR A GENE THERAPY THAT WILL GIVE HER OFFSPRING A HUMAN LIFESPAN.
Cytosine
Adenine
Hydrogen bonds
EXCELLENT WORK, DR. PQ. AN UNEXPECTED BUT NOT UNWELCOME CONCLUSION TO THIS MISSION.
OF COURSE, JUNCTURE. I'VE ALREADY STARTED TREATMENT WITH HOODRAT, BUT ANANSI HAS NOT TURNED UP.
SENSEI WILL RETURN SOON.
"HE'S JUST TAKING IN THE WORLD WITH A NEW SET OF EYES AND EARS.
"LOOKING AND LISTENING FOR THE STORIES OF OTHER STOLEN CHILDREN, CRYING OUT FOR A REUNION."
END.

OSAJYEFO • SMITH 3

BLACK AF

WIDOWS AND ORPHANS

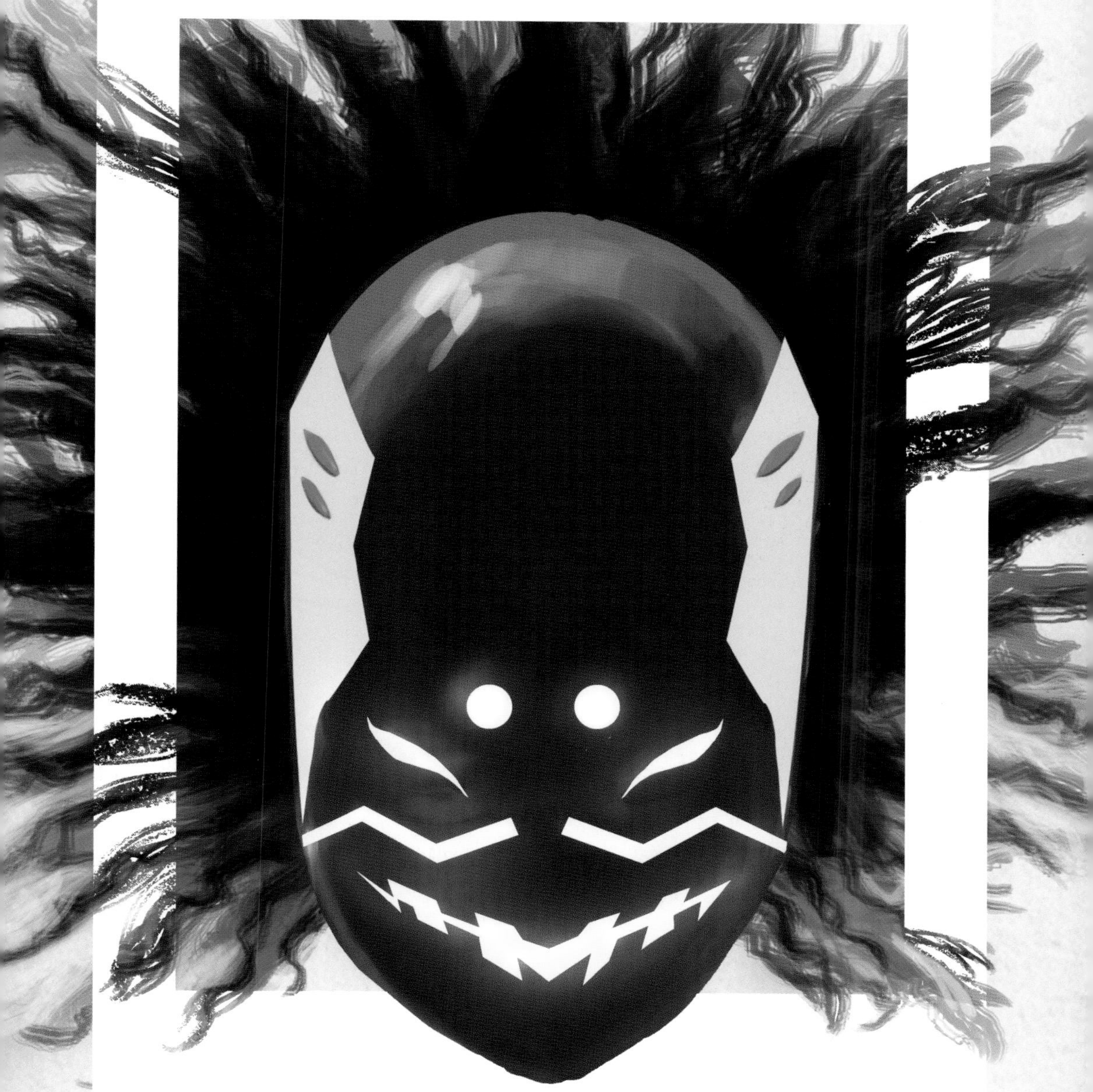

BEHIND THE SCENES

descriptions and designs by ***KWANZA OSAYEFO*** *and* ***TIM SMITH 3***

ANANSI

Anansi was trained almost from birth for one purpose: assassination. Everything else in his life comes a distant second. When not on assignment for The Project he spends much of his free time exploring life through the personas he takes on as a ninja.

At his core, he is an unflinching killer and though he finds no pleasure in death he also feels no remorse. Knowing his lifespan is short, Anansi eagerly explores his humanity to prove he doesn't have to be the killer he was raised to be.

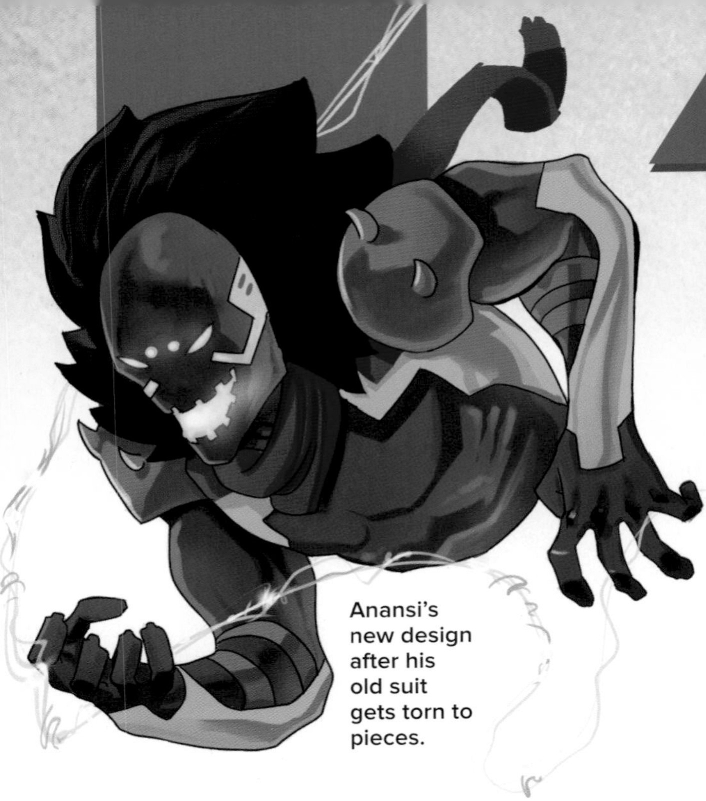

Anansi's new design after his old suit gets torn to pieces.

Played around with the hair to see what works best for a dramatic look.

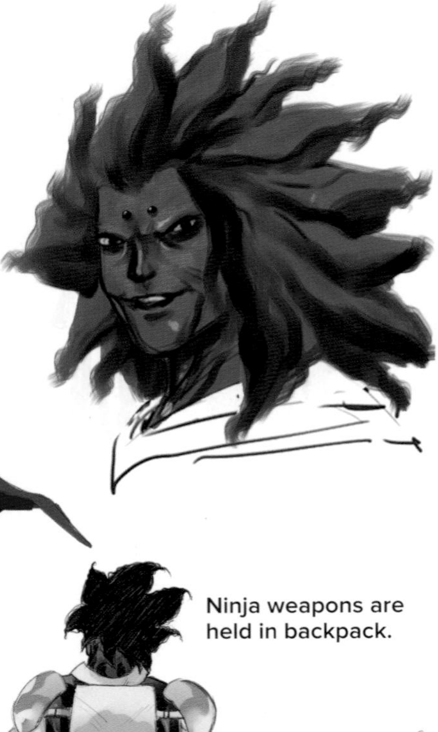

First suit design.

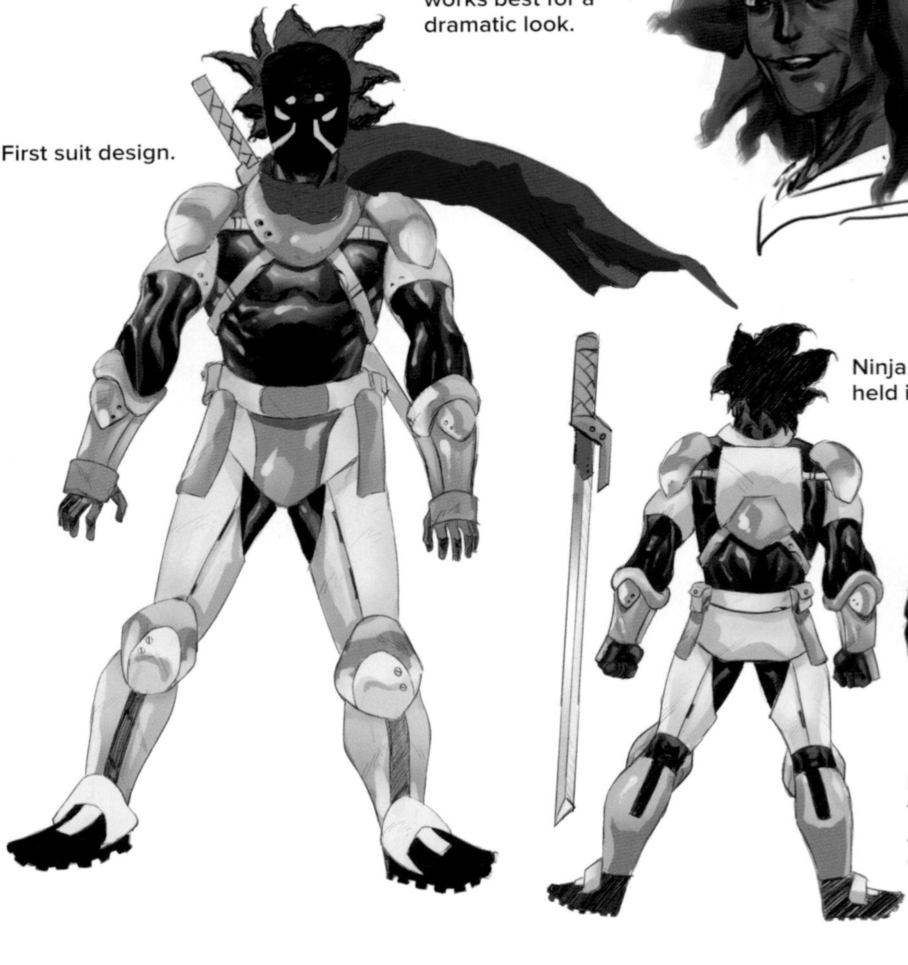

Ninja weapons are held in backpack.

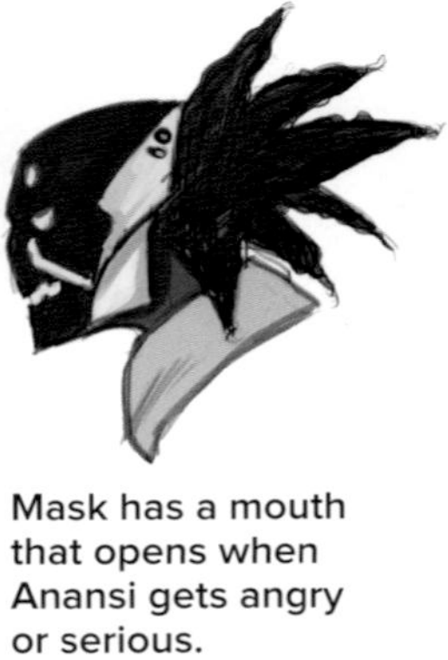

Mask has a mouth that opens when Anansi gets angry or serious.

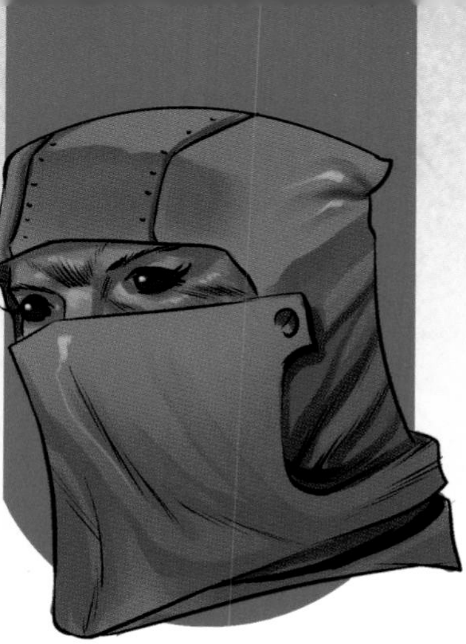

HOODRAT

Chronologically young, Hood Rat is intelligent beyond her years and has a genius level IQ. She's able to grasp complexities very quickly, whether mathematical or social. Her intellect is often in conflict with her animal instincts so she spends a lot of time praying and practicing ninjutsu to keep herself focused. She worries anytime she acts on her urges that she's devolving into her old animalistic state – a place she never wants to return.

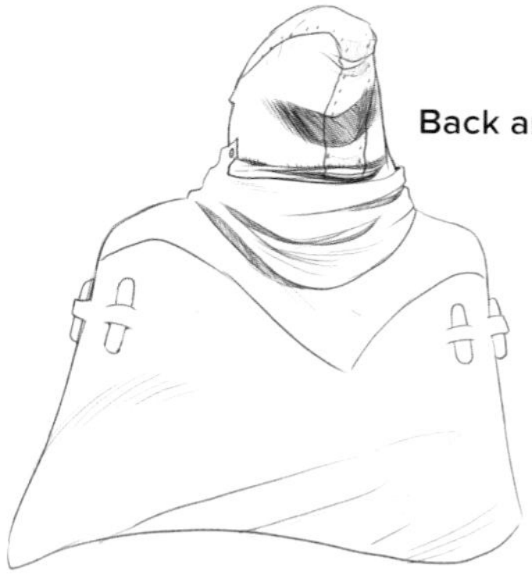

Back and front design.

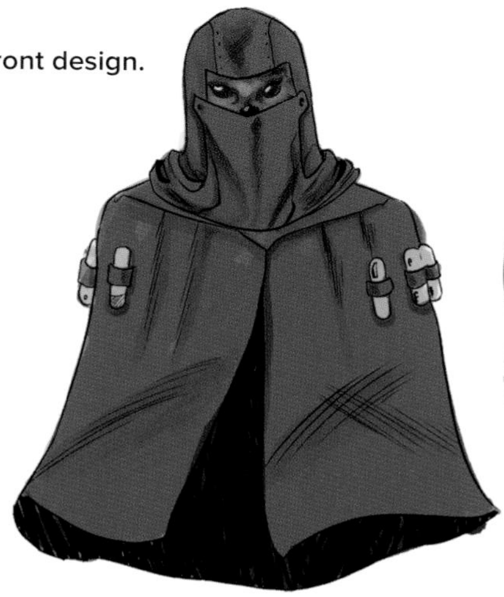

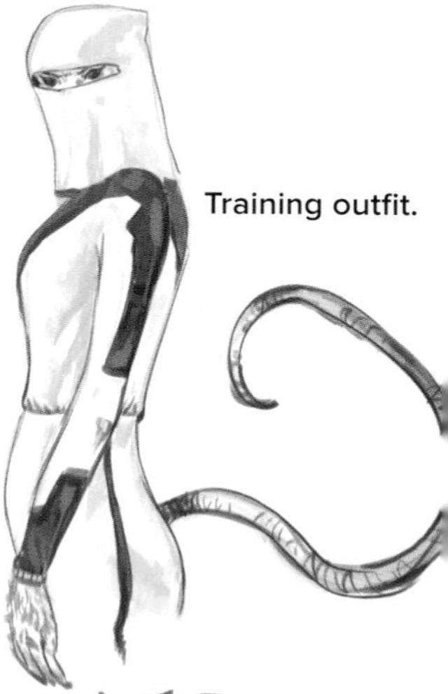

Training outfit.

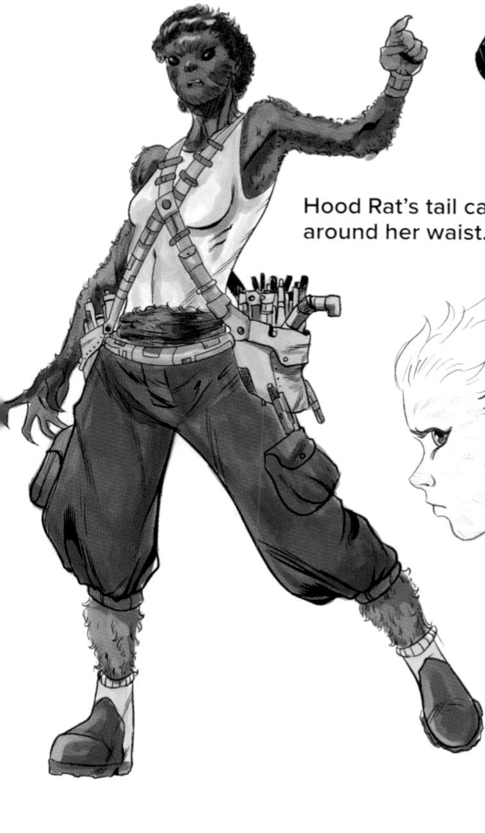

Hood Rat's tail can wrap around her waist.

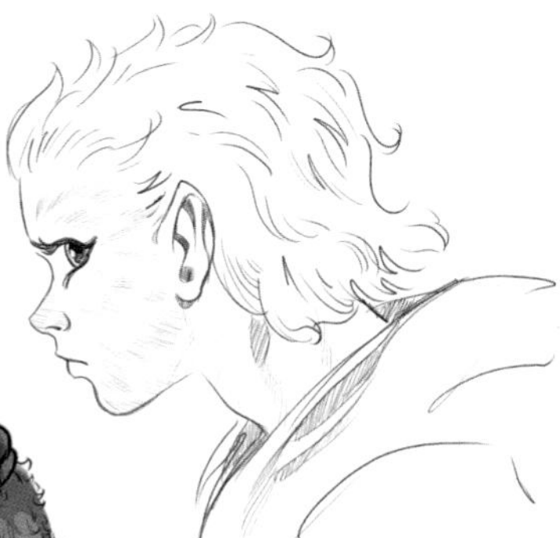

Her face is covered with fur and she has pointed ears.

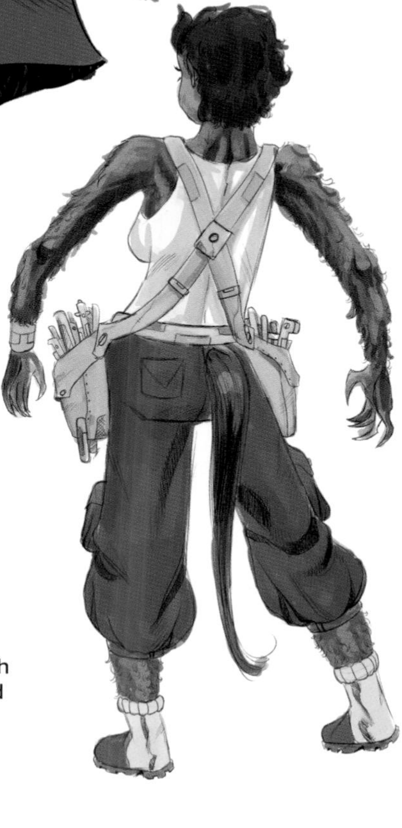

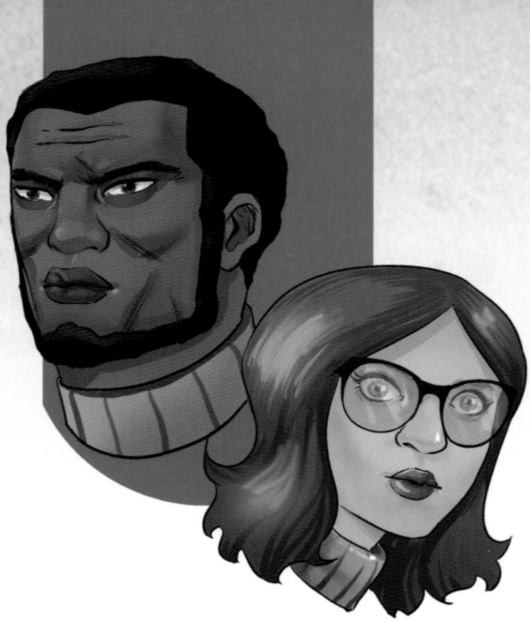

DR. PQ

Dr. Anna Pistorius-Quaife is Chief Science Officer for The Project and a leading authority in biology and quantum physics.

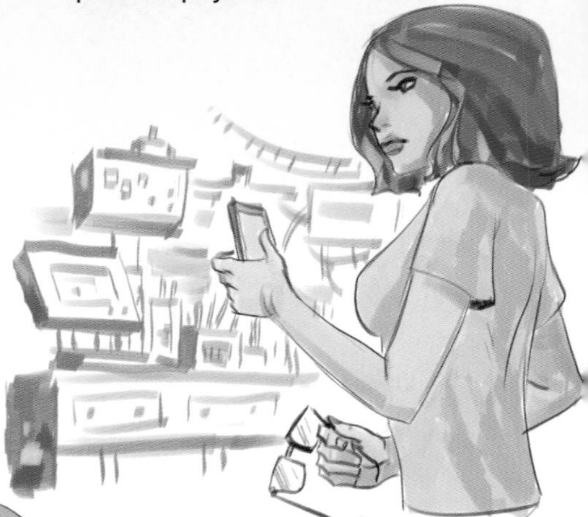

JUNCTURE

Jeremiah Knowles is the global leader of The Project.

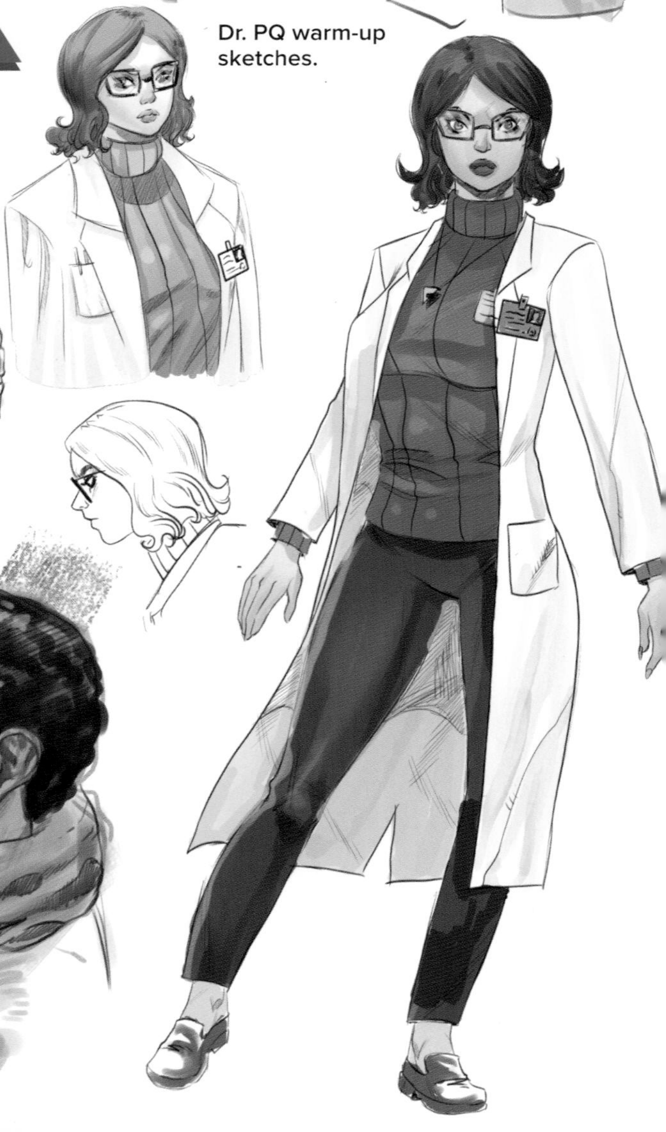

Dr. PQ warm-up sketches.

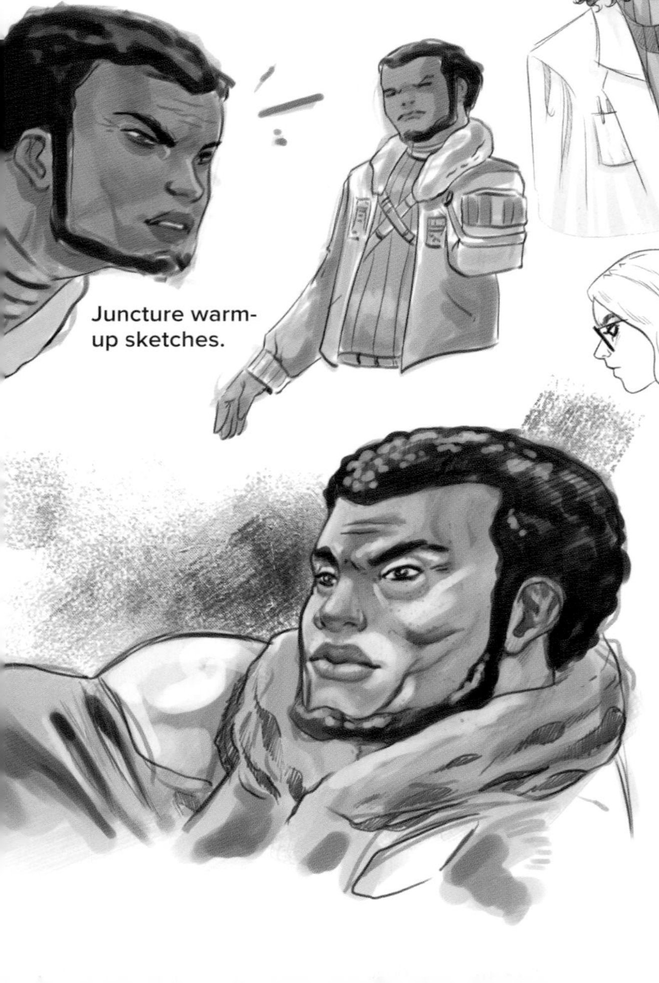

Juncture warm-up sketches.

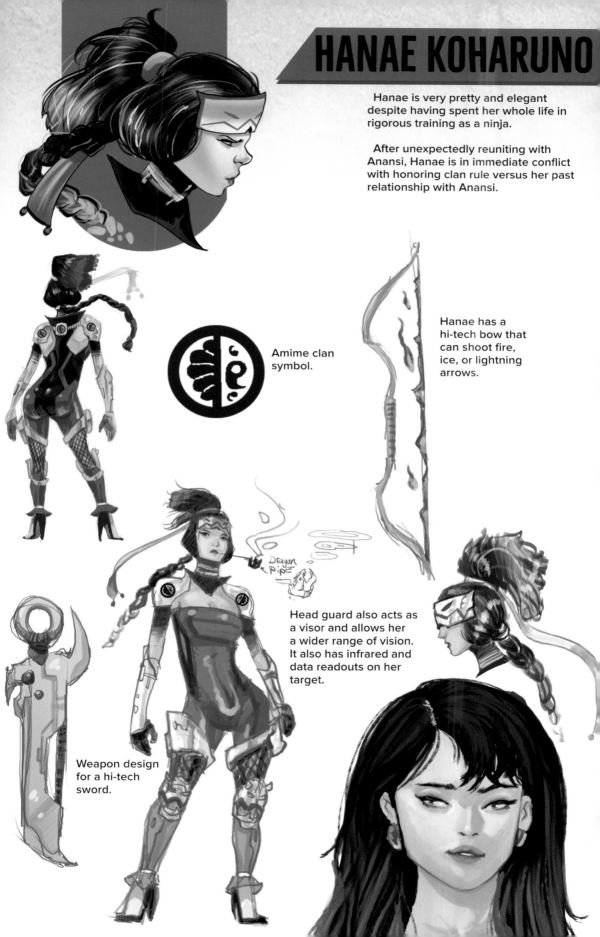

HANAE KOHARUNO

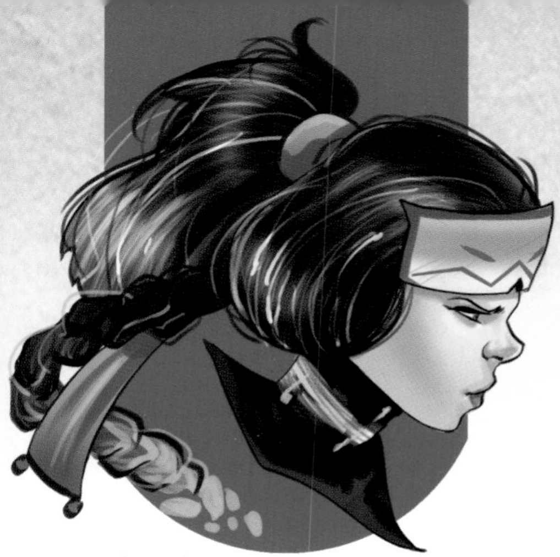

Hanae is very pretty and elegant despite having spent her whole life in rigorous training as a ninja.

After unexpectedly reuniting with Anansi, Hanae is in immediate conflict with honoring clan rule versus her past relationship with Anansi.

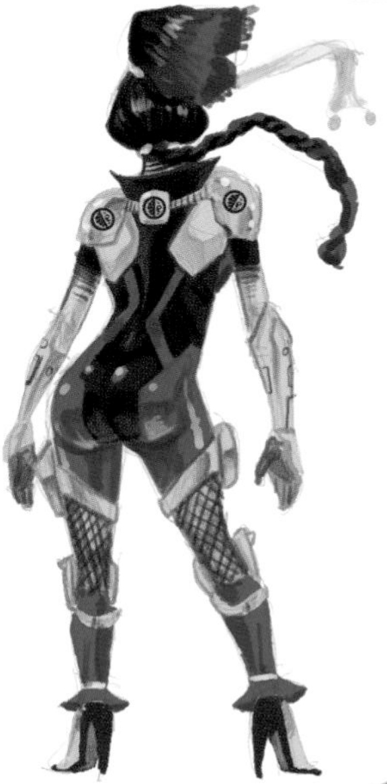

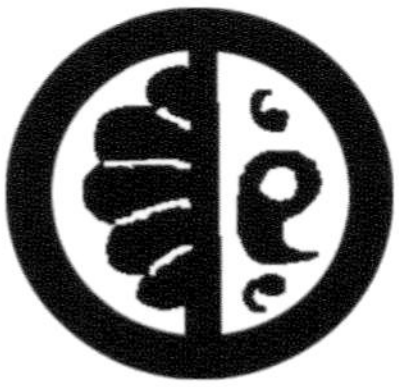

Amime clan symbol.

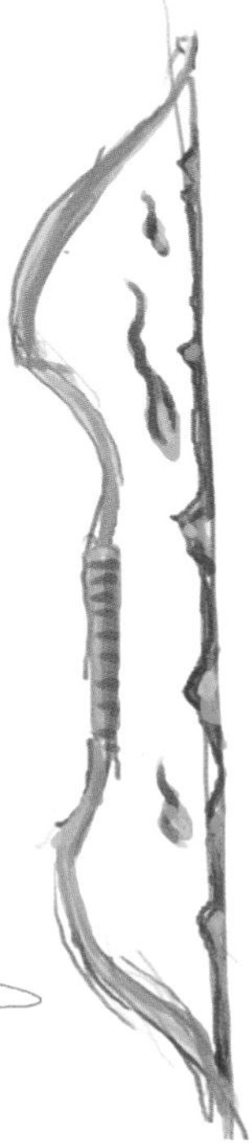

Hanae has a hi-tech bow that can shoot fire, ice, or lightning arrows.

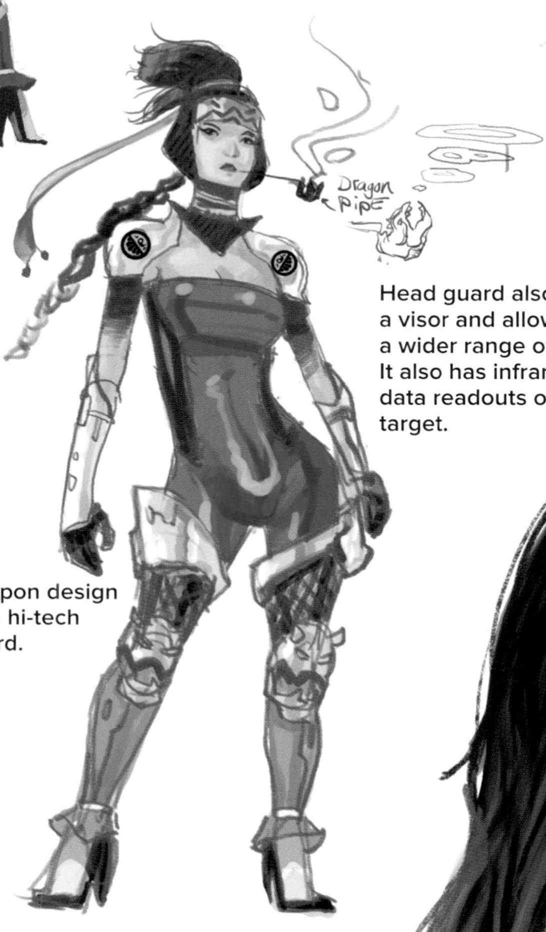
Dragon Pipe

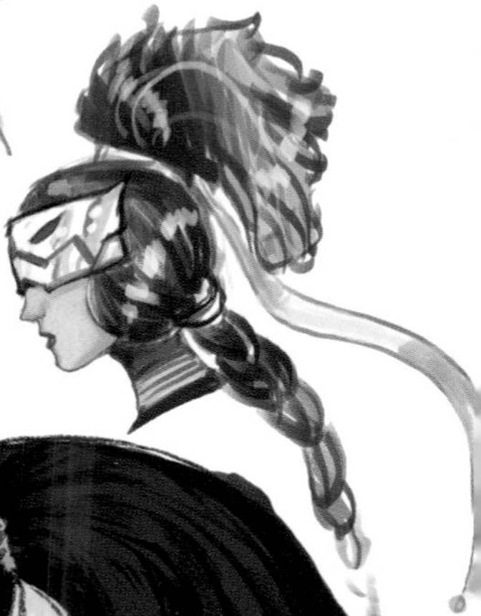

Head guard also acts as a visor and allows her a wider range of vision. It also has infrared and data readouts on her target.

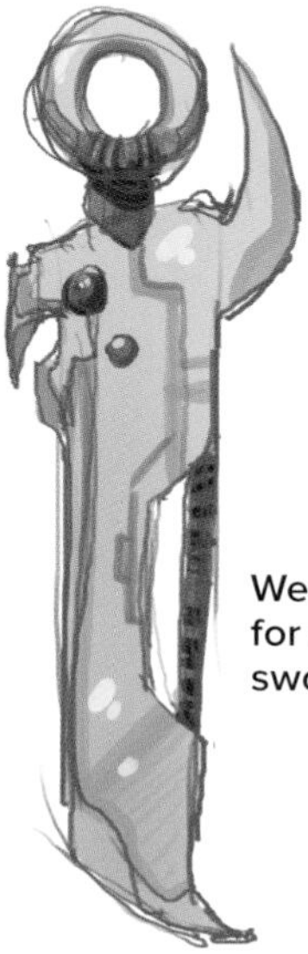

Weapon design for a hi-tech sword.

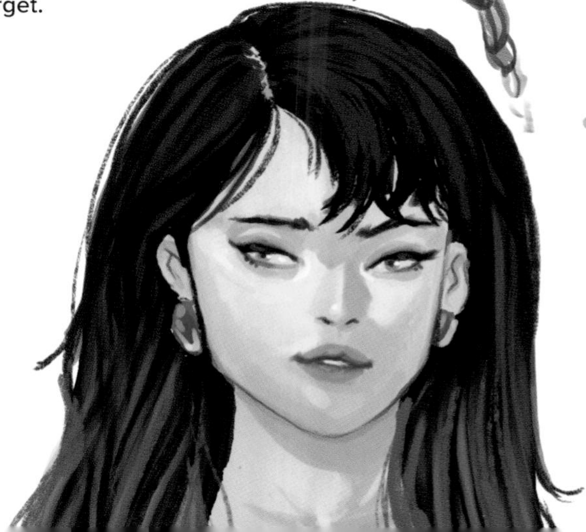

JOROGUMO

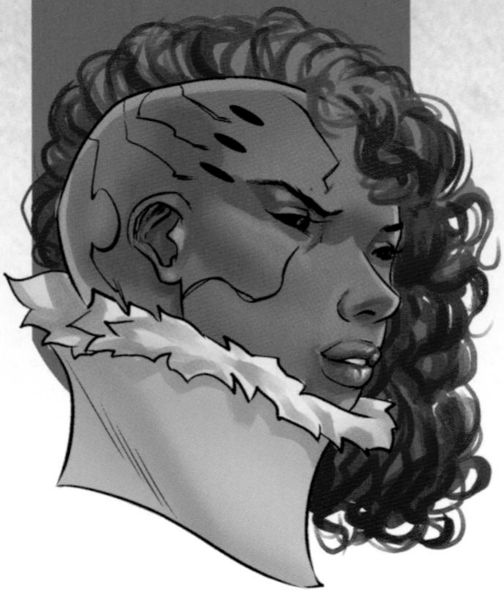

Jorogumo is lithe and muscular because she constantly trains. She has pronounced canine teeth that secrete a venom into whomever she bites, paralyzing or even killing her victims if she bites long enough.

She starts off as a very callous killer but as the story continues she begins to unravel a bit as her revenge isn't bringing her the satisfaction she thought it would. Her thinking is that killing Anansi must be the only thing that will bring fulfilment to her life.

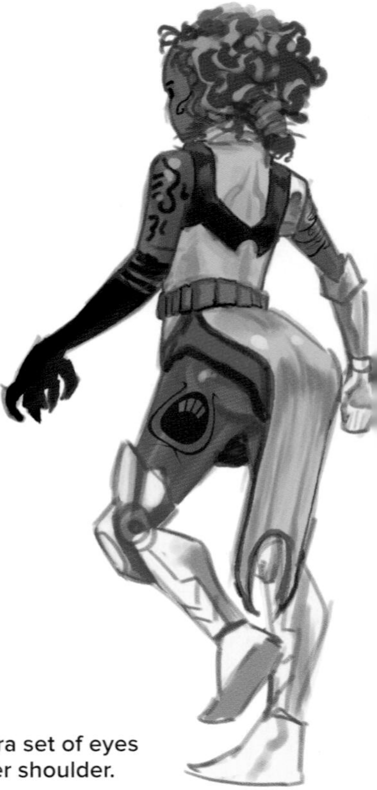

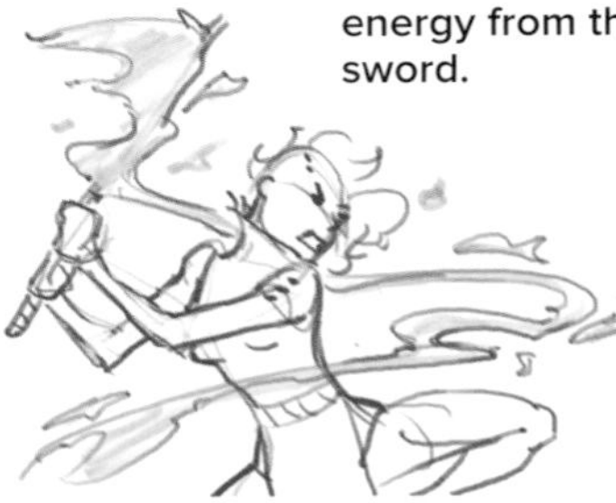

Can channel energy from the sword.

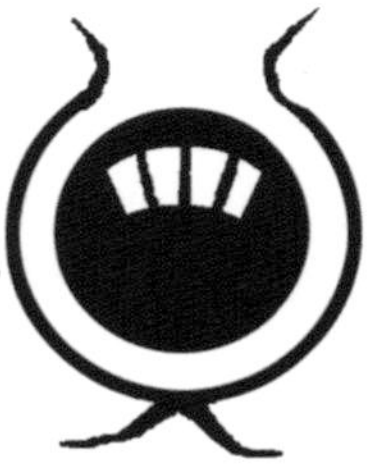

Jorogumo creates a symbol for her new clan.

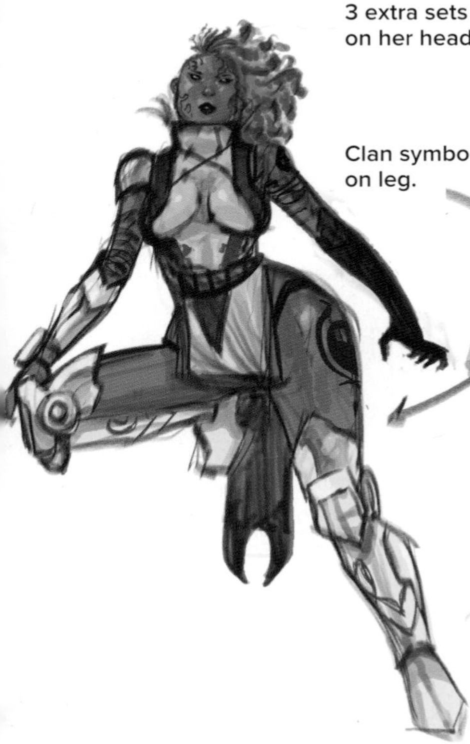

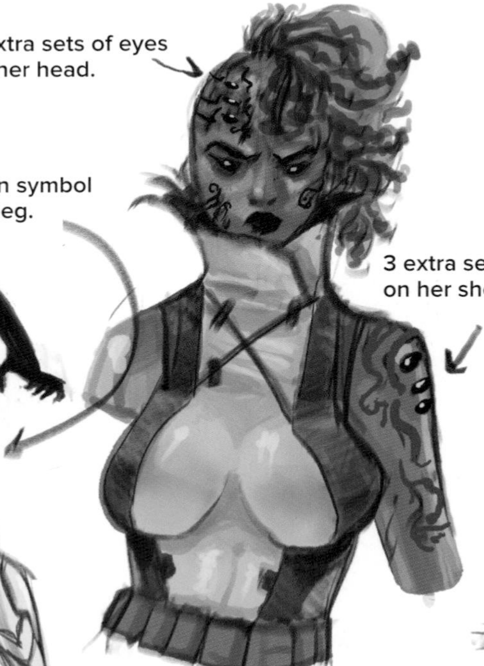

3 extra sets of eyes on her head.

Clan symbol on leg.

3 extra set of eyes on her shoulder.

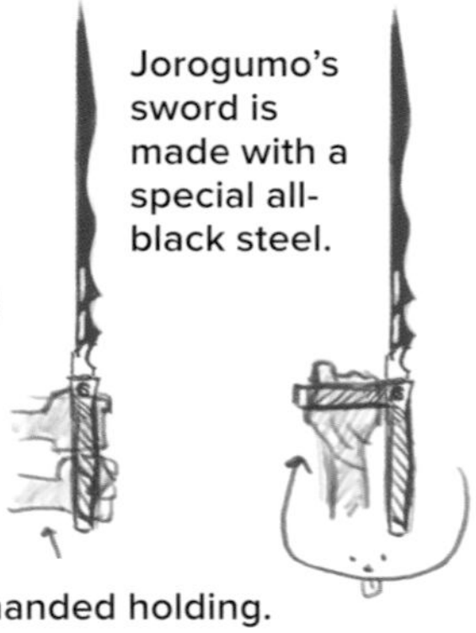

Jorogumo's sword is made with a special all-black steel.

Handle folds out for single-handed holding.

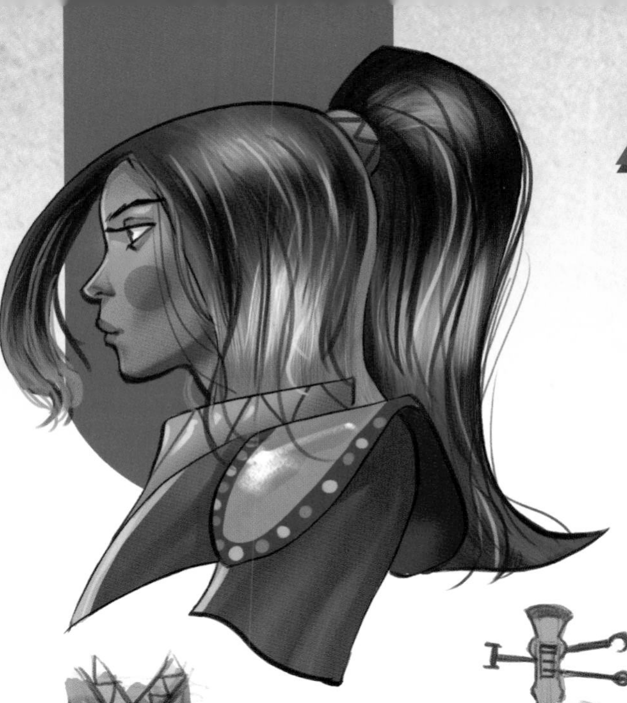

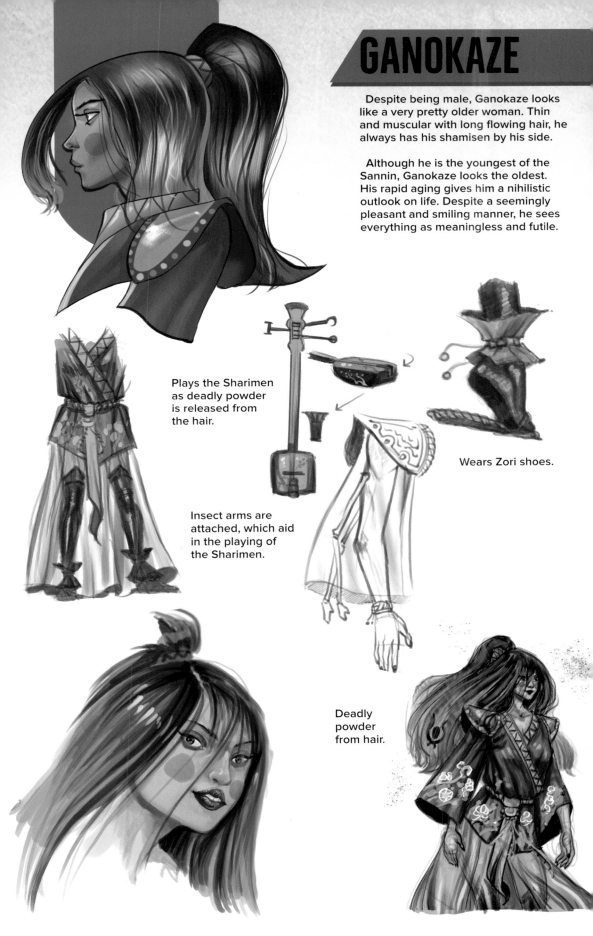

GANOKAZE

Despite being male, Ganokaze looks like a very pretty older woman. Thin and muscular with long flowing hair, he always has his shamisen by his side.

Although he is the youngest of the Sannin, Ganokaze looks the oldest. His rapid aging gives him a nihilistic outlook on life. Despite a seemingly pleasant and smiling manner, he sees everything as meaningless and futile.

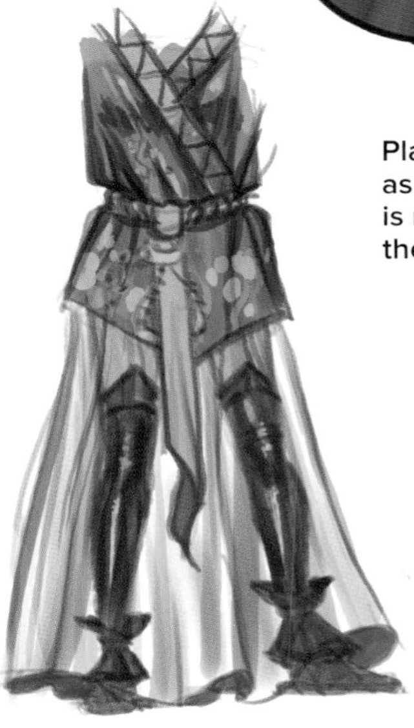

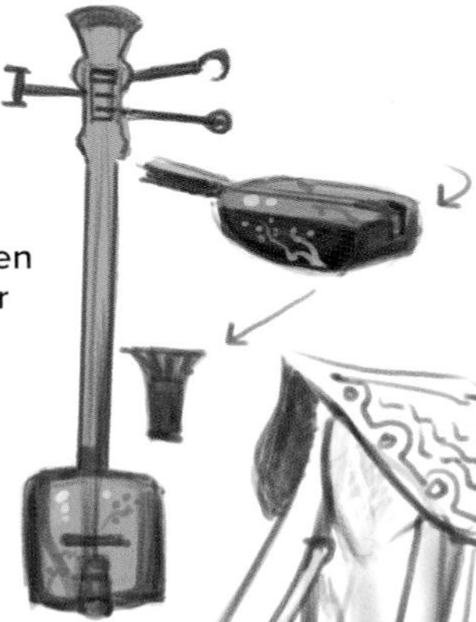

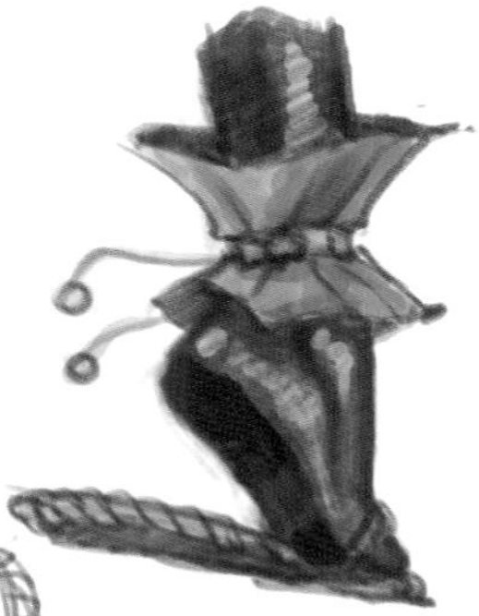

Plays the Sharimen as deadly powder is released from the hair.

Wears Zori shoes.

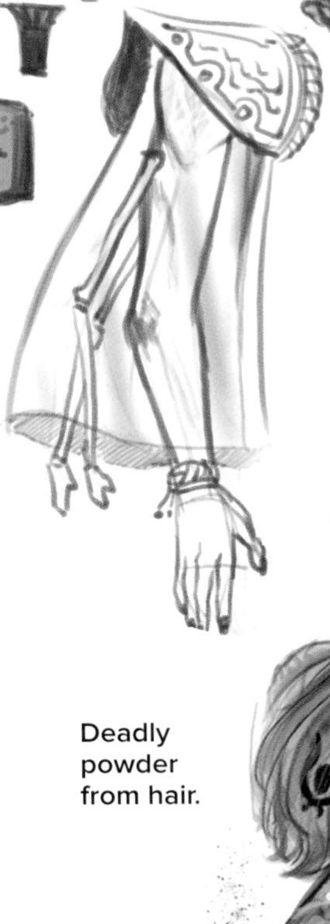

Insect arms are attached, which aid in the playing of the Sharimen.

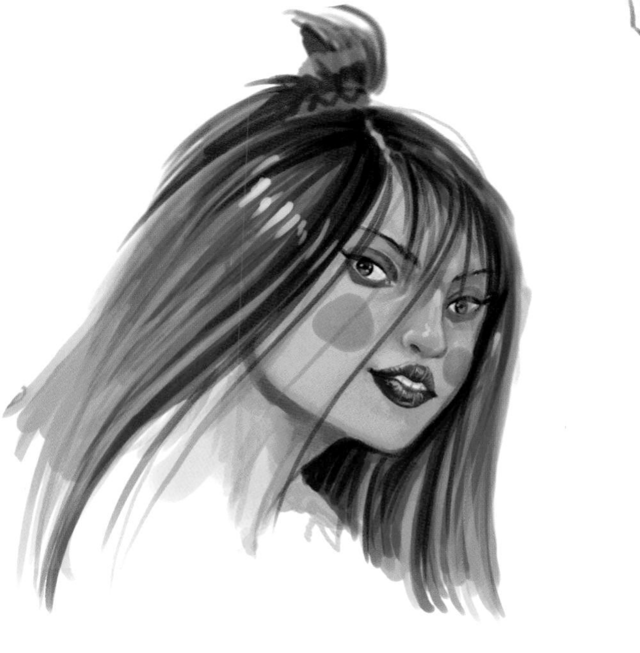

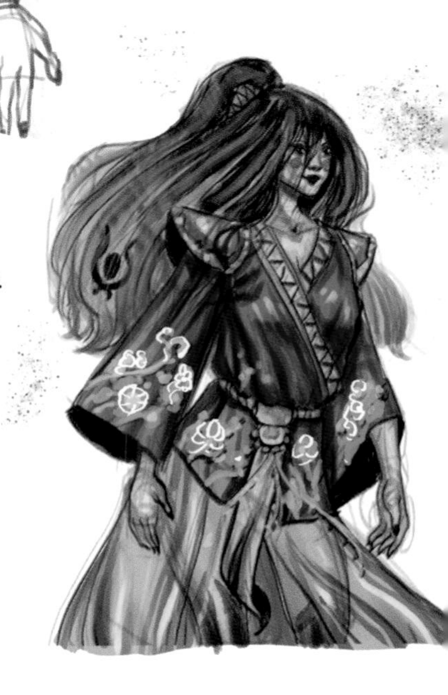

Deadly powder from hair.

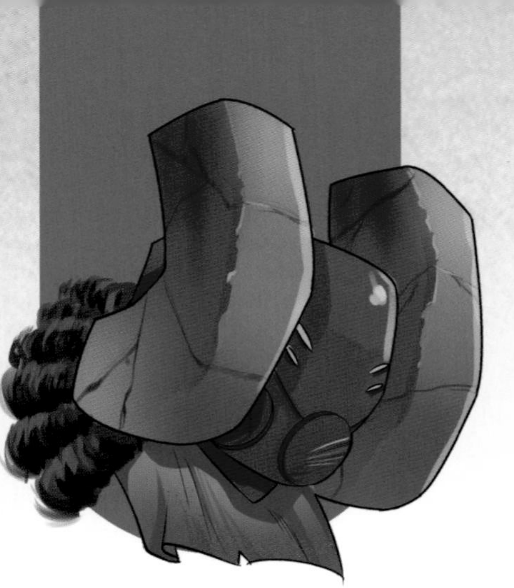

KABUTO

Kabuto is almost seven feet tall. His body is covered with large plates that are impervious to harm, though the spaces in between are normal flesh. Even though the plates deflect attacks, he can still the feel impact when he gets hit.

Much like Ganokaze, Kabuto has is aging very rapidly. Instead of nihilism, he has taken on more of a Bushido view of life. Resolved that he will die, he seeks to save others from this fate and die in peace.

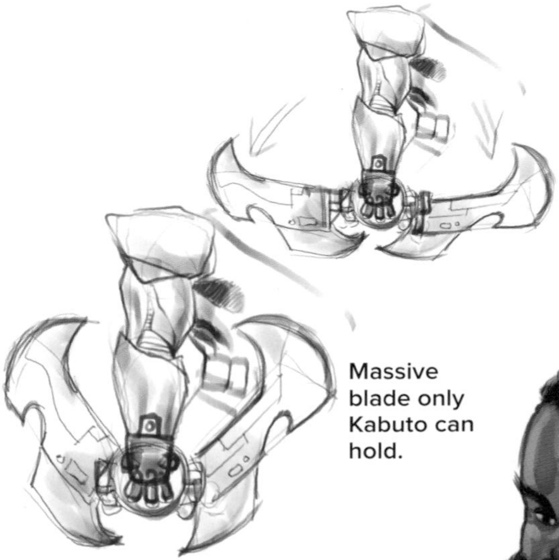

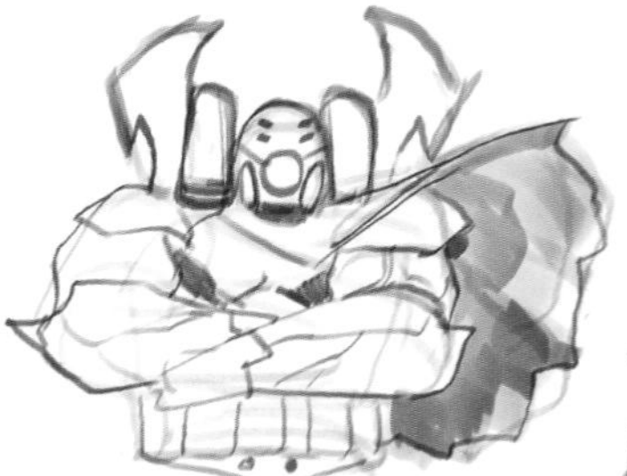

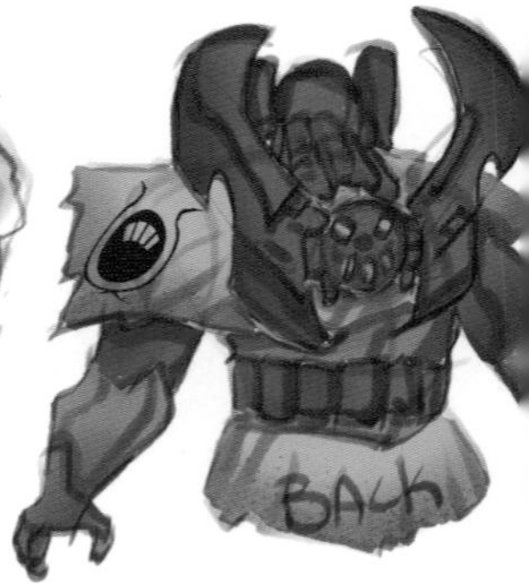
BACK

Massive blade only Kabuto can hold.

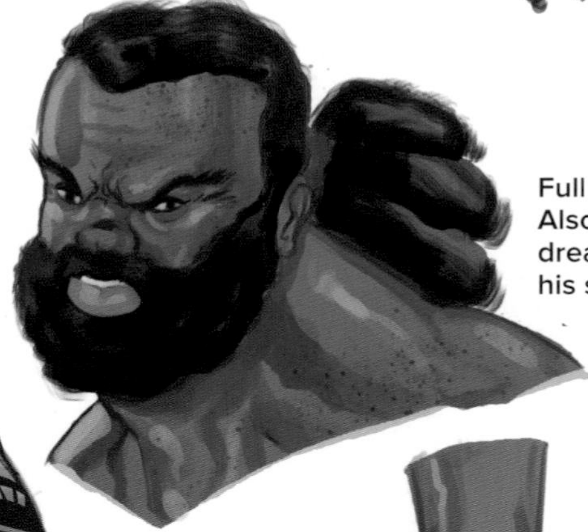

Full beard. Also very massive dreads to match his size.

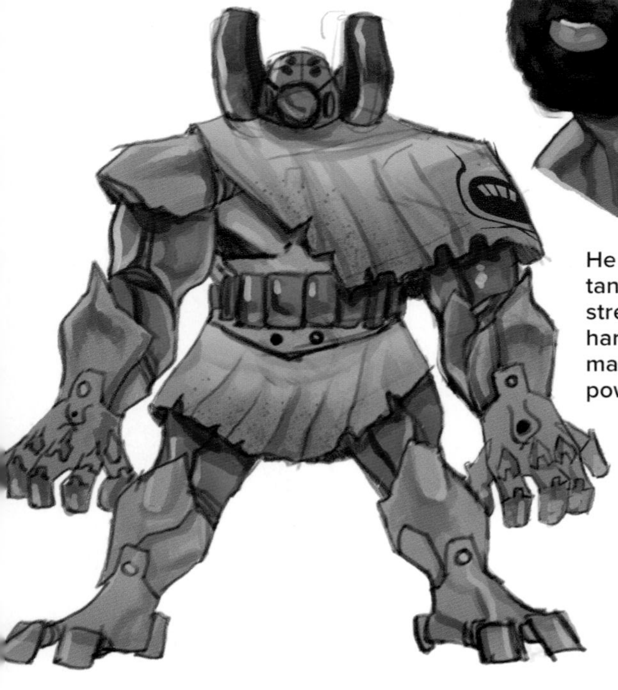

He is a walking tank! His strength and hard exterior make him a power house.

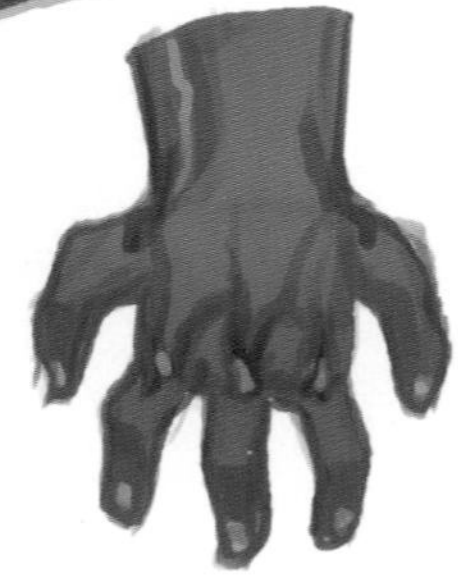

3 fingers and 2 thumbs help him to hold his weapon.

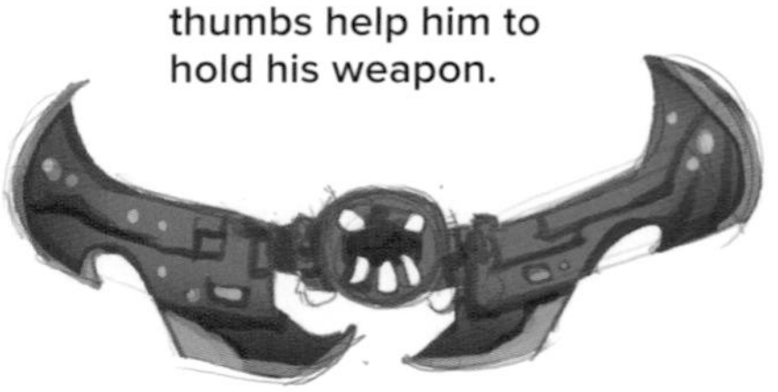

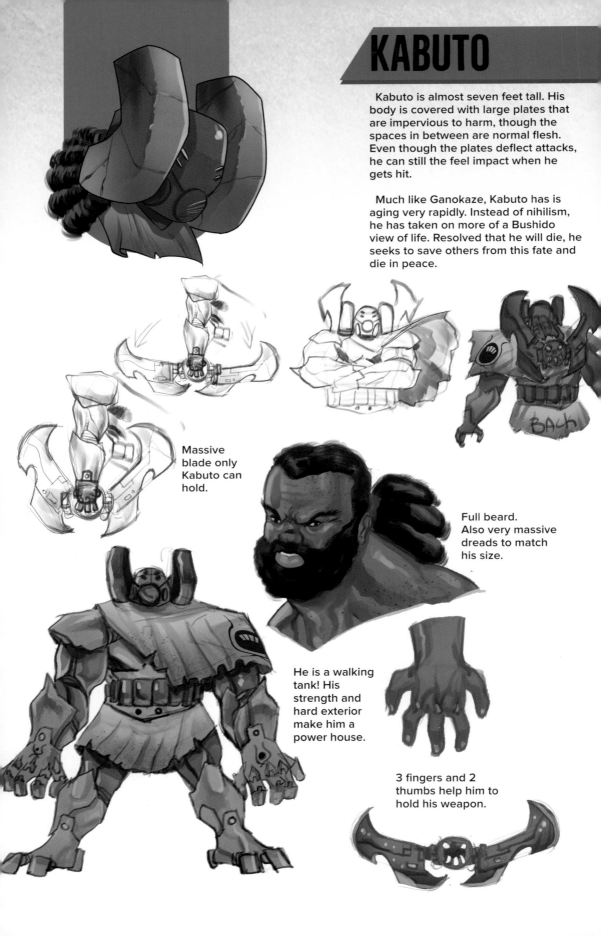

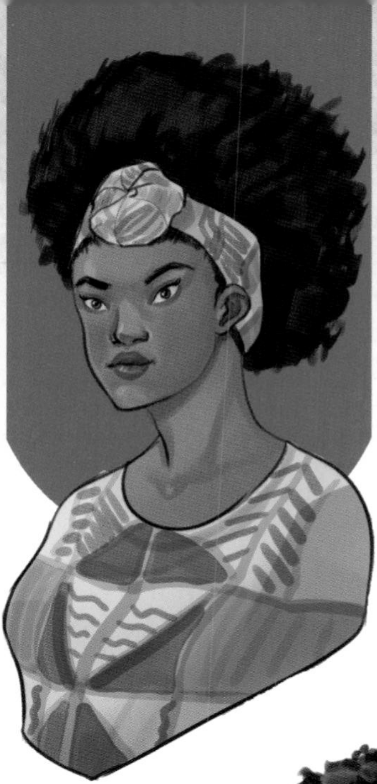

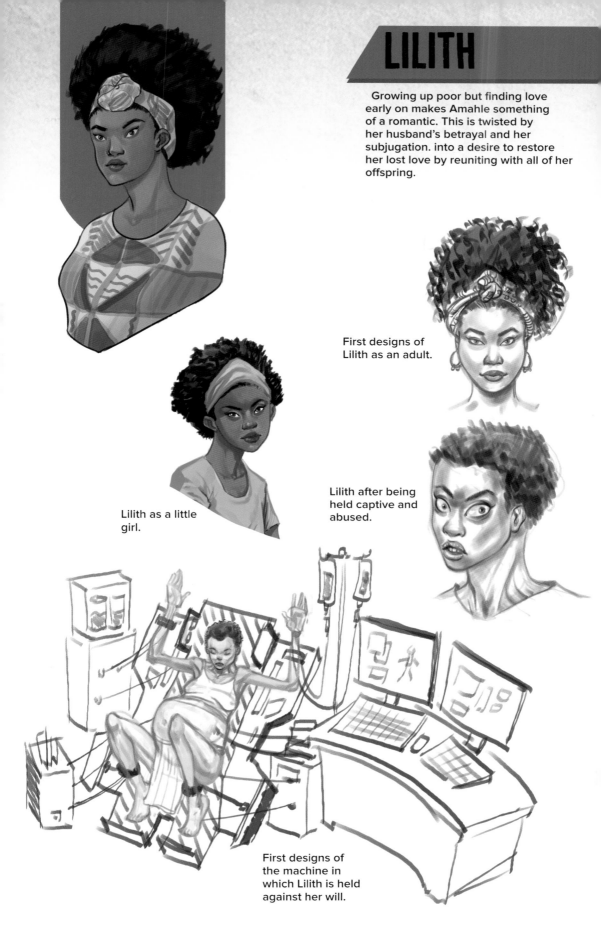

LILITH

Growing up poor but finding love early on makes Amahle something of a romantic. This is twisted by her husband's betrayal and her subjugation. into a desire to restore her lost love by reuniting with all of her offspring.

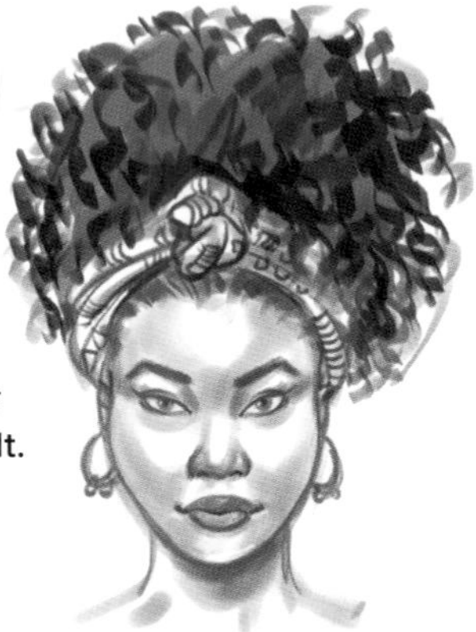

First designs of Lilith as an adult.

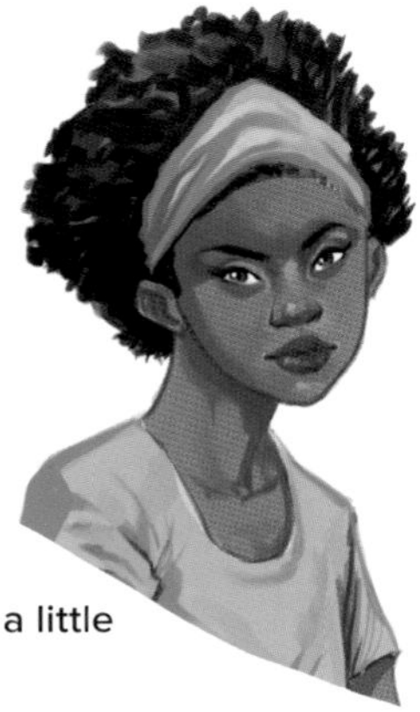

Lilith as a little girl.

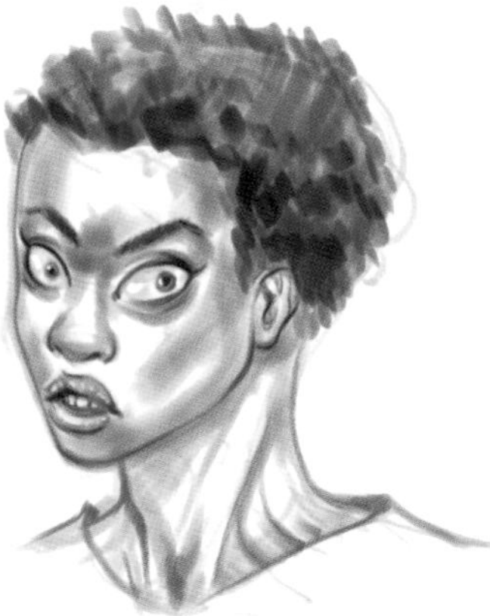

Lilith after being held captive and abused.

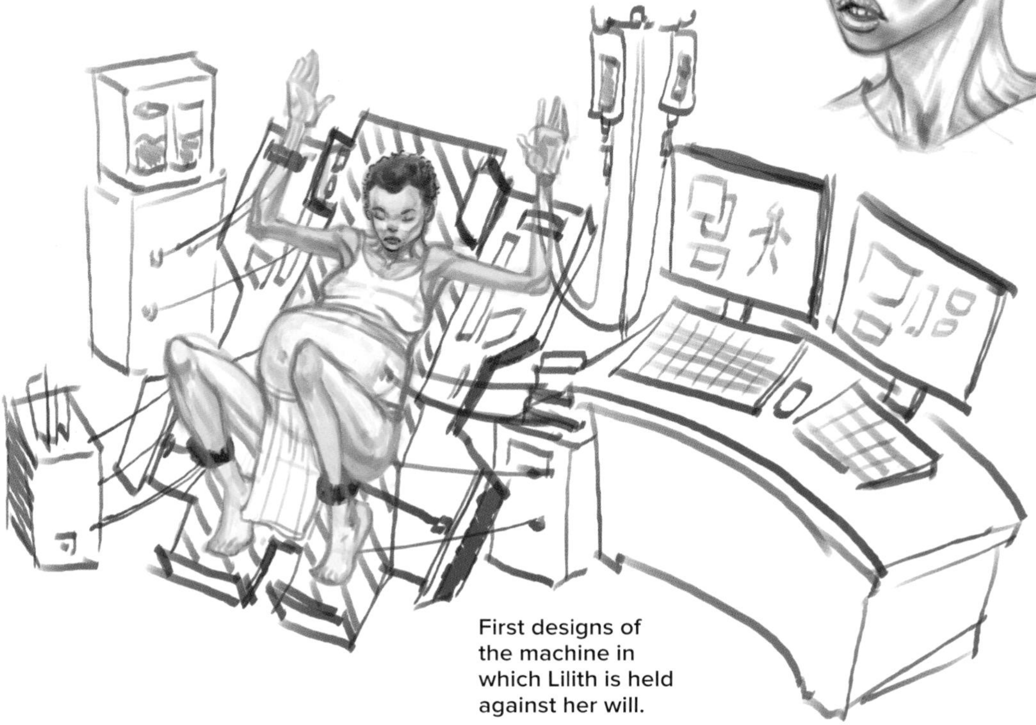

First designs of the machine in which Lilith is held against her will.

MINDGRAPES

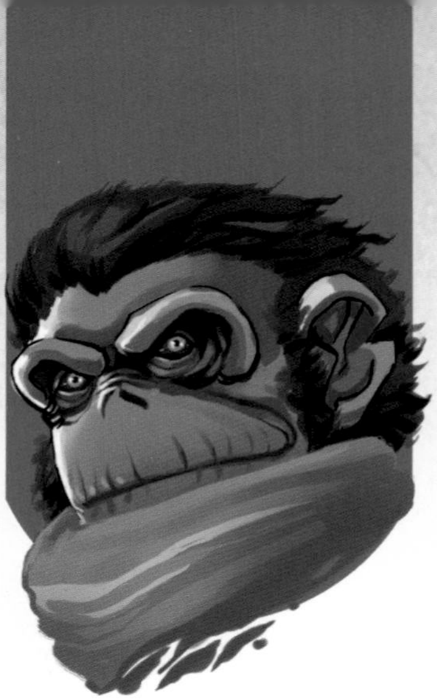

Mindgrapes seems to be working for Lilith at first, but it becomes clear that he's using her as a conduit to manipulate her and his siblings to act on his behalf.

Due to his appearance, Mindgrapes hates humanity more than any member of ONE. If his powers worked on other empowered he'd have taken over the organization.

Warm up sketches of Mindgrapes.

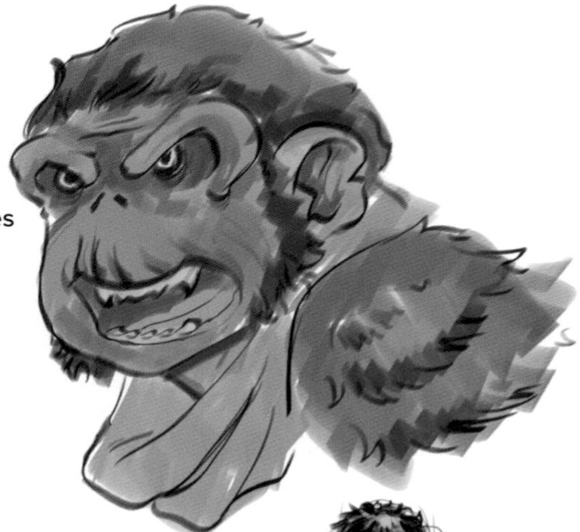

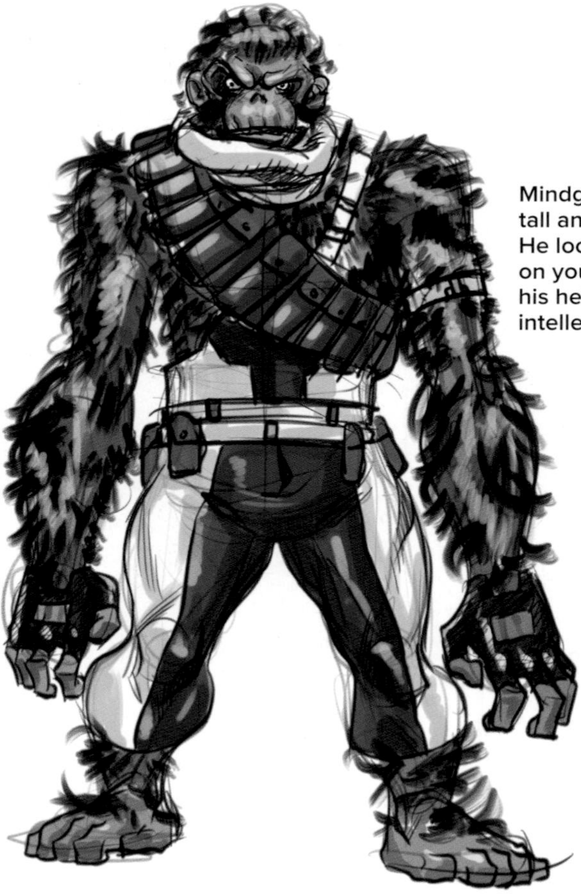

Mindgrapes is tall and massive. He looks down on you from both his height and his intellect.

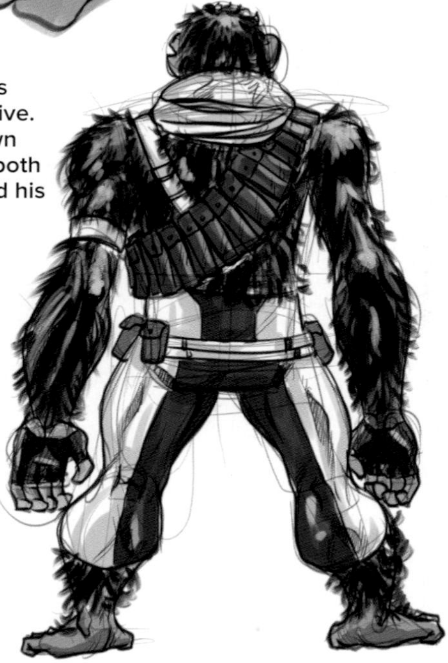

No shoes.

CHAPTER 1 PG.5

Hood Rat relays over comms that the fly-ninja was wounded and can't seem to fly very high. Anansi takes this update as a cue to make a move. He fires razorwire-like weblines from his fingers. The tethers connect with a building and he uses this to wall-run along a pendulum curve and launch himself into the air at the fly-ninja.

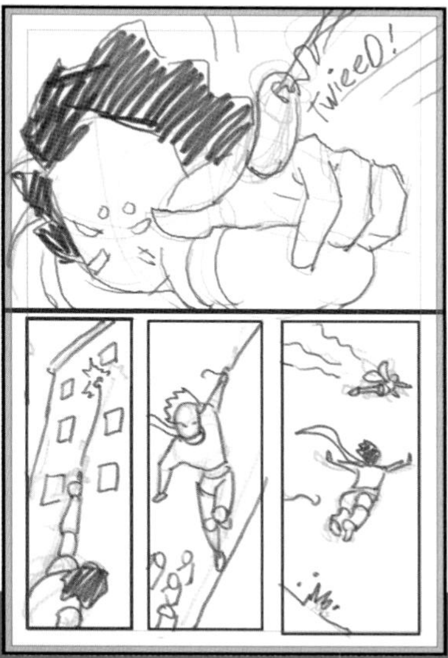

I wanted the first real shot of Anansi to show off his attitude so the reader can get a good feel and sense of him in action.

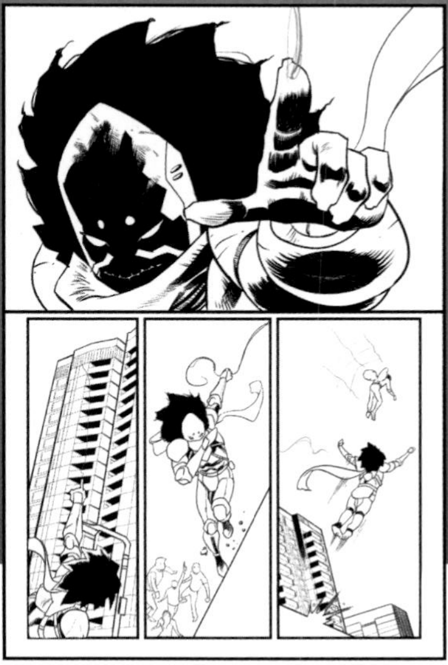

Next, after the rough pencils, our amazing editor Sarah approves the page before moving onto inks!

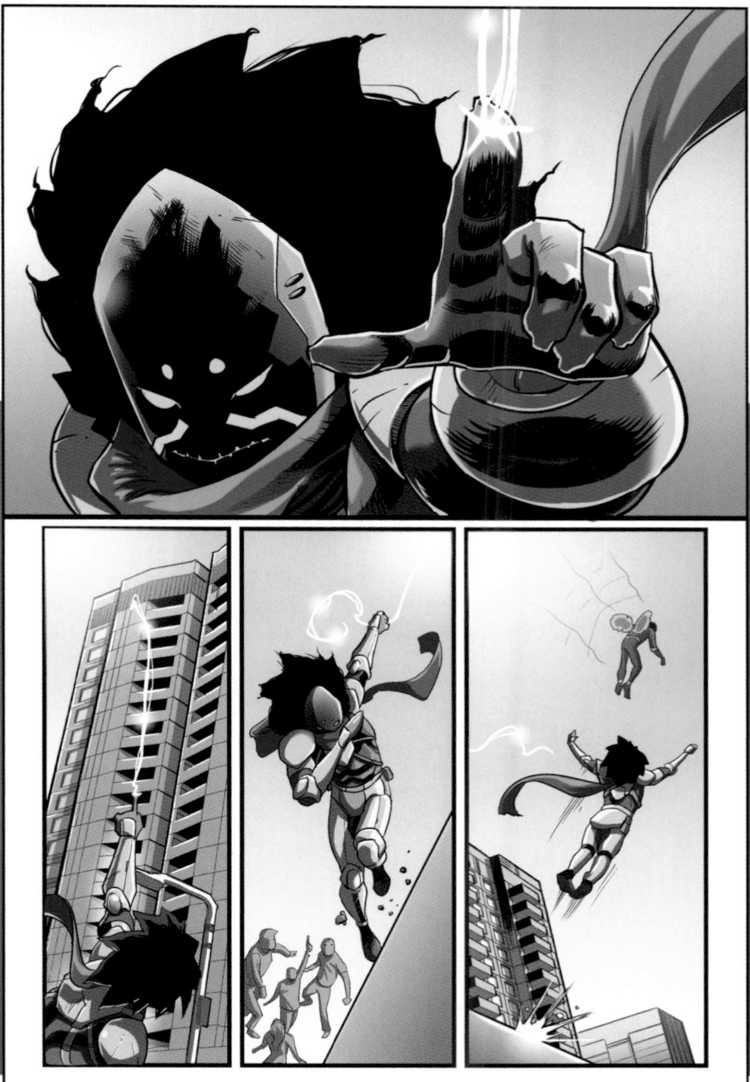

Last step for the page is Derwin's amazing colors gracing those inks. Of course, the lettering is the FINAL step for the page. But you just read Dave's handiwork.

color by: DERWIN ROBERSON

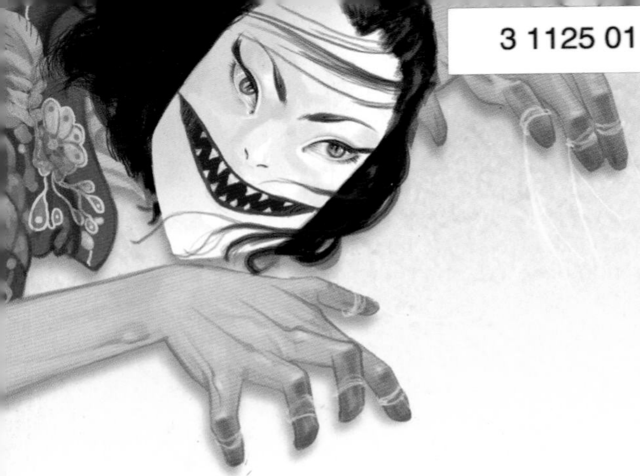

COVER ROUGHS

Here are a few cover layouts. Some worked great as a cover, others looked more like pin-ups than covers.

TS3 creates these thumbnails and Kwanza Osajyefo figures out what works best for the mood and feel of what he is cooking up for the story.

Always best to have another pair of eyes look everything over!

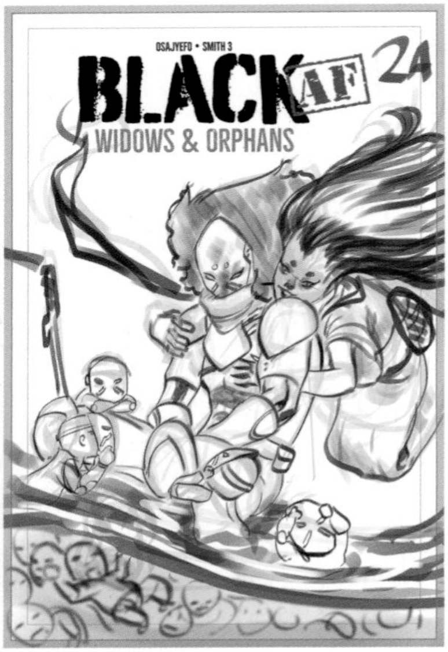
OSAJYEFO • SMITH 3
BLACK AF
2A
WIDOWS & ORPHANS

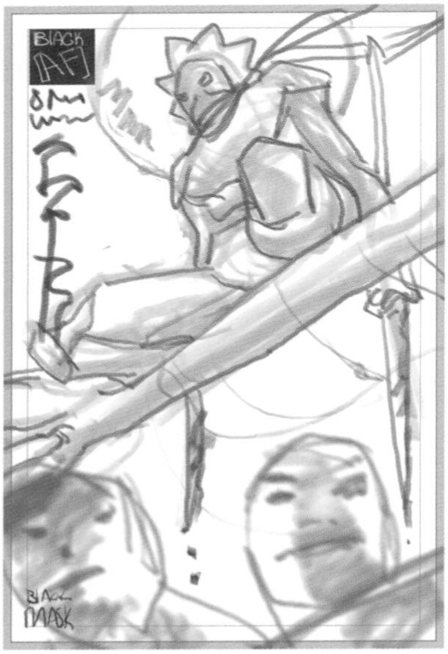
BLACK AF
BLACK MASK

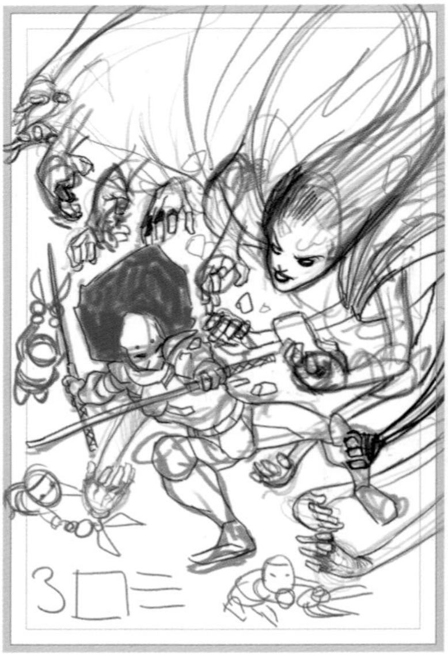

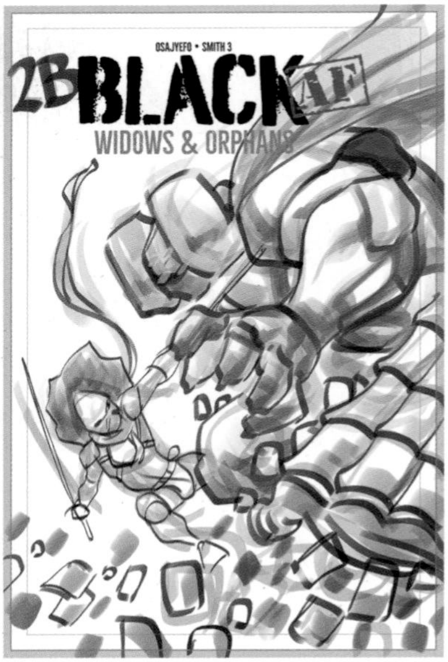
OSAJYEFO • SMITH 3
2B
BLACK AF
WIDOWS & ORPHANS

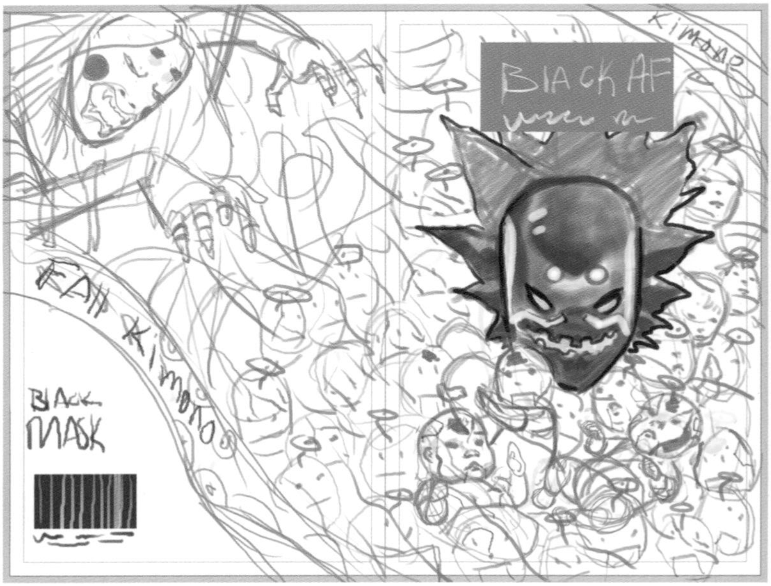
BLACK AF
BLACK MASK